RITA® award-winning author **Leah Ashton** never expected to write books. She grew up reading everything she could lay her hands on—from pony books to the backs of cereal boxes at breakfast. One day she discovered the page-turning, happy-sigh-inducing world of romance novels…and one day, much later, wondered if maybe she could write one, too.

Leah now lives in Perth, Western Australia, and writes happily-ever-afters for heroines who definitely *don't* need saving. She has a gorgeous husband, two amazing daughters and the best intentions to plan meals and maintain an effortlessly tidy home. When she's not writing, Leah loves all-day breakfast, rambling conversations and laughing until she cries. She really hates cucumber. And scary movies. You can visit Leah at www.leah-ashton.com or Facebook.com/leahashtonauthor.

For my grandmother, Marica—
who inspired this story.

Not just with her homeland of Vela Luka, but also with her sixty-five-year romance with Rafé, which was the kind of love that dreams—and romance novels—are made of.

Thank you for all your help with this book. Thank you also for your food, your garden and all your love.

Hvala, Nana.

“You want to kiss me? Right here, in front of hundreds of people?”

He just smiled at her. And *looked* at her—right into those lovely hazel eyes.

He supposed, in theory, it was a ‘don’t stress about it’ type kiss. At least, that was his intention.

He was playing the role of the loving, supportive fiancé, after all.

But also—yes, he wanted to kiss her. If he was honest with himself, he’d wanted to kiss Jas ever since she’d told him off in that briefing.

She closed her eyes, and he watched as she took a deep breath.

When she opened them, she nodded. And then he kissed her.

Her lips were soft and fleetingly cool beneath his own. They were chastely closed, of course—but they shifted against the pressure of his mouth, as if she’d open her mouth for him if only he were to ask.

It was shockingly, unexpectedly sexy—a simple kiss that felt like a promise of so much more. It wasn’t just about the touch of their lips or the mingling of their breathing but of the subtle movement of their bodies, the way they leaned toward each other while still only joined by their laced fingers.

Marko was no longer aware of their audience, or of the ballroom, or even why he’d kissed her in the first place.

All that mattered was the way her mouth fit so perfectly against his.

THE PRINCE'S FAKE FIANCÉE

BY

LEAH ASHTON

First Published in Great Britain 2018
By Mills & Boon, an imprint of HarperCollins*Publishers*
1 London Bridge Street, London, SE1 9GF

ISBN: 978-0-263-93634-6

23-0118

MIX
Paper from responsible sources
FSC™ C007454

This book is produced from independently certified FSC™ paper to ensure

CHAPTER ONE

JASMINE GALLAGHER SAT in the back seat of a sleek, dark sedan, silently observing the passing countryside behind windows tinted almost black.

The road hugged the very edge of the island of Vela Ada, almost touching the perfect blue of the Adriatic Sea. It was late afternoon, and the ocean glittered beneath the glorious summer sun, the azure surface interrupted only by the occasional tall-masted boat with sails in blinding white.

Jasmine's car was the third of three identical vehicles. Leading the small convoy were two of Jas's team: Scott—who was ex-Special Forces—and Heather—who, like Jas, was ex-Australian National Police. Next in line was what was called the 'principal's' car—the person that Gallagher Personal Protection Services had been tasked with protecting. In Jas's career she had provided close personal protection services—what most people outside the industry would call a 'bodyguard'—to a wide range of people: prime ministers, ambassadors, religious leaders, CEOs, celebrities—but this job was a first for her, and a first for her company.

From today—and for the next three months—she was looking after a prince.

Jasmine smiled. *Royalty.*

This was the opportunity of a lifetime for a girl who'd grown up in public housing on the outskirts of Canberra. And further confirmation that those naysayers who told her a woman couldn't be the face of a protection services company were clueless.

Not that Jasmine had ever doubted herself.

The dense forest that faced the harbour thinned as the

convoy approached the city. At a predetermined landmark—a distinctive cast-iron lamp just over a kilometre from the palace—Jas picked up her phone.

'We're approaching,' she said.

As Jasmine ended the call the woman seated beside her shifted in her seat.

'Can you quiz me again?' she asked, her voice just slightly high pitched. Jas met the gaze of their driver, Simon—a retired SAS Commando—in the rear-view mirror, and knew he was smiling. Felicity had been asking for help with her script and backstory ever since they'd picked her up from Dubrovnik airport, and then over the several hours it had taken to drive and then ferry to Vela Ada.

'You've got this,' Jasmine reassured her. 'But we can run through it one more time if you like.'

Felicity nodded. 'Thank you. I know I'm being ridiculous. I *know*, I know this, it's just…' she paused, pushing her long, perfectly curled blonde hair behind her ears '…this isn't a normal acting job, is it? And Marko… I mean, you've met him, right? *Prince Marko...?* He's pretty distracting.'

Jasmine laughed. 'I can't say I personally feel that way, but guess I can imagine why that would be.'

If you were the type to find tall, dark, broad-shouldered Mediterranean princes distracting. Which Jasmine was not. She couldn't afford to be distracted by something as irrelevant as attractiveness in her job.

'Oh, come *on*,' Felicity said, narrowing her eyes. 'You're not that much older than me, and you're not dead, so don't pretend you haven't noticed he's totally hot. And that *accent*. Honestly, he could read a dictionary and make it sound sexy. Why don't Aussie guys sound like that?'

She flopped back into her leather seat, and now Simon—also Australian—was quietly laughing as the car slowed to a crawl to navigate the narrow cobblestone streets of the city.

'So, I met Marko in Rome six months ago, during a break,

while he completed a secondment with the Italian Army and while I was on holiday. It was *terrifically* romantic…'

Jasmine nodded as Felicity spoke. Jasmine had, of course, been briefed on this rather unusual arrangement—although she didn't know every detail that Felicity was running through now. But she wasn't worried—Felicity was whip-smart, and very well prepared. Ivan—the Prince's valet—had told her of Felicity's exceptional improvisation skills as well, so she was clearly an excellent choice. Plus she certainly looked the part—even now, just slightly anxious, the blonde woman oozed class and polish.

The perfect princess. Or rather, princess-to-be.

'And he took me on a picnic to propose—at the Pavlovic Estate.' Felicity paused. 'I mean, can you imagine if that actually happened? If Prince Marko actually proposed to me for real?' She sighed, and closed her eyes as if imagining the moment herself. '*Princess* Felicity!' She shrugged. 'Oh, well, best enjoy it while it lasts. And do my best to make it believable that Europe's most notorious playboy would *actually* settle down.'

'You've got this,' Jas repeated, but then added, more seriously, 'But remember, your engagement might be fake, but no one else knows that. Your security is real. We don't have any intel that suggests Prince Marko is under threat, but if he was—to any potential bad guys, you *are* his fiancée, and you *will* be a princess. So it's important for your own safety that you follow my instructions tonight, and over the next few months. Okay?'

Felicity nodded. 'Of course,' she said.

Jas watched as Felicity straightened her shoulders and adjusted her expression. No longer did even a hint of the actress remain—she was every inch the mysterious fiancée who Marko would be introducing to Vela Ada at tonight's ball.

The car slid to a stop at the security checkpoint at the palace gate.

Now in range, Jas activated her earpiece. 'We're here.'

* * *

Marko sank back into the linen fabric of his couch, and rubbed his temples.

He had a cracking headache, right on top of the fuzzy cloak of fatigue he'd been wearing all week.

Across from him, in separate plush single armchairs, sat his valet, and the head of his new security detail—Jasmine Gallagher. Beyond that pair was a massive window, framed with heavy brocade curtains and so sparkling clean as to appear invisible. Through that—if he looked—he could see the entire east side of the island—a stunning view but also rather useful when the palace had also played the role of military lookout several centuries ago. Built at the island's highest point, Palace Vela Ada had three-hundred-and-sixty-degree views of the tiny island nation—of its single undulating city of red-roofed stone houses, of the tiny towns dotted amongst the vineyards and market gardens that spoke of its rich agricultural industry, and of the boats and yachts that bobbed in the ocean and brought in as many tourist dollars now as the fish.

But Marko wasn't looking at the view, because he didn't really want to be here at all.

He wanted to be back in Italy, he wanted to be the man who had just been promoted to Pukovnik—Lieutenant Colonel—and who had been thrilled at his progress in strengthening ties between the minuscule Vela Adian army and their allies in neighbouring Croatia and Italy. He also wanted to be the man who—much of the time—managed to ignore the reality of being a prince.

Sure, he was treated differently in the army—but it was subtle, now, after years of his adamant refusal to be coddled and protected or elevated to a rank he hadn't earned. He'd earned the respect of his peers through hard work and later through tours of duty. He was Lieutenant Colonel Marko Pavlovic first; *Prince* Marko only really made an appearance at official royal events, and even that was rare, as his brother—King Lukas—seriously had that all in hand.

It was the greatest stroke of luck that Lukas had been born two years before Marko, rather than the other way around, as Lukas had been the perfect king-in-training since birth. He was everything a king should be, leading Vela Ada through the last few years of political unrest as the Vela Adian parliament had been rocked by scandal and corruption.

Now the dust had—almost—settled, but then Lukas had been diagnosed with cancer.

In the week since Lukas had called him, Marko had been in a fog. He was labelling it fatigue, but it was different from that, really. More a heavy weight of uncertainty and fear.

Lukas—and the royal doctor—had assured Marko and the royal family that Lukas's form of cancer was highly treatable, and that his prospects of making a full recovery were extremely good. He'd also gone to great lengths to stress that Lukas's cancer was unrelated to the cancer that had killed their father, the late King Josip.

But Marko couldn't imagine life without his brother. They might be as different as night and day, but there was no one on this planet Marko respected more than Lukas. Nobody.

Marko couldn't say for sure that was how Lukas felt about *him*—but that didn't really matter. Especially not now.

'I need you to step up for me, Marko,' Lukas had said. 'The island can't cope with any more turmoil. My people need to feel safe, they need to trust our government and know that we—the heads of state—are in control and incorruptible. You need to be—for once in your life—respectful of your position. Respectful of your responsibilities. You can't run away any longer.'

Marko had bristled—despite his concern for Lukas he was unable to leave that comment unchallenged. 'No one would ever dare question my commitment to our military,' he'd said, his tone hard-edged.

'Your commitment to training all over the world, you mean?' Lukas had said. 'Italy, Australia, the US, France...'

His brother had sighed.

'Look, I'm incredibly proud of what you've achieved in your career, and what you've done for our defence alliances—but would it have killed you to spend a bit more time in Vela Ada? To actually be visible to your people? To support them in a way that is tangible to them? Especially over the past few years? Instead, all they see of you is photos in glossy magazines. What was the last article on you? Something about top ten royals in their swimwear... I mean, well done on being number one and all...' Lukas's tone had been desert dry '...but honestly—you were with a different woman in every single photo. How do you think that looks to our people?'

'It's none of their business,' Marko said firmly.

'That's the point,' Lukas had said—for the first time sounding as tired and unwell as he really was. 'You're a prince. Their *Prince. It is their business that you'd rather spend your time anywhere but here and with a different woman every week.'*

The phone had been silent for long moments.

'This isn't going to work, is it?' said Lukas. 'I know you're capable of caretaking my role, but perception is the problem. If people don't believe in you, they won't feel safe. And I can't have that. We've worked too hard to prosecute Senator Božić and his allies and rid Vela Ada of this scourge. Look, I know the label's not entirely accurate, but will they believe in the Playboy Prince? Maybe I can still be active, in between treatments. Try and downplay my illness, and don't mention it's cancer...'

His brother was talking faster and faster.

'Stop,' Marko said. 'I'm not the Playboy Prince. Not any more.' He'd paused, trying to work out what he could say to reassure his brother. He hated hearing his usually impeccably calm and measured brother so anxious. He also

hated—as he'd always hated—the way his personal life was even relevant to Vela Adians—and that his brother bought into it too. Surely his years of military service outweighed a selection of photos of him with bikini-clad women? But this wasn't the time for that argument. 'I'm engaged,' he blurted out the moment the idea even partially formed in his brain. 'I wanted to tell you in person. So you needn't worry. The Playboy Prince is no more.'

'Really?' Lukas had been stunned. 'That's perfect. I mean—congratulations!'

'Thank you,' Marko had said, his lips quirking upwards.

'Who is she? I didn't know you were dating anyone.'

Because, of course, he hadn't been. Marko searched his mind and the room for some titbit about this mystery woman he could share with his brother. On the wall of the small hotel room was an aged map of the world, and his gaze fell to the right-hand corner. 'She's Australian,' he said, thinking fast. 'I met her six months ago. How about she comes with me to Vela Ada, next week, so you can meet her?'

'Yes—' Lukas had said, sounding like himself again. 'I'll announce my illness this week and then have a ball a few days later to reassure everyone I'm not about to keel over, and to reposition you as a stable, responsible, engaged caretaker head of state. I like it.'

'A ball, Lukas? That's really not my thing—'

'It is for the next three months, Marko. You'd better get used to it.'

Marko's gaze slid from the view to the people before him. Ivan sat neatly in his ever-present pinstriped suit, listening intently and studiously taking notes. Beside him, Jasmine—also in a suit—was talking of safe rooms, escape routes and tonight's schedule.

'Your Highness,' she said, her tone suddenly steelier. 'This is important. I appreciate that Ivan will probably brief you again later, but for your safety—and for the safety of my team and everyone in the palace—you need to pay attention.'

Now his gaze sharpened. Before he'd simply been aware that a woman in a jet-black pantsuit sat across from him, but she was right—he hadn't been paying attention. He hadn't even really looked at her. This week had been such a blur of bad news, upturning his life and coordinating his impulsive 'fiancée' lie, that he'd simply approved the appointment of Gallagher Personal Protection Services based on the recommendation of Palace Security and thought little more about the woman who headed the company.

Now he properly considered her.

She was quite tall—obvious even when seated thanks to her long, crossed legs and the fact that her shoulders sat almost level with Ivan's. Her hair was dark, and tied back sleekly from her pale skin, with not one stray strand obscuring the curved line of her cheeks and straight edge of her jaw. Right now, that jaw was firm as she studied him with intense brown eyes.

No, hazel eyes, he corrected as he continued to just look at her, and as the sun that streamed through the window highlighted the flecks of gold in her gaze.

She had great eyes, he realised—large and framed with thick lashes and neat eyebrows as black as her hair. And sharp—as if she missed nothing.

Which would come handy in her job, he supposed.

She hadn't missed his perusal. He felt her intent gaze as his continued to track its way down her narrow, ski-slope-shaped nose—with the slightest upturned tip. It was a nose that probably veered closer towards large than small—and it sat above lips that were neither large nor small. Pink though, and glossy.

Her chin—like her jaw—was firm. A stubborn chin, most likely—but again, this was probably a trait useful in her profession.

Overall, he'd say she was pretty. Certainly pretty enough that in any other week of his life he would've noticed that fact immediately. But he barely remembered what his fake fiancée looked like, and he'd met with her via video conference and face to face nearly a dozen times this week.

His gaze slid back up to hers. Actually, her eyes were definitely more than pretty…beautiful, really—

'Your Highness, may I assume that you also spend this much time documenting the appearance of your male security personnel?'

Marko blinked. Jasmine's eyes were hard.

'My apologies—' he began.

'My gender is irrelevant, Your Highness. And I have certainly not been employed for you to look at.'

'No—of course not—'

Marko couldn't remember the last time he'd felt so flustered. He'd say most people who knew him would assume he never was.

'But if we can agree that I'm not to be either ignored, or ogled, from now on, I think we can continue with my briefing.'

Marko nodded, not just a little ashamed of his behaviour. She was absolutely right—he'd had a terrible week, but it didn't excuse what he'd just done.

What was wrong with him?

He needed to pull himself together. He needed to commit to this—to this stupid plan of his—with everything he had.

He needed to do this for Lukas.

And for Vela Ada.

'I sincerely apologise, Ms Gallagher,' Marko said, again meeting her gaze squarely. 'I assure you it won't happen again.'

She raised an eyebrow, but then she nodded. A neat, controlled movement—like all her movements, he suspected.

He didn't like that she clearly didn't believe him. Did Jasmine think he was the Playboy Prince, too? That he was some frivolous, useless heartbreaker who'd abandoned his country and left his brother to deal with all that royalty bother while he flitted around the world enjoying himself?

Probably.

And he wouldn't be able to talk her around, especially after that rather woeful first impression.

He didn't bother to analyse why it mattered what the head of his protection team thought of him—he knew, instinctively, it wouldn't make any difference to the quality of service that Jasmine would provide.

But it did matter.

Maybe because he genuinely *wasn't* the man who—as Jasmine had said—*ogled* his employees. Or maybe it was because if he wanted all of Vela Ada to respect him, he needed to start with the people standing around him.

Or maybe it was just because Jasmine Gallagher had remarkable golden eyes.

CHAPTER TWO

AFTER THE BRIEFING, Jasmine excused herself to escape to her room.

She nodded at Simon in the hallway, stationed outside Felicity's suite, but didn't meet his gaze. The blush she'd somehow suppressed throughout Marko's…assessment? Inventory? She didn't know how to describe it, but her blush was working its way up her neck at a rate of knots. She needed to get to her room before anyone noticed.

Because Jas Gallagher *did not* blush.

Fortunately, her room was adjacent to Felicity's, and so only a few doors down from Prince Marko's. Safe inside, she flopped onto her bed and stared at the ceiling. At the ornately painted ceiling rose and small glittering chandelier, to be specific, because her room was as sumptuous as the Prince's suite. Just significantly smaller.

Although—in the Pavlovic Palace—small was certainly relative. It was actually about the size of her two-bedroom flat back in Canberra.

Jas squeezed her eyes shut.

Palace. Royalty, she reminded herself.

This job was important. Significant, even. It was highly unusual for an external company to provide personal protection services to immediate members of any royal family. Usually such services for dignitaries would be provided by a country's government—either the royal's own government, or, if visiting another nation, by that nation's own police. When she'd been with the Australian National Police she'd often worked on the shoulder of ambassadors, presidents and prime ministers—simply because laws in Australia prevented visiting protection teams from carrying firearms.

This opportunity—possible only because of the lack of suitably qualified Vela Adian protection personnel, and the expediency that protection services were required—was as rare as it got.

So biting off the head of said actual royal was probably not advisable.

Although obviously she was always going to say something. She would never let a client ignore her like that—and then *stare* at her like that—without comment. It wasn't acceptable behaviour. Personal protection didn't work without respect—of her, of her team, of her directions. It was non-negotiable.

But still—had she had to draw attention to the fact she was a woman? It was something she—as she'd told the Prince—considered irrelevant. And hence, it was not a topic she ever engaged in.

Despite contrary advice, she'd always been very visible as the head of her company. There were no surprises to anyone who hired Gallagher Personal Protection Services that the person in charge was a woman. It was a self-selecting strategy—if someone was too closed minded to realise that Gallagher was awesome at what it did, just because she didn't have broad shoulders and a… Well, then that was definitely their issue. Not hers.

She wasn't about to defend or justify or do anything else to explain herself, because of course to tell anyone that being female *wasn't* an issue *because* of x, y and z implied that she entertained their concerns. And she did not.

Actions spoke louder than words. She'd learnt that the hard way after—

Jas dug her fingernails into her palms. *No.* It had been months since she'd thought about what had happened, and she wasn't about to start now. What mattered now was she hated that she'd brought up her gender to the Prince. Why would she do that?

Because he'd made her feel so female...

Ugh.

What was it about Prince Marko? Despite what she'd told Felicity, she *had* noticed how unbelievably gorgeous he was the few brief times they'd met. Because he was gorgeous in person in a way that was surprising, and almost *overwhelming*, despite her being familiar with his looks because...well, if you'd ever picked up a women's magazine, anywhere in the world, you'd heard of the Playboy Prince.

In person, his looks were just more intense: he was taller, broader, and his blue eyes more piercing than she ever could've imagined.

And despite looking like a man who'd received upsetting news about his brother—with the olive skin of his jaw dusted with stubble, his eyes tinged red, and the occasional grey hair in his army buzz-cut dark hair—such dishevelment just made him even more appealing to her: raw, and real.

And for some reason that real prince—after barely glancing at her for almost the entirety of their business arrangement—had decided to stare at her today.

And if she'd thought his looks intense before—being on the receiving end of his concentrated attention was something else entirely.

The instant he'd really looked at her, her blood had run hot and her belly had heated. She'd sat perfectly still as his eyes had travelled across her face—and she was certain she'd briefly stopped breathing as he'd caught her gaze. As she'd begun to feel herself get lost within it...

But then he'd moved on: his gaze like a touch along her nose, her bare lips, and her skin that seemed so pale amongst Mediterranean complexions.

How long had he stared at her?

It had felt like an age—but maybe it was no time at all?

Maybe—and, God, she cringed at her choice of words now—it hadn't been an *ogle* at all?

It would make more sense if it hadn't been, really. She knew she wasn't unattractive, but she was no Felicity. Her nose was a little too big, her hair nondescript and her figure was more athletic than voluptuous.

But she didn't really believe that. He might not have planned to do it—but she knew when a man was checking her out.

Jas's eyes snapped open, and she studied the way the setting sun reflected off the crystal beads of the chandelier above her.

Not that it mattered if Marko *had* checked her out.

What mattered was that she'd spoken without thinking first. She could've made her point in a myriad other ways without drawing attention to the two things she wanted Prince Marko to forget about completely: that she was a woman, and that he'd been appreciating that fact.

A sharp knock on her door snapped Jas out of her self-recrimination.

She sat up, and straightened her shoulders.

She was being ridiculous. What was done was done.

From now on, she would simply revert to being as impeccably professional as she always—usually—was.

Besides, she seriously doubted that the Prince was likely to check her out again—today was surely a blip?—which would make things easier.

Another insistent knock on her door, and Jas was on her feet. A moment later, she opened the door. It was Simon, and Jas blinked, surprised. It was several hours before they would be accompanying Marko and Felicity to the ball.

Simon spoke in a low, urgent tone. 'We have a problem.'

Felicity sat curled up in a brocade wingback chair beside her room's windows—but she'd closed the heavy curtains and blocked the setting sun. The room was lit only by a single bedside lamp, its glow revealing Felicity's evening gown, laid across the bed in a cascade of emerald silk.

'I'm so sorry,' Felicity said brokenly, and Jas ran to her side, dropping to her knees beside the chair.

'Don't be,' she said, gripping the other woman's hand. 'Of course you need to go home.'

Felicity had just received news that her mother and father had been hospitalised with serious injuries following a terrible car accident. Fortunately neither parent was in a critical condition, but there was no question that Felicity needed to be back in Australia to support her family right now—and not in Vela Ada.

'What is Marko going to do, though? He needs a fiancée. I feel terrible, I—'

'Don't stress about it. You just worry about getting home. Can I help pack your things for you?'

Felicity nodded as Jas got back to her feet.

'I'm sure the Prince will sort something out—' Jas began.

'I certainly will,' a deep voice said from behind her. Jas turned to see Ivan and Marko framed in the doorway.

'Your car is ready to take you to the airport,' he said as he approached Felicity. He also dropped to his haunches so he was at Felicity's level. 'I'm sincerely sorry to hear about your parents' accident. I'll make sure you get home as quickly as possible.'

He stood, and offered his hand to help Felicity up. The blonde woman took it gratefully, and then headed for the door.

'My things—' she began.

'I've got it under control,' Jas reassured her. 'I'll get it all sorted and send it down to the car.'

And then Felicity—and Ivan—were gone.

Somehow, Jas had ended up alone in a room with Prince Marko.

She sent him a tight smile, assuming he'd leave in a moment, and busied herself with locating Felicity's suitcase.

She jumped when he spoke just as she opened one of the built-in cupboards. It seemed he hadn't, in fact, gone anywhere.

'This is not ideal.'

Jas couldn't help but grin at that understatement. She knew exactly how much planning had gone into tonight.

'I assumed you would just announce that your fiancée had a family emergency,' Jas said. It was, after all, the only option he had.

Suitcase found, Jas grabbed it and turned—to find the Prince sitting on the edge of Felicity's expansive bed.

The image of Prince Marko in—well, *on*—a bed had her momentarily transfixed.

It was the most innocent of poses—he literally just sat on it, fully clothed in suit trousers, and a crisp white shirt, unbuttoned at the neck.

He wasn't even looking at Jas, his attention, instead, on the dress that lay beside him. The fingers of one hand were absently twisting a fold of the delicate fabric.

And yet being alone in a room with the only man she could remember ever having…*unsettled* her—*distracted* her—the way he had just by *looking* at her was disconcerting.

Despite her personal pep talk only minutes ago, Jas certainly felt less than purely professional right now. She was spending far too long admiring how the breadth of his shoulders was emphasised by the cut of his shirt, and how its slim fit and the musculature it skimmed reminded Jas of his military day job. Again, she had the sense of something raw and hard in Prince Marko, a world away from the perfect Playboy Prince that she had imagined.

'That won't work,' the Prince said, now looking at Jasmine.

The intensity of his gaze—or maybe that was just how he looked at everybody—once again knocked Jas off balance. She looked down, reminding herself of the empty suitcase in her hands, which she was gripping so hard her knuckles had turned white.

'Oh?' Jasmine said, not really following—instead refocusing her attention on her task. She needed to get this bag packed for Felicity, not worry about princes and beds.

'No,' said Marko, 'I need a tangible princess-to-be, someone for the people of Vela Ada to fall in love with. Unfortunately I don't have what my brother has, that innate—'

'Kingliness?' Jas prompted as she skirted the end of the bed to lay the suitcase beside the evening gown, and as far from Marko as she could manage. She had considered laying it on one of the couches, or on the floor, instead—before she'd told herself she was again being ridiculous.

Marko laughed out loud, the sound deep and rich and filling the room.

Jas's head jerked upwards as she only belatedly realised what she'd actually said. *What was it about this man that made her speak before she thought?* 'Oh, gosh, I'm sorry, that was a stupid thing for me to say—'

But he shook his head. 'No,' he said. 'It's perfect. It's exactly why I'm doing this. Vela Ada needs a king right now—but as Lukas isn't available, it's on me. But I'm not—how did you put it?—*kingly* enough and I know it. Put me in a war zone and I know what I'm doing. Put me in front of the population of Vela Ada…and I hate it. I hate the scrutiny of my personal life. I hate how carefully every word and sentence needs to be constructed. I hate balls and cutting ribbons at the opening of things and having to always be gracious and polite and shake everybody's hand…and everyone knows it.' Marko rubbed his temples, his gaze again on the fabric of the dress. 'No one's going to believe I suddenly have all this *kingliness* in me, unless they believe I've actually changed. That I'm no longer the Playboy Prince.'

And that was why he needed an actual, real-life, in-person fiancée.

She got that now. But…

'Why are you telling me this?' she asked, confused. Her hands had stilled on the zip of the suitcase, packing once again forgotten.

He didn't know her. Why would he reveal so much personal stuff to the head of his security detail? She and her team had only known enough of Marko's plan to allow them to protect the Prince and Felicity effectively. Nothing more.

She watched as Marko pushed himself to his feet and then carefully lifted the emerald dress so that it hung from his fingertips before him. It was a stunning dress, with delicate cap sleeves, a sweetheart neckline, and a slim gold belt at the waist. Beneath that, it fell in a full skirt to the floor, in waves of heavy, shimmering fabric.

A crazy possibility—the *craziest* possibility—tickled at the edge of Jas's subconscious.

'Do you think this would fit you?' Prince Marko asked.

'Pardon me?'

Jasmine's eyes were wide in the shadowy lamplight.

But there was no need for Marko to spell it out—he knew Jasmine understood what he'd meant.

'It's the obvious solution,' he said. It had been obvious to him the moment he'd walked into Felicity's room and seen Jasmine there. 'I need a fiancée *tonight* and no offence to Ivan, but you're the only one who knows about any of this who will look good in this dress.'

He gave the dress a little shake for emphasis.

'I'm not an actress, Your Highness,' Jasmine said carefully, her shocked expression now completely erased. Instead she looked very calm, as if she intended to talk him out of this using common sense.

Of course, this whole idea was nonsensical right from the beginning—Marko knew that. But his impulsiveness was only equalled by his stubbornness—and his commitment to supporting his brother through his illness.

'That doesn't matter,' Marko said patiently. 'You'll be

expected to be a little nervous at your first public event—it will be endearing. And, please, call me Marko.'

Jasmine shook her head, ignoring him. 'Haven't you shown a photo of Felicity to your brother? Told people she's blonde? And even today—we arrived in daylight and I'm sure a few palace staff would've seen her?'

Marko shrugged. 'She was my guest. Or your guest, even—easily explained. And fortunately I've told my brother very little. I don't like lying to him.'

Jasmine raised her eyebrows at that contradiction, but Marko wasn't about to explain. It was true though, he had told Lukas very little—partly for the reason he'd told Jasmine, but also because the week had been such a blur. Ivan had become responsible for the details.

'This is ridiculous. I'm a bodyguard, not a princess. No one's going to believe it.'

'Of course they will,' Marko said firmly. 'If I introduce you as my fiancée, then you're my fiancée.'

Jasmine was looking down again, fiddling restlessly with the zip of the suitcase. 'But,' she said. And now she met his gaze, back to the no-nonsense Jasmine he was already familiar with. 'Let's face it, I don't look anything like one of your girlfriends.'

'I'm not having a discussion about the appearance of the women you, or anyone else, thinks I date, Jasmine.' He knew there was an edge to his tone, but it was unavoidable. 'All I will say is that I enjoy the company of many types of women. I can see nothing unbelievable about me dating you.'

He was surprised to see Jasmine's lips quirk upwards. 'Many types…' she repeated.

Marko narrowed his eyes. 'Yes, many,' he agreed. 'I like the company of women. I'm not going to apologise for it.'

Not nearly as many women as Jasmine, or everyone else, seemed to think. But he wasn't about to explain himself to her.

He could see Jasmine thinking. 'Why not make up a

reason why your fiancée is absent tonight, and then find a new actress? You found Felicity quickly. I'm sure you can do it again.'

Marko shook his head. 'No. Tonight is important. Vela Ada just found out their King is seriously ill. Tonight is the night they need to meet my new fiancée.'

Jasmine chewed her lip, and he knew she was scrambling for a reason to get out of this. 'And this fiancée would be *me*. Jasmine Gallagher, right? No fake name?'

Marko nodded. The press would be onto this—as with Felicity, it would've been too high risk to create a false identity, with the consequences of being found out catastrophic. So, it was the relationship that was fake, nothing more.

'So—assuming everyone *does* believe that I am princess material, it'll mean that my friends and family will think I've been hiding this from them for six months.'

'You can say it was at my request,' he said. 'They'll understand.'

'But that would be a *lie*,' Jasmine said. 'I would be lying, not only to everyone in Vela Ada, but to everyone I know.'

'Yes,' Marko agreed. 'Unfortunately that would be the case.'

Jasmine gave a little huff of frustration. 'That's not a small thing.'

'It's not,' he acknowledged. 'But for me, for the King, and for Vela Ada, the benefits far outweigh a small untruth.'

Jasmine raised an eyebrow. 'And for me?'

'You get to be a princess for a while?' he said, a little hopefully.

'Try again,' she said, crossing her arms.

'I'll triple the fee I'm paying you for protection services.'

He watched as her mouth dropped open.

But quick as a flash her lips were arranged in a straight line again. 'I'd argue that doing this could be detrimental to my business.'

'Yet you've been seeing me for six months with no impact on the quality of services you provide.'

Again, Jasmine raised an eyebrow. 'Ha-ha,' she said, as flat as a pancake.

'I have contacts,' Marko said—more seriously now. 'Through the military, and through diplomatic relationships. I promise you that your company will have more work at the end of this, not less.'

She nodded. 'But what about me, personally? I love what I do, not just managing my company. Who will want a princess as their bodyguard?'

'Well,' he said practically, 'in three months' time, you *won't* be a princess. And three months after that, everyone would've forgotten who you are.'

'Ouch,' she said.

He shrugged. 'It's true. And to help that along, I'll make sure to date someone famous on the rebound. Draw the attention away from you.'

Her expression was sceptical. 'So you'll enter into *another* fake relationship after this one?'

Marko grinned. 'No. I'll just ask a good friend of mine who I date occasionally if she'd mind being photographed with me. She has a film out later this year, so I'm sure she won't mind. It's never been her that's been concerned about discretion.'

'You casually date a *movie star*?' But she held up her hand before he could respond. 'No, wait. Of *course* you do. You're a prince. Royalty. Celebrities. They go together. Can't you see that I don't fit into your world?'

'Right now, all that I really care about is if you'll fit into this dress.'

Jasmine's gaze dropped to the dress he still held.

Long moments passed as he watched Jasmine make her decision—and for the first time he seriously considered what he'd do if she said no.

And honestly, why wouldn't she say no? All of her concerns were valid, except, of course, her belief that a relationship between them was unbelievable.

He'd thought her pretty before, during the briefing. He found her even more attractive now—in the soft, warm lamplight. She was right—she probably *wasn't* exactly his type, in that she was more quietly pretty. Not like Felicity, who everyone noticed the moment she stepped into a room. But Jasmine…he liked how she looked at him so directly, and he really liked how she'd challenged him during the briefing, and how she'd questioned him now. She treated him like an equal—exactly as she should, but how so very few people did. It was, again, one of the many things about his royal title that sat so uncomfortably on his shoulders. He wasn't special simply due to the fortune of his birth. He didn't ask, or expect, to be treated differently from anybody else.

'Yes,' Jasmine said, suddenly. 'I'll do it.'

Marko's gaze caught hers as he exhaled in relief. '*Hvala…* thank you,' he said. 'You have no idea how much this means to me.'

She smiled, and he saw understanding in those lovely hazel eyes. 'Oh,' she said. 'I think I do.'

CHAPTER THREE

THE DRESS DIDN'T FIT.

Well, more accurately, it didn't fit *yet.*

Jas sat on the closed lid of the toilet within her—literally—palatial bathroom, having quickly moved her belongings from her previous smaller room into Felicity's suite.

On her lap was the dress, and in her hands—her nail scissors.

It was sacrilege, really, to be hacking away at the lining of a clearly obscenely expensive dress, but she had no other option. Two stylists—for her hair and make-up—were arriving any minute, so she needed to make this dress fit *now.*

It did occur to her that palaces probably had things like royal tailors, or assistants who could dash into the town to buy her more event-appropriate underwear (she wore a well-worn nude strapless bra that was usually beneath nothing more glamorous than a vest top and a pair of cotton knickers printed with purple violets) but she hadn't thought to ask the Prince—no, *Marko*—about them before he'd left the suite looking all relieved and gorgeous.

And so she carefully cut through the figure-hugging dark emerald lining that had been designed to fit a figure with far slimmer hips than hers.

Lining removed, she tried the dress on again.

This time—it made it over her hips. The waist, thank God, fitted perfectly, and the bodice…well…nothing that a few tissues shoved inside her bra wouldn't fix.

Jas straightened her shoulders as she twisted and turned in front of the mirror. It was, honestly, the most beautiful thing she'd ever worn. Its skirt—thankfully made up of enough layers that the lack of lining seemed to make no difference—made lovely swishing sounds as she moved, the silk unbelievably luxurious against her skin. And the gold—and she was pretty sure it was *actually* gold—belt glittered underneath the bathroom lights.

She nodded at herself in the mirror. *Done.* Now, shoes.

She gathered up the heavy fabric of the skirt and headed into the bedroom. On the bureau near the door was a white box labelled with a high-end shoe brand, and inside was a stunning pair of gold heels—that she immediately realised were a size too small.

Why hadn't she checked earlier?

Maybe because she didn't know what the hell she was doing?

Jas met her own gaze in the mirror above the spindly table.

What have I got myself into?

There was a sharp rap on the door, followed by Simon's voice—as he was now, ridiculously, *her* bodyguard. 'Hair and make-up are here,' he said.

'Just a minute!' she said.

Then she scanned the room, wondering if maybe palaces were like hotels—and there would be a phone line directly through to a concierge who could go find her some shoes.

Unsurprisingly, there wasn't.

Again, she met her gaze in the mirror, and again, she straightened her shoulders.

She took a deep breath.

She'd agreed to do this. She'd agreed to do this because she was about to earn her company's entire income from last year in three months—and...because her myriad concerns with saying yes hadn't seemed so compelling when contrasted with the desperation in Prince Marko's gaze.

It hadn't been overt, but she'd seen it. Flashing in and out so briefly before he'd gathered himself again.

Desperation...and also...*vulnerability.* A vulnerability she'd somehow known he'd hated to reveal. But then—he didn't want to be doing any of this, did he? He didn't want to be desperately asking a total stranger to help him, because he'd much rather his brother was healthy and he didn't have to worry about royal balls and acting kingly. Prince Marko wasn't doing this for himself.

He was asking her to do this crazy, ridiculous thing for his brother, and for Vela Ada.

That was why he'd *needed* her to say yes.

And in the end that was what it had come down to.

Because he'd needed her, she'd said yes. A man she barely knew.

It was nuts. Completely out of character for her to be so impulsive.

And yet she'd done it.

For the next three months, she was Prince Marko of Vela Ada's fiancée.

It might not entirely make sense to her—but she was committed now.

And as such—she was committed to sorting out a pair of sparkly shoes.

She opened the door. Outside stood two very stylish-looking women, and Simon.

'Simon, can you please notify Ivan that I require a pair of gold heels in size nine, with a three-inch heel?'

To Simon's credit, he nodded as if this were a perfectly normal request from his boss.

Then she turned to the stylists. 'Ladies, I'll just change into a robe and be right with you.'

'No problem,' said the older lady, with an American accent, 'Your High—' She paused, then blushed. 'Oh! That probably isn't right yet, is it? What should we call you?'

'Just Jas, is fine,' said Jasmine. 'I'm certainly not royalty.'

'Not yet,' said the woman with a grin.

Your Highness.

Oh, wow. Oh, God.

What had she done?

Marko gripped the carved balustrade tightly, his gaze aimed unseeing at the stairs that would lead him to the ballroom two floors below him. He rocked slightly on his heels on the plush carpet, only peripherally aware of the muffled sounds of the string quartet warming up in the distance.

This was both the best, and worst, idea he'd ever had.

As a method to calm his brother during a very stressful time, inventing a fake fiancée was genius. But in every other way it was far from brilliant.

His plan had felt complicated enough when he'd had a trained actress on board. Now…

Now it felt messy.

Now he'd somehow talked Jasmine Gallagher into something he knew she couldn't possibly comprehend. Yes, she'd alluded to the fact she'd be lying to her family, and yes, she was concerned for her business—but she had no idea what it actually meant to be under public scrutiny every moment of the day.

It was life in a fish bowl: a life that he had determinedly escaped. And now Marko had led another woman straight into it, and a woman who—unlike Felicity—didn't welcome the opportunity for a higher profile.

And so he felt bad about that.

But not bad enough to call it off.

Inside his tuxedo jacket, he had a contract for Jasmine that would minimise some of the messiness of the situation with clear expectations and details of his generous remuneration. It was, after all, just a business arrangement. An unusual one, but nothing more—

'Marko?'

He turned at Jasmine's voice, soft—but clear—across the empty landing.

He opened his mouth to say something—but instantly forgot what.

She looked…stunning.

Suddenly, his previous assessments of Jasmine as pretty, or attractive, seemed embarrassingly inadequate.

As did his inability to even notice her until today. He

must have been temporarily blind—or his libido temporarily in hibernation—for Marko to have been so oblivious of Jasmine Gallagher.

He swallowed as she shifted her weight, still a good five metres or so away from him—a wide expanse of carpet between them.

The dress was gorgeous. He'd known that—had been involved tangentially in selecting it if you could count Ivan asking him to approve the designer Felicity had chosen—but on Jasmine it was something else. Her skin—so pale—contrasted against the deep emerald fabric, and her hair—so dark—rolled into a lush smooth arrangement at her nape was a sharp contrast to the severely scraped-back ponytail she'd sported earlier today. Her eyes—still lovely—seemed even larger, and her lips—in ruby red—were lush and glossy.

He watched as she shuffled on the spot again, and then deliberately straightened her shoulders. 'Please say something,' she said, catching his gaze with a piercing look. 'Do I look okay? I feel like the biggest fraud.'

Marko covered the distance between them in a moment, and now he stood close enough that she needed to tilt her chin upwards.

'Lijep,' he said. *'Tako lijepo.'*

Jasmine swallowed. 'Pardon me?' she asked.

'Beautiful,' he said, having not even realised he hadn't been speaking English. 'So beautiful.'

'Oh!' she said, looking mildly stunned. 'Thank you. That's a very nice thing to say.'

'It's true,' he said. 'You look like a princess.'

She grinned. 'I suppose that's the idea,' she said. 'You look very much like a prince, yourself.'

Her gaze flicked over his tuxedo—the crisp white shirt, the black bow tie, the white pocket square.

'No crown?' she asked, her eyes sparkling.

'No,' he said, firmly. His brother had worn one at his cor-

onation, but Marko never had. But he then surprised himself by adding, 'Damn uncomfortable things.'

How did this woman do that? He'd spent the whole week knotted up with tension, and yet now he was teasing her?

Jasmine's lips quirked upwards.

'Well, I am *actually* uncomfortable in these shoes.' She gathered up her skirt so she could poke her heels out from under the fabric.

They were a glittering gold, with a peep-toe front.

'I didn't have time to paint my toenails,' she continued. 'But these were the best match for the dress out of the collection that Ivan somehow sourced for me. It's just they pinch a little. I have no idea how he did it so quickly. It was like he had some secret stash of evening shoes in the palace.'

'Thank you,' Marko said, suddenly.

She shrugged. 'It's okay, I've packed a few plasters in my clutch so my feet will survive. I'm always prepared.'

She was deliberately misinterpreting him, and it made him smile.

'You know what I mean,' he said.

She just smiled. She was quick to smile—and it was a gorgeous smile. Natural and wide.

How had he not noticed before?

'We have somewhere to be,' she said.

'Ah,' he said, 'the schedule.'

She nodded. 'We need to get moving, or my guys downstairs will get twitchy.'

Almost on cue, a member of Lukas's staff came up the stairs, his boots a soft thud on the carpet. 'The King is ready to see you now.'

They were to meet King Lukas and Queen Petra in the Knight's Hall.

Located at the base of one of the four circular…towers? Turrets? Jas wasn't sure, but whatever they were they were large, and round, and located at the four corners of the palace, connected together by long, stone corridors, half clad in dark wood panelling.

Lukas's attendant had announced their arrival, and then quietly disappeared. No security stood at the opened door before them—at such a secure location, there was no need for it. It was why Prince Marko and herself had no escort, and why Jas's team were already down in the ballroom.

To be honest, on nights like tonight, in a secure building, with a strict guest list and no current threat, there wasn't a heck of a lot for security to do. The King's own staff had the perimeters under control—so all Jasmine and her team would be doing tonight was ensuring that events progressed as scheduled, and to keep an eye out for anything unusual. Effectively, they would've just blended into the background—ready if required, but otherwise unobtrusive. The Prince and Felicity would've barely noticed they were there.

Jas certainly hadn't expected to be anywhere near this close to Prince Marko this evening.

She looked up at him, standing so close to her that her shoulder would bump his upper arm if she moved even a little bit.

No. She certainly hadn't expected to be this close to Marko. Tonight, or ever.

'You okay?' he asked, his voice low.

This close, his delicious accent gave her shivers, and she closed her eyes as she took a deep breath.

'Of course,' she said.

She wiggled her toes in her new shoes, welcoming the way they rubbed just a little at the back—the slight pain a useful reminder that this was *actually* happening. She opened her eyes—only to find herself gazing directly into Marko's blue gaze.

She shivered again.

The sound of a man clearing his throat made Jas jump, and she stepped back abruptly from Marko.

'You two lovebirds planning on joining us?'

It was, of course, the King.

Marko's older brother stood in the opened doorway. He was tall—about the same height as Marko, and with similar dark-coloured hair. But Lukas's hair was longer, and peppered with grey. He wore an identical suit to his brother, but he wore it with an ease that Jasmine only now realised that Marko lacked. Lukas wore his tux as if he wore one every day—and, Jas realised, that probably wasn't too far off the truth. A king must attend formal events as regularly as Jas had Thai takeaway when she was back home: i.e. a *lot*.

Jasmine straightened her shoulders and smiled at Lukas. He was easy to smile at—his expression open and welcoming, so different from his more shuttered brother.

And then Marko wrapped his fingers around Jas's hand—and she had to do everything in her power not to gasp.

Fortunately, Lukas had already turned away, gesturing for them to follow him into the Knight's Hall.

Marko had never touched her before—if she excluded a brief, firm handshake when they'd first met several days ago. Marko had barely met her eyes back then, and as such the touch had been warm—but utterly unmemorable.

This was *nothing* like that.

Marko had laced his fingers through hers—an intimate gesture, and fitting, of course, for an engaged couple. But for Jas, the intimacy was shocking, and sent a thrill of sensation up her arm and through her body to finally pool low in her belly.

Jas's gaze flew upwards, but Marko wasn't even looking at her. That probably would've dumped ice water over her unwanted reaction—but then, he squeezed her hand.

Now, she *knew* he was just being reassuring. She *knew* he was holding her hand for show and not any other reason.

And yet…as crazy as this was, as *insane* as it all was, it was so easy, just for a moment, to desperately wish it were all real.

But—since when had Jas Gallagher believed in fairy tales?

Inside the Knight's Hall, Jas gently tugged her hand free. She wiggled her toes again, rocking her heels on the parquet floor.

Queen Petra stood near the unlit fireplace, and she turned to greet them. She wore a stunning red gown, and her blonde hair was piled in an elaborate updo, behind a diamond and platinum tiara.

'Hello,' she said, 'I'm Petra.'

She sounded so normal, as if they'd met at a barbecue, except that she had a fancy accent.

'I'm Jasmine,' Jas said. Something terrifically obvious suddenly occurred to her. 'I'm sorry, am I supposed to curtsey?'

They all laughed. 'No,' Marko said. 'I should've explained. When no one's watching, there's no need for any pomp and ceremony.'

'Absolutely not,' said Petra. 'We're all really normal, actually.'

'Hmm…' was all Jasmine could manage. She was standing in a turret or a tower, with oversized lancet windows, walls full with oil paintings of previous monarchs, and there was a *full suit of knight's armour* standing beside one of the armchairs. 'Normal' didn't really explain any of this.

Lukas laughed. 'Come on, you've been with Marko for six months, you must know by now there isn't anything special about him.'

Marko grinned. 'No, she's already pointed out that I don't have any of your kingliness.'

'Kingliness?' Lukas laughed out loud. 'I like it. I do try my best to be suitably kingly at all times.'

Jasmine silently waited for the floor to open up and swallow her.

Petra saved her. 'Ignore them,' she said. 'Walk with me to the ballroom and tell me all about yourself—I need to know all about the woman who has captured my brother-in-law's heart.'

Petra headed out of the room, obviously expecting Jas to follow. Jas looked to Marko—but he nodded that she should go.

His smile had fallen away, Jas noticed—as had Lukas's.

For the first time, Jas remembered how sick the King was.

'Jasmine?' Petra prompted, and Jas hurried to catch up.

'Can you tell me when I'm supposed to curtsey and stuff tonight?' she asked as they traversed the hallway, skirts rustling in tandem. 'Marko said it didn't matter, but it does to me.'

A white lie, but this level of detail hadn't occurred to her when she'd agreed to this charade.

'Of course,' Petra said. 'I had to learn all this too. It does get easier, I promise. One day it'll be second nature for you.'

'I can't imagine it,' Jas replied, honestly.

Petra paused when they reached the end of the corridor, standing in the palace's huge entry foyer. Behind her twin staircases swept upwards to meet at the first-floor landing and the biggest chandelier Jas had ever seen glittered above them, making the marble floor shimmer and sparkle. Around them palace staff bustled busily, with guests due to arrive any moment.

'Really,' Petra said. 'One day I woke up and the palace felt like home.'

Home?

Jas smiled, relieved she could finally be completely honest. 'I'm sure this place will never feel like home to me.'

After all, in three months' time she'd be back in her real home, and this palace—and this night—would feel like no more than a dream.

CHAPTER FOUR

IT WAS GOING WELL, Marko thought.

For a prince pretending to be engaged and a bodyguard pretending to be in love with him.

His lips curved upwards as he settled back into his chair and absently swirled his champagne.

Actually—that was unfair. Jasmine was doing remarkably well, considering there had been no time to really tell her anything.

He observed her as she spoke to one of the ministers of the Vela Ada parliament, her head tilted as she listened intently to whatever the other woman was saying. The pair stood only a short distance away, between the as yet empty dance floor and one of the many round tables that seated a mix of the most prominent and influential citizens of Vela Ada—from politicians, to philanthropists to entrepreneurs.

Although he'd stood beside Jasmine as they'd greeted the guests with his brother and Petra, and also sat beside her at dinner—they'd barely spoken.

Petra seemed thrilled to have someone else to discuss the realities of adjusting from civilian to royal life with, and had happily taken Jasmine under her wing. And, of course, pretty much everyone wanted to know about his mysterious fiancée, and so there had been a constant stream of interested guests wishing to introduce themselves. At first, Marko had stood nearby, ready to answer or deflect any tricky questions—but there was no need. Jasmine improvised like the actress she said she wasn't—smoothly redirecting conversation to topics other than the details of their supposed relationship, or answering with laughter and ambiguity, allowing guests to fill in the blanks however they saw fit.

With Jasmine doing so well, it had left Marko free to have his own conversations. Which he had: with a retired army general, a prominent business owner, a former Olympian. They were all nice people, and the conversations were pleasant enough—but it didn't take long for him to be over it. In fact, he'd been over it from the moment he'd stood in that reception line, greeting hundreds of people in a blur of handshakes and a cheek-aching smile.

He'd excused himself and headed for his table—then downed his champagne in one gulp.

A waiter immediately refilled his drink—but he resisted downing that one too. Someone was always watching at these events, and the last thing he needed was another Playboy Prince non-scandal to disappoint his brother and pretty much everyone else who knew him.

He didn't want to be here.

He *really* didn't want to be here.

What he'd much rather be doing was hanging out with Lukas. To do anything with him—maybe play pool at the table his brother had in his library. Or watch a movie and drink beer. Or just have something nice to eat. Stuff they hadn't done together in longer than he could remember.

And something he wanted to do, with the person he wanted to spend time with—and *not* in public, and not with the weight of expectation and obligation weighing heavily upon him.

But instead he was here, at a ball, to make other people feel better about Lukas's illness, when *he* certainly wasn't feeling any better about it. Talking to Lukas, or to the royal doctor, had done nothing to ease the spiky ball of worry, concern and fear that had lodged itself in Marko's belly.

If he lost him…

Marko clenched his jaw.

No. He wouldn't even consider it. He couldn't.

His gaze travelled back to Jasmine—searching for a distraction. Maybe she sensed his gaze, as she turned towards him.

She began to smile—but then stopped. Her brow furrowed.

In concern?

He swore under his breath.

He looked away—focusing his attention on his fingers as they gripped the stem of his glass, absently spinning the glass from side to side.

He tensed as Jasmine slid into the chair beside him. He did *not* want to have a conversation about whatever Jasmine had thought she'd seen in his face. Not with a woman he barely knew. Not with anyone.

'Only a few minutes before the speeches,' she said quietly. He turned in his seat to look at her.

She looked—totally normal. No more furrowed brow. No questions in her gaze.

He felt his shoulders relax. *What was wrong with him?*

He was jumping at shadows.

'You don't need to worry about that,' he said, happy to talk about anything. 'Palace staff will let us know where we need to be.'

'It's still my job,' she said, with a shrug. 'I can't switch it off. I'm keeping an eye on my team, too, although it's weird to not be able to talk to them. I feel naked without my earpiece at a formal event.'

Naked was probably not the best word Jasmine could've chosen. Or possibly it was the *best*, as Marko was now extremely effectively distracted from his unwanted thoughts of Lukas, and royal duty and…

Tako lijepo.

God, she was hot in that dress—all pale skin and soft curves.

He caught Jasmine's gaze again as his crept back up to her face. She narrowed her eyes.

Marko cleared his throat.

This is a business arrangement, he reminded himself.

'Is that why you're so good at talking to everyone?' Marko asked, focusing on not—once again—ogling Jasmine, as she'd so accurately accused him of earlier that day. Could it really have only been today? 'You've attended lots of events like this one?'

Jasmine nodded. 'On the other side, of course,' she said. 'I've been in the background—or at times right on the shoulder—of all sorts of conversations. And I've spoken to all sorts of people too. Some VIPs are chatty in the car, or bored when they're waiting for someone or something, and often I'm the only person available to talk to. I guess maybe I've picked up a few bits and pieces, although this is a bit different from a quick chat to a pop star who's nervous before a performance, or talking to a visiting ambassador about kangaroos.' She reached for her own champagne. 'I'm glad you think I'm doing a good job. I just feel like I'm doing lots of smiling and rambling about not much at all.'

'That's all I do,' Marko said. 'Smile, talk about something benign, then nod at someone else's benign conversation while trying to look interested. Welcome to a royal event.'

She nodded. 'Everyone's been very nice to me. And some of the people I've spoken to are really interesting. But it's not,' Jasmine said in a low voice, leaning closer as if to confide in him, 'quite as exciting as I expected.'

Marko laughed out loud. 'No. Being royal is a job. With really great food and wine, but just a job, nonetheless.'

A palace attendant tapped on Marko's shoulder and murmured in his ear.

He stood, and reached for Jasmine's hand.

'Looks like we're up,' he said.

It was time for Marko to formally introduce Jasmine to Vela Ada.

Jas hadn't thought to put her champagne glass down before following Marko to the small stage at one end of the ballroom, and so now she stood beside the King and Queen, with Marko, feeling somewhat as if she were about to give a speech at a really, really fancy wedding.

Although—thankfully—she wasn't scheduled to actually say anything. Her role tonight was to stand beside Marko and look like the loving fiancée she supposedly was.

The loving fiancée part wasn't all that hard. It was all too easy to stand, oh, so close to him—close enough to feel his body heat, and to smell whatever delicious fragrance he wore—something crisp and woody.

And to look up at him—to imagine she was in love with him—was easy, too. He still held her hand—and he squeezed it occasionally, sending shivers of sensation rioting throughout her body.

He did so now, and glanced downwards to hold her gaze. His gaze was reassuring, a *you've got this* message. There was nothing more—not a hint of what she'd seen before: both an unexpected rawness of emotion she'd glimpsed as he'd been watching her from a distance, but also a different type of rawness later—that heat, that *wanting*.

She'd tried to shut it down—she'd glared at him, channelling her affront of earlier that day. But as it had been during the briefing, she hadn't really had her heart behind it.

In fact, her heart had been beating at a million miles an hour.

Now she squeezed his hand back. *I'm fine.*

But she wasn't—not really.

Partly, she was uncomfortable simply standing here—while she'd been at many important events in her career, she'd never been the subject of such concentrated attention. Standing beside someone important on a stage, in her black suit, was *not* the same as wearing a ball gown with a room full of dignitaries staring at her.

She felt terribly awkward in her tight shoes and with her superfluous champagne glass, and it was a constant battle not to fidget.

But she didn't, of course. She was a professional. She could do this.

Lukas was speaking now, in the Vela Ada dialect—and as Jas knew only very few words of the Slavic language, she could only guess at what he was saying.

His voice revealed none of his illness, although this close she could see how lean he was beneath his suit, and the hint of dark beneath his eyes.

Petra stood beside him, looking composed and lovely. And she *was* lovely, and had been all evening to Jas—checking in with her, whispering little hints and words of encouragement. Earlier she'd even given her a crash course in curtseying—although with the only other royals in attendance being the late King Josip's brother and his wife, as Lukas and Marko's mother had retired from public life following her husband's death, she'd only had to worry about it briefly—and in the end it hadn't been that hard at all.

But it was Petra that she was feeling most uncomfortable about—more so than feeling awkward in front of hundreds of guests. Here was a woman dealing bravely with her husband's cancer diagnosis, and Jas was—*lying* to her.

Marko leant down to murmur in her ear, his breath a tickle against her skin. 'Here we go.'

Lukas gestured for Marko to step forward, and Jas stepped up right beside him.

'And now,' Lukas said, in English now, 'I'd like to introduce the woman who will be accompanying Prince Marko as he takes on my royal commitments over the next three months—and who I am looking forward to welcoming into the Pavlovic family: his fiancée, Jasmine Gallagher.'

The ballroom filled with polite applause, and Jasmine just smiled and tried not to look awkward.

Marko then began to speak—again, in Slavic, and as he spoke—and he spoke well—Jasmine took the opportunity to simply watch him.

He stood tall, and powerfully—his shoulders back, his

stance firm—and there was definitely no fidgeting involved. He looked fantastic in his suit, but it did nothing to hide the strength of the man, the solid contour of his biceps and the width of his shoulders evident beneath the expensive fabric. His buzz-cut hair only further enhanced the impression of a man constructed of hard edges—there was no softness to this prince.

She'd noted before that he wore his suit less comfortably than his brother, and she still thought that true. There was a tension to Marko's posture, as if he was out of his native habitat. He'd said earlier that a royal title was just another job, and although she didn't think it was that simple—there were some big perks to being a royal!—she understood his sentiment. And so—knowing he was a highly ranked military officer—she supposed it was army fatigues rather than a tuxedo that was his uniform of choice?

And yet, despite his incongruity in a tuxedo, and despite the tension she sensed in him—and also whatever it was she'd glimpsed in his gaze earlier—he now commanded the ballroom. His ability to do so wasn't unexpected—since she'd met Marko it had been impossible to ignore his magnetism—but *before* she'd met him, she wouldn't have expected it.

She had thought her company had been hired to protect a playboy prince—and the Playboy Prince she had expected was nothing like Marko at all.

Of course she'd seen the photos of Marko in women's magazines. And of course she'd looked him up on the Internet again when she'd first been approached to work for him. And the photos and articles were all the same: about a man who had eschewed a royal life to flit across Europe—and who had seemingly never been photographed with the same woman twice. There he'd been, on the list of World's Most Eligible Bachelors or the World's Hottest Royals or whatever.

None of this had mattered to her, as it had no impact on the job she'd been hired to do.

But she'd been curious.

Even the whole fake fiancée ruse hadn't really given her pause—she and her team had just signed the water-tight confidentiality agreement and been done with it. It wasn't her job to judge the decisions of the rich and famous—no matter how odd or misguided they appeared to her.

Of course, it *had* given her pause when Marko had asked her to take Felicity's place.

Suddenly Marko's lie would be affecting her. And now Marko's lie was *her* lie. She was no longer a bystander—she was part of this.

Ever since her impulsive decision to be Marko's fake fiancée, the weight of that lie had only grown heavier the more real it had become.

And standing here right now, in front of hundreds of people as a man you barely knew announced you to his *country* as something you weren't...well, lies didn't get much bigger than that.

What have I done?

Were the pleas of a man who made her blood run hot enough of a reason to do something so far outside her moral compass?

His reasons at the time had seemed so compelling, the lie so harmless...

But now...

Jas's gaze flicked from Marko back to Lukas.

As she watched he stepped back from where he'd stood beside Marko.

Marko noticed—although to anyone in the crowd they'd never know.

But Jas saw it. She saw the nearly imperceptible inclination of Lukas's head towards Marko, and then Marko's matching gesture back.

Lukas took Petra's hand—and Jas saw how tightly he gripped it. Then he closed his eyes, and released what she imagined was a long-held breath.

Relief.

Petra leant in close to kiss her husband's cheek, and when she turned back to look again at Marko her eyes were glazed with unshed tears.

'Jasmine?'

Marko's voice made her jump, and to her horror it also made the long-forgotten champagne glass dislodge from her fingertips.

It shattered loudly at her feet, to a chorus of gasps from the crowd.

And then—before her brain could catch up with all that it had been coping with today: fake princesses, and ball gowns, and curtseys, and unwell kings, and friendly queens and the way Marko's voice and touch just did all sorts of *things* to her—she swore.

Rather loudly.

CHAPTER FIVE

THE ENTIRE BALLROOM went absolutely silent, after a few bursts of laughter were quickly muffled.

Jasmine's expression as her gaze shifted from the shards of glass at her feet to meet with Marko's own was of pure mortification.

Her lovely mouth had dropped open, and her already pale complexion had turned completely white.

'Marko—I am *so* sorry,' she said, barely above a whisper. 'I don't even really swear that often, honestly, and then to say *that*, here... I don't know what came over me. Oh, God, now I've embarrassed you, and your family, let alone myself and—'

Her words were getting all jumbled—so he reached out, grabbed her hand, and tugged her close to his side. Her eyes widened, but she went silent.

He leant close to her, and whispered roughly, 'Can I kiss you?'

'Pardon me?'

'Let's give them something else to remember about the first time they met Prince Marko's fiancée.'

She just blinked at him.

'Jasmine?'

'You want to kiss me? Right here, in front of hundreds of people?'

He just smiled at her. And *looked* at her—right into those lovely hazel eyes.

He supposed, in theory, it was a *don't-stress-about-it*-type kiss. At least—that was his intention.

He was playing the role of the loving, supportive fiancé, after all.

But also—yes, he wanted to kiss her. If he was honest with himself, he'd wanted to kiss her ever since she'd told him off in that briefing.

She closed her eyes, and he watched as she took a deep breath.

When she opened them, she nodded.

And then—he kissed her.

So it was a simple kiss—a straightforward kiss.

His mouth pressing against hers briefly, nothing more.

But then—when his mouth did touch hers—suddenly, it wasn't brief. Suddenly—he lingered.

Her lips were soft, and fleetingly cool beneath his own. They were chastely closed, of course—but they shifted against the pressure of his own mouth, as if she'd open her mouth for him if only he were to ask.

It was shockingly, unexpectedly sexy—a simple kiss that felt like a promise of so much more. It wasn't just about the touch of their lips or the mingling of their breathing—but of the subtle movement of their bodies, the way they leant towards each other while still only joined by their laced fingers.

Marko was no longer aware of their audience, or of the ballroom, or even why he'd kissed her in the first place.

All that mattered was the way her mouth fitted so perfectly against his.

Something—maybe a cough, or a sigh, or a laugh—dragged Marko backed to reality, and he ended the kiss. But he didn't move far—instead he leant even closer, and in a low, gravelly, drawn-out whisper only she could hear he repeated the exact same curse Jasmine had so loudly exclaimed just minutes earlier.

She laughed, breathily, as he turned back to the podium, and introduced Jasmine Gallagher to Vela Ada.

* * *

The evening breeze ruffled diaphanous curtains as Jasmine stepped through one of the several open French doors that led onto the palace terrace.

The terrace was wide and paved with large flat stones, criss-crossed with decorative lines and swirls of cobblestones. With the sun now set the terrace was lit only by the ballroom behind her, and the many strings of fairy lights that decorated the castle architecture—wrapping around pillars and arches and outlining the notches in the crenelated wall that edged the terrace—and the palace.

In daylight, Jasmine knew, she'd be able to see across the city of Vela Ada—across its undulating sea of red-roofed cottages and out to the pure white sand beaches and the Adriatic Sea.

But tonight she could barely see the outlines of some of the giant trees that grew beside the palace—instead they were simply black shadows against a sparkling, starry sky.

Jas shivered, even though it was a mild late summer evening.

She was alone. And thanks to a quick word to her team, she would remain so.

She took a long, deep breath in an attempt to slow her turbulent thoughts.

She closed her eyes.

No. That was a mistake.

Closing her eyes only reminded her of how her eyes had slid shut as Marko's lips had covered hers.

Her eyes snapped open.

A kiss. It was just a kiss.

For show only.

And as a show, it had been immediately effective. During the kiss itself—which could have taken place over five seconds or five minutes, Jasmine had no idea—she'd been oblivious to her surroundings. But after Marko had stepped away it had been immediately obvious that the mood of the room had shifted.

From a mood that Jas had interpreted as a mix of censure, laughter and pity, the room had transformed into warm approval—as if Marko had beguiled the room as well as Jasmine.

No.

She wasn't beguiled by Prince Marko.

She was *working* for him.

So what if he'd dealt with her clumsiness in the most perfect way, and then introduced her to his people as if he were truly in love with her—with pride and admiration that would've made Jas melt into a puddle of happiness should any of it actually have been real?

That the Playboy Prince was charming was of no surprise to her.

But that he was considerate, and, despite his reputation, clearly extremely loyal to both his brother and Vela Ada—this was a little unexpected.

And that he was a fabulous kisser…

Wait. No, that wasn't surprising. That he'd kissed *her*. Yes—that was surprising.

That was about the last thing she'd ever imagined would happen to her.

Kissed by a prince.

'Jasmine?'

She turned at Marko's voice. He stood across the terrace—a step or two down from the French doors, only his silhouette visible with the bright lights of the ballroom behind him.

Unfortunately, she hadn't been able to ask her team to keep Marko away. Mainly because it would've looked seriously weird if anyone had noticed, and partly because she did *not* want her team to realise how flustered she was by that kiss.

She was a professional, after all.

Even if she smashed champagne glasses and swore at the

most regal and formal of events anyone could ever imagine…

Mentally she gave herself a shake. It was done now. Time to move on.

Even if she could've done with some more Marko-free time. Having him even this close to her had her all prickly and tingly with awareness. It was exceedingly distracting.

'I think it's definitely time you just called me Jas,' she said, and was pleased that she sounded satisfactorily relaxed and normal. Professional.

'Jas,' he said, as if testing it out on his tongue. With Marko's accent, her name sounded about as exotic as it ever, possibly could.

He crossed the terrace, and as he drew near Jas was able to make out his features in the moonlight—the sharp shape of his nose, the strength of his jaw, and the outline of the mouth she'd kissed just minutes ago.

'I'm sorry,' she said abruptly, needing to halt her wayward thoughts. 'About the glass. And the swearing.'

'I know you are,' Marko said. 'But it doesn't matter. That entire room now believes we're in love, and that's all that matters. That is—' he'd stopped now, close enough that if she reached out she could touch the expensive wool of his suit '—if you've decided if you're going to continue in this role or not.'

Jas blinked, surprised. 'You think that's why I came out here?'

She wrapped her arms around herself, rubbing at the wave of goose pimples that dotted her skin.

'Yes,' he said firmly. 'You're having second thoughts.' A statement.

She nodded, because he was right. Or almost right. 'I am,' she said. Then swallowed. 'I mean—I was.'

Something shifted in Marko's posture—a silent exhalation of relief?

'It's all the lying,' Jas said. 'I was worried about lying to my friends and family, but I hadn't thought about how I'd feel about lying to people face to face. Especially people who are close to you, like Lukas and Petra. I feel terrible about it, especially given what they're going through.'

Now Marko nodded, but made no comment.

'But then I saw the way Lukas responded when you took the microphone tonight. It was like the weight of the world had been lifted from his shoulders. And that's when I got why you're doing this—it's all for Lukas. Not Vela Ada, but Lukas.'

'It's the weight of Vela Ada he has on his shoulders,' Marko corrected her. 'He's been carrying it alone for a very long time.'

His gaze flickered away from Jas's as he spoke, and she wondered at his last sentence. But before she could say or ask anything, he continued.

'And yes—you're correct. This is all about Lukas. I couldn't give a damn what anyone else thinks of my reputation, but it does matter to me when Lukas believes it. He sees me as self-indulgent and unreliable. An outsider from the royal family who has shunned all my princely responsibilities.'

'But your stellar military career—'

'Doesn't hide the fact I've avoided anything to do with the palace for as long as I, or anyone else, can remember,' he finished for her. 'I'm not going to sugar coat it, Jas—I've left it all to my big brother to deal with. Lukas knows it—*everyone* knows it. My army career doesn't cancel that out.'

'Okay,' she said. It was about all she could think of to say. She couldn't really comprehend the idea of having to bear such responsibilities purely due to the circumstances of your birth.

'So,' he said, 'thank you—once again—for doing this for me. With you, I appear a changed man. And that's exactly my goal.'

He smiled at her—a gorgeous, grateful and, as always,

sexy smile—and not for the first time this evening, Jas was losing herself in his eyes.

Then, Jas watched as Marko quickly undid a single button of his jacket. In the darkness his black waistcoat seemed to blend into his jacket, and his shirt was as white as the moon.

It took her a moment to realise that he was holding his lapel to show her the lining of his jacket. Part of a white envelope poked out of an inside pocket.

'I've had Ivan write up a new contract—based on Felicity's, and it contains the contract terms and your remuneration details.'

A contract. Money. Of course.

What else had she thought Marko was doing?

She mentally gave herself a little shake—*clearly* it had been too long since she'd had a date if a man unbuttoning his suit jacket made butterflies flutter inside her.

'The confidentiality statement is a little more comprehensive than the one you've already signed, and it also outlines your role in more detail than what we've discussed.'

Jas nodded, but she was trying to remember when her last date was. Surely it wasn't that long ago? It had been in London, at the end of a short four-day job with an international cellist. She'd had a really nice dinner—a rack of lamb with this amazing rosemary breadcrumb crust and…what was his name again?

It was probably not great that she'd remembered her meal but not the name of her date. Although that was probably also unsurprising as she'd just realised that it had been over a year ago. Fourteen months, to be exact.

Marko was still explaining the contract, and she *knew* she should be paying attention. But she'd read it later anyway before she signed it, and right now she needed to reassure herself that it was simply *logical* that one kiss from a prince had her all starry eyed—just through the lack of any form of romantic male contact in so long.

It wasn't anything about Marko, especially.

'It details all the responsibilities of the role, including, of course, the kissing policy, amongst other things—'

It was important to Jas that Marko's kiss *wasn't* special, because she'd already learnt the hard way how badly professional life and relationships could conflict. Plus, while—

Wait. Kissing policy?

'Pardon me?'

Marko's teeth were a perfect white as he smiled. 'Just seeing if you were paying attention.'

'So there isn't a kissing policy?' Something else occurred to her, and she added more stridently, 'Or an *anything else* policy?'

Marko had long ago let his jacket fall closed, and now he raised his hands in mock surrender. 'I assure you there is not. I would never ask you to do anything that you didn't want to do.'

She thought back to those moments after she'd smashed that glass: *Can I kiss you?*

No, he wouldn't ask her to do anything she didn't want to do.

It was impossible in the fairy-light-lit almost darkness to read Marko's gaze, but in the silence he was definitely looking at her.

She sensed, rather than could clearly see, his lips curve into a grin.

Had he stepped closer?

Suddenly the air between them felt hotter—and infinitely more electric.

'Unless,' Marko began, and his voice was all low and impossibly even sexier than normal, 'you would like there to be a kissing policy?'

The atmosphere fairly crackled now.

Had she moved closer? Someone definitely had, as no longer would she need to reach far to touch the fabric of his suit. Not very far at all.

A sudden breeze made the towering trees beside the terrace rustle in the darkness, but the sound barely registered in Jas's periphery.

Instead, her gaze remained on Marko, and, while she desperately wished she could see him more clearly, there was no questioning the hotness of his gaze, or her certainty that Marko would be seeing a matching heat in hers.

It would be so, so easy to close the gap between them. To run her fingers along the fine wool that covered his broad shoulders and then entwine her hands behind his neck. To allow herself to fall into him—to press her body close against his, and to kiss him very differently from before. This time with open lips and tongue and…

'You mean a no-kissing policy?' Jas said suddenly, and sharply, brutally yanking her traitorous libido back to reality.

And the reality was that this was *not* real. Prince Marko was a client. She was a professional.

Marko stepped back.

'You can have Ivan add it to the contract if you wish,' he said, not missing a beat.

As if the last few minutes had never happened. As if Jas had imagined the almost magnetic pull that she'd felt between them.

Jas straightened her shoulders.

Thank goodness she'd pulled herself together before she'd done something stupid.

He was the Playboy Prince, after all.

He probably seduced every woman he met. She'd just happened to be the closest one available.

And the fact she hadn't felt that way—that he'd made her feel special rather than one of many—was just a mark of what a player he was.

'We'd better get back inside,' Marko said. 'We don't want to miss out on dessert. Have you had Vela Adian pastries before? Our chef is famous for his *pršurate* and *hroštule*.'

Jas just nodded and followed Marko back inside. At the top of the steps, and just before they walked through those gauzy curtains again, he took her hand in his. Once again he casually laced his fingers with hers, and once again he smiled at her.

Still that made her heart do a little flip.

But she ignored that entirely, and instead smiled right on back.

And silently decided that she *would* be adding that no kissing clause.

It would make things between them crystal clear.

There would be no more kisses from the Playboy Prince.

CHAPTER SIX

MARKO FOUND JAS sitting at the only table on the dining room terrace the next morning.

Her attention was focused on her open laptop, and she didn't immediately notice his approach.

She sat at the table where the King and Queen generally had breakfast together, but Lukas and Petra had left early that morning for the Pavlovic Estate where they'd be based during Lukas's treatment. It was also the table where the previous King and Queen—Marko's parents—had taken their breakfast.

'My mother and father used to like sitting here,' Marko said when he stood beside Jas. 'My mother used to get Lukas and me to count all the boats we could see in the harbour.'

Her head jerked upwards at his voice, and she blinked in surprise as she met his gaze. 'Sorry,' she said, 'I was in my own little world.' Then she turned to look out to the ocean. As always, boats dotted the view, and even from this distance Marko could make out colourful towels decorating the white sand of a beach, and a flock of seagulls hovering above the water.

'I can't imagine waking up to this every morning,' Jas said, turning back to Marko. 'My mum's flat had a balcony with a view of the neighbouring building, and I used to eat breakfast cereal in front of the TV while she got ready for work.'

'We had a chef,' Marko said. 'Lukas and I used to ask him to make us dinosaur-shaped pancakes.'

Jas laughed out loud. 'I'm glad I didn't know there were some kids on the other side of the world with their own chef each morning, as otherwise I might not have been so happy with my Weet-bix.'

'But you were?' Marko asked, curious.

'Happy, you mean? With my Weet-bix and a balcony with a herb garden instead of a view?'

He nodded.

'Yes,' she said, now looking at *him*, curiously. 'Very much. It was just Mum and me, but we laughed a lot. Even at the brick view when we first moved in.'

But Marko didn't elaborate, and instead placed his coffee on the table. Jas's brow wrinkled.

'You want to sit with me?' she asked.

'Unless that's a problem?' Marko said, surprised.

The kiss last night could've complicated things, but Jas had made her feelings clear with her 'no-kissing' clause.

He had wondered, for more than a moment, if maybe they could build on that kiss they'd shared, and discover where the electricity he'd felt would lead them. Out on that ballroom terrace, it had momentarily been all he could think about.

Sex definitely hadn't been a requirement of his fake fiancée, but it could certainly make things over the next few months more fun.

Or—as he'd belatedly realised—more complicated.

He'd never had a relationship stretch from weeks into months, and so there was no doubt that any physical relationship between himself and Jasmine would come to an end well before Lukas returned. And where would that leave them? Best case, it would end amicably and their business relationship would continue as before.

Worst case, it would end acrimoniously and continuing to persuade Vela Ada they were in love would be impossible.

So, yes—Jasmine's 'no-kissing' clause was definitely a good thing.

Even if he had to remind himself of that as he admired her long legs revealed by denim shorts and tan sandals that criss-crossed just past her ankles.

'Oh, no,' Jas said, shaking her head. 'Of course not. I just didn't expect you to.'

'I think the staff would think it strange if we didn't keep each other company.'

'Oh!' Jas said. 'That makes sense.'

She seemed to relax at that explanation, and she snapped her laptop closed and moved it aside.

'Well,' she said, 'if we have to sit together, it probably is a good idea if we talk a bit about ourselves. You know, the kind of stuff that we should know given we're engaged.'

Marko didn't feel he *had* to sit with Jasmine at all. In fact, he'd come out here because he'd been looking for her—not because of the role she was playing for him, but because he was wondering how she was after last night. After their… uh…*conversation* on the ballroom terrace there'd been little opportunity to talk, and she'd said very little when he'd handed her the contract outside her room later on.

'How are you feeling?' he asked. 'After your first royal engagement?'

Jas tilted her head, as if confused. 'I'm fine,' she said. 'Why wouldn't I be?' She reached for her own coffee. 'Now, let's start with the big questions: how do you like your coffee?'

Jas had been *almost* glad at Marko's interruption.

Almost, because she'd already determined that time spent with Marko was not exactly relaxing. Around him, she wasn't herself. She wasn't calm, she wasn't together.

She did *not* like that.

But—Marko's interruption had allowed her to save her reply to her mother's email as a draft, rather than finish it. A reply to an email that had consisted of an official palace photo of Jas beside Marko, Lukas and Petra as they'd welcomed guests to the ball, and a subject line of question marks.

That was definitely going to be the worst part of all of

this: lying to her mother. She had several missed calls on her phone as well from family and friends—but she'd responded to only one: her mum. Although she'd cheated and called her when she'd known she'd be at her yoga class, and had left a voicemail.

'I'll send you an email and explain everything.'

Explain things how, exactly, Jas?

The confidentiality agreement she'd signed as part of Gallagher Personal Protection Services already meant that telling her the truth was not an option. Her latest contract—which she'd sign once Ivan had added the no-kissing clause she'd requested—only made the requirement for secrecy even more iron clad.

So yes—she'd have to lie to her mum. And so yes—briefly—she'd been glad for Marko's interruption. Even as she'd noticed how fantastic he looked in faded jeans and a T-shirt that did more than hint at the power of his chest and shoulders.

But then when he'd sat down, her tummy had done all that ridiculous flip-flopping again, and it had been concentrating on their *business* relationship—which was, of course, all this was—that had helped her to refocus.

From the coffee discussion, their conversation had flowed to other easy topics: favourite movies, food, holiday destinations. She'd asked him more about his childhood, curious at the almost wistful look in his gaze when she'd mentioned her Weet-bix and TV breakfasts. She wasn't even sure if it was possible for Prince Marko *to* look wistful, but the discovery that he'd had private tutors until university helped to make a bit more sense of why the simplicity of her youth might have seemed appealing to him. Although she definitely wouldn't have said no to 'all you can eat' dinosaur pancakes.

'So why join the police?' he asked.

A member of the palace staff had magically appeared once they'd each finished their coffees, and now fresh coffee and pastries sat between them, their delicious aroma mingling with the clean scent of the giant firs that surrounded the palace.

Jas smiled. She'd been asked this a million times before.

'I always knew I would,' Jas replied. 'Since I was a little girl. My mum and I didn't have a lot of money, and for a long time after my dad left we were waiting for public housing. So we both slept on couches, always feeling like an imposition on mum's friends and acquaintances and hyper-aware of overstaying our welcome. We had absolutely no control over our situation, and I hated it, and I hated how much my mum worried.'

She reached for one of the pastries—a piece of strudel packed with apples, sultanas and cinnamon.

'So, I guess it's no surprise that I grew up into someone who likes to be in control of things. And for some reason I thought that if I was in the police, I'd be in control. I mean—of course I was also attracted to the idea of protecting people—and I have a really strong sense of right and wrong, too—but there was a lot about the allure of having authority. Of being in charge in a situation.'

'And is that what you experienced?'

Her lips curved upwards. 'Not the way I expected. There was a lot of frustration too—of being part of some great police work that sometimes led to soft or no sentences for the bad guys. And then there were the people—mostly men—who had real issues with a woman in the force. It was exhausting having to prove myself all the time—to the members of the public who'd talk to my junior male partner more than me, and even within the job itself. When I made it to the ANP, and protecting the Prime Minister, it felt even more like a boys-only club.'

Jas stopped talking, unsure why she was going into so much detail. The Prince didn't need to know all of this.

'So that's why you started your own company?' Marko asked.

No.

Her stomach roiled in a familiar, unwanted, visceral reaction to the real reason she'd left the ANP.

She'd started her own company because she'd made the mistake of falling in love with a sergeant within her department. A man who she'd found out, too late, had definitely not loved her back. A man who'd betrayed her in the most—

'Yes,' she said, forcibly halting the direction of her thoughts. 'That's exactly why I did.'

She'd answered his question completely normally—she seemed to be getting better at channelling her usual, measured self around him—and yet Marko was studying her as if she'd said something he didn't believe.

Jas looked down at the untouched pastry still in her hand. She took a bite, but barely tasted it.

This was the second time in two days that she'd allowed memories of the past to clutter her brain.

But she could *not* allow that.

And so she dusted off the icing sugar that had fallen onto her fingers, and met his gaze again. Steady and assured.

'So,' she asked calmly, 'why did you join the military?'

Now he looked away—out over the trees that covered the hill the palace was built upon. But he was looking at Jas again when he said: 'Because I hated this place.'

Jas felt her mouth drop open, but before she could say anything footsteps alerted her to Ivan's arrival.

'We have an hour before we need to depart for your school engagement, Your Highness, Ms Gallagher.'

Marko nodded sharply, then stood, and left without a word.

Because I hated this place.

Why would he say that?

He sat in the back seat of one of the fleet of low, dark palace sedans, with Jasmine beside him. They were heading to an elementary school in one of the lower socio-economic townships of Vela Ada, where he'd be representing Lukas at the announcement of a palace-funded literacy programme.

Why would he say that?

His dislike of royal responsibilities was well known, but he'd certainly never said anything like that before. He didn't even think he'd said it to himself privately.

Had he hated growing up in the palace?

Did he still hate the palace now?

He kept asking himself those questions as the car slid over undulating roads that narrowed as they approached the town, but he found himself unable to answer.

By the time the convoy of three cars pulled onto a grassy verge to allow a small truck laden with a family of goats to pass, he'd managed to shove the questions aside.

It didn't actually matter, after all.

Whether he liked the palace or not—and all it represented—he was living there for the next few months.

That was all that mattered.

The woman he'd be living with for that time was currently chatting to the driver and to the bodyguard sitting in the passenger seat.

No—not chatting. She was running through the plan for this school visit, reminding her team of the school's layout from a reconnaissance visit she'd led two days earlier. She then noted the possible exit points should there be any need to evacuate the Prince.

'And his fiancée,' Marko reminded Jas.

She slid a glance in his direction, and her lips quirked upwards. 'I'll be fine,' she said drily.

His gaze flicked over her. She wore a navy blue and white summer dress that was part of a wardrobe of clothing that Ivan had sourced under the guise of lost luggage. Sleeveless, but with a high neck and shirt-style collar, it was fitted to her waist before flaring out to a full skirt that finished not that far above her contrasting pale pink sandals. She looked lovely, with her hair styled into a low bun and swept from her face. But when he met her gaze again, she also looked imminently capable. A woman most definitely still able to do her job, regardless of the height of her heels.

It occurred to Marko, as the car came to a stop outside the school's three-storey building, that in the unlikely event that he and Jasmine *were* attacked by an unknown threat—then with his military training and Jasmine's skill set, there probably didn't exist a more difficult royal target in the world.

He was smiling as the driver opened Jasmine's door, and still was when he joined her on the footpath. He took her hand and laced his fingers with hers in an action that had quickly become second nature to him.

'What are you grinning about?' she asked, tilting her head up to look at him.

It was a warm day, and the sun was hot against his unbuttoned charcoal suit jacket. The sun also made Jasmine's skin glow, highlighting the subtle curves of her biceps and the quiet strength in her lean physique.

'I was just thinking how I almost *want* someone to try and take us down,' he said. 'Good luck to them—you and I would end it before it even started.'

Jasmine gave a shocked, loud laugh, and then clapped her hand over her mouth. When she removed it, she was still grinning. She shoved him in the shoulder with her spare hand.

'You nong,' she said, her eyes twinkling.

'Nong?' he asked, confused.

'You know, like a ning-nong? A bit of an idiot?' She brought her hand to her mouth again. 'Whoops, I'm probably not supposed to call you an idiot, am I?'

But Jas didn't sound at all concerned that she had.

Marko just found himself still smiling at her.

She squeezed his hand, and then, on tiptoes, whispered in his ear, 'While I tend to agree that we *are* pretty well qualified to defend ourselves, I just want to make it clear that you are *not* to go all superman on me should anything go down. My team is in charge, and you follow our orders, understand?'

He squeezed her hand back. 'Understood.'

She stepped back, just as Ivan loudly cleared his throat.

For the first time, Marko realised there was a small welcoming party—who he knew must be the school principal and local government officials—and about twice as many photographers only a few metres away.

He'd been so focused on Jas, he hadn't even noticed them.

He glanced down at Jasmine, who was still smiling. 'They probably think we were being all lovey-dovey,' she whispered.

He smiled back at her, but he knew he'd never been lovey-dovey in his life.

The school visit was going well, Jas thought.

As far as she could tell, given she could barely understand a word anyone was saying. The kids had seemed really excited to meet Prince Marko, anyway, and Marko himself had seemed pretty relaxed. Certainly more so than at the ball—last night she'd noted the tension in his shoulders and jaw, and today it was barely noticeable. In fact, aside from when one of the journalists had asked a question about the King, rather than the literacy programme, he'd seemed positively content—even laughing along with the kids as he read to a half-circle of nine-year-olds a book illustrated with zoo animals.

Jas didn't feel quite so relaxed. She had no official role—neither had Felicity at any of these events—and so subsequently she simply got to hover near Marko and look…she didn't know. Supportive? Fiancée-like? In love?

Surely Felicity would've been fine, looking effortlessly natural in any surroundings.

Instead, Jas had found herself standing as if she were on a job—legs just slightly apart, her hands loosely linked in front of her. Her gaze scanned the crowd in the classroom—

from Marko and the children and their teachers through to the small bank of invited journalists and photographers huddled at one end of the room.

As always, she was looking at faces and hands, faces and hands, searching for something impossible to define, the slightest sign of something *not quite right…*

Wait. Stop.

She unlinked her hands and gave them a little shake. She shifted her weight and moved her feet closer together.

Her team had the room under control. Today, that wasn't her job.

Her job was to stand still and look elegant. Or something like that.

CHAPTER SEVEN

JAS WAS STANDING beside Marko in the school's entry foyer, preparing to leave, when Ivan approached and murmured something to Marko in Slavic.

Instantly, Jas felt Marko tense.

'No. Not today,' he said. Firmly.

Ivan replied in an urgent whisper, but all Jas could make out was *paparazzi*.

But Marko didn't even reply. Everything in his expression still said *no*.

Ivan might have sighed, but he was too professional to reveal too much in *his* expression. But Jas would guess he was annoyed. Very annoyed.

A moment later Ivan had had a word with Heather from Jas's team—who was leading the team today—but Jas knew what was going on. They were going to be using their alternative exit.

She nodded as Heather explained that paparazzi now congregated outside the school, and how they would reach their new pick-up point, although of course Jas was familiar with it. No matter how low the risk, you *always* had more than one way in and out.

Of course, none of this was unusual. Principals went off-script all the time, and dealing with it was part of her job. And yet…

Why hadn't Marko said something to her?

With Ivan sent out the front to answer a few questions—and act as a distraction—Jas and Marko were led by their protection team out of the school building, once Simon had reported back that the way was clear.

Marko didn't make eye contact with her as they walked.

Which didn't matter, of course. Why should he? He didn't owe her an explanation.

She shouldn't expect one.

But before, outside the school, she'd felt a camaraderie between them. A closeness…

Wait. *Stop.*

If anything she should be annoyed as the head of his protection detail. *Not* as his fake fiancée.

Although she shouldn't be annoyed, because it was her job not to be.

Jas gritted her teeth. She was being *ridiculous*.

Outside, the school was nothing like a typical school back home in Australia. Rather than being surrounded by acres of lush green playing fields, this school was right in the middle of the town, with houses either side in the familiar cream brick, red-roofed style seen throughout the island. Out the back, there was a bitumen-paved play area, painted with lines in overlapping colours to allow for a variety of sports and lunchtime games. Trees lined the tall brick boundary, providing privacy as they walked briskly and silently—but for the tense click of Jasmine's heels.

Through a rear access gate, and down a narrow, cobblestoned laneway—they avoided the most direct route to the street parallel to the school entrance. Instead they continued onwards, behind several terraced cottages, before emerging onto a quiet street perpendicular to the main road—and a moment later their car with its blackest black tinted windows rolled to a stop before them.

They were inside the car, and on their way before it would've even occurred to a single paparazzo that Marko and his new fiancée were taking rather a long time to exit the school.

This was partly because the milling paparazzi didn't expect Prince Marko and his new fiancée to avoid them.

After all, although this particular event had not been

publicly announced ahead of time, and school staff and students had been sworn to secrecy, the moment royalty turned up anywhere word was going to get out. And the palace had expected there would be substantial interest in Marko's princess-to-be.

So, while the media inside the school had been palace-selected, and all photographs and content related to the literacy programme would be palace-approved—a relief to Jasmine, given her bodyguard-like behaviour at times—today's schedule had allowed for brief questions from any waiting paparazzi. It was, after all, in Marko's best interests to endear himself to the media given his role was to reassure the people of Vela Ada that all was well, despite Lukas's illness. He needed to be portrayed as competent, approachable...*kingly*, really.

Marko had certainly known this.

And yet here they were—already out of the town and amongst paddocks full of vineyards or dotted with goats.

No one had said a word since they'd left the school building.

Jas desperately wanted to say something now.

But to say what, exactly?

That he should've told her his plans to...well, escape really.

Ideally, yes. He should've. But that was something to debrief him about in private later, not to snap at him now as their car raced through the countryside.

Especially as—and only now, as she observed Marko, did she acknowledge it—Marko still radiated tension.

Mentally, Jas took a step back. This wasn't about her—certainly not about her affront due to not having been informed of what she suspected had been Marko's split-second decision to leave.

It was strange, this sudden escape. As was Marko's reaction to Ivan earlier.

That tension she'd first felt when she'd been standing beside him in the school foyer had definitely not dissipated. Here in the confines of the car, it felt amplified.

None of Marko's body language invited conversation.

But even so, words danced on the tip of Jas's tongue. Different words now—not to lambaste him, but instead to ask him what was wrong.

She felt they'd made progress today: they'd very clearly outlined the ground rules of their business relationship following that somewhat of a *hiccup* at the ball. And they'd had a good chat this morning at breakfast, and Marko had even teased her when they'd arrived at the school.

Teased?

Or flirted with her?

Jasmine dug her fingernails into the palms of her hands.

Nope. She was not going to even *consider* that possibility.

As she needed to keep reminding herself: charming women was what Marko did. It was who he was. He probably flirted so often—anywhere and with anyone—that it was a subconscious reflex.

As she'd determined last night—it was *not* about her.

But even so, they were building a rapport, weren't they? And that was critically important to the success of this ruse.

Although did that mean Marko would welcome her concern?

She doubted it, but still, her eyes traced the hard, angry shape of his jaw uneasily: Marko was *not* okay.

The car jerked slightly as it went over a pothole, and yet Marko remained resolute in maintaining his attention on the lovely—if a little repetitive—surrounding fields.

He couldn't really be any clearer in his wish for silence, but Jas couldn't help herself.

'Marko?' she began.

He spoke—but it wasn't a reply.

'Turn here,' he said, to their driver. It was more of a bark, really. Definitely a demand.

The driver didn't hesitate—lurching the car to a speed

capable of making the turn with copious application of the brake, and then accelerating down the un-signposted lane.

'Where are we going?' Jasmine and Heather asked at exactly the same time.

Marko's attention was back out the window. 'This is palace property,' he said curtly. 'We won't be disturbed.'

Heather didn't look very comfortable. Jasmine wasn't comfortable either—she did *not* like going off schedule.

But equally—if they didn't know where they were going, then any threat didn't know either. Their job was to safely get the principal through his day. Wherever that day might take him.

And today, it would seem, it was down a compacted gravel lane, where occasional loose pieces of stone pinged against the underside of this extremely expensive car.

Marko had hoped that when the familiar gravel lane eventually led them to an equally familiar sandy track, he would relax.

But when the car came to a stop—ill equipped for the deep beach sand ahead—he didn't feel even the slightest loosening of the tension that enveloped his neck and shoulders, and caused his head to pound.

Everyone was talking to him—Heather, the driver. They wanted to know what they were doing here, but honestly—wasn't this the point of being a prince? To occasionally do random stuff without explanation?

Actually—not everyone was talking. Jasmine had remained silent since her soft question ten minutes earlier.

He couldn't even look at her.

He'd been aware of her attention since he'd decided to leave the school. At first, he'd sensed her censure—which hadn't surprised him. But later, that censure had shifted to concern. She'd been *worried* about him.

He did *not* like that.

Marko yanked off his dress shoes and socks, rolled up

his suit pants, and climbed out of the car and into the salt-tinged air.

It was a decent hike from here to the beach—up and down over several hills that eventually became sparse, scrubby and rocky as the ocean neared.

He shrugged off his jacket, and he gripped it with white knuckles as he took big strides over that last hill—and could finally see the water.

The sky was cloudless today, perfect above the crystal-clear water of the small, absolutely private beach. Near the shore, he could see straight through to the rocks lining the ground beneath the waves, although about ten metres in the water went sharply from light aqua to deep navy blue, where—as Marko well knew—the water abruptly deepened as suddenly as an underwater cliff.

He and Lukas had swum and snorkelled at this beach their whole lives. Not recently though—it had been…ten years? Or more? He'd been at university, and his father had still been alive.

This place—and the small, hidden cottage that sat set back from the stone outcrops now above him as he negotiated the rocky path down to the shore—had once been the only place Marko had ever felt he could escape to. Lukas had felt the same way.

Here they'd been safe from prying eyes, and from anyone's expectations.

So it should be no surprise it was where he'd gravitated to today.

Now at ground level, Marko clambered over rocks in so many shades of grey—most no bigger in circumference than a dinner plate—a mix of smooth and square and sharp edges.

He remembered the easiest path through the rocks, although he was sure it had been many years since anyone had trod it. He couldn't imagine Lukas here now—his brother was just too important, too busy, too serious.

Finally reaching the coarse sand of the one patch of rock-free beach, Marko sank to the ground, discarding his jacket in a careless pile of charcoal fabric.

And then he put his head in his hands.

He was being an idiot. Such an idiot.

Such an idiot.

What had Jas called him? A nong? A ning-nong?

Well—a far stronger word was required when he'd literally just *run* from the first intrusion of paparazzi he'd had to deal with since his return to Vela Ada. An intrusion he'd expected and yet had, apparently, been unprepared for.

He swore loudly—violently and creatively—at himself and into the sanctuary of this beach that absolutely nobody knew about.

Something—a rock knocking against its neighbour—tugged his attention from his self-flagellation.

It was Jas.

About two-thirds of the way down the steep path to the beach—but facing away from him, as if beating a fast retreat.

He did *not* want anyone on this beach with him.

Jas looked over her shoulder, fleetingly meeting his gaze.

'I'm sorry,' she called out. 'I thought—' A pause, but she didn't elaborate. 'I was wrong. I'm sorry. I shouldn't have disturbed you.'

Then she continued her climb, her long dress flapping in the ocean breeze.

For about another metre.

And then, as Marko watched, a rock beneath Jas's bare feet wobbled dramatically, and despite her arm-waving attempts to regain her balance she crashed to the hard ground with a shocked cry.

In moments, he was beside her, crouching to assess how badly damaged she was.

The breeze had tugged long strands of her dark hair free, and whipped them about her face as she looked up at him.

'I'm fine,' she said, very firmly.

But then she shifted, as if about to get up—and winced.

'You're hurt,' Marko protested.

She shook her head. 'Just give me a moment,' she said. 'It's nothing.'

He watched as Jas wiggled her left ankle—and winced again.

'It's something,' he said grimly. 'Here.'

He stood and offered a hand to assist her up, which she took a moment to grasp.

'I'm really sorry,' she said as she came to her feet, balancing on her uninjured foot. 'You—'

But then she wobbled again, and was suddenly falling towards him.

He grabbed her reflexively, and he wasn't particularly gentle, his hands gripping her firmly at the waist. Even so, he didn't stop her fall entirely, and with a surprised, feminine *oomph* she landed against his chest, her hands sandwiched between them.

There was a long moment of silence.

A long moment where Marko was absolutely aware of everywhere Jas's body was pressed, firmly, against his. They'd kissed last night—but they'd never been this close before. Chest to chest, hip to hip.

Jas flattened her fingers against Marko's chest, but otherwise she didn't move a muscle, her gaze apparently trained on the buttons of his shirt.

'I am *so* sorry,' she said, yet again, but Marko wasn't really paying attention.

Instead, he shifted his hands from her waist, bent his knees—and swung Jas up into his arms.

She gasped against his shoulder as he headed to that small patch of sandy beach—safe from Jasmine's apparent aptitude for identifying hazardous rocks.

There, he sat her down on the sun-warmed sand, and—without giving his actions too much further consideration—

sat himself down beside her. He propped his hands behind him, and stretched his legs out alongside Jasmine's.

Then, he looked at her.

Her usually pale skin was tomato red. 'You're blushing,' he said, surprised.

She touched her cheek. 'You think there's a reason I shouldn't be embarrassed after interrupting a clearly private moment, falling on my backside, and then causing a prince a permanent back injury having to heft me down that hill?'

Marko was mildly affronted. 'I can assure you I had no problem carrying you, Jasmine.'

It had been the opposite of a burden having her soft, strong, warm body curled against his chest.

She seemed about to argue with him—but then turned her attention to the horizon. Not a single sail boat interrupted the view.

'This place is amazing,' she said.

He nodded. 'It's a special place for me.'

Her clothing rustled as she attempted to stand again, and he reached out to lay a hand on her leg—on her thigh—to stop her.

Immediately he removed it, not intending his touch to have been so intimate. But, he didn't want her to go.

Or rather, she couldn't go. She'd hurt her ankle.

That was it, right?

He rubbed his forehead in exasperation.

'Stay,' he said. 'I don't mind that you're here.'

As he said it, he realised it was true. Only minutes ago he'd grimaced at her unwanted arrival—and yet now her presence was almost comfortable.

But not quite. Because that underlying current between them—and it was constant, no matter what clause they agreed to—hadn't gone anywhere.

That sat together in silence for a while.

It was mid-afternoon, and the sun quickly heated Marko's skin. He removed his tie and made quick work of his shirt—

unbuttoning the cuffs and rolling them up to his elbows. His shirt had been pulled out of his dress pants, most likely when he'd picked up Jas, but his skin still prickled beneath his clothing—and if Jas weren't here he probably would've stripped off and dived into the water, and worried about the lack of a towel and other practicalities later.

'I used to come swimming here with Lukas,' he found himself saying, his gaze focused on the crests of the small, lapping waves. 'It felt like the only place on the island where we could totally relax—and where no one was watching.'

'Or asking questions,' Jas prompted. 'Like the media outside the school today.'

Marko shifted to face Jasmine, unsurprised she'd guessed why he'd come here.

'Yes,' he said. 'No paparazzi to bother us here.'

But also no palace staff, and once Lukas was sixteen—no minders. Not one person to observe or comment on their behaviour. Or to advise and pre-empt how they *should* behave.

'Were there more paparazzi than you'd expected today?' Jas asked, her voice gentle.

He didn't want her concern.

'No,' he said. 'It was exactly as we'd all expected.'

Her unspoken question seemed to whirl in the breeze: *And so why did you run away, then?*

But he didn't have to answer that. He didn't need to explain anything to Jasmine, or to anyone.

Except…

That he did.

His whole life he'd rebelled against all that was expected of him. Since adulthood he'd divested himself of pretty much all royal responsibilities, aside from those related to his military career.

But those days were over.

At least, for now.

'Do you know what the paparazzi would've asked us if we'd walked out?' Marko asked, still staring at the waves.

Jas seemed to realise it was a rhetorical question.

'They wouldn't have asked about the literacy programme, or about the kids we met today,' he continued. 'They wouldn't have cared about how investing in literacy will change these kids'—and many other kids'—lives. They wouldn't have cared about anything important.' He paused. 'Instead, they would've asked about your dress. Or your shoes. And I can *guarantee* there would've been some stupid *Playboy Prince* comment—because, of course, that's who they want people to think I am, because it gets them clicks and sells their magazines.'

'And you didn't want to answer those questions?'

'Not today,' Marko said. He rubbed his forehead again. 'Even though I know I need the media onside. Even though I know I could've just ignored the stupid questions and said my piece about the literacy programme and be done with it. All I needed to do was play nice, and play the role that Lukas needs me to play. Play the game like a good boy. For *once*.'

'But you couldn't,' Jas said neutrally.

Marko waited for the question—for the *Why?*—but it didn't come.

Maybe that was why he decided to explain.

'The first girl I kissed, I kissed at my fifteenth birthday party. It was at the family estate, and not at the palace. We were under this tree practically in the middle of the property, with the lake behind us.'

Jas gasped. 'I know that photo,' she said. 'She had blonde hair, right?' Marko nodded. 'And that was your *first kiss*?'

'Yes,' he said. 'We were over a kilometre from the road, but a photographer with a telephoto lens decided to trespass and he obviously got close enough for that shot.'

'Wow,' Jas said. 'I don't know how I'd feel if my first kiss was documented and then printed and reprinted for the rest of my life. Although, I wouldn't have expected a photographer to be lying in wait behind my local fish and chip shop when Josh from Calculus stuck his tongue down my throat.'

Marko couldn't help but laugh.

'That *is* pretty terrible, though,' Jas said, more seriously now. 'You were still a kid.'

'I was,' Marko said. 'And so was she. It was my first experience being personally targeted by the media. Until then, I'd just been photographed with my parents. This was different. And Sofia—the girl I kissed—was mortified. For a few weeks, she and her family were hounded by the media. It was ridiculous. A private moment—a private memory—was ruined.' He managed a grin now. 'Although I did learn to be more creative with where I kissed girls from then on.'

'I bet,' Jas said drily.

'It didn't stop after that. For some reason, suddenly Lukas and I were being followed everywhere we went. I used to hate how confined I felt in the palace, but now I felt that way *everywhere*. Didn't matter what I did, the media was there. I got drunk for the first time at uni—and there they were. I woke up with a hangover and a headline on the front page of the paper.'

Marko shifted his weight on the sand so he was facing Jas.

She'd pulled her legs up and wrapped her arms loosely around her knees.

'Lukas handled it really well. He just accepted it as part of the deal. I guess he had to—he was the heir to the throne, and so he'd carried that responsibility from birth. He just conformed to what was expected of him. I did try for a while, for a few years at least. But then my father got sick...'

Marko stopped. Swallowed.

'Anyway,' he said, 'eventually I figured, if they want photos of me drinking, or kissing girls—then I'll give them to them.' His lips quirked. 'And also, I was eighteen, so it wasn't like that was a hardship.'

But Jas wasn't smiling with him.

'Your dad had cancer, didn't he?' Jas asked.

'A different type from Lukas,' Marko said firmly. 'And with my father, they think maybe his military service in

Vietnam caused—' He stopped again. Swallowed again. 'Anyway. It's different, and treatments are further advanced now, and Lukas's prognosis is excellent.'

He sounded as rehearsed as Lukas's oncologist.

Jas just nodded, and tightened her arms around her knees. He sensed she was trying to work out the right words to say, but that was the thing—there weren't any.

She could hardly reassure him that she was sure Lukas would be okay.

'Look,' Marko said, before she had a chance to say anything. 'The short explanation is: I only found out my brother had cancer this week. I'm doing fine most of the time, but when Ivan told me it was time to go and face those damn stupid questions today, I just couldn't. I couldn't go outside and pander to the media that didn't give a crap about me when they photographed me self-destructing as my father was slowly dying. I couldn't. I—'

His voice cracked. Just like the scared twenty-year-old almost-man he'd once been.

He stood up, and was walking towards the water before he'd even realised what he was doing, his hands unbuttoning his shirt, then his trousers.

In boxer briefs only, he stood for a moment on the smooth rocks in the shallows, the water lapping against his knees.

And then a moment before diving into the water, he looked over his shoulder. At Jas—still sitting on the sand—just looking at him.

'You coming in?' he asked.

CHAPTER EIGHT

JAS HAD NOT joined Marko for a swim.

Common sense had prevailed, as had the reality that she had known this man for less than a week, and that she worked for him. Swimming with Prince Marko in her underwear was *not* an option.

But…oh, it had been tempting.

She'd seen photos of him shirtless before—and after what he'd revealed she felt terribly guilty for being part of the audience that drove photographers to intrude on Marko's life—but those photos really did not reveal how…*devastating* a shirtless Marko was in real life.

She'd known he was fit and strong, and she'd known he had muscles. But she hadn't known the way the sun would paint every hard edge of his body with gold, and she hadn't known how she would feel when the owner of all those delicious hard edges was looking at *her*.

When he'd surfaced after diving into the water…and that water had sluiced over his broad shoulders and down his pectorals and the occasional dark hair on his chest…

She had literally fanned herself with her hand.

And then quickly stood up, and made her way back to the car. The pain in her ankle now no more than the slightest echo of an ache.

As she'd put the distance between herself and a nearly naked Marko, she'd been able to focus instead on their conversation, and what he'd revealed to her.

Her heart ached as she imagined a teenage Marko grappling with growing up—and later grieving the death of his father—in front of a paparazzo lens. And it ached some more at the emotions the Prince was attempting to deal with now: fear for his brother balanced with the responsibility of acting as Vela Ada's head of state—while faking an engagement.

This was big stuff. Huge.

No wonder he'd run today.

But he couldn't do it again. She knew he knew that, and somehow she was certain that there wouldn't be a repeat of today.

There was a steeliness to Marko—a sense that once he decided upon something he was unwavering in his determination to follow through. His successful military career reflected this. As did, Jas suspected, his extraordinary playboy reputation. As he'd told her today, once everyone—the media, Vela Ada, the world—had decided he was a player, he'd just run with it.

Her lips curved upwards; she didn't think doing so had been *entirely* a hardship for Marko.

However, after today, she was aware there was more to Marko than his reputation.

He was much more than just the Playboy Prince.

The next day, there were no royal engagements scheduled.

Jas, once again, had breakfast out on the terrace. However, today Marko didn't join her.

But, aside from an early morning run that Jas knew about only because two of her team had accompanied him, Marko didn't leave the palace all day.

Even so, Jas didn't lay eyes on him.

Instead, she spent the day working—not as a fake fiancée, but as the owner of a rapidly expanding personal protection services company. And after a day playing princess, she definitely had a lot to do.

Apart from remaining abreast of the two assignments her two other teams were currently engaged in, she also needed to plan ahead for Prince Marko. She might now be standing by his side in a different capacity, but she was still in charge of his protection. So her team needed to be out visiting upcoming venues, and liaising with Ivan and other palace staff about scheduling and logistics.

Frustratingly, Jas herself could no longer lead the scouting trips, although her team were more than capable of doing that without her. Even so, she asked for video footage to be taken where possible—even though she had each location's building plans, it wasn't quite the same as seeing a venue for herself.

In the evening, she ate dinner out on the terrace.

She told herself it was because the weather was glorious—warm with a breeze that carried the scent of conifers and just the slightest hint of the ocean—but when she found her gaze drifting to the French doors *once again*, she knew she was just lying to herself.

She had hoped Marko might join her.

Why?

As they'd driven home from the beach yesterday, Jas had barely spoken a word to Marko. If she'd expected becoming his unexpected confidante would lessen the constant tension between them, she'd been patently, spectacularly wrong. His impromptu swim seemed to have washed away any chance of that happening. Back at the palace the Prince had excused himself to his rooms—and there he had remained.

Why was she surprised?

Because, really, wasn't it *normal* that things were a bit weird between them now? She'd gatecrashed an intensely private moment, and because of that—and *only* because of that—he'd been rawly honest with her. After all, why else would he tell her—effectively his employee—something so intensely personal?

Jas would bet her beloved vintage saucer collection that Marko wasn't one to confide in random strangers.

And that was who she was: a random stranger.

Just as he was a random stranger to her.

Who'd kissed her.

Who'd made her heart flip and every childhood fairy tale come true when he'd carried her in his arms.

Jasmine laid her knife and fork firmly on her dinner plate, loudly enough to make a noise and make the attentive wait person—*everyone* who worked in this palace was attentive—who'd just walked out the French doors startle.

The interruption as her plates were collected was timely.

It *did not matter* that Marko had kissed her—it hadn't been real. And it also *did not matter* that she thought about his lips on hers more often than she should—which was never—or about how being carried by someone so strong and powerful had taken her breath away.

Or that he'd asked her to come swimming with him in her underwear.

Jas squeezed her eyes tight.

Maybe he'd intended for her to swim in her dress. Or—more likely—because *he didn't think of her that way*, a nearly naked Jasmine Gallagher was of no concern to him.

Yes. That was definitely it.

Her phone rang, vibrating against her water glass.

Her mother.

Jasmine sighed.

She must have received her email, finally sent late the night before.

'You're actually marrying a *prince*?' her mum said, barely giving Jas an opportunity to say hello. 'This is not some elaborate April Fools type thing? I did not dream that my only daughter was on the front page of the *Canberra Herald*?'

'It's September, Mum,' Jas said, because it was the only thing she was actually allowed to refute.

'Jasmine Sadie Gallagher, this is *not* the time to be cute.'

'I know,' Jas said. 'I'm sorry, I don't know how to explain.'

That, at least, was honest.

Jas took a deep breath, and repeated what she'd written in her email. 'Marko asked me to keep this secret. He didn't want our relationship scrutinised by the media unless it went somewhere.'

'I'd say it's gone somewhere, Jas,' her mum said. 'And surely he would've understood that your own mother is an exception, and you could've said that I was trustworthy. It isn't like I would've told anyone, you must know that.'

The hurt was obvious in her mum's voice, and it made Jas feel ill. She couldn't remember lying to her mum since she was a teenager—and what she was lying about now was far more important than that one time she'd wagged school to go to the movies, and Jas *still* felt a little guilty about that.

'I'm sorry, Mum,' she said again. 'I really am.'

She couldn't wait until this charade was over and she could tell her the truth. No matter what her contract might say, she wasn't living the rest of her life with this lie hanging over the most important relationship in her life. Her family *was* just her and her mum. It always had been.

'So you'll be living there? In Vela Ada?'

Jas chewed her lip. 'I guess?'

'You *guess*? Isn't that the kind of thing you should discuss *before* you get engaged to royalty, Jasmine?'

This was horrendous. Guilt wrapped itself heavily around her shoulders.

'And, Jasmine, I was reading about this prince of yours, because I thought surely my daughter wouldn't marry a man who seems to have had sex with everything that walks in Europe—but, *no*, it is *that* prince. You know what he's called, right? The *Playboy* Prince? Why would you want to marry someone like that?'

Jas's head pounded with the effort to not blurt out everything.

Or to cry.

Her mum thought she was losing her daughter to the other side of the world to a man she didn't know, and none of that was true.

Right now, Jas genuinely hated herself for getting tangled up in this mess.

'He's not really like that, Mum. You can't believe everything you read in the tabloids.'

At least Jasmine believed that herself now. Marko was so much more.

'So all those photos with different women are what—all his closest friends?'

She knew her mum was just doing her job as a mother. She was supposed to be worried, she was supposed to be concerned—and yet Jas found herself snapping back at her.

'Actually,' she said firmly, 'most of those photos were taken years ago. More recently, Marko has rarely been photographed with women he's dating. The tabloids just like to reuse old photos, or make up stories with recent photos of him alone, particularly whenever he dares to go to the beach somewhere—and then speculate about who he might be dating. Just because an article says he dated someone, doesn't make it true.'

Last night, Jas had spent several hours discovering this all for herself.

Yes, Marko had probably deserved his playboy reputation, but the media were the ones who persisted with it—not Marko. But, Jas imagined, writing about how Prince Marko had settled down and now had a fiercely private personal life wouldn't sell many magazines, or get many clicks on social media.

There was a moment of silence, as if her mum was digesting this information.

'I'm sorry,' her mum said, eventually. 'I know you're no fool. You wouldn't be marrying him if he was really like that. I should've known. It's just that, after—'

Jas knew what was coming, and found herself gripping her phone so hard it hurt.

'—after what happened with Stuart, I can't help but worry about you.'

Now it was Jas's turn for a moment of silence.

'That was more than three years ago, Mum,' she said, doing her best to sound perfectly calm. 'It's not an issue any more.'

'But what he did…' The anger in Jas's mum's voice was familiar, and very real. 'After something like that, I'd hate you to trust the wrong man again.'

Jas shook her head, even without her mother there to see it. 'That *won't* happen again, Mum. It hasn't. Marko isn't the wrong man.' She swallowed. 'He's the right man. You don't have to worry.'

'Have you told him about Stuart?'

Jas had to hold back a hysterical burst of laughter. *Tell Prince Marko?*

For a crazy, maniacal second, she imagined quietly sitting down with Marko and explaining in a matter-of-fact tone exactly what Stuart had done. And what she'd done, just before Stuart had so irretrievably shattered her trust, in her misguided, desperate act of supposed love…

'Of course I've told him,' Jas said, with calmness that she certainly did not feel. 'We're engaged.'

'How did he—?'

'Mum,' she said firmly. 'Please. I don't want to talk about it.'

Thankfully her mum let it go. For now, at least.

But how *would* Marko respond?

It was the most rhetorical of questions. She'd *never* tell him.

She could probably guess, though. He'd respond like every other person who knew: *Jas, what were you thinking?*

Of course, everyone hated Stuart too, but they still asked the question. And really, once they asked that, all their vitriol directed at her ex became irrelevant.

Because it was their judgment that she remembered. That she felt—still—deep inside her.

Marko wouldn't be any different.

Wouldn't he?

Jas shoved that question out of her mind.

Her mum spoke for a few more minutes, but Jas remembered none of it when she eventually hung up.

Instead, she sat back in her chair, and stared out across the trees and out to the city of Vela Ada—now identifiable only by a mass of lights, with the day shifting into darkness as they'd talked.

He's the right man.

Well, that certainly wasn't true—at least, not outside this charade. That right man for her might, in fact, not even exist. In the past few years since Stuart, Jas had begun to wonder if there were *any* right men, for anyone. If love, and especially the concept of *one true love*, might not be an actual attainable thing.

After all, she'd loved Stuart.

Or thought she had.

A French door opened, and someone, somewhere, turned on the fairy lights that must decorate every outside space at the palace.

It was Marko who had stepped outside.

But as he did Jasmine pushed back her seat, and got to her feet.

'I'm sorry,' she said. 'I was just going to my room.'

She managed a smile as she walked past him, but that was all she could manage.

She couldn't remain out here, in the aftermath of lying to her mother and the unwanted reminder of her disastrous recent history with men, and simply talk to Marko.

So she didn't.

It was for the best, this new understanding between Jas and Marko.

It was an unspoken understanding, but in the almost week since he'd invited Jas to swim with him, it would appear they'd both separately come to the same conclusion.

This was strictly a professional arrangement.

No more friendly banter—unless they were being observed, of course. No more flirting. And *definitely* no more deeply personal revelations.

What had come over him, on that beach, to tell Jasmine so much?

He'd never spoken of his past, or of his father, to any woman. To anyone. Once he'd used to share most things with his brother, but those days had long passed, even before Lukas's coronation.

So to confide in Jas was definitely out of character.

That had made him feel…not exactly uncomfortable around her, but it had certainly added another layer to the tension already between them.

Despite Jas's no-kissing clause, the hum of attraction had not suddenly ceased to exist. It certainly hadn't gone anywhere when he'd so impulsively invited her into the ocean, and it persisted now, despite their carefully strict professionalism.

And it was amongst this attraction that there was now this added tension: Jasmine knew something about him that no one else did.

He *hated* that.

Today he was with Jas at a morning tea for a charity for which Lukas was patron.

It was a relatively small event, held at a hall in the city, which Lukas attended with Petra each year.

Consequently, they'd been greeted by waiting media as they'd exited their car.

Which Marko had handled with no problems at all.

As he'd handled every interaction he'd had with the media since that damn, stupid escape from that school.

Because he'd needed to. Now was not the time to be so self-indulgent. Of course, he still hated the media intensely—it was just now he was bothering to hide it.

He was *not* going to give anyone a headline that would

worry Lukas. Instead, he would be the dutiful Prince that Lukas needed him to be, and smile, and nod, and answer—or deflect—inane questions.

It wasn't easy for Marko, but it was getting easier, one plastic smile at a time.

Currently, his plastic smile was aching with overuse, as he and Jas wrapped up their latest conversation. Alone, just briefly, before Ivan subtly brought the next group over. It was constant at these events—a steady stream of people and questions and politeness, carefully managed so that he and Jas could meet as many guests as possible.

There was a soft *clink* as Jas replaced her teacup on the delicate saucer she held. The sound drew his attention—and just briefly Jas met his gaze, and smiled.

'I don't know how Lukas and Petra do this,' she said. 'One week of it and I'm already exhausted.'

Marko nodded. This was their third event for the week—not including her welcome ball. The school visit, an art gallery opening, and now this charity function. 'He's very stoic, my brother,' he said. 'And also just genuinely interested in everyone. He could extract the life story from a lamp post, and find it fascinating.'

Jas laughed. 'You aren't using lamp posts as a metaphor for the people of Vela Ada, are you, Marko?'

'No!' Marko said. 'If anything, I'm the lamp post. And also not very good at asking leading questions.'

'So you're a taciturn lamp post,' she teased, tilting her head as she studied him. 'Interesting.'

Her eyes sparkled with humour.

'You know,' he said, 'this *isn't* actually the most ridiculous conversation I've had today.'

Jas grinned. 'I know. *Are* you going to be guest judge at the Vela Ada National Dog Show?'

'I expect so,' Marko said drily, 'seeing as detailing my lack of qualifications wasn't much of a deterrent. And how about you—will you ensure I never stray by baking Baba Lucija's *madjarica* cake for me every Sunday?'

'No,' Jas said firmly. 'Although the recipe looked good, so I'm going to keep it.'

Ivan was approaching with the next small group.

Jas took another sip of her tea, and then leaned close to Marko, standing on her tiptoes so only he could hear her.

'You're good at this,' she said, firmly. 'Nothing lamp-post-like about you, I promise.' He looked down to meet her gaze, surprised.

Jas narrowed her eyes, as if considering something.

'Well, maybe you could smile a bit more.'

'More!' he whispered, disbelieving. But Jas gave nothing away as to if she was teasing, or genuine—as surely it was physically impossible for him to smile *more*? Jasmine simply smiled at him, serenely.

And so Marko, of course, found himself smiling too—and this time, as he was introduced to their latest guests, it was a smile without the faintest hint of plastic.

It had been nice to make Marko laugh.

She'd tried, for a whole week, to be strictly professional, but she was just spending too much time with the Prince to maintain it. So after the lamp-post incident, she began to relax a little around Marko again—chatting with him in the car on the way to events, and talking more freely at the events themselves.

But outside the royal events they attended—and in the second week there were only two—Jas backed off again. Even when they met for a meal—and they were scheduled to have at least one together each day as part of their ruse—Jas didn't encourage much conversation.

It was just easier that way.

No confusion, no chance she'd misinterpret Marko's innate, rather smouldering charisma as having anything to do with her specifically. They were just two people working together. Professionally.

So they would eat breakfast, or lunch, or dinner—usually out on the terrace—in a not quite comfortable almost silence. Marko began bringing along whatever book he was reading—generally autobiographies or science fiction—while Jas would manage Gallagher Personal Protection Services.

Which didn't mean that at times Jas didn't want to ask him questions. About what it was like growing up in this palace—and *why* he'd hated it so. About his obviously complex relationship with his brother. About all sorts of things.

But she never asked, of course. Because it was none of her business.

Midway through Jas's third week as fake fiancée, they headed for Vela Ada harbour for a sailing regatta. Terraced houses huddled close to the water, overlooking everything from rowboats to yachts, all moored along narrow jetties, bobbing gently in the undulating sea. Crowds milled near the water's edge, kids dangled their legs into the water, and couples drank dark coffee in cafés. When they'd arrived, there'd been a large crowd waiting for them, but now they'd finished an extended meet and greet the crowd had dispersed somewhat, and they were being led to their exclusive VIP marquee.

It was a beautiful day, the sun warm on Jas's shoulders, revealed by the drop sleeves of her white summery dress. The novelty of the beautiful clothes she got to wear still hadn't worn off, and Jas had never felt more sophisticated than she did right now in her wide-brimmed, fashionably floppy hat and dark, oversized sunglasses.

She also still felt like a total fraud, but, miraculously, now three weeks in, the people of Vela Ada continued to embrace her as their future princess. Three weeks of shaking hands, and small talk, and smiling—and countless newspaper and magazine articles—and Marko's plan continued to go to plan. Everyone actually believed she was Marko's fiancée.

It was crazy, really.

Although the real reason anyone believed any of this was because of Marko.

In public, he played the affectionate fiancé in the most natural, casual ways: he took every opportunity to hold her hand, he was forever touching her—the small of her back, her shoulder…

And the way he *spoke* to her. And about her…

It was beautiful.

It made her *feel* beautiful.

And in those moments, a part of Jasmine let herself believe it was all real.

Only a very small part, the part of her that in the dead of night couldn't remember why their no-kissing clause had seemed so essential—but a part of her, nonetheless.

She'd seen that part of her in some of the many photographs taken of her. She tried to avoid paying attention to them, because—unfortunately—becoming a fake princess-to-be had not suddenly made her effortlessly photogenic. But she was human, and so she'd looked herself up on the Internet. And amongst the photos that made her cringe at her awkward expression or an unflattering angle (Marko, without exception, always looked devastatingly handsome) there had been images of her simply looking at Marko. And in those images it was easy to see why Vela Ada—and the world—thought they were in love.

Because her gaze was that of a woman besotted.

It had scared her at first—her mother's warning warring with her own determination to never be so romantically stupid again—but then she'd started paying attention to Marko's gaze in those photos.

And his—while not besotted—told its own story. His gaze was that of a man with all sorts of delicious plans for the woman he was looking at. A gaze that made her shiver.

It was also a gaze that was absent the moment they left the public eye.

At the palace, there were two people with a business arrangement and a no-kissing clause.

So, they were *both* pretending. They *both* could separate fact from fiction.

Marko's wrist bumped against hers as they walked along the marina, and then—in an action that was now so familiar—he laced his fingers with hers.

In a reaction that was also familiar, Jas's belly flipped over, and electricity zipped up her arm.

But she ignored all that, and, because it was her job too, she looked up at Marko and smiled.

Her eyes were hidden behind her dark glasses, but his weren't.

And when he smiled back at her, and squeezed her hand, looking at her as if she were the only woman for him in the world…

She simply acknowledged, once again, what a remarkably good actor he was.

CHAPTER NINE

JASMINE MIGHT THINK he was good at this—at mingling with all these total strangers beneath an open-sided marquee where waiters constantly circulated with obscenely expensive champagne—but Marko did not feel that way at all.

He was getting more practised, certainly. He now didn't feel he needed to wrack his brain for things to say, and instead he found words and platitudes spilling easily from his mouth. The people he met—and honestly, most were really very nice people—seemed happy enough, anyway.

Obviously he was no Lukas, but then, he wasn't trying to be. He was playing a role for a defined period of time, and the people of Vela Ada seemed okay with that. He had no doubt that Jasmine was having a huge influence on his acceptance into this role, and that having her by his side was the reason why he was attracting crowds that rivalled the King and Queen's at events. Without Jasmine, he was simply the absent, disreputable Prince, but with her, he was—according to the headlines—a changed man. A changed man who had come *home* to Vela Ada.

Home?

No. Vela Ada wasn't his home. But this perception fed perfectly into the narrative that he and Jasmine had created, and for that he was grateful.

He'd spoken to Lukas earlier this morning, just before his brother had begun his day of chemotherapy. He was doing as well as could be expected, he'd said. And he'd asked about Jas.

So, everyone believed in his relationship with Jas.

This was good, right? Exactly what he'd wanted?

'Your Highness?'

Marko blinked. The older couple standing in front of him were looking at him curiously.

See? This was why he was no good at this. He'd just completely checked out of this conversation.

He took a long sip of his champagne, and glanced at Jas.

He'd meant to shoot her a look of thanks for carrying the conversation, but then he noticed the way her lips were arranged in a tense, straight line.

'We were just discussing how lovely it is that you've settled down,' the older man said. Marko glanced at the name tag pinned to the lapel of his suit jacket. He didn't recognise the name, but the seafood business printed in italics beneath it, he did. The largest in the country.

Marko nodded without a lot of commitment, wondering what he'd missed. He could sense the tension in Jas, despite the gap between them.

'Yes,' said the woman. She was beautiful, with white-blonde hair wrapped into a polished chignon. 'And to choose such a *successful* woman. How nice.'

'I'm very proud of Jas's achievements,' Marko said, but a little warily now. 'She is exceptional at what she does.'

There was a glint to the woman's gaze when she looked at Jas that Marko did not like.

'But it must have been hard giving up your old lifestyle,' the man said.

'I haven't left the military,' Marko said. 'I'm not sure what you mean.'

But he did, of course. The surname on their name tags suddenly clicked into place, and a half-formed memory of a young woman with hair the same colour as in that chignon.

He turned to Jas, taking her hand. He lifted his gaze in search of Ivan, to signal that this conversation was over.

But the older couple weren't paying attention, seemingly intent on delivering their message.

'So many *beautiful* women,' he said, in a chummy, 'just

between us men' type tone. 'Models, actresses, the most stunning women in Vela Ada. And with all that choice, you chose Jasmine.'

He smiled at Jas in a way that made Marko feel violent.

'You *must* be very proud of her,' the woman said. 'Of all that she's *achieved*. Because, well—'

The woman whipped her hand in front of her mouth, and laughed, as if she'd accidentally let something slip, instead of carefully constructing this entire conversation.

Jas gripped his hand tightly, but she murmured, 'It's okay. I'm fine.'

But this really wasn't fine. Anger bubbled inside him, and the urge to tell these people exactly what he thought of them—and loudly—was almost impossible to resist.

Yet resist it he did.

Because if he didn't, if he made a scene, it would be in the papers, it would be all over the Internet. And he suspected that was exactly what this couple wanted.

So instead, he faced them both again.

'Jas is the most remarkable woman I've ever met,' he said, in a deliberately calm and low tone. 'Now, if you'll excuse me, I—'

The man's words were muttered beneath his breath, but neither Marko nor Jas misheard: *It'll never last.*

'Ivan,' Marko said, more loudly now. His valet stepped closer. 'Please escort this couple to the exit.'

He didn't bother to provide a reason. He just wanted them gone.

In fact, he also wanted to be gone. From this marquee, from all these people, and from anyone who had an opinion on him, or Jas, or their relationship.

'Want to come for a walk?' he asked Jas.

They didn't leave in a hurry. Instead, Marko politely made his way through the crowd, explaining that he wanted to show Jasmine *Mjesto za Ljubljenje*.

Everyone smiled when Marko said that, although Jas had no idea why, her efforts at learning basic Slavic phrases not having extended to those words. *Za* might mean 'of'? She couldn't remember.

'Where are we going?' Jas asked—partly because she was curious, but mostly because Marko couldn't just walk off into the distance. Her team still had a job to do.

'*Mjesto za Ljubljenje* is up there—' Marko gestured to where the harbour curved and merged into a rocky beach. 'On the other side of those trees.'

'That's still part of the exclusion zone,' Jas said, referring to the area surrounding the marquee that had been cleared for anyone but guests. Palace security patrolled the edges of the zone, ensuring the privacy and security of the Prince—and mostly to keep the paparazzi at bay.

'Exactly,' Marko said. He turned to Scott and Simon, who had materialised at their sides. 'So, guys—could you keep your distance?'

Marko needed some space; it was obvious to Jasmine in every tense line of his body. *She* needed some space, actually.

Which was silly. Because as much as she appreciated Marko's defence of her, and as much as she acknowledged that such rudeness towards anyone—let alone your country's Prince and his fiancée—was utterly outrageous…

That couple had been right.

Marko would *never* have chosen her, from all the women he'd had to choose from—and who he would have to choose from again, once this was over—based on her looks.

To have it so baldly stated was definitely a direct hit to her vanity.

But in reality…it didn't actually matter.

He hadn't chosen her—for any reason—and he never would.

So, alone, Jas and Marko went for a walk.

He still held her hand, although it was obviously for show—given they remained in full view of the marquee.

He didn't say a word, he simply walked briskly, his gaze straight ahead.

He only paused—and dropped her hand—when they passed the last mooring to reach the edge of the marina, and Jas needed to stop to take off her heels. Marko removed his shoes too.

They now walked along the sandy beach of a narrow point that stretched out from the town. With no buildings and covered in a mix of tall trees and scrubby plants, it was a stark contrast to the bustling crowd behind them. But Jas still sensed she was being watched, and it wasn't until they'd rounded the top of the point—and were hidden from view—that she began to relax.

'It's all national park here,' Marko said suddenly. 'It extends along the coast for a few kilometres. There are walking trails, some picnic spots and a few lookouts, but not much else.'

'It's beautiful,' Jas said. And it was. Their only company was the ocean, and the white yachts that dotted it as they took part in the regatta Jas had almost forgotten about. 'It's hard to believe we're so close to the city.'

He was still walking. A bit faster now, so Jas had to lengthen her own stride to keep up.

'I'm very sorry about before,' he said. 'I think they must be the parents of a woman I dated briefly. Seems they maybe had hopes of marrying into royalty.'

Jas shrugged. 'It's okay.'

Marko stopped. The beach had narrowed here, and water lapped almost against their toes.

'It's not okay,' he said, facing Jas. It was mid-afternoon and the sun made him squint.

The sea breeze had loosened Jasmine's hair from its bun, her hair no longer contained by the hat she'd forgotten back at the marquee.

'No, really,' Jas said, 'it is. You must get so frustrated with how everyone refers to your past. That guy made it sound like—'

'No, Jas,' he said, interrupting. 'Don't make this about me. They were very offensive towards *you*.'

Jas crossed her arms in front of herself. 'So they were mean to me.' She shrugged again. 'So what? I'm pretty tough, remember?'

She raised her eyebrows and smiled, but Marko was refusing to play along.

'It wasn't acceptable,' he insisted.

Jas wrinkled her forehead, confused. Why was he so stuck on this? 'Thank you very much for your chivalry back there, but, please—don't worry about it. I'm really fine. Besides—'

But then she snapped her mouth shut.

'Besides what?'

Now it was Jas's turn to start walking, and she did so with big, urgent strides. Did they really need to have a conversation about how much less attractive she was than all his *real* past partners?

'It doesn't matter.'

He caught up with her effortlessly, and they walked together, gentle waves occasionally covering their feet, the water cool against her skin.

'You told me, that first night, that you don't look anything like the women I date,' he said shrewdly. 'You don't still believe that, surely?'

'It really doesn't matter what I think,' Jas pointed out. 'Everyone else seems to believe it's plausible we're engaged—except this couple today—and that's what's important.'

'I disagree,' he said.

'With what? That everyone believes we're really engaged? Or that it's not important they do?'

She was being deliberately obtuse, not understanding why Marko wanted to have this conversation.

'I disagree that you don't look like a woman I'd date,' he said.

He stepped in front of her, forcing her to stop.

Jas made herself look up at him, and tucked long escaped strands of her hair roughly behind her ears.

'That's very kind of you to tell me that,' she said neutrally. 'And trust me, I think I have relatively good self-esteem—but I'm not delusional, Marko. I'm no supermodel. Heck, I wasn't close to being the most beautiful girl in my year at school—or probably even in my *street*—let alone the most beautiful woman in Vela Ada. That couple kind of had a point. If you were, in fact, *actually* engaged to me, it *wouldn't* be for my looks.' She grinned now. 'It would definitely be my sparkling personality that won you over.'

But Marko wasn't smiling.

'Do you really think so little of me that you think looks are all I care about?'

'No,' Jas said. 'It's just—'

'Based on what you've read in magazines and photos you've seen, you know what kind of man I am? Just like that couple thought they knew me?' He swallowed. 'Despite the amount of time we've spent together, that's *still* the man you think I am? Despite what I've—'

He stopped abruptly.

Despite what I've told you. Jas *knew* that was what he'd been about to say.

But he wouldn't say it. Jas also knew that Marko still hated what he'd revealed to her on that beach.

Jas shook her head. *'No,'* she said.

But, she realised, even though she'd defended him to her mother, part of her, maybe, still labelled him as the Playboy Prince.

'Okay,' she said. 'I'm sorry. I probably have made unfair assumptions. But why are we even having this conversation? It doesn't matter if it's my looks or my personality or whatever that you're attracted to, because *you're not* attracted to me. Remember? This isn't real.'

Jasmine stepped around Marko, and continued down the beach.

She hugged herself as she walked, unsure why she felt so agitated, and frustrated that her cheeks had definitely heated into a telling blush.

She was *just* working with Marko. None of this mattered.

It was only her ego that was bruised, not her heart…

Her heart?

Ha! She couldn't help but smile. Now she *was* being delusional. Sure, Marko was very handsome. And charming. And, it turned out, smart, and complex, and thoughtful, and he laughed at her jokes…

But she'd always known that he wasn't really interested in her. He'd flirted with her, maybe. Checked her out, that first time they'd met…but—that was what he *did*. Right?

Because he was the Playboy Prince…

Except, he wasn't. Not really. She knew that.

She shook her head, as if trying to shake these unwanted thoughts free.

No. He might make her tummy flip over, and her skin tingle—but that didn't mean there was anything more there. She was only human, and he *was* gorgeous. But she knew that was all it was—an attraction she was very capable of controlling. A physical attraction, nothing more.

The beach sand had merged into rocks—large and flat, and arranged like a natural, gradual staircase. Jasmine made her way up them, her strappy sandals still in one hand. She didn't look back, but she knew Marko was behind her.

At the top was a large, flat space, paved in small square cobblestones in differing shades of cream. At the centre a line of dark grey stones formed a square, and inside that even smaller pavers formed the words *Mjesto za Ljubljenje.*

It seemed she had found Marko's destination.

Jas stepped into the square—it felt as if that was what she was supposed to do—and let her sandals drop to the ground.

It must be a lookout point, Jas decided. The view was certainly spectacular—from here she could look back towards the city of Vela Ada, its red-roofed buildings peeking out beyond the trees of the national park as they covered the undulating hills. And ahead of her was the ocean, a sparkling, perfect azure, the horizon only interrupted by yachts and foaming waves.

Marko stepped into the square.

Suddenly, with Marko beside her, the square seemed tiny—barely big enough for the two of them, their feet covering most of the writing.

'What does it mean?' Jas asked. She attempted to pronounce it. *'Mjesto za Ljubljenje.'*

'I worked out why we're having this conversation,' Marko said, ignoring her current question to reference a question she hadn't really wanted him to answer. 'Why what that couple said bothered me so much, and why I don't like you being so okay with it.'

They both kept staring out to the ocean, not looking at each other, and not touching.

Jas hated how she was feeling right now, an unfamiliar mix of embarrassment and hurt that she knew was misplaced. Why wouldn't Marko just move on from this? She wasn't fragile; she didn't need him to try and make her feel better.

'It's because I didn't like those people saying you weren't beautiful, and I don't like that you think you aren't.'

Jas rolled her eyes, turning to look up at him now. 'Seriously, Marko, there is a *lot* more to me than how I look. I'm genuinely, totally fine. You don't have to say nice things to make me feel good about myself.'

'I'm not saying it to make you feel better. And I know there is so much more to you than your appearance—I know there is so much more to everyone than their appearance.

But—the thing is, I particularly like your appearance, and it turns out it's important to me that you know that.'

'You *particularly like my appearance*?' Jas said, her lips quirking upwards. 'Well, that's a new one. I'll file that compliment beside the *Well Done for Trying* stickers I got as a kid, or that one time I received a "sound" rating in a performance review from a sergeant who really didn't like me. What does "sound" even mean in that cont—?'

'Jasmine,' Marko said, cutting off her stream of words. 'Stop. I'm trying to tell you I think you're beautiful, and you're too busy being facetious to listen.'

'I wasn't being—' she argued, automatically. And then stopped. 'Pardon me?'

'I said I think you're beautiful. Really beautiful, actually. And I *am* attracted to you. Very much so.'

'But—'

'I'm actually a bit confused why you would ever think I *wasn't.* You knew I checked you out that first time we met. You knew I liked kissing you, and was angling to kiss you again later that night. And you knew I invited you to swim with me that day, and, believe me, my dreams have done their best to imagine how you would've looked in your underwear if you'd said yes. In your wet underwear, actually.'

Oh, God. Marko's deep, delicious voice sent shivers down her spine.

She closed her eyes, and took a long, deep breath.

'But since that day at the beach, you've been so different when we've been alone. You've kept your distance,' she said.

'So have you,' Marko pointed out.

'I was being professional.'

'So was I,' he said. 'But I was putting aside the attraction between us. I certainly wasn't pretending it didn't exist.'

'I haven't been pretending!' Jas said, narrowing her gaze. 'I'm just not as arrogant as you, assuming that every person I meet is melting into a puddle of lust in my presence. *You* don't even know if I'm into you. Maybe I'm not.'

He just looked at her steadily, with infuriating self-assurance in his gaze.

'Maybe you weren't pretending,' Marko continued now, his voice low. 'Maybe it was just plain old denial. Because, surely, you feel this too.'

He reached out, taking her right hand, and lifting it to his chest. Jas stretched her fingers out, until her palm was flat against his heart.

'Can you feel that?' he asked hoarsely.

His heart beat like a drum beneath her touch.

Jas wasn't capable of doing much more than nod, and so that was what she did.

Then Marko's fingers curved around her wrist to press gently against her skin—against her own pulse, a pulse that beat every bit as rapidly as his heart.

She watched as Marko's lips curved into a knowing smile, but then her gaze met his, and all she could concentrate on were his eyes. Eyes that were hot with want—for *her*.

But, Jas realised only now, that wasn't a complete surprise. Since the moment they'd met, electricity had sparked between them, and that connection had only grown since then with every touch, every word, and every laugh.

So he'd been right, she had been denying this, for reasons beyond professionalism. For such professionalism didn't require denial, it simply required restraint.

She didn't *want* to want Marko, because Marko was not the right man for her. Even now, as she stood within the spell of his words and his proximity, she knew he was not the man who would mend her still-broken heart, or who she could trust to never hurt her. Because Marko, while not exactly the playboy he was portrayed as, was also not going to fall in love with Jasmine Gallagher from Canberra. In just over two months' time he would return to his military career, and to a world that would not involve her.

Of that she had no doubt.

'Marko,' Jas said, attempting to sound serious, but ending

up soft and breathy. 'As it appears we both have thrown professionalism out the window, can I just confirm something?'

'Anything,' he murmured.

He was brushing his thumb against the sensitive skin of her wrist, making it nearly impossible for Jas to think aside from wondering how something so simple could make her knees feel so weak.

'Uh—' she began, then swallowed. Straightened her shoulders. 'This is important,' she said—partly as a reminder to herself. 'I just want to be clear what this is. So if we tear up the no-kissing clause, we'll be *not* not kissing for how long, exactly?'

Marko raised his eyebrows. 'I don't think it's necessary to update our contract, Jas.'

'But not beyond these three months together, right?'

The look of horror in Marko's gaze told Jas everything she needed to know. It also made her laugh out loud.

'Wow, Marko—way to freak out,' Jas said. 'Don't panic, I'm thinking something fun and easy too. I'm on the same page.'

And she most definitely was. Especially now there was *no* danger she might start imagining a future for them that would never be.

Marko seemed to have decided he'd had enough of talking. He stepped closer, almost sandwiching their hands between them—but not quite. Still, they only touched above his heartbeat, while the ocean breeze tangled her skirt against his legs.

'Mjesto za Ljubljenje,' he said, now so close she had to tilt her chin up to meet his gaze. 'You asked before what it means.'

Jas curled her toes against the smooth shape of those words against her feet, and nodded, although right now all she cared about was getting closer to Marko.

'It translates to Place of Love,' he said, in a rough tone that did delicious things to Jas's insides. 'But in English, people usually call these places a kissing spot—which is what it's intended to be.'

'There's more than one?' Jas asked, her gaze travelling downwards to his lips.

'Mmm-hmm,' Marko said. 'Across the island, and also throughout Croatia. One of many ideas we've borrowed from our neighbour.'

'An *excellent* idea,' Jas said firmly. But she was getting impatient now. What was Marko waiting for?

His lips—the lips she couldn't drag her gaze away from—had formed into a smile. God, he *knew* what he was doing to her. But, with her hand against his heart, she also knew *exactly* what she was doing to him.

He was just as affected by her nearness as she was by his. And with that knowledge came power. And with the clarity of expectation they both now had—came freedom.

Suddenly she remembered something: whispered words from a night that seemed a lifetime ago.

She stood, on tiptoes, to speak almost against his lips. 'Can I kiss you?' she said, repurposing Marko's own words.

'You, Jasmine Gallagher, can do anything you want.'

And so Jas was smiling as she bridged the tiniest of gaps between them to press her mouth against his.

At first, their kiss had many similarities to that one in front of the glitterati of Vela Ada. His lips were warm, and tasted of just a hint of the salty breeze—and remained closed. As if he was waiting for her.

Like then, they were joined only by their hands and lips, and like then, it was incredibly, impossibly sexy.

A kiss that promised *so* much more, and now—now there was no question that there was definitely so much more to come.

But it was as if because of that knowledge they'd both decided to build the anticipation, to wait just that little bit longer. To allow the heat that had already built between them to keep on building until every fibre of their bodies felt engulfed in flames.

And so, when Jasmine's lips finally opened against Marko's, and he brushed his tongue against hers, the sensation was so incredible, so overwhelming, that Jas—strong, capable, always together Jas—felt her knees give way.

But she fell no further than into Marko's arms—that were there so quickly it was as if he knew what would happen, or maybe he had fallen into her as well.

It didn't matter; all Jas knew now was that her hands were twined behind Marko's neck and his hands were at her waist and back, pressing her close against him.

To be *held* against Marko was just something else entirely. After weeks of sparks from simply holding hands to now have his chest, his hips, his thighs pressed hard against hers was enough to make Jas sure she would ignite.

Or combust into that puddle of lust she'd teased Marko about but had always been revealingly close to the truth.

Marko did something to her in a way that she'd never experienced before.

It had her believing in things she had no place believing: that love and happy ever afters were actually possible.

Although—obviously—not with Marko.

She moved her mouth from Marko's, to take a deep breath and try and right her rioting, silly thoughts. But Marko only took the opportunity to press kisses against her jaw, working his way to the sensitive skin of her neck and below her ear.

He murmured something against her skin, foreign words that could have meant anything, but still practically made her swoon.

This was *not* the time for thinking, it was for *feeling*, and so Jas simply closed her eyes and let sensation take over.

Her own hands traced patterns against his neck and shoulders, and brushed through his army-short hair. She worked one hand back to his front, in an attempt to undo his tie in a quest to touch more of his skin—but she soon gave up and simply slid a button undone. Then two.

Marko's hands were searching for bare skin too, one making its way to her bare shoulders, his fingers sliding just slightly beneath the fabric below her shoulder blades.

Then he was kissing her mouth again, and if the kiss had begun as Jasmine's it was now all Marko's as he kissed her thoroughly with lips and tongue—at times teasing her with his mouth, or allowing her to tease him—and then he'd take control in a way that made Jas lose sense of anything. When she was lost within his kiss.

Eventually, Jas—or Marko, she had no idea—broke their lips apart, and they stood, foreheads still touching, as they each took deep, harsh breaths.

'Do we need to go back to the marquee?' Jas asked when she was again capable of speaking.

'Probably,' Marko said, but his smile was wicked. 'Lukas definitely would.'

'Are we?' Jas prompted.

Marko took a step back, and his gaze travelled across Jasmine—with now familiar heat in it—from her eyes, to her lips, then down to the askew bodice of her dress and her breasts that still rose and fell rapidly.

Jas took Marko in too—his own heavy breathing, that gorgeous olive skin she could see where she'd so artlessly yanked his shirt open…and the promises in his piercing blue gaze.

'We're not going back to the marquee,' Jas said.

'No,' Marko agreed, lacing his fingers with hers as he led her back down the rocky steps. 'We—most definitely—are not.'

CHAPTER TEN

He'd never slept with a woman in the palace.

This realisation—in both senses of the word—came to Marko as the dawn crept its way around the edges of his curtains.

Although, he wasn't so much looking at his curtains as looking at Jasmine—her shape revealed in increasingly more satisfying detail as the morning light gradually entered his suite.

She lay, fast asleep, naked, beside him. She had her back to him, his sheets caught up around her waist, but leaving her back bare. While he'd been contemplating the realisation that Jas was the only woman who'd lain beside him here, he'd only been able to see as much as the darkness would allow: not much more than her silhouette, her hair a dark wave against the crisp whiteness of her pillow.

But now, he could appreciate the pale alabaster of her skin, and the gentle curve of her spine. He could recognise the smattering of freckles he'd discovered last night on her shoulders, and he could be grateful that his sheets did not hide the smooth roundness of her bottom.

And he could also wonder at how he felt, having a woman here. In the palace. With him.

Last night, it hadn't even been a consideration. *Nothing* had been more important than returning home, and kissing Jasmine again. And again.

It also would've been ridiculous to go anywhere else.

They were supposedly engaged. To take her to a hotel would've been ludicrous, if it had even occurred to him.

But it hadn't. So here he was, with a woman in his room.

He supposed, up until now, bringing a woman into the palace had never been a possibility. The palace wasn't the place to bring a one-night stand—and yes, at one stage, he'd had his fair share of those—but it equally wasn't the place to bring any woman he'd been seeing.

To do so would imply too much—it would imply a relationship, and a relationship was something he'd never had.

But even if he had—if something had stretched from weeks to months with a woman—the palace was not the place he would've wanted to take her.

This place, to Marko, was a place of suffocation. And of scrutiny and surveillance. Here he was controlled by the expectations of his birth, of his family, his brother—and of everyone in Vela Ada.

Here there was no pretending that he wasn't a prince. Here it was *all* he was.

He'd never wanted to bring a woman into that. To put her through that.

Yet, despite all that—here Jas was. In the palace, and in his bed.

So—how did he feel about it?

Not great.

But also—not entirely bad.

Not even close to bad, actually.

His unease at the situation was more an itchiness in his subconscious—an awareness that he should be feeling regret right now.

Yet he didn't. He wouldn't say he felt comfortable, exactly. But equally, he didn't want Jas to leave his bed any time soon.

The realisation surprised him, but, as he watched Jasmine roll onto her back, still asleep, one arm out-flung and now almost touching his shoulder, it probably shouldn't.

It was because Jasmine had come to his room with no expectations.

In her typical way she hadn't even allowed him to kiss

her without determining exactly what she was getting into—much like the way she had her team scout out venues before events. Jas was *always* prepared in her professional career—and it would seem she approached her personal life in the same way.

Marko smiled as he reached that conclusion.

Jas made him smile a lot, he'd discovered. When they'd both backed off after his accidental divulgement at that private beach, it had felt like the right decision. But within days he'd missed the way she teased him, and her willingness to say whatever popped into her head.

Fortunately, it hadn't lasted long, and he supposed he should've realised he and Jas were always heading in this direction, and into bed. Right from the start he'd been drawn to her, he just hadn't realised how strongly until meeting that silly couple with their misplaced jealousy.

Although, that wasn't entirely true.

He'd known how strongly he was drawn to Jasmine from the moment he'd kissed her that very first evening. He'd just, as he'd told Jas, not pursued it.

Jas had been right to keep things professional between them. And he'd needed to minimise any complications amidst this exceedingly complicated deception. He couldn't risk anything going wrong, because he needed to keep everything together for Lukas.

But yesterday…

Suddenly, he hadn't been able to pretend any more.

And because of Jasmine—because of who she was—so straightforward, so structured—he *knew* she had no expectations beyond right now. Whether it led to tomorrow, or a week, or the rest of their three-month contract—it *would* end eventually. Jas was not imagining herself as a future princess, and as such there was no significance in her lying here beside him right now.

None.

So that must be why he felt fine.

Actually—as Jas's eyes fluttered open and her lips formed into a sleepy, sexy good-morning smile—he changed his mind.

Right now—as he leant forward to kiss the beautiful, naked woman in his bed—he felt pretty damn fantastic.

Given the nature of Jas's career, she'd never been particularly active on social media. You never knew how a person with nefarious intentions might track or monitor a client she was looking after, so it wasn't as if she could ever post a selfie of herself at work or anything. Nevertheless, she did have social media accounts, even though she'd been ignoring the hundreds of messages she'd received since the news of her 'engagement' had become news across the world.

Soon after she and Marko eventually emerged from his suite for an extremely late breakfast on the terrace, Marko had been called away for something royal-related by Ivan, and while she'd waited for him to return she'd logged into her account on her phone.

Slowly she weeded through her messages—ignoring those from people she didn't know at all, and also those from friends of the 'we went to kindergarten together but I probably wouldn't recognise you in the local supermarket' variety.

To the rest—some of her friends from the police academy, and the small group of women she'd gone to high school with that she still always made sure to catch up with when in Canberra—she sent short messages that didn't invite extended conversation.

Yes, I'm really engaged to a prince. I'm sorry we had to keep it secret until now, I hope you understand. Don't worry—I'll tell you all the details when I'm next home.

And by then, of course, it would all be over.

Jas still didn't feel okay about lying to her friends, but for some reason, now, it didn't feel so impossible.

Maybe it didn't feel so much of a lie now that she had *some* form of relationship with Marko? Other than a business relationship, of course.

Jas smiled. Yup, it was definitely more than a business relationship, now.

To wake up this morning the way she had—with Marko there, simply looking at her, with the *most* remarkable expression in his eyes… And then…

Well.

It had been pretty damn spectacular.

Jas looked up from her phone at the sound of Marko's footsteps. It was a little cooler today, and he wore jeans and a faded T-shirt. He hadn't bothered to shave that morning, and Jas thought the shadow of stubble across his jaw made him even more impossibly handsome. Like a slightly more dangerous version of Prince Marko. His expression, however, was serious.

'My apologies,' he said. 'There is a protest going on outside the Vela Ada courthouse.'

Marko briefly kissed Jas before he took the seat across from her, the simple action still making her shiver.

It took her a moment—just a moment—to recall what he'd just said. 'Anything I need to know about?'

Anything that could increase Marko's threat level needed to be considered by her team.

He nodded. 'Senator Božić is being sentenced today. Unfortunately his supporters aren't letting go of their conspiracy theory, or their resolute belief in his innocence.'

Jas was familiar with the situation, of course. The senator's corruption had been discovered twelve months ago, shocking the people of Vela Ada and having far-reaching impacts. Dozens of contracts had been cancelled as the corrupt behaviour had been investigated, with Božić taking bribes to influence tender decisions for several capital work projects.

Businesses had collapsed amidst the scandal—with thousands of innocent workers also losing their jobs.

It was a very messy situation, and one where King Lukas had taken a far more visible role than was usual for the head of state of Vela Ada's constitutional monarchy—given Lukas reigned over Vela Ada, but he did not rule it. That was the role of the elected government.

But the situation had required a sense of unity despite a fractured parliament, and so Lukas had done his best to hold his country together.

It was primarily why Prince Marko had been needed in Lukas's absence. In times of turmoil, there was something satisfyingly reassuring in the stability of Vela Ada's royal family.

'Lukas—and I—have faith that the investigation was fair and the outcome was correct, and to be honest I'd thought that the protests were over now that the government is helping the innocents caught up in all this…'

Jas had read about how employees of the businesses involved had received one-off payments to go some way towards off setting their financial losses. But not all, of course.

'But it seems not,' he added, then rubbed his forehead in a gesture that had now become familiar to Jas. He did it in contemplation, and also frustration, she'd discovered.

'So there'll be a briefing with Palace Security and the police?'

Marko nodded.

'I don't imagine this will increase my threat level—the issue that these people have is not with me, or even with Lukas.'

He was probably correct. 'When is it?'

'During the opera tonight,' Marko said.

'Of course it is,' Jas said, frustrated. 'But I'll still need to go to the briefing. I'm not delegating this. I'll just meet you at the opera later.'

It wasn't even a question.

Marko smiled, and looked utterly unsurprised. 'I've already organised a car for you.'

* * *

Jas arrived at the royal box about ten minutes before intermission.

Even in the muted light, she was stunning in her navy-blue floor-length gown, and with her hair swept up and off her face. She wore jewellery borrowed from the royal collection, so sapphires and diamonds glittered at her ears and décolletage.

Marko stood to greet her, intensely aware that the whole theatre was no longer paying attention to the performance of *La Bohème*—but was instead focused on Jasmine's arrival.

A vague reason had been provided by the palace for Jas's tardiness, although it was possible some members of the public might have guessed at the real reason, given the events of the day. It didn't really matter. There was, of course, intense interest in Jas's career and how she might—or might not—continue to run her business once she was a princess.

But, given that wouldn't actually happen, there'd been no need for Marko or Jas to provide anything but the barest of answers when asked about it.

Although, if Jas had *actually* been his fiancée, Marko definitely knew the answer.

There was no way she was giving up her career.

He remembered her adamant expression as she'd told him so clearly that she wouldn't be delegating tonight's briefing. Nope. She would *not* have walked away from a career she so obviously loved.

He smiled now as Jas reached his side. He took her hand, and, as always, laced his fingers with hers.

He kissed her—he was definitely taking advantage of this waiver of the no-kissing policy—and then whispered in her ear: 'How did it go?'

'No official change to the threat level, as there's been no credible threat to you, or Lukas. But I'm going to bring in a couple of extras from my team, anyway—I should've done it earlier, really.'

'Why?' Marko said as they settled back into their seats. 'You, and your team, have done an exceptional job.'

'Thank you,' Jas said. 'But I can't possibly be as focused on my protection role while acting as your fiancée. Especially now.'

Below them, the orchestra and soprano were reaching a crescendo, and Marko sensed—thankfully—that the eyes of the theatre were no longer on them.

'Especially now?' Marko asked. He still held her hand loosely, and now drew little squiggles on the delicate skin of her wrist with his thumb.

Jas bumped her shoulder against his, and he could see her smile even as she concentrated on the performance below. 'Don't pretend you don't know exactly how distracting you are.'

And—just because he could—Marko then told Jas—very quietly—all the distracting things he would like to do to her, right now.

If they weren't at the opera, with two bodyguards standing just metres away.

Then later, back at the palace, they did all those distracting things, together.

The next week was…fun.

Fun didn't seem quite the right word, given Jas was, technically, working, but it was definitely accurate.

When she was with Marko, she always seemed to be smiling.

Whether he was teasing her into a laugh, or guiding her through a crowd with the lightest touch at her waist, or patiently translating conversations into English for her—around Marko, she just smiled.

They'd fallen easily into a new normal pattern of behaviour post the 'no kissing' clause. Both wary of any sudden change notifying keen royal watchers of something being up, they were careful not to become dramatically more affectionate in public.

But then, Jas thought Marko was seriously unlikely to *ever* be particularly affectionate in public.

Jas knew that Marko never forgot the scrutiny they were under.

With no further protests following the incarceration of the corrupt senator, and no further intel received from the police, Jas and her team—now expanded by two—simply continued their routine of royal engagements.

This week they had another school visit—this time a secondary school—then a charity auction, and finally, on the weekend, they visited a winery that through its innovative viticulture and harvesting techniques—so Marko told her—was putting the wines of Vela Ada on the international stage.

It was another warm day, and Jas's heels sank slightly into the rich soil as she walked beside Marko between rows upon rows of grape vines. Just ahead of them, the winery owner was their tour guide, and a small group of palace-approved photographers, plus Marko's bodyguards, followed behind.

Their guide didn't speak English, but Jas was taking the opportunity to just enjoy her surroundings. For almost four weeks now she'd spent all her time either at royal engagements, running her company or—for the last week—alone with Marko.

It had all been a blur, really—and stressful at times, too.

As she'd told Marko right from the beginning, she was no actress. And so acting in her fake-fiancée role had been far from easy for her. Even though she'd been playing a variation of herself, any question put to her about their relationship was an opportunity for her to accidentally expose Marko's deception, and she'd felt the weight of that responsibility heavily on her shoulders.

Plus, she was also responsible for Marko's *actual* safety. So there was that, too.

It was probably ridiculous that she felt more comfortable theoretically saving Marko's life than mingling with the Vela Ada hoi polloi—but it was the truth.

Although, now, she definitely did feel herself relaxing into the role. She and Marko knew their back story inside out, and her lies flowed far more easily. She'd also got a lot better at smiling for the cameras—and also *much* better at not looking herself up on the Internet. Nothing was gained from viewing the hundreds of photos taken every time she was out in public with Marko, and definitely not from reading any of the comments. Unsurprisingly, a lot of people weren't super happy such an eligible bachelor was no longer—apparently—available, and she'd stumbled across some not-so-nice remarks.

A brisk breeze whipped its way across the valley, ruffling the loose curls that her stylist had arranged her hair into this morning. Jas smoothed her hair back behind her ears as she looked out across the vines and the undulating hills, and breathed in the scent of damp soil and clean, crisp air.

She might be more relaxed in her role, but it still didn't feel any less crazy. If she stopped for a moment—like now—it just seemed even more fantastical. Right now she could hear the click of a photographer behind her, and of course she knew exactly where her team had positioned themselves to protect Marko—but they were also protecting her.

Marko and the guide had stopped, just ahead. Marko was watching as he waited for her to catch up, his gaze sliding down the shape of her polka-dot sundress before returning to her face with an appreciative smile.

He held out his hand for her as she approached, and then leant forward to press a kiss to her cheek.

As his lips pressed against her skin—just for that moment—Jas allowed herself to indulge in the fantasy that her life had become:

A princess with bodyguards, a hair stylist *and* a make-up

artist, a bottomless closet of designer clothing and a constant schedule of glamorous events to attend…

And her very own prince.

Sort of.

Just for a short while.

CHAPTER ELEVEN

JAS WOKE UP before Marko.

He slept flat on his back, she'd discovered. With one arm hooked above his head, and the other hand either across his chest or—just the one time—flung out and laid over hers.

Almost as if he wanted to hold her hand as she slept.

Ha! Jas rolled her eyes as she studied him. Right. She was not one given to overly romantic notions, especially now.

She sat perched on the edge of the bed as she watched his chest rise and fall. She was dressed in T-shirt and jeans, her feet bare and her hair still wet from a shower.

She would much rather stay in bed with Marko. They'd had a late night following a formal dinner with visiting French diplomats and also—she really liked lying in bed with him. And just looking at him—even now, after ten mornings of waking up beside Marko, the novelty had not worn off.

Ten mornings?

Jas mentally recounted before confirming to herself that—yes—it had definitely been ten mornings since she'd last woken up in her own bed. At the moment, the adjacent suite was used more as a closet than a bedroom, and each evening it literally hadn't even occurred to her to return to her own room.

Should it?

Her phone vibrated briefly on the bedside table, signalling she'd received a new email, and the sound was a welcome distraction.

She had a conference call to attend with her team in Hong Kong, but she still had a few minutes before she needed to leave. So she picked up her phone and settled back against the velvet bedhead for a few minutes of email-checking and mindless internet checking.

But the moment she saw the new email her stomach plummeted.

The email wasn't signed, and the address was one of those free ones, with a meaningless jumble of letters before the '@'.

But its intent was clear. Jas didn't need to open the attachments to know exactly what they contained.

And know exactly what this faceless person would do with them if she didn't do what he or she wanted.

'Jas?'

Marko had woken, and he'd propped himself up on one elbow.

But for once all those acres of gorgeous olive-toned skin were no distraction. Jas's brain simply raced around in every direction, desperately trying to form a coherent thought, let alone a coherent action.

What was she going to do?

'Jas,' Marko said, more firmly now. 'What's going on?'

He sat up, and she could see concern in his gaze.

It was *really* tempting to just blurt it out—to tell him about the email, and the piece of her past that it represented. To share her panic with him and have him help her work out what on earth her next steps might be.

She almost did—she could feel the words, all ready to go, right on the tip of her tongue: *A few years ago I dated a guy I thought was perfect, but...*

But to reveal something so personal, so embarrassing, so painful…

To dump all this on Marko…

Why would she do that? He wasn't her partner; he wasn't her boyfriend.

Their relationship, such as it was, was not based on anything beyond laughter, sex and their fake engagement. Since that afternoon at the beach they had not shared anything personal with each other.

It had been about fun, and mutual attraction.

And that was the way it needed to stay.

If anything, this email simply underlined that. She did *not* want to ever confuse sex for something it wasn't, ever, ever again.

She remembered how her mum had asked if she'd told Marko about her past, and she'd lied so easily.

Well—here she was. It was actually happening. It was the stuff of her nightmares, and Marko *would* need to be told now, but he didn't need to know right this instant. And he definitely didn't need all the messy, emotional details.

On the phone to her mum that day, she'd told herself how he'd react if she did—how he'd judge her. Back then, she'd wavered—but based on what? Why on earth would Marko be different from everyone else?

She looked at him now, and it was so tempting to tell herself that he *would* be different. That if she told him now she wouldn't be left awash with shame and regret.

But that was as silly a romantic notion as Marko holding her hand as she slept.

'Nothing's going on,' she said brightly. Then smiled.

It was a fake smile, though. The first fake smile between them.

Did Marko realise that?

For a moment, she thought he wasn't going to let her get away with it.

But then, maybe he came to the same conclusion Jas had. Their relationship wasn't about intimacy beyond the physical, and it certainly wasn't about sharing secrets.

'Okay,' he said. 'Good.' He sat up, and swung his legs onto the floor. 'I'm going to go get some breakfast.'

Jas nodded. 'Enjoy!' she said, with that same false breeziness.

Then she got out of bed, put on her sandals, and left Marko's room.

After breakfast Marko went for a run.

Quite a long run, and with his security detail shadowing him, so it was no surprise that by the end of it he was being tailed by a news station van and a paparazzo on a bicycle.

But honestly, today, he didn't really care.

Maybe this was how Lukas dealt with all the attention and intrusion—by just immersing himself within it, rather than fighting it?

If someone really wanted to buy a magazine, or visit a website, that had a photo of him drenched in sweat and breathing heavily, then let them. He didn't care.

Marko's lips quirked upwards. He knew that tomorrow he would definitely care again, just today he couldn't be bothered.

Last night, just before dinner, Lukas had called.

They'd been speaking regularly, but for the first time Lukas had sounded different. Tired.

Really tired.

And he'd told Marko about the ulcers in his mouth, and how they were actually worse than the hours of being hooked up to the cocktail of chemicals that would—Marko desperately hoped—save Lukas's life. He'd joked about his hair loss too, about how for the first time he was the one moulting all over the bathroom, rather than Petra with her mane of golden blonde hair.

Lukas had been deliberately upbeat, and so had Marko.

And it wasn't as if Lukas's fatigue were a surprise. Cancer treatment was exhausting, and Lukas being tired didn't necessarily mean that anything was wrong.

None of what Lukas was experiencing indicated that anything was going wrong.

But still, Marko worried.

Back at the palace, Marko had a shower.

As he grabbed the soap out of the niche in the wall that held his toiletries, he knocked over Jas's little bottle of face scrub. As he righted it he remembered Jas's expression from earlier, as she'd stared, white as a ghost, at her phone.

Something had been wrong; it had been obvious in every tense line of her body, and in her parody of a smile.

But she hadn't wanted to talk to him about it.

Just as he'd decided not to talk to Jas about his concerns for Lukas last night.

Last night he'd told himself that he could handle it. What value was there in confiding in Jas? Of confiding in anyone? He'd managed well enough this far into his adult life without doing so.

Except for that day at the beach—but then, he had no plans to repeat that.

So he could hardly challenge Jas for doing the same—for handling things on her own.

And if there was anyone who could handle anything life threw at her, it was Jasmine Gallagher.

He raised his face into the firm spray of water, squeezing his eyes shut as water sluiced over his body.

But, even as he instinctively knew that she probably wouldn't want or appreciate his concern, he couldn't just switch it off.

He got out of the shower, towelled himself dry, and made a decision.

He didn't need to know the details—but he needed to go find her.

Right now. And make sure she was okay.

After her conference call with her team, Jas organised for Ivan to come meet her in the small *salon*—as the palace staff referred to the small reception room where Jas had been working over the past few weeks—to discuss the email.

She sat on a brocade single armchair with spindly legs, the small coffee table before her holding her now-closed laptop, her printer and a small mountain of printed plans, maps and schedules.

Her makeshift office was quite incongruent with the room full of antique furniture and the oil paintings of—Jas assumed—Pavlovic ancestors, all with identical severe expressions.

Ivan sat across from her, in a matching armchair, and listened as she explained her situation, and her suggestions as to what they should do next.

Fortunately, Ivan agreed with her approach, but there were others within the palace that would need to be consulted—there were protocols and procedures to be followed and expert advice to be canvassed.

But first, they needed to tell Marko.

As if reading their minds Marko materialised at the doorway.

'Jas,' he said. 'I was—'

But then his gaze drifted to Ivan, and he went silent.

Ivan stood, immediately. 'I'll leave you to discuss this with His Highness,' he said.

'No,' Jas said, more sharply then she'd intended. 'I think it's best that you stay.'

Ivan barely raised his eyebrows as he resettled in his chair. He was good at his job, Jas had to give him that. The epitome of discretion.

She stood, straightened her shoulders, and said to Marko: 'Please, take a seat.'

She was being deliberately formal. They had a situation to deal with, so it made sense to be so, she'd decided.

Marko just nodded. She'd become used to him kissing her, or at least touching her, whenever they were in close proximity.

He did neither now. She didn't *want* him to, right now, of course. But still, she definitely noticed that he didn't.

Marko took a seat on the two-seater armchair between Ivan and Jas, but he turned his body to face her, and not the valet.

'Jas,' he said firmly as she took her own seat. 'Are you okay?'

She nodded, equally firmly. 'Of course. We have a situation I need to brief you about.'

His expression was unreadable. 'Okay.'

Jas took a deep breath.

'This morning I received an email from an anonymous sender who is trying to blackmail me,' she began, ensuring her tone was matter-of-fact. 'He has some photos of me.' She swallowed. 'Uh, naked photos of me, that he will release to the press if I don't meet his demands. Which are basically for me to pay him a lot of money.'

Marko simply nodded.

Jas desperately searched his gaze for his reaction, for the glint of *something*.

Shock. Disappointment. Disgust.

But she saw nothing.

'Fortunately the photos are relatively tasteful. I took them myself, actually, selfies…' She swallowed again. 'Anyway. While I definitely wouldn't have chosen for the photos to be seen by anybody, and I'd actually hoped to never see them again—Ivan and I agreed that the best thing to do is to defuse the situation by issuing a press release about their existence. If I'm lucky, this person will then just disappear. Or maybe he'll publish the photos, or sell them—I don't know. But at least we get to start the narrative, rather than respond to it.'

'Ensure any media organisation who publishes the photos is blacklisted by the palace,' Marko said in a clipped, authoritative tone. He still held her gaze, but Jas could still read nothing in it.

'Of course,' Ivan said.

'Plus explore any legal options we have.'

For the next few minutes, Ivan discussed next steps with them both, but Jas barely participated.

What was Marko thinking?

Right now, needing to know what Marko thought was killing her—more than the photos, more than anything.

Ivan stood up and exited the room.

Marko's gaze had barely moved from hers, either. It was excruciating.

But then, the moment Ivan left them alone, something in his eyes shifted.

Jas squeezed her own eyes shut, and let out a long, slow breath as her stupid, naïve bubble of hope that Marko would be different painfully deflated.

'You must think I'm such an idiot,' she said, eyes still closed. 'Naïve, right? Stupid? Thoughtless?'

All the words she'd heard before echoed in her brain.

'I should've thought to tell you earlier, but I was so sure the photos had been deleted. And that my ex would never—' She stopped. No. Marko didn't care about the details. He was just like the rest of them. Was it too much to ask that just *one* person wouldn't blame her?

No, not just one person. *Marko.*

She'd *so badly* wanted him to be different. The realisation that he wasn't shocked her as much as the arrival of that awful email.

'I'm sorry—' she began.

'Jas,' he said firmly. 'Stop. You have nothing to apologise for.'

Jas shook her head, eyes still closed.

She was being ridiculous, even within this ridiculous situation. But she couldn't bear to see the judgment in his eyes.

He was saying the right thing, but he didn't really mean it.

'Look at me,' he said, louder now. Demanding. Then more softly. 'Jas, please.'

Finally, she did.

It was still there, in his gaze. What she'd seen.

But now—now that she took more than a moment to acknowledge it, to interpret it—she realised what she was really seeing.

The look in his eyes matched his body language—the tension in his shoulders, the bulging of his biceps, the way his hands had formed into fists.

He was angry. Furious.

But not with her.

Definitely not with her.

'You have nothing to apologise for,' Marko repeated. 'You're not the one threatening to circulate stolen photographs.' That he thought the person doing so should be *very* sorry was obvious in his poisonous tone. '*You* haven't done anything wrong.'

Jas sagged a little in her seat, disbelieving.

'Jasmine,' Marko said firmly. 'You aren't stupid, or naïve, or thoughtless. I would *never* think that.' Then he shrugged. 'Besides, why wouldn't you take naked photos of yourself?' He grinned now. 'You're hot.'

The comment was so unexpected amidst all the tension that Jas burst out laughing.

But now he was more serious again. 'I know all about how it feels to have your privacy invaded, Jas. I'm so sorry you're going through this.'

His words were sincere, and for a moment Jas was tempted to say more. To let him know there was more to the story. To trust this man who hadn't judged her, who wasn't angry with her—who hadn't blamed her for any of this.

But instead, she said: 'But I don't think anyone's got a photo of you *naked*, Marko.'

'True,' he said. 'Want to take some?'

This time, they laughed together.

They didn't take any naked photographs.

Instead, Marko left Jas in the salon to continue working, while he filled his day working with Ivan and the palace protocol staff to determine the best way to protect Jasmine from the *vrag*—the devil—who was blackmailing her. Privately, he imagined exactly what he would do if he ever met the guy, and it definitely involved him *never* being able to hurt Jas again.

Although, it wasn't as if Jas needed him.

She'd worked out her plan of attack without him, and had included him in the discussion as a stakeholder she was bringing up to speed. *Not* as her...*what*, exactly?

Guy she was sleeping with? He *was* that.

Boyfriend? No.

But surely that lack shouldn't move him behind *Ivan* in the chain of communication?

It appeared it did.

Maybe that shouldn't sit so uncomfortably with him, but it did. Who would've thought—Marko Pavlovic was disappointed that a woman *hadn't* told him something obviously private and emotional?

Actually, he realised, it wasn't disappointment he was feeling.

He was hurt.

Which was stupid, and selfish, as what Jas was going through was definitely *not* about him. And he knew that Jas had gone to Ivan based on the premise of their relationship: casual, fun. No deeply personal secret revelations.

But still, he wished she'd come to him, first.

Did that mean he wanted *more* than fun with Jas?

He hadn't worked that out by the time he went down to meet her for dinner, once again out on the terrace. He didn't really even know what it would mean if he did.

But as it turned out, he didn't need to work out anything—or maybe it had been worked out for him—because shortly after he sat down at their table, a member of staff passed on a message from Jasmine:

'Ms Gallagher sends her apologies. She's having an early night tonight.'

After dinner, Marko was unsurprised to discover Jas had not spent her early night in his room—which had been effectively hers for a week and a half—but in her own.

So into his own bed Marko collapsed, alone.

Jas did not have a good night's sleep.

She was most of the way through a very strong coffee when Marko strode out onto the terrace the following morning.

She hadn't been sure whether she'd even see him today. They had nothing scheduled, so there was no requirement for them to do so. And after yesterday—and especially after last night—would he even want to?

Would he have seen her decision to spend the night alone as a snub?

Or would he not even care? Would he have been thrilled to have some time to himself?

Last night she'd told herself that he *wouldn't* care. He might be a bit annoyed she hadn't told him personally that she was sleeping in her own bed, but seriously—ten nights in a row sharing a room was surely enough. They needed a break from each other.

But, as she saw him now, with dark smudges under his eyes that she couldn't read at all, she wasn't so sure.

Even so, she did exactly what she'd planned.

She stood up, and met him as he approached.

She rose on tiptoes, and pressed her lips to his cheek in greeting.

She *didn't* want what they had to end, not yet. But last night…

Last night it had scared her how much she'd wanted to tell Marko everything. To cry in his arms—rather than alone in her room—at the embarrassment and overwhelming sense of hurt and anger she felt deep within her bones. How *dared* Stuart—or one of the men with whom he'd shared her photos, or even, although it was a slim chance, whoever had hacked into his account—do this to her?

But would Marko want to just hold her while she cried?

She didn't know. It wasn't fair to expect he would. And so she had slept—a little—alone.

'Did you have a good night's sleep without me hogging the covers?' she said brightly as she stepped back. His unshaved jaw had been rough against her lips.

But Marko didn't answer her.

Instead, he stepped forward, and dragged her into his arms.

And, without a word, he kissed her. Kissed her thoroughly, until her eyes slid shut and her arms wrapped behind his neck, desperately pulling herself closer.

Kissed her until her knees felt useless, and she wished the hands bunched in the fabric of her singlet could whip it over her head, and she could push his own T-shirt up so she could press even closer against him, skin to skin.

Kissed her until she had no idea about anything but how his lips and tongue felt against hers, and how hard and strong his body felt pressed against her own.

Then, he stepped back.

They were both breathing heavily, and now she could certainly read Marko's gaze—there was no doubt she was seeing a mirror of the want and need in hers.

But then, suddenly, all of that was gone.

His expression was once again indecipherable.

It was so abrupt, Jas would've hardly believed he'd just been kissing her if she couldn't still taste him on her lips, and feel the abrasion of his stubble on her skin.

'I'm visiting Lukas today,' he said. 'They'll expect you to come with me.'

Not—*I would like you to come with me*. And not even a question as to whether she'd like to go.

Marko expected her to accompany him out to the Pavlovic Estate today to visit his brother and his wife.

But he didn't actually want her to come. He just needed her to, because they were supposed to be engaged.

'Okay,' she said. 'No problem. I'll go get changed.'

It was her job, after all. She shouldn't feel weird about it—that Marko didn't really want her by his side as he visited his unwell brother.

It made sense. This was definitely beyond the boundaries of their fun, short-term relationship. Just as yesterday's photo saga had been, too.

Boundaries were good. *She* was the one who'd been so sure to strengthen them last night.

Maybe it was just the contrast—to share a kiss that felt so intense, and so intimate…and now to feel a million miles apart?

Yes, Jas decided. It was.

It had to be.

CHAPTER TWELVE

GIVEN THEIR ENTIRE relationship had evolved from a fake relationship, Marko wondered if maybe it was to be expected that interactions between himself and Jas could sometimes feel false.

But the thing was, they hadn't until now.

Even right at the beginning, when they'd barely known each other.

Even then, Jas had always been genuine. She'd always been herself.

It was why he'd kissed her before, out on the terrace.

When she'd asked how he'd slept—and he'd *known* it was a line she'd prepared as he'd recognised the subtly different tone she'd used with reporters when reciting the story of how they'd supposedly met—he'd *hated* that she was pretending for him.

And so he'd kissed her. To see, maybe, if the spark—no, the fireworks—between them was fake, too.

But it wasn't. That connection between them, the physical one, anyway, burned even brighter, if anything. For long moments after he'd finally stepped away from her he'd had no idea what his plans for the day had been, beyond kissing Jas a hell of a lot more.

Then he'd remembered.

So, here they were.

In just a single car today, with security based at the estate where his mother lived full time after retiring from public life after his father's death, and where his brother would be living for the duration of his treatment.

The car entered between tall stone pillars and a wrought-iron gate, then weaved its way down a long, winding driveway to reach the house.

Compared to the palace, it was a very modest building, just two storeys tall and built out of stone and a red-tiled roof like nearly every other house across Vela Ada. It had sprawled from the original centuries-old building with a succession of additions by previous generations, and at the rear a white-painted pergola stretched across much of its length, covered in lush, twining grape vines.

As their car came to a stop Petra and his mother raced from the front door to greet them.

Behind them, moving much more slowly, was Lukas.

But to even see him outside, the sun glinting off his brother's dark hair, did much to release the vice-like pressure on Marko's chest.

Just as he went to exit the car Jas grabbed his hand.

He went still. They hadn't touched, or spoken, since they'd left the palace.

'I won't get in your way,' Jas said, meeting Marko's gaze. 'I promise.'

There was lots more in her hazel eyes: concern—for him?—an attempt at reassurance, understanding…

'I know,' he said. He'd never doubted she'd understand what he needed today. 'Thank you,' he added.

And as he said it he realised his thank you wasn't only because of what she'd said, but also simply because she was here with him.

Then he got out of the car, and strode over to his family, before he could consider for a moment what that might mean.

Petra took Jas for a tour of the surrounding landscape while Marko caught up with Lukas.

They walked through an olive grove that stretched in rows from the rear of the grand old home, and then past a small orchard to a large vegetable plot. Clumps of lavender and rosemary scented the air, and the sun ducked in and out from behind powder-puff clouds.

Petra did most of the talking as she described the history of the property and the Pavlovic family—but when they arrived at the vegetables, she clapped her hands together in excitement.

'Now *this*,' she said, 'is the only good thing to come out of Lukas's illness—I finally have time to garden.'

Jas noticed the freshly sown rows of dirt, and the carefully handwritten signs stuck into the ground before each one. Then there were the established rows—of beans and tomatoes winding their way up stick pyramids, and other neat lines of green fronds that Jas couldn't identify. Their signs were of no help: *krumpir*, *mrkve…*

'You grew all this?' Jas asked, surprised.

She couldn't imagine Petra working in a garden—even now in casual jeans, blouse and sandals she was just *so* elegant. But as Jas watched the Queen absently yanked some recalcitrant weeds from the rich, dark brown earth.

'Yes,' she said, beaming. 'I come from a family of market gardeners. Growing up, I was in charge of at least one crop for the weekly *tržnica*—a market—and I've never really lost interest in growing my own vegetables. I just don't get much of a chance nowadays, although I do help the chef with her herb garden at the palace.'

'You met Lukas at university, right?' Jas asked, trying to connect the dots as to how the daughter of market gardeners became a queen.

Petra smiled. 'Yes. In Split. A long way from my family's market garden in Korcula,' she said, reading Jas's mind. 'My father was very old-fashioned, and he was so worried that tertiary education would make me leave Korcula Island for ever. And as it turns out, he was right.'

'Do you ever miss it?' asked Jas.

Petra shrugged. 'Sometimes. Not so much Korcula—or even Croatia—but my family, definitely. And also the simplicity of that life.' She paused, then smiled. 'Why? Are you missing Australia?'

'A bit,' Jas said honestly. 'It's been so crazy these last few weeks, I almost crave my normal life in Canberra.'

'*Almost* crave,' Petra said, her gaze knowing. 'I'd bet Marko is pretty good at distracting you from your home-sickness.'

Jas gave a shocked laugh.

Petra shrugged. 'I'm married to his brother, remember,' she said. Then winked, before heading down along a row of lettuce, pausing occasionally to pull up more rogue weeds.

Jas hurried along behind her.

'It's great to see Marko so happy with you,' Petra said, over her shoulder. 'My mother-in-law is *very* proud of Marko for stepping in for Lukas, so I've seen heaps of the photos and footage of you together.'

Jas didn't really know how to respond to this. The *Queen* and the *Dowager Queen* of Vela Ada had been looking at photos of *her*?

Well, of Prince Marko mostly, she was sure.

But her, too.

Another thing to add to her list of things she'd never thought would happen to her.

Along with contributing to the fact the photos making an elderly woman happy were based on a lie.

Although…if she was honest, they *had* been having fun together at the many, many events they'd been attending. So the smiles Petra and the Dowager Queen had seen had been real, at least.

Petra had stopped and was looking at Jas as if waiting for her to say something.

'Um—' Jas said. 'Aren't engaged people supposed to look happy together?'

'I'd hope so,' Petra said, 'but Marko…' She paused. 'I haven't seen him like this since before his dad passed away.

Even today—I know he's worried about Lukas, but there is just something *different* about him.'

'He's taking his role seriously,' Jas said. 'He knows he needs to get better at engaging with the public, and with the media, even though it doesn't sit comfortably with him. He's working really hard.'

Too late, Jas realised how defensive she sounded. As if she was trying to convince Petra that Marko *wasn't* actually happy.

Petra just studied her curiously, and then turned and walked off again—this time a few rows over. She dropped to a squat to pick a handful of plump red strawberries from amongst clusters of deep green leaves, and then stood and gave half of her harvest to Jas.

'Lukas is complicated,' Petra said. 'I know Marko is complicated too. I've known him nearly fifteen years, and I don't *really* know him. Not really. So, maybe I don't actually know if he's happy or not.'

Jas shook her head.

What had she done?

How had such a simple conversation gone so wrong?

It would've been so easy to just smile, and laugh, and say something about how happy she and Marko were. That was what Petra had expected her to say. It was what *anyone* would say.

It was what she'd said when responding to a hundred similar observations over the past few weeks. She'd even got creative and embellished: they'd been *blissfully* happy, and *incredibly* happy and *happier than I thought was possible!*

But as it had been that very first night, when she'd first met Petra, there was something about the Queen that made Jas find it near impossible to lie. Or not even lie—but to speak for Marko.

Because, what did she know about how happy Marko was? Who was she to speak for him? Beyond their physical relationship, she knew nothing about what he was thinking or feeling. He'd said not a word about Lukas's illness to her since that day at the beach. He'd confided nothing in her, about anything. Sure, he smiled a lot around her, but was he truly *happy*?

So she racked her brain for something to say…*anything* to say that would stop Petra looking at her so seriously. Preferably something that was also true.

'Marko makes *me* happy,' she said.

The words came out in a rush in the end, before Jas could stop them.

Petra's gaze was wise and assessing. 'Good,' she said simply. 'Now, try the strawberries.'

Lunch had been fine.

He, Lukas and their mother had been settled in their chairs beneath the canopy of grape vines, a literal feast spread out before them upon a blue-checked tablecloth, when Jas and Petra had returned from their walk.

Jas had come straight over to kiss him, briefly, on the cheek. In that instant he'd inhaled the scent of sun and the sunscreen on her shoulders, plus her familiar citrus and spice perfume.

But she hadn't lingered; instead she'd taken her seat across from him and barely touched him again until they'd left. She'd charmed his mother over lunch and laughed at all of Lukas's terrible jokes—but with him she'd still been as distant as she'd been all morning. Maybe even more so, actually.

But not in a way that anyone else would notice, although Marko certainly had.

In the car on the way home she'd asked him about Lukas, but Marko had been pretty matter-of-fact: he was doing as well as could be expected. Prognosis was still good.

After that it had just been silence.

Silence until now, as they stood, alone, together, in the hallway outside both of their rooms.

It was late afternoon.

Marko had vaguely considered going for a run. Or going down to the gym in the palace basement.

He didn't know what Jas planned to do with the rest of her day. Work, probably.

'Jas—' Marko said, and then stopped.

He'd meant to say he'd see her that evening for dinner, but found he couldn't.

'Jas,' he started, again. She just stood there, looking at him, her hands loosely knotted in front of her. She looked beautiful, even with her hair in a simple ponytail and without the efforts of her make-up artist. His gaze was locked with hers, and in hers he saw…uncertainty? Or was he just projecting how he suddenly felt? 'I—'

But Jas halted his words when she stepped close, curled her fingers into his hair, and pulled his mouth down to hers. Hard.

It was a determined kiss, almost an *angry* kiss, and definitely a frustrated kiss.

Marko kissed her back with all of his own frustration of the past twenty-four hours, and of the way things with Jas now didn't feel easy. He kissed her with frustration that she wasn't bumping her shoulder against his when they walked, or asking him to teach her Slavic swear words in the car. Her eyes weren't sparkling when she looked at him, and her lips weren't quirking at even the silliest little joke he'd make.

He didn't fully understand what had happened, but he knew he didn't like this new distance between them. Right now, the best way to remedy that seemed to be to get as close as it was possible for two people to be.

Thankfully, as Jas yanked his shirt upwards and popped open his buttons, she certainly seemed to be thinking the exact same thing.

His own hands tugged the elastic from her hair and then slid beneath her silk blouse to caress hot, perfect skin, and press her as close against him as possible. His hardness against her softness, her breasts squashed against the bare chest her impatient fingers had now revealed.

He somehow backed her against the door to her room, and part of him was lucid enough to reach for the door handle—before he was completely distracted by the way Jas was shifting her hips against his.

Then all he could focus on was lifting her up so she could wrap her jeans-clad legs around his waist, and kissing her harder: hot, and long, and raw.

At some point, as he kissed Jas's jaw and neck and made his way downwards, she suddenly whispered in his ear: 'I think we have company.'

He followed her gaze to an obviously hastily abandoned bucket and mop, lying haphazardly down the hall.

He grinned as he finally opened the door to Jas's suite.

'I'll apologise to the staff later,' he murmured.

He could feel Jas smile against his cheek as he carried her into the room. 'They'll understand,' she said. 'Everyone thinks we're madly in love.'

Marko took a moment to laugh in response, her blithe comment oddly jarring. But he didn't have time to think about it, in fact, now that he'd deposited Jas onto her bed, and she was looking up at him, her shirt and bra askew, and her eyes hot and seductive…

Right now was definitely not the time for thinking.

Right now was all about how Jas made him feel.

Jas closed her eyes as she let the warm water pour over her, the shower pressure just high enough to provide a satisfying sting against her scalp.

When she opened her eyes, Marko—also in her shower with her—smiled.

He reached out, running a finger beneath her left eye. 'I hadn't realised you were wearing make-up,' he said.

'Are you nicely saying I have panda eyes?' she asked as

she reached around him for her face wash—before remembering it was still in Marko's bathroom.

The realisation was irrationally annoying—after all, she'd first realised she was face-wash-less this morning, and she'd managed well enough then.

But now, with Marko here…

Should she bring her face wash back? Or leave it where it was as now she'd go back to staying in Marko's room? Or should she buy another one, so that she and Marko could continue to be all free and casual and non-committal about whatever they had going on?

Marko's finger now traced the smudge beneath her other eye, and then, so gently, traced the shape of her cheekbones, jaw, and then lips. His touch—so sensual, and so delicate, in delicious contrast to the water still firm against her back—made her eyes slide shut.

'What are you thinking about?' he asked, low and soft.

'Toiletries,' she muttered.

'Pardon me?'

Jas's eyes snapped open. Marko looked at her curiously.

He stood very close to her. They'd showered together before, but Jas hadn't tired of looking at Marko soaking wet. He was almost beautiful rather than simply handsome, with water droplets caught in his eyelashes, and the hard, wet edges and planes of his shoulders, chest and abdominal muscles.

'Jas?' he asked.

'I want to know where to put my face wash,' she said honestly.

'Okay,' he said, his brow creasing. 'Is this a metaphor for something?'

She nodded. 'Yes. I don't like not knowing what's really going on here. It's been weird between us since yesterday—and I don't like it.'

'Neither do I,' Marko said bluntly.

He was looking at her intensely, but Jas couldn't interpret it.

'What do you want?' he asked.

Ah—Jas could understand it now. It was subtle, but there. The tension in his shoulders, and in his jaw. Just as she'd felt when she'd made her joke about them—apparently—being madly in love.

'I wanted to tell you about the photos yesterday,' she said. 'I thought it wasn't appropriate to—I mean, it was pretty serious. Not really part of our fun and no-strings arrangement, right?' Even though she wasn't cold, she rubbed her hands up and down her upper arms. 'But I realised that I don't like having sex with someone that I can't talk to about stuff like that. I mean—I love having sex with you, but—'

She shook her head, trying to refocus.

'Look, for as long as this lasts, I'd like to be able to talk to you. And I want you to talk to me. Otherwise, maybe it's best I just go get my face wash from your bathroom, and we end this now.'

Jas realised, too late, that she could very well be about to be dumped while naked.

But then—of course—she hadn't planned any of this.

'For as long as this lasts,' Marko repeated.

Jas nodded. 'Yes,' she said. 'Whether it's for another week or the rest of my time as your fake fiancée.'

Only now did Marko release the tension in his shoulders.

Oh—he'd thought she was asking for more—something beyond their contracted time together.

Marko makes me happy.

Everyone thinks we're madly in love.

Her own words echoed traitorously inside her head.

No.

This was never about for ever. She didn't *want* for ever. Or rather—she didn't trust it.

Plus, that didn't even matter—Marko *clearly* didn't want for ever, anyway.

But did he still want 'right now'?

Marko still hadn't agreed with her. His gaze travelled across her face, and Jas realised she was holding her breath.

Then—he stepped out of the shower.

He grabbed a fluffy white towel off a hook, and as Jas watched rubbed himself dry, and then wrapped it low around his hips.

Then, he grabbed another towel, stepped back to the shower, and reached behind Jas to turn off the water.

Suddenly, Jas was freezing cold, regardless of the room's perfect climate control.

'Here,' he said, handing her the towel. 'I've been wanting to talk to you about Lukas for days, but I'm not going to talk about my brother and my dad while you're standing in front of me naked in the shower.'

Jas gave a shocked burst of laughter.

Then she took the towel, and said gently, 'You can talk to me any time.'

'I know,' he said with a crooked smile. 'How about we start now?'

CHAPTER THIRTEEN

MARKO HADN'T MADE his decision when he'd got out of that shower, or even as he'd wrapped the towel around his waist.

If Jas had told him about being blackmailed as soon as she'd received the email, he definitely would've listened, and he definitely would've been there to support her—but clearly, she hadn't believed that. And to be honest, she really had no reason to believe he would.

But being prepared to listen to Jas—in fact, *wanting* to be there for Jas—was quite another thing from revealing his own emotions to her.

He hadn't been willing to share anything with anyone for such a long time, he wasn't even sure if he was capable of doing so now.

But in the end, it had been Jas—standing in the shower, as naked and vulnerable as it was possible to be—that had made his decision obvious.

He wasn't walking away from her.

It seemed that right now he needed Jas in a multitude of ways: bodyguard, fiancée, lover and now...confidante.

But now was not for ever.

And now was what he needed.

They sat, sprawled, on Jas's unmade bed, both wearing their monogrammed palace bathrobes. He'd organised for dinner to be brought up to the room, and they each held glasses of *maraština* wine.

He just talked.

About Lukas, and what it was like growing up with him. And then about his father. About how he'd felt when his father was first diagnosed with cancer, and how—after he'd got over the initial shock—he'd been so adamant that his dad would be okay. Because, of course, his father had had access to the world's best oncologists, the most cutting-edge treatments—Marko had been so sure that doctors and science would cure him.

Or maybe it had just been his way of dealing with it all.

His dad actually *had* responded well to his initial treatment. But a year later the cancer had returned, and that original treatment had been less effective a second time. Other treatments hadn't worked. And then—initially slowly, but later far more rapidly—his strong, fit, powerful father had deteriorated. And eventually, with his mother holding his dad's hand and Lukas and Marko on the other side of the bed, holding onto each other…his father had died.

He'd rushed out of the hospital blindly.

People had been yelling—his brother, his mother, their bodyguards—for him to stop, to wait.

But he couldn't. He'd just needed to move. To not be in that hospital room any longer, sitting across from his horrifically still father.

So he'd raced out of the main entrance—which, of course, had been stupid. What had he expected? If he'd thought it through for even a second he would've known what to expect. He would've known that to run anywhere but out of that door was a better option.

But he hadn't been thinking, he'd been feeling. Feeling emotions he'd barely been aware he'd possessed. Pain and grief and this deep, echoing sense of loss that made him feel sick and empty and impossible. As if this couldn't possibly be happening. His father couldn't possibly be dead.

King Josip's death hadn't been announced yet, so he supposed it wasn't entirely the paparazzi's fault. Because, really, they hadn't known they were photographing a son who had just lost his dad. A man who hadn't even begun to think about concealing his grief. A man who shouldn't have had to conceal anything.

Later he would, though. Over the next days, and weeks, and months he would draw a curtain over how he really felt.

The papers had got their photographs that day. And of course they'd published them, even when they had heard of the King's death. That was definitely the paparazzi's fault. To print those raw photos that exposed everything, exposed emotions he hadn't even been able to let his mother and brother see, and yet they'd been shown to the world...

But he'd learnt, of course. Years later, he was still hiding.

Until now. Until Jasmine.

'I don't want Lukas to die,' Marko said, sinking into the pillows and staring up at the ceiling.

It was such an obvious thing to want, and such an obvious thing to say—and yet he hadn't said it, to anyone, until right at this moment. He'd barely allowed himself to think it.

He heard a clink as Jas rested her glass somewhere, and then the rustling of sheets as she crawled across the bed to where he lay, propped amongst a mountain of pillows.

She met his gaze briefly, and he nodded his permission just before she settled in beside him, curled against his side, her head resting on his chest.

She rested one hand against his chest, and one of his hands found itself in her hair, absently tangling the long strands loosely around his fingers.

'I know he's doing well. I know he's supposed to survive this. But I still worry. I just—'

His voice cracked, and he swallowed.

'I try to be positive for Lukas. I mean, it doesn't help anyone if I'm all doom and gloom. And he seems pretty upbeat too, but then—maybe he's doing the same as me?' Marko shook his head as this occurred to him. 'Maybe all the Pavlovic men are being stoic and non-communicative about how they really feel.'

'I'd say that's a strong possibility,' Jas said, and he could hear the smile in her voice.

Marko talked a bit more, and none of it was anything

groundbreaking, or unexpected. He didn't have an epiphany or anything.

But it still helped. Just voicing the fears he'd kept locked in his head seemed to help, even if the fears themselves weren't going anywhere.

After a while Marko fell silent, and he watched as Jas rose and fell against his chest as he breathed. Eventually, Jas shifted, and hauled herself further up his body, so she could kiss him on the mouth.

With her lips still brushing his, she said: 'Thank you for trusting me.'

He kissed her back, because that was it exactly—the reason why he'd been so intensely private for so many years: trust.

First, it was the obvious type of trust. The trust that the person he told was not secretly recording the conversation with plans to sell it to the highest bidder.

Secondly, and—he realised—more importantly, trust that the person he told would not change their opinion of him once he did. *This* was what he'd been unable to find until now.

Maybe it was something to do with the intensity of their current arrangement: the fake fiancée lie they shared, the amount of time they were spending together, the incredible sex…

Whatever it was, he *did* trust Jas to see him for the man he actually was.

And that was…liberating.

He laughed out loud. *Liberating?* Now he *was* having some sort of weird, out-of-body epiphany. And an overreaction. He liked having Jas to talk to—it was no more than that.

'Laughter,' Jas said, her head now back on his chest, 'is not the reaction I'm looking for when I'm wrapped around a man in nothing more than some terry towelling.'

Immediately Marko rolled Jas onto her back as she shrieked with laughter, so he loomed above her, his hands bracketing her face.

'Is this more like it?' he asked.

But as he watched he saw the playfulness fade from her eyes.

'Want to see some naked photos of me?' she said.

He said no, quite firmly, but Jas persisted.

'I don't need to see them,' he said.

'Odds are you're going to, eventually,' Jas pointed out. The palace's press release was scheduled for the following day.

'No, I won't,' Marko said. 'Anyone who looks at those photos is a—' And he then said a string of Slavic words that—from the few she recognised—Jas was pretty sure were the foulest, filthiest terms possible.

Jas gently pushed against his shoulders, and immediately Marko rolled away. Jas sat up, and then reached for her phone on the bedside table.

'I *want* you to see the photos,' she said. Then, looking up from the screen, she added: 'I think I need you to. Up until now everyone—except the original recipient—who's seen them has done so without my permission. I'd like to make a decision for someone to see them—and that someone is you.'

'Everyone?'

But she'd get to that in a moment. For now, she simply handed the phone to Marko.

He just held it—without looking anywhere near it—for what felt like ages, and so Jas scooted off the bed to the bureau, where their bottle of white wine still nestled in its ice bucket, although it was mostly ice water, now.

She'd left her glass on Marko's bedside table, so she strode over to it, aiming for nonchalance. 'Would you like another?'

He shook his head.

'Just look at the stupid photos,' she said. *'Please.'*

And then, with her back to him, she busied herself with pouring a glass of wine. Reflected in the mirror above the bureau she saw Marko finally scroll through her phone, and as he did she closed her eyes and breathed out. Long and slow.

She took a long, long sip from her glass before she finally turned around to face Marko again.

He'd laid the phone screen-down on her bed.

'You look beautiful in the photos,' he said quietly.

'Thank you,' she said. 'I remember being pretty pleased with them at the time.'

Marko nodded, but didn't say anything more.

She knew this was her cue—after all, she'd just allowed Marko to talk, and now it was her turn.

'Umm—' she began, and then stopped. Swallowed, and straightened her shoulders. 'I had a boyfriend a few years ago,' she said, her tone now strong and clear. 'Stuart. We worked together, actually. He was a sergeant. Not in the same unit as me at the Australian National Police, but we shared the same building, and worked together on some jobs.' She still held her wine glass, but now she just swirled the liquid around a bit, and didn't drink. 'He was a few years older than me. Very handsome, very successful, and very well respected. And very charming. I fell for him, hard. It wasn't like any other relationship I'd had—although, honestly, I haven't had that many.'

If Marko found any of this uncomfortable, he didn't reveal it in any way.

'We'd been together a few months, although we hadn't told anyone at work. Stuart had been really clear on that—and he made it sound like he was protecting *me*. That if things didn't work out between us, that it wouldn't look good if I was the girl who'd had some fling with a guy at work.' She paused now, to let her gaze drift from where it had been focused on her phone, to meet again with Marko's. 'Obviously that's stupid—why should *I* be the one worried about my reputation, and not him? But that was just the culture really—I worked with eighty-five per cent men. I knew they *would* judge me. Back then, though, that reality didn't make me angry. I just accepted it.'

Briefly, Jas considering moving to sit beside Marko, but she felt as if her bare feet were glued to the plush carpet.

'Anyway, after a few months I guess I sensed that maybe Stuart was drifting away. He cancelled on me a few times. Wasn't always sleeping over. That kind of thing. Although when we were together he still said all the right things—which I now know was more about keeping me on the hook rather than having any basis in truth. But at the time, obviously, I didn't realise that. And I *did* want the spark of the start of our relationship back. So—I decided to send him some sexy photos.'

Jas did take a long drink of her wine now.

'So it was all my idea, not his, if that's what you're wondering. And at the time, it was kind of fun. I mean, it felt pretty risqué, a bit naughty…'

She closed her eyes.

'Actually, even now, I'm not ashamed of the photos. Not at all.'

Her tone was challenging, as if she expected Marko to argue with her.

'You did nothing wrong,' he said, repeating his words from yesterday. 'The photos are beautiful.'

She shook her head, not really wanting to acknowledge a compliment right now. 'My mistake wasn't in taking the photos, but in who I sent them to. And I worked that out *very* quickly. I took the photos on a Saturday night, and Stuart loved them, of course. We spent the day together on Sunday. And then, on Monday, at work, things were different.'

Jas finished her wine, then placed it, with hands that were shaking just a little, onto the tray beside the ice bucket.

'I told myself I was being paranoid. That I was imagining things. But by lunch it was obvious what had happened—there was too much smirking, or suddenly cut-short conversations for it to be anything else. Stuart wasn't responding to my text messages, and he wouldn't answer his phone, so in the end I had to go into his office to confront him. I asked if he'd sent the photos to anyone, and he promised on his mother's life that he hadn't. But—and maybe he did have a shred of humanity, or maybe he realised that I was about to start screaming at him—he did admit to showing them to a couple of the guys.'

She rolled her eyes. *A couple of the guys.* Right.

The moment he'd admitted what he'd done had been shocking. Part of her, even then, hadn't wanted to believe it was real. That the man she'd thought she'd loved would do something like this to her.

And aside from that, the gross invasion of her privacy was simply horrific. To think of so many people having looked at her body, judged her body, without her consent…

Even now her stomach churned.

'I watched him delete the photos from his phone, and then I went straight to HR to find out what I could do. I couldn't keep on working in those conditions. Team is everything in the police, and now I felt like I could trust no one. I'm sure some of the guys didn't look at the photos. Many, probably. But who had?

'So I asked if I could make a complaint or something. Do *something*. Have some sort of agency, you know? But the couple of people I spoke to focused more on the fact I'd taken the photos, rather than the fact Stuart shared them with what felt like half the department. They seemed to care more about *my* "poor decisions" than Stuart's. I have no idea if their view reflected the relevant policy or procedure or whatever, but I wasn't about to find out. I've told you before about the frustrations of being a woman in the police force, but most of the time I could deal with it. I could focus on the bigger picture. From that moment, as the worst day of my life suddenly became *my* fault, I'd had enough. So I quit.'

'And started Gallagher Personal Protection Services,' Marko added.

'Yes,' she said, with a brief, broad smile, 'I did.'

Marko stood up, and walked to Jasmine.

He reached out, and untangled her hands from each other—although she hadn't even realised she'd been twisting and untwisting her fingers together until his touch halted her. He held both her hands gently, and waited while Jas slowly lifted her gaze from their joined clasp to meet with his.

'Dragi moj,' Marko said, so softly. 'I'm really sorry that this happened to you, and that, because you're helping me, it's happening again.'

'I'll be fine,' she said. 'I'm tough. I can handle it.'

'I know you will,' he said. Then he shook his head. 'Jasmine Gallagher, you are remarkable.'

Then he kissed her, as tears—for no reason Jas could fathom—made her throat feel tight and her eyes prickle.

When they broke apart, he spoke against her lips—just as Jas had spoken against his earlier. 'Thank you for trusting me.'

Jas closed her eyes. She *did* trust him.

Dragi moj.

It was a phrase that she *did* recognise—an endearment she'd looked up after hearing it between Lukas and Petra, and between other couples while she'd been in Vela Ada.

My dear one.

It was hardly an extravagant display of affection—Jas *knew* it was just Marko offering her comfort. And yet—he'd never called her that before, and those simple words…said so softly in Marko's delicious, dark accent…

They'd made her heart ache. And dream, just fleetingly, of so much more with Marko.

But, while she knew that she could trust him with her past, and that he would *never* do anything like what Stuart had done to her…

It wasn't photos or secrets that she feared when it came to the Prince standing before her.

What scared her was how she was going to stop herself from trusting him with her heart.

CHAPTER FOURTEEN

IT SEEMED SUCH a shame to wake her.

Marko sat on the edge of Jas's bed, fully dressed. He'd been up for hours, his whirling thoughts making it impossible to sleep.

For the first time in his life he'd used his royal status to be unreasonable—he'd woken Ivan up well before five a.m., and shortly afterwards a very sleepy Palace Communications Secretary had been driven through the palace gates.

A long, at times heated, conversation had then been had—and now Marko was satisfied with what was going to happen next.

He just needed Jasmine to approve.

As if she sensed the direction of his thoughts, Jas's eyes fluttered open. She'd fallen asleep in his arms, in her bathrobe, as they'd watched some action movie they'd both taken great glee in dismantling for copious inaccuracies.

'Why bring a SWAT team if the detectives are going to go in first?'

'That is not *how you hold that firearm.'*

'Are they really going to touch all that evidence?'

'Dobro jutro,' Jas said now.

Pillow creases on her cheek did nothing to distract from how gorgeous she looked—her hair tumbled across her pillow, and her eyes almost green in the early morning light.

'Good morning to you, too,' he said. *'Kako si?'*

She shook her head, laughing. 'Nope, I've got nothing. I've exhausted my grasp of your language.'

'How are you?' he tried again, his lips quirking.

'Ah,' she said, 'I *do* know that one.' She stretched expansively, reached her arms up above her head, so her fingers grazed against the bedhead. 'Fabulous,' she said, making the word as long and elastic as the movement of her body.

'I'm glad to hear that,' he said.

Jas seemed to register now that he was dressed, and must have seen something in his expression. She pulled herself up so she was sitting.

'What's wrong?' she asked.

'I've just heard that our legal team and the police have had no luck in tracking down the person or persons attempting to extort you.'

Jas shrugged, but he saw the flicker of disappointment in her expression. 'Isn't that what we expected?'

'Yes,' he said. 'But I'd hoped…'

She nodded. Yes, she'd hoped too. 'So we're going ahead with the press release today?'

'Yes,' Marko said. 'That's what I wanted to talk to you about.'

Jas looked at him curiously. They'd both already approved the content yesterday.

'I've changed the phrasing of the release, slightly,' Marko said. He handed the piece of paper he'd been holding to Jas.

She read through it carefully, occasionally flicking her gaze upwards to meet his.

'This is more than a slight change,' she said. 'The original press release was from the palace. This is from you.'

'There's something else,' Marko said. 'Rather than just releasing it, I'd like to make a video of me reading it, and release that instead.'

'Why?' Jas's tone was direct, almost accusatory. It surprised him.

'Because what happened to you a few years ago was not acceptable, and what's happening now is not acceptable. I think that message will be stronger if it comes from me personally, rather than with just the palace letterhead.'

Jas shook her head. 'You don't have to do that, Marko.

I'll be out of the public eye in a few months' time. It's not like I'm really Vela Ada's future princess that you need to defend.'

He didn't understand her reaction. 'I know I don't have to do this. But I *want* to. Last night… I was so angry about it I couldn't sleep. I watched you sleeping in my arms and hated how helpless I felt.'

'I don't need you to protect me, Marko.'

Jas stood up and walked over to the window, pulling the curtains all the way open, so sunlight now flooded the room. Before the room had felt sleepy and fuzzy edged, now everything was hard and stark.

Marko didn't move from where he sat on the bed, giving her the space she seemed to need.

'But that's the thing, Jas,' he said. 'I can't protect you from stuff like this. Clearly, I *haven't*. And you didn't sign up for this—this *never* would've happened if you hadn't agreed to help me. I've put up with this rubbish my whole life, but to drag *you* into it, to drag my fiancée into it, and in this way… It crossed a line.'

Jas turned from the window to face him. She'd crossed her arms, and was hugging herself tightly. 'But I'm not really your fiancée.'

Her lips quirked upwards, but only momentarily.

'That doesn't matter. Why do you think I've never fallen—?'

He'd been thinking *married*, but he'd almost said *fallen in love.*

He mentally gave himself a shake. That didn't matter either.

'I've never addressed the gossip and lies published about myself before. The palace has a legal team to deal with the libellous, but anything simply fictional I've let slide. And in my silence I've created space for my grossly exaggerated Playboy Prince persona and I am not going to create space for the violation of your privacy in this way by yet more silence.' He held Jas's gaze unwaveringly as he spoke. 'A carefully worded press release in palace-speak is not good enough. I want anyone, anywhere in the world who considers publishing your photos to know that I, *personally*, will go after them should they do so. And I will do everything in my power to destroy them.'

For long seconds the room was completely silent.

Jasmine uncrossed her arms. 'Destroy seems rather a strong word,' she said, with half a grin. 'How exactly would you do that?'

But her smile did not reach her eyes, which gleamed with…unshed tears? He couldn't imagine Jas Gallagher crying.

'Details,' he said, with a wave of his hand. 'Believe me, I'd find a way.'

And he would.

He stood, and strode to stand before Jas.

'So?' he asked. 'Do you approve?'

She nodded, then tilted her chin upwards to look up at him. She'd blinked away any tears—or maybe they'd never existed.

'Just one thing,' she said. 'Can I do it with you?'

Marko smiled. 'I was hoping you'd say that.'

Jas and Marko filmed their statement in the Knight's Hall.

They sat together on a small baroque-style couch with an ornate, gold-leafed frame, with their hands linked together and rested casually on the red velvet upholstery as they each read from the teleprompter.

Marko was dressed in a charcoal suit, and Jas in an elegant cream boat-neck dress. Her hair and make-up were professionally styled and applied—and it all felt very formal for not even nine o'clock in the morning.

Marko spoke first in the Vela Ada dialect. Immediately afterwards, he repeated what he'd said in English.

Jas knew exactly what he was going to say, and yet, still,

his words made her throat feel tight, and her fingers grip his more firmly.

Partly it was because, well…it was pretty damn confronting to be faced with the reality that immediately after this statement was released there was a high probability naked photos of her would end up in cyberspace.

If she thought about that too long she'd want to curl up in a hole somewhere and never face the light of day—or the judgment of Joe Public—ever again.

But the emotions she was feeling—embarrassment, regret—were losing a battle against the bubbling elation she felt about what they were doing.

Initially she'd balked when he'd told her his plans. She'd hated the idea of someone else fighting her battles for her. Of doubting her ability to look after herself.

But as he'd stood before her in her room, in front of that amazing view of Vela Ada, she'd slowly realised that Marko wasn't trying to fight anything *for* her, he wanted to go into battle *beside* her.

And as hard as she might have tried to convince herself—at first—that he would do this for anyone, she didn't actually believe that.

For all their talk of fun and no expectations—and she *still* had no expectations—she knew that right now there was a connection between them. Right now she had Marko beside her in every sense of the word. And right now, that was exactly what she needed.

Marko was speaking of his long history and poor relationship with the media. Of his journey from anger to apathy when it came to how he'd been portrayed, and his regret that he had not made a stand earlier.

He spoke, heartbreakingly, of the cruelty of being photographed during the worst time of his life as his father died—of having images of his grief only a click away, and impossible to escape.

'You may say this is the price I pay for being a prince,

but, as grateful as I am for my privileged life, it is still *my* life, and I have the same rights to privacy as everyone else. Just as Jasmine does, too.'

Marko shifted his gaze from the teleprompter to meet her own.

'And, of course, this is not about me.'

Marko squeezed her hand as Jas steadied her gaze on the teleprompter.

'Several years ago,' she began, 'I sent some naked photos of myself to my then boyfriend, and later, without my permission, he shared those photos with others.' Jas swallowed. 'I want to make it clear that even now I do not regret taking those photos. I am not ashamed of them. However, they are personal photos taken with a very specific audience in mind. An audience I *chose*. I never wished for anyone to ever see them without my permission, and when that happened it was awful—and the way I felt I wouldn't wish on anyone. I made a mistake in putting my trust in a man who did not deserve it. I do not regret taking those photos, but I do not want anyone else to see them.' She paused. 'Should these photos be released, I am putting my trust in you. I am trusting you to respect my privacy, in the way that everyone on this planet should have their privacy respected.'

Jas repeated her statement in carefully practised Slavic.

And then—her part was done.

She was still being filmed as Marko finished their statement, so she couldn't relax, as such. And yet, she definitely did feel as if a weight had been lifted.

A weight she'd been carrying for years—and that insidious voice that had blamed herself for what had happened, that had told her she was stupid, naïve, and blinded by love, had finally been silenced.

She'd known, logically, that she'd been the victim. She'd known that if she *had* decided to pursue charges against Stuart the law was on her side.

But that hadn't mattered in the end. Everyone she'd told

had been shocked she'd taken the photos, and had struggled to understand why she'd done it. Only Marko hadn't cared about any of that. He hadn't judged her. Instead, he'd understood her.

'I ask you to remember that she did not choose to fall in love with a prince. She fell in love with me.'

Marko's words—unexpected and definitely *not* part of the script—dragged Jas's attention back to the man beside her. She met his gaze, confused and disoriented. *Why say that?*

But he answered the question in her eyes with a kiss—soft and brief.

When his lips lifted from hers, the camera crew started talking quickly, and Marko got to his feet, reaching out a hand for her.

He chatted to the woman behind the camera for a minute, before turning to Jas.

'Let's leave them to edit,' he said. 'I hope you don't mind my ad-lib at the end. The crew loved it though, thought it was a nice touch.'

A nice touch?

Jas knew she shouldn't feel so disconcerted by a sentence so in keeping with their supposed engagement.

To hear talk of *love* now, just as she was finally letting go of her own self-flagellation, which had been so closely linked to her—again supposed—love she'd felt for Stuart, had left her flustered.

She'd thought she'd loved Stuart, but she realised now much of her pain had been that of betrayal, and not of lost love. Love had never existed between them, no matter how badly Jas might have wanted it to.

But with Marko…

No.

That was impossible. She'd known him only weeks. She'd lived thirty years without telling a man that she loved him. Without truly falling in love. She knew that now.

So to fall in love with Marko, a man with no interest in a relationship, let alone love…

No. To fall for Marko was a self-fulfilling prophecy of pain and disappointment. As she'd known right from the very beginning, Jasmine Gallagher was no princess. Without the circumstances that had thrown them together, Marko would never even have noticed her in a crowd.

He might have noticed her now, and they might have some sort of a connection…but to extrapolate that to be love would be as naïve as the trust she'd placed in Stuart.

Marko had led her to the wide hallway outside the Knight's Hall. He was looking at her curiously.

'Jas—'

'I'm just going to go up to my room,' she said quickly, not quite meeting his gaze. 'I'd better call my mum before the video goes out.'

'I'll see you at lunch?' he asked.

She shook her head. 'No. I—' A beat passed. She'd been going to say she was feeling unwell, but she didn't want to lie. 'I think I need some time alone, if that's okay,' she said. 'These last few days have been…overwhelming.'

In so many different ways.

Marko frowned. 'Are you sure?' he said. 'I don't like leaving you alone—'

'Marko,' Jas said, much more sharply than she intended. 'I am *fine*. I promise. I just need some space.'

Marko nodded just as sharply as she'd spoken. 'Let me know if you need me,' he said abruptly.

Then he walked off down the hallway, to where, Jas had no idea.

Leaving Jas to head for her room.

Just like a few days earlier, she told herself that having some space was a good idea.

Back then, she'd been worried about blurring the lines of their relationship—from fun to serious. From superficial to sharing their deepest secrets.

But those lines had now been erased.

Let me know if you need me, he'd said.

And that was the thing, of course.

She didn't need Marko. She just needed to remind herself of that.

CHAPTER FIFTEEN

'She did not choose to fall in love with a prince. She fell in love with me...'

Why had he said that?

Marko stood beside Jas later that evening, in the historic Vela Ada City Hall. They had yet another event, this time honouring some of Vela Ada's most generous citizens—people who had dedicated their lives selflessly to others. Foster carers, disability campaigners, philanthropists—it was a diverse group of very good people, and a heartening reminder that such people existed, given that it had taken mere minutes after their videoed statement was released for Jas's photos to end up all over the Internet.

The police and the palace were managing the situation as best they could. Jasmine was handling it brilliantly.

She'd emerged from her room appearing refreshed, and certainly without that almost panicked look she'd had after they'd finished filming. She'd hidden it well, but he'd noted it the moment it had appeared—which was the moment he'd mentioned her—apparent—love for him.

He shouldn't have gone off script, but at the time it had felt right.

While videoing the statement had helped to channel some of his anger at the whole situation, it hadn't helped to abate it. And much of that anger was still directed at himself. This *was* his fault. As he'd said—Jas hadn't chosen this.

But mentioning love, even faux love, even if his intent was to show that Jasmine had done nothing to deserve any of this, was a mistake.

He should've known, given his own reaction to Jas's joke

about them being 'madly in love' when they'd been surprised by that cleaner in a passionate clinch. He still couldn't work out how he'd felt—other than he hadn't found the joke amusing, and he didn't really know why.

Also, he hadn't allowed himself to think too much about it. He wasn't a man who had ever spent much time reflecting on *love*, in any context.

So why mention love, especially on camera?

He could lie and tell himself it was all part of the role he was playing—of a loving, concerned, protective fiancé.

But he wasn't really playing that role. He was genuinely concerned, genuinely protective—even if Jas insisted she didn't need him to be, and was probably right. The only thing false about the situation had been the fiancée bit. And the bit about Jas loving him.

She was in sparkling, princess form tonight. She'd grown into her role over the weeks, and now she effortlessly charmed everyone she met. Even tonight, as Vela Ada buzzed about the 'photo scandal', she was flawless. Dressed in a form-fitting deep red dress and holding a glass of pink champagne, she chatted easily beside him. It was Marko who was discombobulated.

The gentleman who had been speaking to him, Marko realised belatedly, had disappeared at some point as Marko had been lost in his own thoughts. Jas bumped her shoulder against his arm, and glanced up at him, asking him a wordless question: *You okay?*

He nodded.

Why do you think I've never fallen in love?

He'd almost asked that question of Jas earlier that day, and now he asked it of himself.

He knew the answer. Since the very first girl he'd kissed, he'd known he couldn't bring someone he loved into the suffocating, scrutinised life of a royal. He would not allow the woman he loved to be defined by her relationship with him—to become nothing but the royal title that marriage to Prince Marko would bestow.

To love him, and to marry him, was to lose too much of herself. He would not wish the way his life was invaded, and judged, and labelled on his worst enemy, let alone the woman he loved.

Yet—here he stood. Beside a woman who had had her privacy violated in a way that was more horrendous than *any* he had experienced. Yet she still stood beside him.

Was that due to her contract and hefty fee?

Even considering that possibility felt like a betrayal.

No, he knew Jas Gallagher. As he watched her now she straightened her shoulders and smiled. She was every inch a strong, resilient woman. And that was no façade.

Something—a sudden movement—caught Marko's eye.

A split second later, an exclamation from the surrounding crowd followed:

'*Nož! Nož!* He's got a knife!'

And then Marko saw it—a flash of a silver blade, the whites of the knuckles of the man that gripped it fiercely.

The movement of that blade towards him.

Instinct took over—his army training allowing him to instantly assess the threat, to move to disarm the—

But then, in a blur of a jet-black suit, the man was gone, tackled to the ground by Simon. In the same instant Jas had her arm around him, guiding him into a crouch. At his other hip materialised another person from Jas's team, and together they ran for the exit—an exit Marko hadn't even been aware existed, but Jas clearly did, guiding him there with total confidence.

The whole time, she was barking instructions to her team.

It felt wrong—totally wrong—to be fleeing from a threat.

He wanted to stay—he wanted to make sure the threat was disabled. He wanted to assist with clearing the room, with ensuring no other threats lurked, waiting.

But that wasn't his role.

He wasn't Lieutenant Colonel Marko Pavlovic today, and he certainly wasn't a bodyguard.

He was the target.

Now through the door they ran down service steps, three pairs of feet somehow almost perfectly in sync with each other. Jas's feet were in stockings only, her spiky heels obviously discarded for haste.

The other bodyguard paused at a heavy access door, talking urgently into his earpiece. Then the door was opened from outside, where two more from the team waited and then—perfectly timed—their car arrived. Moments later he and Jas were in the back seat, and well before anyone could consider details like seat belts they were off—just as Marko heard sirens approaching in the distance.

'You okay?' Jas asked finally.

He nodded. 'Perfectly.'

From the front seat, Scott turned. 'Suspect arrested,' he said. 'Simon is fine.'

Beside him, Jas breathed a heavy sigh. 'Great job, everyone,' she said.

Then she turned to Marko, her mouth kicking up into a triumphant grin. 'Now that,' she said, 'was a lot of fun.'

'Fun?'

It was several hours later, and Jas lay beside Marko in his bed. He was propped up on one elbow, his gaze trained on hers.

The room was lit only by a single lamp, all that had been needed for doing what had seemed logical after a threat to Marko's life: make love.

No. Jas corrected herself. *Have sex.*

The night had been a blur after their escape from City Hall and then the necessary reports to police. They'd barely had a chance to talk.

Jas smiled up at him. 'You know exactly what I meant. You do so much training—for months and years—for *exactly* those moments. And for it to all come together so perfectly… yes, it was awesome.'

'I hate that I put you in danger.'

Jas snorted. 'Are you serious?'

'No,' he said, 'hear me out. What if that guy had gone for you?'

'He wouldn't have got near me. I could've disarmed him, but I wouldn't have needed to. My team was onto it.' Jas narrowed her eyes as she studied him. 'It is literally my job to deal with this stuff, Marko.'

'But it isn't your job to be the target. With me you're a target.'

She shook her head. 'I wasn't. That guy was one of Senator Božić's supporters. He wasn't angry with me, he was angry at your brother—and you, as his proxy. Not me.'

'But another time it could be you.'

She raised an eyebrow. 'I've known that from the start. That's why we have bodyguards, Marko. It's why you employed my team.'

Marko rolled, moving his body until he was above her, his hands tangled in her hair.

The intensity of Marko's gaze shocked Jas. The sudden intimacy—the way he was holding her so gently, his thumbs tracing her jaw and cheekbones—made her breath catch.

He kept his weight mostly off her, but they still touched all the way along her body—breast to chest, hip to hip, skin to skin.

'What if something had happened to you, Jas?' he asked.

She held her tongue when it would've been so easy to retort that she could look after herself.

She knew that wasn't what Marko wanted to hear right now.

So she remained silent, letting him speak.

'I could've stopped that guy,' Marko insisted.

Jas nodded. She knew that.

'And I understand that it isn't my role. But I *hated* how

helpless I felt. How I was reduced to being a helpless prince you had to protect.'

Jas narrowed her eyes. 'You'd better not think it's your job as a man to protect me,' she said. 'Or that it's not my job to protect you.'

'No,' he said, with the slightest quirk of his lips. 'It's our job to protect each other.'

Oh. Those words did those funny flip-floppy things to her heart.

She didn't like that, and so she started talking in her no-nonsense work voice: 'If you want a more active role in your protection we can probably involve you more closely. Engage you in our tactics—'

'That isn't what I meant, Jas,' he said gently.

He bridged the gap between them, pressing his mouth to hers. As were all their kisses, it was sweet, and sexy…but this one was also almost frighteningly intimate…

Jas wrenched her lips away. 'What did you mean, then?'

Marko held her gaze again. In the muted light his expression was like nothing she'd seen before—intense but open. As if, for the first time, he was revealing everything to her.

Then he rolled away.

Jas propped herself up onto her elbow to study him.

But his gaze now was unreadable.

Jas considered pushing him for an answer. Part of her needed to—she *needed* to know what he was thinking, she needed to make sense of the ache in her heart and the whirling in her head…

But the other part of her felt the adrenalin that had kept her buzzing drain rapidly out of her system. Suddenly, she was so very tired.

She crawled to Marko, wrapping her arms around his chest, and burying her head in his shoulder.

She breathed in the clean scent of his skin, and listened to the beat of his heart beneath her ear.

'Jasmine?'

Only now did she allow the reality of tonight to settle on her shoulders. Only now did she make tonight about something other than a successful job.

Until right now, it had been fun. It had been about her team, and about their successful extraction of their principal. She'd been all arrogant bluster and cocky satisfaction.

But as she listened to Marko breathe, she finally let herself embrace the fear that it was her job to compartmentalise.

Not fear for herself, or fear of their attacker tonight.

'What if something had happened to you, Marko?' she said, oh, so softly, against the rise and fall of his chest.

CHAPTER SIXTEEN

MARKO CANCELLED ALL royal engagements the following day.

Instead, in a single car, Jas and Marko went to the beach. To Marko's isolated, private beach.

This time, he was prepared. They had an oversized beach umbrella, colourful plush towels and a gourmet picnic basket complete with wines from a Vela Ada vineyard. It was a gorgeous day, the sky clear except for the slightest wisps of cloud, and the ocean all perfectly still shades of blue.

After falling asleep last night with Jas curled against his body, they'd barely spoken. Marko had woken before Jas and gone for a long, punishing run. When he'd returned, Jas had already headed to her *salon* to work. Although when he'd interrupted her shortly after to invite her to the beach, she'd accepted immediately.

Maybe she understood, or shared, his need to escape?

But escape from what, exactly?

Even here—in this perfect, private, place—Marko hadn't relaxed.

He lay on his towel, wearing nothing but his board shorts, trying to enjoy the beat of the sun against his skin, and the sound of the waves lapping against the shore.

But it wasn't working.

At his side lay Jas. She was wearing a green and white polka-dot bikini, a broad-brimmed white straw hat and oversized sunglasses, and held a book in her hands that she appeared completely absorbed by.

But—her body seemed tense too. Or was he just overthinking things?

He didn't know what was wrong with him. This didn't feel

like a normal reaction to an attempt on his life—especially as he'd never actually felt his life was in danger.

Last night…

Last night his brain had been busy with thoughts of Jas, and today all he'd wanted to do was spend time with her. Only her—no one else.

So here they were. But things between them weren't how he wanted them to be. He was tense, and she *was* tense. Out of the corner of his eye he saw her bouncing her foot, just slightly, against the sand. She was fidgeting, and Jas didn't fidget.

He should probably talk to her. Talk to her properly, not the slightly stilted small talk they'd managed in the car.

But last night they *had* been talking, and he'd stopped. She'd stopped, too.

What he wanted between them, right now, was for it to feel easy. But last night hadn't felt easy. It had been the opposite of easy.

Now wasn't easy either.

He stood quickly, shoving himself up from the sand.

'Marko?'

He didn't look at her. 'Just going for a swim,' he said.

In the water—which annoyed him by not being bracingly cold and rough but instead warm and languid—he immediately leapt into a powerful freestyle, heading for the horizon.

He swam and swam and swam—heading well past the boundary of the cove. When he finally stopped to tread water, the ocean had pushed him slightly around the edge of a peninsula, so now he could no longer see their private beach. In fact, where he swam now, he could see nobody. There was not one boat, not one person on the shore, nothing.

He lay back in the water, and stared up at the almost cloudless sky.

What was up with him?

Jasmine Gallagher.

The answer was so obvious; she'd been all that filled his thoughts—as he'd slept, as he'd run, and as he'd swum.

Over the past few days the concept of their relationship being fun or casual or easy had become farcical. With Jas he'd shared more than he'd ever shared with any other woman—but what did that mean?

What did it mean that last night he'd felt a fear that he'd never before experienced—the fear of losing the woman he…

What?

Loved?

No. It was too impossible.

Even considering the possibility seemed ridiculous. They'd been together only weeks, known each other not much longer.

But even if it was possible, it didn't actually matter.

Because—after last night—he knew, inarguably, that he'd been right to never drag a woman into his life in any permanent way. Jas's privacy had been irretrievably invaded because of him, and last night she could've been *killed* because of him.

That wasn't acceptable.

Marko turned back onto his belly, and swam back the way he'd come. As he entered the cove he saw Jas standing at the end of the narrow jetty that stretched out from the far end of the rocky beach, and where he and Lukas had fished what felt like a hundred years ago.

So he swam to Jas.

At the wooden jetty, he hauled himself out of the water to stand beside her.

He realised, belatedly, that she was glaring at him, and her hands were placed firmly at her hips.

Then, before he had any idea what she intended, said hands were pressed forcefully against his chest—and, throwing her entire weight behind it, she shoved Marko straight back into the ocean.

They hit the water almost simultaneously, then surfaced less than a metre apart.

'What the hell, Jas?' he exclaimed.

She was treading water furiously, her hair slicked back, and her hazel eyes sparked with anger.

'What the hell, *Marko*?' she retorted. 'Someone tried to kill you yesterday, and *you* just went for a swim and *disappeared*. How do you think I felt when I looked up from my book and I couldn't see you?'

'I wasn't in any danger, Jas,' he said, attempting a soothing tone.

'But I didn't know that!' she snapped. 'How could you be so bloody—?'

Her voice cracked, and she looked away, her eyes squinting in the bright sunlight.

He swam closer to her, reaching out to brush her fingers beneath the water with his own.

He'd scared her. Properly scared her. His brave, strong Jasmine.

'I'm sorry,' he said. 'I didn't think.'

She snorted. *'Obviously.'*

She turned and swam the short distance back to the jetty. As he watched, she pulled herself out of the water, and then perched herself at the very end of the structure so her toes just dipped into the sea.

He followed suit behind her, and a minute later he was sitting beside her, the sun quickly evaporating the sheen of water from their skin.

Jas didn't think she'd ever been as scared as she'd felt when she'd realised Marko wasn't in the cove.

She'd raced down the jetty, searching the water desperately for him, while shouting his name.

Two from her team were waiting for them in the car above the dunes as Marko had insisted that they be allowed to relax in privacy. After last night, Jas had been too emotionally exhausted to argue. Plus, no one knew about this beach, and they'd made sure they weren't followed. But as her feet had drummed against the wooden jetty boards she'd lambasted herself for her stupidity. If something had happened to Marko…

But then she'd seen him, swimming strong, easy strokes as he swam into view from beyond the cove.

It was only now, with Marko sitting beside her on the jetty, that her breathing returned to normal.

'What's going on, Marko?' she asked abruptly.

Suddenly it seemed pointless to pretend any longer.

'Between us?' he asked.

She knew he knew what she meant, so she didn't bother to respond. All day things had been weird between them. Last night had been intense. And, it appeared, a turning point.

At least for Jasmine.

'I don't know what's going on,' Marko said finally. 'This isn't what I expected when I kissed you at *Mjesto za Ljubljenje*. This is…more.'

More.

He shifted beside her so his body was angled towards hers. She did the same, tipping her chin upwards so that she could meet his gaze.

He was as handsome as always, even under the harsh Mediterranean sun that made his eyes crinkle at the corners.

'More what?' she said bluntly.

He laughed and shook his head. 'You're not making this easy, Jas.'

'*This* isn't easy,' she pointed out.

'No,' he conceded. 'This…*us* isn't easy.' Jas watched his Adam's apple as he swallowed. 'I've never felt like this with another woman, Jas,' he said. 'I know that.'

Jas nodded.

'What do you think is going on?' he asked, after a while.

She shrugged. 'Something that I want to last longer than

my contract,' she said simply. 'So I need you to let me know if that's what you want, too, as otherwise…'

Here her bravado faded away.

'Otherwise?' he prompted.

'Otherwise,' she said, channelling her sensible, direct self, 'I think it's better if we end it now. I had the last man I thought I loved break my trust and my heart. I'm not going to wait around for that to happen again if it's only inevitable.'

She was making it sound like if she walked away now it was 'no harm, no foul'—but the ache already in her heart told her very, very differently.

But Marko didn't need to know that.

It's our job to protect each other.

If he really believed that, if he really felt that, then…

'The last man you thought you loved?' Marko said. 'Love?'

His expression wasn't shocked, exactly. More thoughtful. As if turning the idea over in his head.

'Maybe,' Jas said. 'One day.'

Like, possibly, yesterday.

But Jas wasn't allowing herself to think about that too much. And she certainly wasn't going to tell Marko.

She might have let her dormant dreams of love and happiness and rainbows bubble towards the surface—but she hadn't allowed them to bubble over. She'd learnt something, at least, from Stuart. Her trust, and her heart, weren't so easily offered up now.

If Marko loved her—or *could* love her—she'd know soon enough.

It's our job to protect each other.

So she needed to know: were they a team, or not?

'Love…' Marko repeated.

'Yes,' Jas said firmly. *'Love.'*

His gaze drifted out towards the horizon. 'I don't know, Jas. I've never been in a long-term relationship. I've literally never brought a woman home to the palace, or to meet my mother, until you. This is different, it's unfamiliar—'

Jas pushed herself up to her feet, suddenly annoyed. 'Marko, this isn't about the past. Hell, if we're going to dwell on the past you'd think I've got a pretty good reason to be cautious, don't you think? Yet I've got the guts to tell you how I'm feeling, and you can't even answer a simple question. *What do you think's going on between us, Marko?*' She looked up at the sky, the sun blinding her. 'I need you to tell me.'

Jas squeezed her eyes shut against the glare, suddenly realising there was no 'maybe' or 'one day' when it came to Marko. She loved him.

The realisation made her throat tight and her eyes sting.

When she opened her eyes, Marko was also on his feet. She met his gaze, strong and steady.

His was steady too. No looking away from her now.

'I'm a prince, Jasmine. My life…the life you would have with me… I don't think you understand what you'd be getting into. I don't think it's fair to—'

'You don't think I'd understand?' Jas said, furious now. 'Don't patronise me. The last month I've been literally beside you every step of your royal life. I've survived the paparazzi, an assassination attempt and a nude photo scandal. I think I get it, Marko.'

'But it wasn't real, Jas.'

Shocked, Jas turned on her heel, unable to be close to him right now.

How could he say that, when the past few weeks had felt more real than anything she'd ever experienced?

Halfway down the jetty his hand closed around her wrist. When she tried to tug away, he pulled her effortlessly against his chest, wrapping his arms tightly around her.

'I'm so sorry, *dragi moj*,' he said into her hair. 'I didn't mean it like that. The way I feel for you *is* real, I promise you. What we've had is real. But this whole time you've had an end date. You've known it's not for ever. It's different when it is. When you take on the burden of the world's scrutiny for the rest of your life.'

For a long moment Jas just stood in his arms, her cheek pressed against his chest. She kept her eyes squeezed shut as she listened to his heartbeat, and sank against the rise and fall of his breathing.

Then, she stepped away.

'That's just an excuse, Marko,' she said. 'I have a life in Australia and a business that takes me around the world. This stuff is complicated, I get it. But it's surmountable, to me. Nothing is insurmountable for the man I love.'

There. She'd done it. She'd said it.

Her declaration of love seemed to hang between them, their world silent beyond the murmur of the waves.

Then he shook his head. 'It's not an excuse, Jas.'

She put her hands on her hips. 'Is it love, then—this thing between us? This thing you can't explain? Do you love me?'

Marko's gaze searched her face, tracing her eyes, her nose, her lips.

Jas kept her gaze steady, even as her heart drummed against her chest, and her throat felt so tight she could barely breathe.

'I don't know, Jas,' he said finally as Jas desperately tried to work out what was going on behind his eyes. His expression was unreadable, but his gaze…

Then, he took a deep breath, as if he'd made a decision. 'No, Jas,' he said. 'I don't think it's love.'

Jas hadn't said a word.

Instead, she'd let *his* words hang between them, long enough that they began to feel tangible—as if Marko could reach out and snatch them back.

I don't think it's love.

But he didn't take the words back. He just stood there and watched, and waited, as Jas's bravado began to crumble.

But only for an instant.

Of course, Jas wasn't one to crumble. She was a fighter, his Jasmine. That was what she'd been doing, here on the jetty. Fighting. For him, for herself. For them.

His Jasmine.

She wasn't, of course. He had no right to even think such a thing as he watched her walk away from him. Her pace regular and determined. No more crumbling.

But also, no more fighting.

She'd fought for him, but he'd made his decision.

It was the right decision, for him. For both of them.

He knew that, absolutely, as the sun beat down on his bare skin, and his toes gripped the splintering boards of the jetty.

He followed her, but a while later.

His pace was slow. His limbs felt heavy—as if all the fight had seeped out of him.

Which made sense. The fight was over.

But then, why did he feel as if he'd lost?

CHAPTER SEVENTEEN

Three days later

MARKO SAT BENEATH vines heavy with grapes, a glass of wine in his hand.

Lukas sat beside him, his mostly untouched lunch on the table before him. They both stared out across the olive groves. Inside, their mother was attempting to teach Petra how to make her secret version of *crni rižoto*—black cuttlefish risotto—and occasionally their bursts of laughter would travel outside to where Marko and Lukas sat in silence.

It wasn't an uncomfortable silence. Lukas was still fatigued from his latest round of chemotherapy, and he'd explained to Marko last time they'd spoken that he often found it hard to follow conversations—he was just too exhausted to pay careful attention.

But that suited Marko today, to just sit here and not make conversation. And to let his mind drift. To not *think* too much.

The past few days had been a blur. After the disaster of their day on the beach, he and Jas had returned to the palace. Jas had been adamant she'd continue her role as his fiancée, although Marko had disagreed. Continuing their lie seemed ludicrous now, although Jas had eventually convinced him that 'breaking up' was the worst thing to do given the turmoil and scandal of the past few days. Vela Ada and the palace needed their relationship to appear solid and unbreakable.

Yes, but what did Jasmine need? What did he need?

But he hadn't asked those questions, and they'd instead

avoided each other in the palace, and then both acted their backsides off when they'd headed to open a new oncology ward named after Marko's father.

But spending time with Jas had been excruciating. To stop himself from touching her in all the ways that had become second nature—guiding her through doorways with a hand at her waist, holding her hand, standing just close enough so their arms brushed together…

Although he'd held her hand to help her out of their car when they'd arrived at the hospital. And that had almost been worse—to touch her, but know it was only for show…

This morning, Ivan had brought a message to him. Jas would like to return home for a week for her mother's birthday.

He didn't doubt it was her mother's birthday, but he also knew she'd had no plans to go home for it until today. His instinct had been to go talk to her, to tell her to take all the time she needed. And that he was so sorry. So sorry he couldn't give her what she needed. So sorry he couldn't love her.

Instead he'd sent Ivan back with his approval, and not long after he'd watched from the terrace as she'd left—with her bodyguards—for the airport, in one of the palace cars. Behind tinted windows he couldn't even see her, and briefly he'd fought the instinct to race down the stairs and go after her. And…

What, exactly?

Nothing had changed. He still knew he'd made the right decision.

'Marko?'

Marko blinked, turning to face Lukas. Lukas was looking at him like someone who had been trying to get his attention for some time.

'Sorry,' he said. 'Just thinking.'

'About Jasmine?'

Marko took a long sip of his wine. 'Pardon me?'

Lukas grinned. 'Come on,' he said, 'I'm sick, not stupid. Obviously there's trouble in paradise.'

Marko shook his head. 'Everything's fine. I thought you didn't like talking much at the moment.'

'And I thought you didn't like lying to your brother, and you've got pretty good at that.'

Marko put his glass down on the wooden table. 'I don't know what you're talking about.'

Lukas sighed. 'I know that you're not really engaged to Jasmine. I suspected right from the start—it seemed exactly the type of crazy thing you would do. Petra disagreed with me and was positive it was all real—until you both visited here, and then she worked it out, too. But we weren't going to say anything, because, honestly—it was a genius idea. No one cares about their King having a serious illness when they've got a new princess to get excited about.'

'Glad to be of service,' Marko said drily. There was no point at all in denying any of it. It had been years since he and Lukas had been close, but once they'd shared everything. Lukas still knew him better than almost anyone. Except Jas…

He mentally gave himself a shake. No, he wasn't going there.

'You have been,' Lukas said, his expression serious. 'I know you hate all the royal stuff, and, honestly, I didn't know how you'd manage stepping in for me. But you've been brilliant, exactly the Prince that Vela Ada needed.'

'Except for the photo scandal, and the assassination attempt—'

Lukas shrugged. 'You couldn't have responded better to either. You and Jasmine have captured the hearts of everyone. Vela Ada has fallen in love with you.'

Love.

That damn word again.

'It's remarkable, really,' Lukas said. 'How real your relationship has appeared.'

Marko met Lukas's gaze. He knew what his brother was thinking; he knew his brother thought there was more to him and Jasmine than a contract.

Marko stood up. 'She's an incredible—'

He was going to say *actress*, but found he couldn't.

Instead, he tried again: 'She's incredible,' he said simply.

But it's not real.

Turned out he couldn't say that, either.

Marko then walked away, almost jogging really, down the slight slope to the edge of the olive grove, not wanting to discuss any of this with his brother.

A breeze rustled the leaves that surrounded him as he strode between the olive trees.

Lukas didn't call out to him, but Marko had known he wouldn't.

After a while, he did break into a jog. Then a run.

But no matter how fast he ran, he couldn't escape from what he knew, and what he'd always known.

What he'd had with Jas was real. He'd told her that, on that jetty, but at the time it hadn't been enough.

This morning, it hadn't been enough. He'd convinced himself it wasn't.

But now, he wasn't so sure.

Ainslie, Canberra

Jas's mum hadn't actually organised anything for her birthday. On her birthday, Jas had simply arrived, unannounced, on her mother's doorstep—managing to avoid the Australian media thanks to a private plane and the excellent organisation of the palace and Australian diplomatic staff.

She'd now been here two days and although she hadn't left the house—and poor Simon and Scott were absolutely bored out of their brains—it still seemed the media were clueless. And for as long as that lasted, Jas was eternally grateful.

Because all she felt capable of doing right now was sleeping and watching romantic comedies in her teenage room.

She'd also cried for some time on her mother's shoulder—and promptly broken her confidentiality contract by telling her everything.

But it had helped to do so. So much.

It was Friday night, and her mum was hosting her book club in her blue weatherboard cottage. Jas was hiding in her room, as she absolutely knew that her mum's friends wouldn't be able to keep her presence a secret. They wouldn't go to the media, obviously, but they'd definitely tell one of their kids, and then…

Anyway, the upshot was she was stuck in her room. Her mum had brought her a platter of cheese and biscuits, and she'd curled herself up on her bed in her oldest, comfiest jeans and a T-shirt from a gig she went to when she was seventeen. Simon and Scott were sharing the tiny spare room, and the whole situation was ridiculous if Jas thought too much about it.

About halfway through her movie, there was a sharp knock at the front door. Her mum's house was small, and every sound travelled from one end of it to the other.

Consequently, Jas also heard the sound of the book club ladies' voices rising, and then—a deep male voice.

Jas slid off her bed and was brushing the crumbs from her clothes as her mum knocked on her bedroom door.

'Jas?' her mum said. 'You have a visitor.'

Jas smiled a tight smile as she followed her mum down the hallway. Immediately behind her were her bodyguards—both probably relieved to be able to leave their room.

Her mum only had a single, small living area—an open-plan kitchen, dining area and lounge.

Currently, it was full.

The book-club ladies were spread between the kitchen and lounge, each with a champagne glass and an inquisitive expression. With her and her bodyguards adding to the space, it was definitely crowded, and that was before Jas included the person that everyone was staring at—Prince Marko of Vela Ada. Who currently stood beside her mother's over-crowded hat stand, and in front of a framed piece of Jas's primary school artwork.

She'd missed him.

That was her first thought when his gaze locked on hers.

He was dressed as if he'd come straight from a plane, in jeans, T-shirt and sneakers and with tired smudges under his eyes.

He still looked gorgeous.

Behind him, beyond the still-open front door, were the rest of her team.

'Jas,' he said—and to hear his voice again made her shiver. 'I'm sorry.'

Jas took a long, deep breath. Then walked over to him, and grabbed his hand. She tugged him past the book club, past her mother—and her mother's concerned expression—and straight past Simon and Scott.

'No one is to follow us,' she said firmly.

Then she led Marko down the hallway, and outside.

Outside there was a simple patio, paved with recycled bricks that Jas and her mum had laid a decade earlier. A liquid amber provided shade during the day—but now, at night, its canopy of branches simply acted like a veil between them and the star-sparkled sky.

Jas dropped Marko's hand.

'Why are you here?' she asked.

'I needed to see you,' he said. 'And I needed to tell you something.'

Jas waited.

'I told you once that I hated the palace. Do you remember?'

She nodded. Yes, back when they'd first had breakfast together.

'But, of course, it was never about the palace itself,

but who I was when I was there. At the palace, I'm Prince Marko. I'm not a senior military officer, I'm not a man with his own hopes and dreams and I'm certainly not a man with his own private life. I'm a prince, and that role is one I've never felt comfortable playing.'

Jas's eyes had adjusted to the darkness—not that she needed to be able to see to feel the intensity of his gaze.

'I've spent most of my life rebelling against the expectations of my family and Vela Ada, and hating the scrutiny I've been under my whole entire life. I've been judged, and found wanting, for as long as I can remember.'

'Marko—' Jas began, but he shook his head, silencing her.

'I may now complain about it, but I've been complicit in the lie of the Playboy Prince, hiding behind that façade rather than working out who I *actually* am. Not just who I am perceived to be. With you, Jasmine Gallagher, there's never been a façade. You've never treated me as anything but the man you see in front of you. You see me, you saw me…with you I'm just Marko, and what I had with you is about as real as anything I've ever experienced in my life. Even though we were only together because of a lie.'

Jas wanted to reach for him, but she kept her hands still, twisting her fingers in the fabric of her jeans instead.

'I've never had a serious relationship, Jas, because I've told myself I would never bring someone into a life I hated—a life of scrutiny and judgment. The past few weeks, this belief has been seemingly vindicated—after all, what sort of monster would I be to drag a woman into a life where her privacy is violated, and her life is under threat?' He swallowed. 'That's what I was telling myself that day on the jetty, Jas. I held onto it—onto what you quite rightly called an excuse—and held onto it tightly, right up until you flew back home to Australia.'

'What changed?' Jas asked, trying her best to tamp down

the butterflies beginning to flutter in her belly. What was Marko saying?

'I found out Lukas knew from the start that our engagement was a lie.'

Jas gasped, but Marko just grinned.

'No, it's fine. No one else knows, except Petra. And probably my mum.'

Oh, God. But now was not the time to worry about all her lies to royalty.

'But it got me thinking, Jas, about what else I've been lying about. Like, for example, the lie I was telling myself that my decision to let you walk away was about *protecting* you. When it was never about that. It was about protecting myself. All these years I've told myself that I'd never drag someone I loved into a world I hated, but really—I think maybe I was just scared that no one would genuinely love me enough to look past all that. To put up with the paparazzi, and having their lives turned upside down—for me. For Marko, not Prince Marko.

'Or,' he continued, 'maybe I just hadn't met the right person.'

He stepped closer to her, but now he looked unsure. For the first time, ever, Jas saw uncertainty in Marko's gaze.

'Jasmine Gallagher,' he said, in his delicious, deep accent, 'I love you. I still don't know for sure if you'll want to run away from life as a princess in a few more weeks, or months or years...but I love you. So I need to trust that you might love me enough to stay.'

Jas reached out, lacing each of her hands with his, in an echo of the first time they'd touched as they'd walked into the Knight's Hall that very first night together.

Still, his touch made her shiver.

'I love you, Marko,' she said. 'I love the man you are: a man of strength, and loyalty and integrity. I don't care about the prince stuff, I just know I love *you*, and that's all that matters to me. You've taught me to believe in love again, to trust in love again. And I promise you, I'm not going anywhere.'

She stood on her tiptoes to kiss him, and instantly he was dragging her close, and kissing her until she was incapable of thinking, and certainly incapable of remembering she was in her mum's backyard. For long minutes her world was Marko, and the incredible, extraordinary way he made her feel.

When they finally broke apart, breathing heavily, they just stood there smiling at each other.

'It probably wouldn't be very polite of me to whisk you back to my hotel without properly introducing myself to your mother and her friends.'

'No,' Jas said, grinning. 'Not very kingly at all. Definitely not the behaviour of a prince.'

She reached up to pull him down for another kiss, then whispered against his lips, 'Luckily, we're just Jas and Marko tonight.'

Marko kissed his way up to her ear. 'And Jas and Marko are in love.'

'Yes,' Jas said as she kissed him again. 'We most definitely are.'

EPILOGUE

Twelve months later, Kirribilli House, Sydney

'YOU'RE DOING IT AGAIN,' Marko murmured against Jas's ear.

Even now, after all this time, his proximity made her shiver.

Jas shrugged, and relaxed her bodyguard stance. She'd been scanning the crowd scattered across the perfect, sloping grass outside the Australian Prime Minister's Sydney residence: *faces and hands, faces and hands*. 'I can't help it,' she said. 'It's still part of me.'

Especially when she was so close to the Prime Minister—and, in the background, a few familiar faces from her old workplace. Four years ago, she'd worked here, at this spectacular one-hundred-and-fifty-year-old home with sweeping views across the water to the Opera House and the Sydney Harbour Bridge.

She'd been the one in the shadows, or on the shoulders of members of Australian parliament or visiting dignitaries. Today, as wait staff in starched white shirts circulated with silver platters of canapés, *she* was one of those visiting dignitaries. As was Marko, of course, plus King Lukas, and Queen Petra—stunning, as always, in a raw silk dress and a tiara that caught every ray of the sun.

And Prince Filip. Aged nine months, on his first royal tour of Australia.

Fast asleep on the Dowager Queen's shoulder—Marko's mother was unable to face even a few weeks without her only grandchild— and with hair as golden as Petra's, Filip had no idea of the life ahead of him. The heir to the Vela Ada throne, born three months after King Lukas had returned to his rightful place in the palace—his treatment successful, his long-term prognosis excellent.

Unsurprisingly, Marko had not been upset that Filip had bumped him one place down the line of succession. Although he did worry for his tiny nephew. What if, like Marko, Filip was less than kingly?

Because, even now, Marko didn't exactly revel in his royal duties. The difference was that now he didn't pretend they didn't exist. Since Lukas has returned, Marko had still continued to attend the occasional royal engagement—in between his military commitments—to lessen the load on his still-recovering brother. The time Marko was spending at Vela Ada had also strengthened the relationship between the brothers, as Marko had finally torn down the playboy façade he'd been hiding behind for so long.

Jas had attended some of those royal engagements, too. In between her Gallagher Personal Protection Services commitments, of course. Although now she was—reluctantly—unable to work out in the field. A bodyguard who needed bodyguards of her own wasn't particularly useful.

Marko tugged on her hand, dragging Jas's attention away from a sleeping Filip.

'Want to go for a walk?' he asked.

'Can we do that?' Jas asked wistfully. The entire garden party mingled on the house side of a hedge that bordered the lawn. Beyond that the ground slid abruptly away to the harbour.

Marko shrugged. 'Speeches are done, why not?' Then he grinned. 'Besides, I'm a prince. Who's going to stop me?'

Well, potentially the Prime Minister's security detail—although, as they walked hand in hand beyond the hedges and to a stone-paved path that snaked between lush green gardens, no one halted their progress.

Eyes were trained on them, though. Strategically positioned amongst the gardens, at the perimeter, and even in bobbing boats on the harbour. Kirribilli House would be one of the most secure places in Australia, so this was hardly a private stroll.

The path eventually became steps, and those steps eventually made it to a jetty.

'Alone at last,' Jas said, with a grin, as they stood on the wide, wooden boards of the jetty.

'Not exactly,' Marko said, nodding towards the most visible guards out on the water.

Jas shrugged. 'Close enough.'

There were guaranteed to be some paparazzi out on the water too. Outside the exclusion zone, but close enough with a telephoto lens.

But it didn't matter.

Well, not enough for Jas to want to be anywhere else right now. Since they'd landed in Australia it had been a whirlwind. Here on this jetty, with Marko, it felt as if they finally had some space to breathe. If someone wanted to take a photo of that, then so be it.

It would only be a photo, after all.

A photo of Jasmine standing beside the man she loved.

Oh, she knew that a tabloid might splash a lurid headline on it—maybe *Prince Marko and his Aussie fiancée in harbourside tiff!* Or *Aussie Jasmine's shock declaration: set the date or it's over!*

It was ludicrous, the stories that could be written from the most benign photographs, but that was her life now. And, despite many, many shouty headlines, she and Marko were still very much in love. What the glossy magazines wrote had no bearing on their relationship. It didn't matter.

A photo couldn't hurt them. Heck, a naked selfie hadn't even been able to.

Because what they had was real and authentic—regardless of a photographer's lens, or a tabloid journalist's interpretation.

A breeze ruffled Jas's hair and pressed the silky fabric of

her dress against her legs. Jas had been staring out towards the skyscrapers of the Sydney CBD, but she realised now that Marko was instead staring at her. She turned to face him.

'I've been thinking,' Marko said, very casually. But his grip on her hand was suddenly much firmer. 'About our engagement.'

Jas's smile was slow. 'Our fake engagement?'

'Yes,' he said, 'that one.' He paused. 'I wondered,' he continued, 'if you'd like to make it real.'

'Right now?' Jas said, grinning like an idiot, but also a bit surprised. 'Surrounded by security and photographers?'

'I'd planned to ask you back home, at our beach,' he said, but then he grinned wickedly. 'But then I kind of liked the idea of some paparazzo finally actually photographing something significant and real, and having no idea.'

'Plus we'll get photos of the moment,' Jas pointed out. 'About time we got something useful out of them.'

Marko took her other hand in his, so their fingers were perfectly laced together.

'Exactly,' he agreed. 'Although I'd really rather they were photographing a *yes*.'

Jas met Marko's gaze as he looked at her, losing herself, for the millionth time, in the silvery blue of his eyes.

'Yes,' she said softly. 'It's definitely a yes.'

Then Marko leant towards her, and whispered against her lips.

'*Dragi moj*, let's give them something worth photographing?'

Jas sighed against his mouth. 'Yes, please.'

Then they kissed.

And when they did, they weren't the playboy and the bodyguard, or even the Prince and his princess-to-be.

They were just Jas and Marko.

In love.

* * * * *

If you enjoyed this story, check out these other great reads from Leah Ashton

BEHIND THE BILLIONAIRE'S GUARDED HEART
THE BILLIONAIRE FROM HER PAST
NINE MONTH COUNTDOWN
WHY RESIST A REBEL?

All available now!

"You know, I'm getting the feeling that the two of us have more in common than just Ray Maddox."

The husky note in his voice was so sexy it was almost like he was kissing her. The idea caused her nostrils to flare, her breathing to quicken.

"Why?"

Her murmured question put a faint smile on his face and then his head was bending downward, until his lips were hovering a scant few inches from hers.

"We've both lost parents. We both ride horses. And, uh, we're both standing here beneath the desert stars—together. It's like fate."

The warning bells going off in Tessa's head were deafening, but the clanging noise was hardly enough to make her step back and away from him. Something about him was pulling at the deepest part of her, urging her to touch him in ways she'd never wanted to touch a man before.

"This isn't fate," she tried to reason. "It's—crazy."

His soft chuckle fanned her face. "It's okay to be a little crazy once in a while."

* * *

Men Of The West: Whether ranchers or lawmen, these heartbreakers can ride, shoot—and drive a woman crazy…

THE ARIZONA LAWMAN

BY
STELLA BAGWELL

First Published in Great Britain 2018
By Mills & Boon, an imprint of HarperCollins*Publishers*
1 London Bridge Street, London, SE1 9GF

ISBN: 978-0-263-93634-6

23-0118

MIX
Paper from
responsible sources
FSC™ C007454

This book is produced from independently certified FSC™ paper to ensure responsible forest management.

For more information visit: www.harpercollins.co.uk/green

Printed and bound in Spain
by CPI, Barcelona

After writing more than eighty books for Mills & Boon, **Stella Bagwell** still finds it exciting to create new stories and bring her characters to life. She loves all things Western and has been married to her own real cowboy for forty-four years. Living on the south Texas coast, she also enjoys being outdoors and helping her husband care for the horses, cats and dog that call their small ranch home. The couple has one son, who teaches high school mathematics and is also an athletic director. Stella loves hearing from readers. They can contact her at stellabagwell@gmail.com.

To April May Townsend with love.
Thank you for being a friend and dedicated reader.

Prologue

"Tessa, you are now an heiress."

The legal document Tessa Parker gripped with both hands looked real enough, and Orin Calhoun was the closest thing she had to a father. He would never lie to her. But the words he'd just spoken didn't make sense.

Staring at the rancher, she asked in an incredulous voice, "Are you making some sort of joke?"

Orin glanced over to Jett Sundell, longtime attorney for the Calhoun family and the Silver Horn Ranch.

"Help me out here, Jett."

The younger man left his comfortable seat in an armchair to walk over to Tessa.

"The document is genuine, Tessa. I've already read the will in its entirety and talked at length with the deceased man's attorney. He assures me his client had full control of his faculties at the time he made out this bequest." Jett placed a steadying hand on her shoulder. "In short, a man by the name of Ray Maddox has willed you a sizable piece of property in southern Arizona. Along with a very tidy amount of money, which is already waiting for you in a bank account with your name. Congratulations, Tessa."

Her hands began to tremble violently, causing the document to fall unheeded to her lap.

"That can't be!" She stared wildly up at Jett then swung her gaze over to Orin. "I don't know anyone in Arizona! This has to be some crazy mistaken identity!"

Orin held up a hand to calm her escalating doubts. "According to the attorney in Prescott, your identity has been verified several times over. He's assured Jett that you are the correct beneficiary."

"So the next step we need to discuss is what you want to do with this windfall," Jett continued while directing a meaningful glance at Orin. "If it were me, Tessa, I'd want to take a look at the property before I made the decision."

"Yes, but Tessa isn't you," Orin retorted. "She hardly needs to go traipsing off to Arizona to look at a piece of land she doesn't need. Her home is here on the Silver Horn with us. It won't be difficult to locate a trustworthy real-estate agent to handle all the details of selling it."

Frowning, Jett walked over to his father-in-law's desk. "Orin, I understand that Tessa is like your daughter but—"

"*Like* a daughter! Hell, as far as I'm concerned, she *is* my daughter! And as such—"

"You want her to have every opportunity to be happy. She's been willed a small fortune by someone who obviously cared a great deal for her. It would hardly be in her benefit to get hasty and dump the property before making an effort to see the place."

Orin rose from his chair and began to pace around

the large, plush study. "It's not like I'm a pauper, Jett," he argued. "I can give Tessa whatever she needs. And, frankly, she's too young and inexperienced to go off to Arizona alone!"

The idea of Orin as a pauper was just as laughable as Tessa being an heiress. Orin and his father, Bart, owned the Silver Horn Ranch, one of the largest, most profitable spreads in the whole state of Nevada. The family possessed holdings in gold and silver mines, oil and gas companies, along with other lucrative stocks. To say that Orin could supply her with whatever she needed was very true, but she would never accept wealthy gifts from him, or anyone in the Calhoun family. She was a Parker and possessed her own brand of pride.

"Tessa is twenty-four years old. She's just acquired a college degree," Jett reminded him. "She's certainly capable of making a trip to Arizona. And making decisions about her own future."

The arguing between the two men pushed Tessa to her feet. "Orin, you've given me a home here on the Silver Horn for the past eleven years. As much as I love you, Jett is right. I'm not about to make a hasty decision about something so—life-changing. Anyway, right now I… I'm so shaken I can hardly think! But I can tell you one thing. If a person cared enough about me to leave me a small fortune, then I'm going to make the effort to travel to Arizona. To see the place and find the reason behind this."

Jett gave her a thumbs-up. "Atta girl, Tessa. Now you're talking."

Orin stopped his pacing to glare at the both of them. "Go ahead, encourage her," he goaded Jett. "For all we know there could be something sinister behind this whole thing."

Jett rolled his eyes. "Orin, the man has passed away. And, according to Mr. Maddox's attorney, he had no family to speak of. On top of that, he was a decorated sheriff of the area. I hardly read sinister in the will."

Relenting somewhat, Orin walked over to where Tessa stood near his desk. "Tessa, are you sure your mother never talked about this man before?"

If Monica Parker had still been living, she might've been able to explain this sudden and unexplainable inheritance. But her mother's life had ended eleven years ago in a traffic accident.

Tessa's mind spun crazily as she tried to recall, to make any sort of connection to Ray Maddox. "I never heard Mom say that name. Or mention she was acquainted with anyone in Arizona. This man…he must have known me—somehow. I won't rest until I find the connection."

Orin's stern expression softened to a wry smile. "I imagine I'd feel the same way. It's just that I've always had you close and under my wing." Lifting her hand, he patted the back of it. "And I guess a part of me is afraid you won't come back. That you'll find something down there in Arizona we can't give you."

Her heart full of mixed emotions, she gave the big rancher a reassuring hug. "You've already given me so much, Orin. There's nothing else I need."

His smile turned knowing as he stroked the top of her head. "Oh, yes, Tessa, darlin'. There are plenty more things you need. Like a good man to love. Children to raise. A home to keep."

"Stop it." She sniffed. "You're going to make me cry all over your white shirt."

He squeezed her tight. "Damn the white shirt," he said gruffly. "I have plenty of them. I just have one of you."

"I won't be gone forever, Orin. Just long enough to find out why Ray Maddox wanted to give me his home and money."

Chapter One

The hot May sun was slipping behind a ridge of jagged mountains as Tessa steered her white Ford truck off the road and stared up at the sign arched over a wide cattle guard. Bar X Ranch.

This was it. Her ranch. Her property.

Even though she was seeing it with her own eyes, she was still struggling to wrap her mind around the idea that it all belonged to her. It seemed impossible that a bank in Prescott had an account in her name holding an amount of money that would take a person like her years and years to earn. Everything about the situation was still all so confusing and incredible.

Fighting back a wave of emotional tears, Tessa put the truck into motion and drove through the entrance of the ranch.

A half mile later, after she'd driven through a spectacular view of rock formations and fields of Joshua trees, she parked the truck in front of a rambling house painted pale green and trimmed with a darker shade of green. The structure was shaded by several ancient cottonwoods, while a huge bougainvillea covered in vivid purple blooms sheltered one side of a small porch. Nearby, beneath a set of paned windows, bushes of red and white roses grew thick and climbed along the dark green shutters.

She'd not expected to find anything so beautiful or charming. For a moment, after she'd climbed from the truck, all she could do was stand and stare and wonder about the people who'd lived behind those walls.

The sound of an approaching vehicle pulled Tessa out of her swirling thoughts. She turned to see a beige SUV with emergency lights on the top and a sheriff's emblem painted on the side. Now what? Had someone reported her as trespassing?

Curious, she stood watching as a man stepped out on the driver's side. He was dressed in blue jeans and boots, with a black cowboy hat and a khaki shirt. The long sleeves were decorated with official-looking emblems, while a badge was pinned to the front left pocket. Even from a distance, she could tell he was young but older than her. His tall, muscular body appeared to be in perfect condition and his quick steps were rapidly closing the space of ground between them.

"Hello," she said once he was within earshot. "Can I help you?"

He came to a stop a few steps in front of her and, with the back of his forearm, pushed the brim of his cowboy hat back off his forehead.

"I'm Joseph Hollister. Deputy Sheriff of Yavapai County," he said to identify himself. "I saw your vehicle turn into the entrance of this property. Since your truck is carrying Nevada plates, I figured you might not be aware this ranch is currently unoccupied."

Was he naturally a suspicious man, she wondered, or was he simply a very dedicated lawman? Either way, he was definitely something to look at. His thick, coffee-colored hair was just long enough to curl around his ears, while his deeply tanned complexion told her he spent long hours in the Arizona sun. He had a square jaw, the type that looked as though it could take several punches and never flinch. However, all this was just a gorgeous backdrop to his eyes. Even from a distance, she could see the brown orbs were full of golden flecks, a color that reminded her of dark, potent whiskey.

"I'm Tessa Parker," she told him. "And, yes, I'm from Nevada. Between Carson City and Reno, to be exact. And, yes, I know the ranch house is currently vacant."

His razor-sharp gaze slid over her as though he was sizing up her honesty.

Tessa tried not to bristle. After all, the man didn't know the first thing about her. And he was a deputy sheriff.

"The Bar X is obviously a long distance from Carson City. So what brings you all the way down here, Ms. Parker?"

She straightened her shoulders. "I'm here to see my new property. Is that some sort of crime?"

Tessa didn't know why the tart question had popped out of her. It wasn't like her to be testy with anyone. Particularly a law official. But the suspicious look in his eyes was setting her on edge.

"No. No crime at all. If it *is* your property. Do you have your identification with you?"

If a flying saucer suddenly landed next to them, the situation wouldn't be any more bizarre, Tessa thought.

"I have more than my identification," she crisply informed him. "I have all sorts of legal papers with me—if you'd care to see them."

"That isn't necessary," he said. "Your driver's license will be sufficient."

Turning back to the truck, Tessa fished the plastic-coated card from her purse and handed it to him. As she watched him scan the information, she noticed his hands were big and brown, the backs lightly sprinkled with dark hair. There was no sign of a wedding band on his left hand. But that didn't surprise Tessa at all. He didn't have the softer attitude that most married men possessed.

He suddenly glanced up at her and Tessa's breath caught as his brown eyes looked directly into hers.

"I happened to be well acquainted with Ray Maddox, the man who used to live here," he informed her. "And since he passed away, there's been no talk of this place being put on the real-estate market."

"You've made the wrong assumption, Deputy Hollister. I didn't buy this place. It was willed to me by Ray Maddox."

This news caused his eyes to widen with surprise then narrow to two skeptical slits. "Willed? Are you a relative?"

"No. Not that I'm aware of," she said bluntly. "In fact, I don't think I ever met Mr. Maddox."

He folded a pair of strong-looking arms across his broad chest and suddenly Tessa was wondering if Orin had been right. Maybe it had been foolish of her to make the trip down here alone. This man looked like it wouldn't bother him one iota to arrest her.

"I've heard plenty of cock-'n'-bull stories in my line of work, but this beats them all. Ray Maddox was hardly a fool. He was the sheriff of Yavapai County for more than twenty years. He wouldn't just will his property to a total stranger."

Tessa opened the truck for a second time and collected a large manila envelope from the console. Lifting her chin to a challenging angle, she handed the legal documents to him. "Since you have the idea I'm some sort of criminal, I think you should look at this."

His stern expression was all-professional as he made a quick scan of the papers and then carefully inserted them back into the envelope. "I'm sorry, Ms. Parker. It's my job to be cautious. And I think you'll agree this is a rather odd occurrence."

An ache had developed in the middle of her forehead and as he continued to watch her closely, she tried to rub it away with the tips of her fingers.

"I can't deny that." She turned her gaze to the front of the house and suddenly felt herself close to tears. "The attorney handling Mr. Maddox's estate informed me that his client had been a sheriff and a well-known figure in the area."

"That's right. A beloved figure. He retired about five years ago."

"It's all so incredible," she said in a thoughtful daze.

After a long stretch of silence he asked, "Were you—planning on staying here tonight?"

She wiped a hand through her straight brown hair before she nodded. "Yes, I am," she answered then took a shaky step toward the house. "I'm sorry. I need to sit down."

Recognizing she was teetering on her feet, he leaped forward and wrapped a supporting hand around her elbow.

"Here. Let me help you to the steps."

He guided her over to a set of wide stone steps built into a mortar-and-stone retaining wall.

Once she was sitting, the deputy took a seat on the same step, careful to keep a respectable distance between them.

He said, "I'm not sure it's a good idea for you to stay here alone tonight, Ms. Parker."

"Why? Is this a high crime area?"

"Crimes are rarely committed around here. I'm speaking now of your emotional condition."

Tessa straightened her spine. She might appear fragile to this man, but she prided herself in being tough and capable.

"I'll be fine, Deputy Hollister. I've been driving since early this morning. Nearly seven hundred miles, to be exact. I'm tired and haven't had much to eat today. And then seeing this place—I'm sure you can understand it's all a bit overwhelming."

"That's why staying in a hotel in Wickenburg and having a nice meal would be a better option for you tonight. I'm not even sure if the utilities are still turned on in the house."

He must be thinking she was too stupid to plan ahead. Or perhaps he thought she was the impulsive sort who didn't think five minutes ahead of her. Either way, she wished he'd simply go. Just looking at his broad shoulders and rugged face was playing havoc with her senses.

"Everything is on and ready to go," she said. "All I need to do is carry in my bags. And I can certainly manage that task."

"If you insist on staying, I'll carry your bags for you," he told her. "In a few minutes. After you've gathered yourself."

How was she supposed to compose herself with him

sitting a few inches away looking like he'd just stepped off the screen of a gritty Western movie? With amber-brown eyes fringed with black lashes, lips that squared at the corners and dared a woman to kiss them, he certainly had the appearance of a tough leading man.

Looking away, she swallowed and wondered what had happened to the breeze she'd felt earlier. All of a sudden the heat index felt worse than triple digit.

"Do you always patrol this area?" she asked while wondering what her chances had been of meeting this man.

"I don't exactly patrol it," he answered. "I was on my way home. I live with the rest of my family about five miles from here on Three Rivers Ranch"

Surprise tugged her gaze back to his face. "Family? You have a wife and children?"

A shuttered look wiped all expression from his face. "No. I'm not a family man. I meant my mother and siblings. I have three brothers and two sisters."

"And you all live together."

"That's right. My family has owned Three Rivers for a hundred and forty-five years. We wouldn't know how to live anywhere else."

She wasn't sure if the last was said in jest or if he was serious. Even though Joseph Hollister's face was very easy on the eyes, it was difficult to read. So far she got the impression he was a very sober young man.

Her curiosity pricked, she asked, "Oh. Does your ranch boundary touch mine?"

"Only for a short distance. On the east side. You see, our ranch covers about seventy thousand acres."

A number that made her one thousand acres seem minuscule, Tessa thought. "I see. So that makes us neighbors."

His thick, dark brows lifted ever so slightly. "So it seems. That is, if you're planning on sticking around."

She drew in a long breath and let it out. "I've not made any definite plans yet. This inheritance has all happened so suddenly and—unexpectedly."

"Well, I'm sure you have a family back in Nevada to consider first."

Except for the Calhouns, she'd been without a family ever since her mother had died. But she was far too emotionally weary to go into that part of her life now. Especially with this Arizona lawman.

"I do have people back there. But no husband or children. I'm only twenty-four," she said, as if that explained everything.

Up until now, the sporadic sound of a two-way radio could be heard through the open window of his SUV, but he'd basically ignored the crackly exchange. However, his trained ear must have caught something in the dispatcher's words that called for his attention because he suddenly rose to his feet.

"Sorry," he said. "I need to answer that call."

He quickly strode off to the vehicle and Tessa used the moment to climb the remaining steps and cross a small yard with fresh-cut grass and a bed full of yellow and purple irises. At the front door, she fished a key from the pocket on her jeans and let herself into the house.

A small entryway with two long windows and a lone potted cactus led into a spacious living room furnished with a mixture of comfortable furniture, a TV and several table lamps. Paintings and enlarged photos of area landscapes decorated the cream-colored walls, while rugs woven in colorful southwestern designs were scattered over the hardwood floor. Along the front wall, heavy beige drapes covered the windows and blocked out most of the waning sunlight.

Everything about the room felt warm and welcoming, as if it had been waiting for her to walk in and make herself at home. The odd sensation left goose bumps on her arms and she tried to rub them away as she walked over to a big brown recliner. The soft leather was slightly faded on the headrest and she wondered if this had been the retired sheriff's favorite chair. Had he sat here watching TV or reading? Or simply dreaming about life?

Oh, God, why did it matter so much to her? Why did questions about her mysterious benefactor keep pushing and prodding her?

Her fingers were trailing thoughtfully over the worn headrest when Deputy Hollister stepped into the room.

His boots thumped against the hardwood floor and from the corner of her eye, Tessa watched him move around the shadowy space, his keen gaze surveying the surroundings as though it were a crime scene.

"Everything looks just like it did when Ray was here. I imagine Sam has been keeping it all cleaned and dusted. That's Samuel Leman," he explained. "He's worked for Ray for more years than I can remember."

Tessa had imagined she'd be exploring the house on her own. The last thing she'd been expecting was to have a sexy deputy give her a guided tour. Especially one that appeared to have been well acquainted with the late sheriff.

"I see. Does Samuel live here on the property?"

His gaze landed on her and, without even realizing what she was doing, she pulled her hands away from the recliner and stuffed them into the back pockets of her jeans.

"No. After Ray died, he moved to a little house about

three or four miles from here. You passed it on the way. A peach-colored stucco with a bunch of goats out back."

Yes, she vaguely recalled the place.

"Most folks around here assumed Ray left his place to Sam," he continued. "After all, he was the one who hung around and took care of him after his lungs quit working."

Was this man implying she didn't deserve the place? The notion disturbed her on many levels.

Moving away from the chair, she started toward a wide, arched opening. "Look, Deputy Hollister, you can be frank with me. I'm quite certain that you, and everyone else who knew Ray Maddox, isn't going to understand his last wishes. How could they? I don't understand them myself. And I'm certainly not thinking I deserved everything the man had worked for in his life. But that's the way *he* wanted it. Not me."

The deputy followed her into a breezeway and Tessa paused, uncertain as to which direction she wanted to go first. Certainly not to the bedrooms. Not with this man right on her heels.

He said, "I didn't mean to sound like I'm accusing you, Ms. Parker. Or that I thought you were undeserving. It's just that Sam was such a loyal employee for many long years."

She let out a long breath. "Then I can only hope that Mr. Maddox left his employee something. As for me—" She broke off and lifted her hands in a helpless gesture. "I have just as many questions about all of this as you probably do."

He opened his mouth as though to say something but must have decided against it. After a pause, he gestured to a pair of swinging doors off to their left.

"The kitchen is over there. The bedrooms and a study are to the right."

Tessa headed to the kitchen and since he'd taken it upon himself to join her, she decided Deputy Hollister clearly wasn't in a hurry to get home. Or perhaps he felt it was his duty to make sure she was safe and sound before he left the premises.

"This is beautiful." She walked over to the left side of the room where a large bay window created a breakfast nook. Beyond the paned glass was an incredible view of distant jagged mountains and rocky bluffs. Closer to the ranch house, the desert slopes were filled with sage, saguaro and blooming yucca.

Another wave of emotion caused her voice to quaver. "Is this my land?"

"Most of it. Your boundary stops before it reaches the mountains. The most productive grazing area runs to the east toward Three Rivers," he explained. "Before Ray became ill, he ran about fifty to a hundred head of cattle. After it became impossible for him to care for the herd, he sold out. I can tell you, giving up his cattle and horses hurt him about as much as the lung disease."

"I believe that. I live on a large ranch in Nevada. I see firsthand how much the livestock means to everyone who cares for them."

She glanced over her shoulder to see he was studying her with an air of faint surprise.

"So you're used to living in the country."

"Absolutely. This place is closer to a town than what I'm accustomed to." She turned and walked over to a long row of varnished pine cabinets. Another wide window sat over a double porcelain sink. After turning on the water to make sure it was in working order, she gazed out at the small backyard shaded by two huge Joshua trees. It was a cozy area with a small rock patio furnished with a pair of red motel chairs and a tiny white table for drinks.

"It's fifteen miles from here to town," he informed her.

The skeptical sound in his voice put a faint smile on her face. "Yes, I know. The Silver Horn is double that amount of miles from Carson City."

"The Silver Horn," he repeated thoughtfully. "I think I've heard of that ranch."

"The Calhouns own it. Bart and Orin Calhoun."

"I'm not familiar with—uh—" Deep thought put a crease between his brows and then he snapped his fingers with recognition. "Now I remember. My brother Holt purchased a broodmare from that ranch about four years ago. She's been a dandy."

"The Calhouns are known more for their quality horses than anything," she told him.

He walked toward her and Tessa found herself backing up until her hips bumped into the cabinets.

"But your name isn't Calhoun," he pointed out.

"No. It isn't." As far as she was concerned, she didn't have to explain anything else to this man. She rubbed her palms down the front of her jeans. "Uh, if you'll excuse me, I think I'll go get my things."

"I'll help you."

Tessa let out a silent groan. Was the man never going to leave? Aloud she said, "Thanks. I do have several bags."

What are you so antsy about, Tessa? A normal woman would be enjoying the company of a good-looking man. And Joseph Hollister definitely fits that description. What are you afraid of? That you might actually allow yourself to be attracted to the deputy?

Trying to ignore the taunting voice in her head, she walked past him and out of the kitchen.

As Joseph followed Tessa Parker out to her truck, he mentally cursed himself. What the hell was he doing?

He'd already investigated the situation and made certain no one was going to vandalize his late friend's home. He'd checked this woman's credentials and everything appeared accurate. She had a legitimate reason for being on the Bar X Ranch, so why was he still hanging around when he should've left a half hour ago? Because she looked like a walking dream?

Her slim, angular face was dominated by startling blue eyes, prominent cheekbones and a soft, wide mouth. Straight, caramel-brown hair hung nearly to her waist and though she was far more slender than his usual taste in women, she was nicely curved in all the right places. Her creamy skin was smooth and soft, like she'd been living in a tropical climate rather than the dry west. Furthermore, she carried herself with class and grace.

Yeah, all those things were pleasant to a man's eyes, he conceded. But in Tessa Parker's case, it had been the vulnerable wobble in her voice and the emotions flickering in her eyes that had tugged at something inside him. Even if she did have a family back in Nevada, she seemed to be very alone. And that notion bothered Joseph far too much.

"I'm sure I brought much more than I need," she was saying as she opened the back door on the truck. "But since I was uncertain about how long I'll be staying, I wanted to have plenty."

She placed two very large suitcases on the ground, along with a pair of duffel bags. Joseph picked up the suitcases, both of which were quite heavy.

"I'll get these," he said. "If the duffel bags are heavy, leave them. I'll fetch them later."

"Thank you," she said, "but I can manage."

Joseph followed her back up the steps of the retaining wall and into the house. Along the way, he found himself watching the sway of her slender hips and the curtain of thick hair moving gently against her back.

In the living room, she placed the bags she'd been carrying on the rug and turned on a table lamp situated near the recliner.

Joseph asked, "Where would you like for me to put these?"

She gestured to a spot on the floor near the other bags. "Just sit them down there. Both bags have wheels. I'll deal with them later."

For some idiotic reason he felt a wash of warm color burn his face. "I can see they have wheels. But they're both very heavy."

An impatient, even wary expression crossed her face and it dawned on Joseph that he was making her uncomfortable. But then he had to remember he was a stranger to this woman. He couldn't expect her to behave as though he was an old friend.

"Well, yes, they are. But—" She broke off with a shake of her head then gestured toward the archway. "All right, let's go."

She started out of the room in a long stride and Joseph fell into step behind her. As they made their way down a narrow hallway, the scent of her flowery perfume teased him like a gentle ocean breeze.

"I don't suppose you have any idea which bedroom Mr. Maddox used, would you?"

Her question snapped him out of his dreamy cloud. "I've only been as far as the study," he admitted. "It's the first door on your right. Why do you want to know about Ray's bedroom, anyway?"

Pausing in the middle of the hallway, she turned to look at him. "This is probably going to sound silly to you, but I'm not sure I'd feel comfortable about staying in Mr. Maddox's room."

"I don't understand why you'd feel that way. This is your house now."

As soon as he'd said the words, he wished he could take them back. They sounded insensitive, even rude. And she didn't deserve that. Not unless she turned out to be a complete fraud.

Seemingly unoffended by his tart remark, she said, "That's true. But I'm a stranger in this house. I feel it would be more proper for me to stay in a guest room."

Even though she'd told him she hadn't been acquainted with Ray Maddox, she seemed to want to respect him and his memory. Joseph had to admire her for that.

"Well, let's have a look and maybe we can figure out which room was Ray's."

Nodding in agreement, she moved on down the passageway and opened a door on the left. Peering inside, she said, "I very much doubt a man used this bedroom. I'll stay in this one."

Joseph followed her into the bedroom and placed the cases at the foot of a queen-size bed. When he looked up from the task, he saw the pretty heiress standing in the middle of the room, gazing around with a look of awe on her face. Everything was in white. Even the antique-style furniture.

He said, "I don't know what you're thinking, but all this stuff looks new to me."

Clearing her throat, she walked over to a long dresser with a scallop-edged mirror. Lying on the glass top was a matching brush and mirror with silver-engraved backs. The set was the fancy sort, like the one his mother kept for sentimental reasons.

Joseph watched her pick up the brush and rub her fingers across the soft bristles. "I think you might be right. Did a woman live here with Mr. Maddox?"

"Not since his wife died. And that's been several years ago."

Tessa shifted her gaze to the bed, which was covered with a fluffy down comforter and pillows edged with lace. "How odd to find a room like this in a widower's house."

"Maybe Ray had all this fixed for you," Joseph suggested.

She looked at him, her lips parted with surprise. "That's a crazy notion. Ray Maddox didn't know me."

"He had some sort of connection to you. And he obviously made plans for you to be here."

The notion appeared to rattle her. She quickly placed the brush back on the dresser top then, bending her head, she fastened her hands around the front edge of the dresser as though she needed to support herself.

As Joseph watched her, he was assaulted with all sorts of urges, the main one being to put his arm around her shoulders and assure her that whatever was bothering her would eventually right itself. But he'd only met her a few minutes ago. Even if she did need comforting, he had no right to get that personal.

"I'm so confused. I'm not sure what to think anymore." With her head still bent, she slanted a look at him. "That's why I have to stay long enough to find answers."

The notion that she might be here for an extended length of time filled Joseph with far too much pleasure. He tried to ignore the sappy reaction as he walked over to a pair of large windows and made a show of inspecting the locks.

"What are you doing?" she asked.

He could feel her walking up behind him and then her lovely scent was floating around him.

"Making sure the locks are secure," he answered.

"I thought you said this was a crime-free area."

He allowed the curtain to fall into place before he turned to her. With only two short steps separating them, he could see little details about her face that he'd missed earlier. Like a faint dimple just to the left corner of her lips and the fine baby hairs tickling her temples. Her skin was so smooth it appeared to have no pores and he wondered how it would feel beneath his finger. Like cream on his tongue, he figured.

"A person can never be too safe," he said. "Have you ever stayed alone before?"

That wasn't actually his business, either. But he told himself it was his job to make sure she was capable of keeping herself safe.

"Not out like this. But I'm not the timid sort."

He wanted to tell her only fools were not afraid but stopped himself. Compared to his thirty years, she was very young. Not to mention determined to stand on her own two feet.

"I can assure you, Ms. Parker, my mother would be more than happy for you to stay with us on Three Rivers. We have plenty of room. And she loves company."

She looked away and Joseph couldn't help but watch the rise and fall of her breasts as she drew in a deep breath and blew it out.

"Thank you for the invitation, Deputy Hollister, but I'll be fine. There's no need for you to be concerned about my safety.

"That's my job."

Like hell, Joseph. As a deputy of Yavapai County,

you don't go around inviting women to stay at the family ranch. You're stepping out of line and you know it.

She said, "You must be a very conscientious lawman."

No. At this very moment, he was being a fool. But Joseph was hoping like heck she wouldn't notice.

"The offer has nothing to do with me being a deputy. I'm just being neighborly."

"Oh."

The one word caused his gaze to land on her lips. As he stared at the moist curves, something fluttered deep in his gut. In his line of work, he met up with all sorts of women, but he'd never met one who'd made him think things or feel things the way this woman did.

Clearing his throat, he fished a card from his shirt pocket and handed it to her. "If you need anything, my number is on there. And if you decide to visit Three Rivers, it's easy to find. When you leave the entrance to your property, turn right and follow the road until you reach a fork. Take a left and you'll see the ranch sign. Someone is always at home."

She folded her fingers around the card and bestowed him a warm smile. "Once I get settled, I might just do that. And thanks for your help."

"Sure. So I…better get going and let you get on with unpacking."

He forced himself to step around her and as he started out of the bedroom, she fell into step beside him.

"I'll show you to the door," she told him.

The polite gesture was hardly necessary, especially when he was far more familiar with the house than she was. But he was hardly going to turn down a bit more of her company.

Damn it, somewhere between Wickenburg and the Bar X something must have happened in the workings of his brain, he decided. He wasn't in the market for a woman. Especially one that would only be around for a few days and then gone.

When they reached the front door, she accompanied him onto the porch and surprised him by offering her hand. Joseph clasped his fingers around hers and marveled at the softness of her skin, the dainty fragility of the small bones.

"It's been a pleasure, Deputy Hollister."

A pleasure? It had been an earthquake for Joseph. As he continued to hold her hand, the tremors were still radiating all the way down to his boots.

"Uh, well…maybe we'll see each other again before you go back to Nevada."

She gently eased her hand from his. "Yes. Maybe."

Well, that was that, he thought. "Goodbye, Ms. Parker."

He left the porch and as he walked out to his vehicle, he resisted the urge to glance back. But when he eventually slid behind the steering wheel, he couldn't help but notice she was still standing where he'd left her.

When he started the engine, she lifted her hand in farewell. The sight filled him with ridiculous pleasure and before he could turn the SUV around and drive away, his mind was already searching for a reason to see her again.

Chapter Two

Joseph had planned to tell his family about Tessa Parker as soon as he arrived home. But he'd hardly gotten a mile away from the Bar X when he'd been called back to work to help deal with a three-vehicle accident on the highway—a result of loose cattle and drivers blinded by the sinking sun.

By the time the cattle had been rounded up and the vehicles cleared away, it had been well after midnight. When he'd finally gotten home, everyone in the house had already gone to bed.

But this morning as Joseph, and most of the family, sat around the dining table eating breakfast, he wasted no time in relaying the news. Starting with Tessa introducing herself and ending with her promise to stay until she found answers.

"Ray left his property to a complete stranger? I can't believe it. He wasn't the fanciful sort. In fact, he was a steadfast rock. That's why he was sheriff of Yavapai County for twenty years. He was a man everyone could depend on. There has to be more to this situation."

The statement came from Maureen Hollister, the matriarch of the family. Tall and slender, with dark brown hair slightly threaded with gray and a complexion wrinkled by years of working in the blazing desert sun, she was a picture of beauty and strength. And Joseph had expected his mother to react to the news in just this way.

He said, "I was shocked when she hauled out a handful of legal documents to prove she wasn't a trespasser."

Maureen pushed her empty plate forward and picked up her coffee cup.

"I'm glad you happened to be going by the Bar X whenever she arrived, Joe," his mother said. "Except for Sam, no one ever goes near the place. If I'd spotted a strange vehicle there, I would've thought someone was trespassing."

For the past five years, since Joel, her husband and the father of their six children, had died suddenly, Maureen had accepted the reins of Three Rivers Ranch with a calm yet fierce determination to continue the legacy of the ranch and the Hollister family name. Now at sixty-one, she showed no signs of slowing down.

Joseph took his eyes off his plate to glance down the long dining table to where his mother sat next to her late husband's chair. Ever since his death, Joel's spot at the head of the table had remained empty. A fact that everyone in the family tried to ignore.

Across from Joseph, his oldest brother, Blake, was frowning thoughtfully.

"I visited Ray in the hospital a day before he died. Unfortunately he was too sedated to talk," Blake commented. "Let's hope he was in his right mind when he made out his will."

Next to Blake, the middle Hollister son, Holt, spoke up. "I stopped by Ray's house about a week before he went into the hospital. He was hooked up to oxygen, but he could still talk. That day he appeared to make perfect sense. He told me Sam had driven him around the ranch earlier that morning. He was telling me how happy he was with the way everything looked."

"Poor man. Seventy was far too young for him to die."

Joseph glanced to his left, where his sister, Vivian, was sitting at his elbow. At thirty-three, with shoulder-length chestnut hair, she was pretty in a wholesome way. It was just too bad her ex-husband hadn't appreciated her, or their daughter.

"Any age is too young, Viv," Joseph told her.

"Yes, but Ray had such a tragic life," she observed. "What with his wife being disabled and bound to a wheelchair all those years. I always thought he deserved so much more."

"Ray loved Dottie," Maureen pointed out. "It broke his heart when she passed away."

Holt, who was also head horse trainer for Three Rivers, reached for a biscuit. As he tore the bread apart, he said, "Ray was a widower for years and never bothered to marry again. That was the sad part."

"Sad!" Joseph blurted in disbelief. "You're a good one to talk, Holt. You've gone through women like a stack of laundered shirts. And you've never bothered to marry any of them!"

Holt frowned as he slathered the piece of biscuit with blackberry jam. "Well, you sure as hell aren't married, either, little brother."

"From the way Joe talked about this Ms. Parker, I'm thinking he's getting the idea on his mind," Vivian teased.

Joseph didn't rise to his sister's bait. He figured if he protested too loudly the whole family would become suspicious about him and the lovely stranger from Nevada. And that was the last thing he needed.

"As a deputy, I'm supposed to take in details," he said flatly.

"From the description you gave us, you certainly took in plenty of details about the woman," Vivian said slyly.

"Except the most important one." Blake spoke up, "Like why she ended up with Ray's place."

Being the eldest son of the family, Blake had always taken his position as manager of the ranch very seriously. But then, Blake had always been the serious-minded one of the Hollister kids. There was rarely any joking going on with him. Whenever he did try to be funny, it was so dry he wound up getting more blank stares than chuckles.

"We'd all like to know that, Blake," Maureen interjected. "But, frankly, it's none of our business. And it would look mighty suspicious if Joseph started interrogating her for information."

"Amen. Thank you, Mom," Joseph told her.

Holt leaned forward, his gaze encompassing everyone at the table. "As far as I see things, it would be damned awful if we sat around and let someone take wrongful possession of our old friend's property."

Joseph tossed down his fork and shoved back his chair. "Holt, you can accuse the woman all you want, but she has legal, binding documents. And, by the way, she lives on the Silver Horn Ranch in Nevada."

His brother's jaw went slack. "Are you joking? You mean the ranch I bought Lorna's Song from?"

"That's right. She volunteered that piece of information on her own. I didn't ask for it."

A sheepish expression stole over Holt's face. "That ought to be easy enough for you to check out. I guess the woman is legitimate."

"I'm certain of it," Joseph said bluntly.

Maureen put down her coffee cup as her gaze traveled over her children. "The way I see it, the questions are about Ray, not Ms. Parker. And we really should keep our noses out of the situation. Still, it would be neighborly of me to stop by and welcome the young woman to the area."

Blake smirked while Vivian gave their mother a clever smile.

Joseph said, "I got the impression Tessa has plenty of questions, too. Maybe you'd be a help to her, Mom."

"I have a Cattlemen's Association meeting in Prescott early this afternoon," Maureen said. "I might stop by the Bar X on my way out."

Joseph rose and walked down to the end of the table to drop a kiss on his mother's cheek. "Thanks, Mom. I'm off to work. Don't look for me until much later tonight. I've got extra duty," he said.

Vivian wailed out a protest. "Again? You worked half the night last night!"

He grinned at her. "A deputy's work is never done, sis."

He left the room with the group calling out their goodbyes amid reminders for him to stay extra safe. A morning ritual that never failed to make him feel loved and wanted.

Inside the kitchen he found Reeva, the family cook, standing at the cabinet, peeling peaches that had come straight from the ranch's own orchard.

Poking his head over the woman's shoulder, he asked, "What's that going to be? Cobbler?"

"No, I'm making preserves." The bone-thin woman with an iron-gray braid hanging down the center of her back turned and poked a finger in the middle of his hard abs. "You don't need cobbler. It'll make you fat."

Chuckling, he said, "Well, I wouldn't have gotten to eat it, anyway. Got to work late tonight, so don't bother saving me any supper, Reeva."

"But Uncle Joe—you said you'd go riding with me this evening! Have you forgotten?"

Joseph glanced across the room to see Hannah, Vivian's ten-year-old daughter, sitting at a small round table with a bowl of cold cereal in front of her. At the moment, she looked crestfallen.

"Hey, Freckles, I thought you were still in bed." He walked over to where she sat and planted a kiss on top of her gold-blond head. "Why are you eating in here? You're too young to be antisocial."

She wrinkled her little nose at him. "Sometimes I don't want to hear all that adult stuff. It's boring."

"And Reeva isn't boring?" He looked over at the cook and winked. "Reeva, I hope I'm as cool as you are when I get to be seventy-one."

Reeva let out a short laugh. "Cool? You'll be using a walking stick."

Grinning, Joseph turned his attention back to Hannah. "Sorry, honey, I have to work this evening. A buddy needed time off. We'll have to ride another evening. Maybe Friday. How's that?"

She tilted her little head to one side as she contemplated his offer. "Okay. But if you cancel again, you're going to be in big trouble," she warned.

"I'm not going to cancel on my best girl," he promised.

"Not unless there's an emergency." Reeva spoke up.

Joseph walked over to a long span of cabinet counter

and picked up a tall thermos. No matter what was going on in the kitchen or with the rest of the family, Reeva always made sure his coffee was ready to go to work with him.

"Let's not mention the word *emergency*." He started toward a door that would take him outside, but before he stepped onto the back porch, Hannah called out.

"'Bye, Uncle Joe. I love you."

"I love you, too, Freckles."

"I don't have freckles!" she wailed at him. "So quit calling me that!"

Laughing, Joseph shut the door behind him, trotted off the wide-planked porch and out the back gate to where his vehicle was parked on the graveled driveway.

The summer sun was just peeping over the rise of rocky hills on the eastern side of the ranch. The pale light filtered through the giant cottonwoods standing guard at both ends of the three-story, wooden house. The spreading limbs created flickering yellow patches on the hard-packed ground, which stretched from the yard fence to the main barn area.

Already, Joseph could hear the ranch hands calling to each other, the broodmares neighing for breakfast, and a pen of weaning calves bawling for their mommas. A hundred feet to the right of the main cattle barn, a big bunkhouse built of chinked logs emanated the scent of frying bacon.

Not one of the ten ranch hands who worked for Three Rivers would sit down to eat until every animal in the ranch yard had been fed and watered. It was a schedule adhered to ever since the original Hollisters had built the ranch back in 1847.

If Joseph took the time to walk out to the holding pens, he'd find Matthew Waggoner, the ranch foreman, making sure the using horses were already fed, watered and saddled for the day's work.

As for Chandler, the second eldest son of the Hollister bunch, he was rarely seen at the breakfast table or hardly ever attended the evening meal. He started his days long before dawn and ended them well after dark, tending to his patients at Hollister Animal Clinic located on the outskirts of Wickenburg. Joseph admired his brother's dedication, but in his opinion, Chandler gave far too much of himself to the clinic and the ranch.

Still, none of the Hollister brothers had given as much to Three Rivers as their father, Joel. He'd given his life. In the end, the authorities had ruled his death an accident, but Joseph would never accept the decision. If he had to search for the rest of his life, he would eventually find out who'd killed his father.

A few miles away, on the Bar X, Tessa sat at the bay window in the kitchen with a cell phone jammed to her ear. Between sips of early morning coffee, she tried to answer Lilly Calhoun's rapid-fire questions.

"The house? Oh, Lilly, the house is just beautiful and charming! And the views from the front and back are stupendous! There are all kinds of magnificent rock formations and Joshua trees are everywhere. Out on the range, the sage is blooming and the yard around the house is full of roses and irises."

"Sounds like a paradise," Lilly replied. "And I've never heard you so excited. I'm happy for you, Tessa. Really happy. So what about the rest of the ranch?"

Lifting the mug to her lips, Tessa's gaze followed the sloping landscape until it reached a big white barn and maze of connecting holding pens. Yesterday evening before dark, she'd explored the big building and discovered a room full of tack and a pair of yellow tabby cats. Both had shied away from her efforts to befriend them.

"From what Deputy Hollister told me, Mr. Maddox's failing health forced him to sell all the livestock. It's rather sad seeing the barn area without any horses or cattle around."

There was a long pause before Lilly asked, "Who is Deputy Hollister? I thought you'd settled all the legal stuff before you left for Arizona."

A flush heated Tessa's face. Not for anything would she admit to Lilly that she'd spent half the night thinking of the handsome deputy and wondering if she'd ever see him again.

"The deputy just happens to be a neighbor," she quickly explained. "He stopped by yesterday, right after I arrived—uh, just to say hello." She wasn't about to add that he'd carried in her bags and stuck around to give her a tour of the house.

"That's good. Orin will be glad to hear you have a trustworthy neighbor. I don't have to tell you he's like a father bear. By the way, did you know he's already started searching for someone to take your job as the Silver Horn housekeeper?"

Tessa had been thirteen when she'd been orphaned and gone to live with the Calhouns. At first, the elaborate, three-story ranch house had been overwhelming to her. Especially when she'd been accustomed to living with her mother in a very modest apartment in Carson City. But in no time at all she'd come to love the isolated country life and the wealthy family who'd taken her in like one of their own. And as soon as she'd grown old enough, she'd gone to work as a housekeeper for the family. Not because they'd expected her to repay them, but because she'd wanted to give back to them as best she could.

"He told me before I left. He believes I won't be returning to the Silver Horn anytime soon."

"That's not his reason. Orin understands that when you come back to Nevada, you'll be putting your college degree to use and finding a real job. Not working for us."

Tessa's gaze swept over the spacious kitchen with its varnished pine cabinets and stainless-steel appliances. To her surprise, she'd already found a huge supply of canned and packaged food in the cupboards and even some fresh things in the refrigerator. She supposed the sheriff's old ranch hand had laid in the supplies for her arrival. It was all so odd, yet in a way, completely comforting.

"I have so much here to absorb. I can't think about searching for a job right now, Lilly. Not until I learn about Sheriff Maddox and his connection to me."

"Perhaps your deputy neighbor can help you with that," Lilly suggested. "Could be he worked for the man."

Regarding Ray Maddox, Tessa figured Joseph Hollister could be a wealth of information. But would it be smart of her to approach the man for any reason? He already had her thinking things that brought a fiery blush to her face. She didn't want to feed this instant infatuation she'd developed for the sexy lawman.

Suddenly the back of Tessa's eyes were stinging with inexplicable tears. "Lilly, this is still so surreal and hard to explain. Something—some strange connection came over me whenever I walked into the house. It felt like I was supposed to be here. Now I'm so emotional I'm going around dabbing a tissue to my eyes."

"Well, it's not every day that a woman becomes an heiress—completely out of the blue. You have every right to be emotional. I'd be a blubbering idiot."

Trying to swallow the lump in her throat, she slowly stood. "I just need a few days to digest everything, Lilly."

"Uh, just in case you're interested, Rafe fired Thad yesterday. He won't be back."

The mere mention of the young man's name left Tessa cold. Not more than three months ago, Rafe had hired the guy to work on the fence-mending crew. The moment he'd spotted Tessa, he'd come on to her like a house on fire. At first she'd liked his boyish grin and playful teasing. She'd even gone on a few dates with him. But he'd quickly begun to expect more from her than she'd been willing to give. When she'd abruptly ended all connection with him, he'd retaliated by telling the other ranch hands he'd never had any serious intentions toward her. That she was only a cheap housemaid.

"Rafe needn't have done that for my benefit," Tessa said flatly. "Thad needed some lessons in being a gentleman, but he could still build fences."

Lilly snorted. "The only thing Thad wanted to work was his mouth. I say good riddance."

The ugly incident with Thad had made Tessa wonder how other people viewed her. When she'd told Joseph Hollister she lived at the Silver Horn, she'd not mentioned she'd worked there as a housekeeper. Was the deputy the type of man who'd look down on her for holding a menial job?

Forget it, Tessa. Joseph might be a super-nice guy. But you don't have any business wasting your thoughts on him. Your home is in Nevada. You're here to look over this property and make a reasonable decision about what to do with it. Not to strike up a romance with a lawman you met less than twenty-four hours ago.

Tessa's thoughts were suddenly interrupted with Lilly expressing the need to end the call.

"Sorry, Tessa, I have to hang up. I hear Austin screaming at his sister."

With their conversation over, Tessa went to the bedroom to change out of her pajamas. As she tossed a pair of jeans onto the bed, she gazed around the beautiful white room. Just being in it made her feel like a princess.

Deputy Hollister had seemed to think the late sheriff had actually prepared this room just for her. Most folks would find that eerie, Tessa thought, but strangely enough, it made her feel wanted. And that was the best gift the late sheriff could've given her.

A few minutes later Tessa was in the barn, trying to lure the cats from their hiding place, when she heard a vehicle drive up somewhere in the ranch yard.

Thinking it might be Deputy Hollister stopping by, she put down the pan of food and hurried out of the big barn. But instead of seeing the Yavapai County lawman's vehicle, she spotted a red-and-white Ford truck with a crunched passenger door.

Pausing in her tracks, she watched an older man with a crumpled straw hat and a short, grizzled beard climb from the vehicle. His worn jeans were stuffed into a pair of tall, yellow cowboy boots while a faded red shirt with long sleeves was buttoned tightly at his throat.

As he moved toward her, Tessa noticed his gait was a bit uneven. Whether the slight limp was because of his leg or some other problem, she could hardly say. In any case, she decided this had to be Ray's ranch hand.

She walked across the hard-packed earth to greet him. "Hello. I'm Tessa Parker. Are you Mr. Lemans?"

"Yes, ma'am. I'm Samuel Lemans—just Sam to you. I work for Ray." Grimacing, he shook his head. "Excuse me, ma'am. I said that wrong. I *did* work for Ray."

Tessa extended her hand to him and as he gave it a firm shake, she noticed his palm was as tough as rawhide and his face as crinkled as dry leather. From what she could see beneath the brim of the mangled hat, his thick hair was a mix of black and gray and his eyes were the color of a black bean. Yet in spite of his hard-weathered appearance, the gentleness in his gaze put her instantly at ease.

"I met Deputy Hollister yesterday and he mentioned you," she explained. "I want to thank you, Sam, for keeping everything looking so beautiful."

"Glad to do it. I'll keep on taking care of things until you don't need me anymore. That was Ray's wishes. And I aim to see them carried out."

"Well, I'll see that you get paid," Tessa assured him. "Mr. Maddox left me a sizable sum."

He scowled. "I don't want pay, Ms. Parker. Ray has already taken care of that. You don't worry about a thing. If you need me, I'll be here. If you don't, that's okay, too."

Tessa was totally bewildered. This man and his late boss were making things so easy for her to stay here. Had that been another of Ray's wishes? To make her want a permanent home on the Bar X?

"I don't know what to say, Sam. This is hard for me to understand." She passed a hand over her damp brow then made a sweeping gesture with her arm. "I don't suppose you can tell me why Ray—uh, Mr. Maddox—left me this ranch?"

He lifted the crumpled straw hat and scratched the top of his head. "I expected you to ask me and I wish I could give you an answer. Ray never talked to me about such things. The only thing he told me was that, after he died, a young lady would be getting this property and his money. I gave him my promise to keep on working around the place—that's how Sheriff Ray wanted it."

Disappointment stung Tessa. Evidently this man and Ray Maddox had been more than boss/employee. If Ray hadn't given Sam any sort of explanation about her and the will, it was doubtful he'd discussed the matter with anyone else.

"He didn't say anything about me?" She persisted.

"Ray didn't talk about his private life. And I didn't pry. If he'd wanted me to know more, he would've told me. Anyway, Sheriff Ray always did the right thing. I expect he had good reason to do this for you."

Sam's lack of information hadn't helped to explain anything. But she wasn't going to let it discourage her. Somewhere, someone had answers and she fully intended to find them.

Hiding her disappointment behind a warm smile, she said, "Someday I'll find his reason. For now I'm going to enjoy being here."

With a wistful look in his eyes, he glanced over her shoulder to the empty holding pens. No doubt there had been a time when the dusty corrals would've been filled with weanling calves or cows to be tagged and doctored. Now the ghostly silence of the working area was a sad reminder of happier days.

"You going to hang around until the place sells?" he asked.

Though his question was quite reasonable, the weight of it staggered her. Already the idea of letting this place go was very unsettling. On the other hand, she had to make smart choices for her future. And her life was back in Nevada. Strange, how she had to keep reminding herself of that fact.

"I—I haven't made any definite decisions yet, Sam. Except that I'm not going to be in any hurry about making plans. So I would be grateful to you if you'd come by and help me see after things."

"Sure thing. I'll be around first thing every morning."

For the next half hour Sam helped her make friends with the cats and gave her a detailed tour of the barn and ranch yard. Afterward, she invited him to a cup of coffee on the backyard patio.

Although he wasn't exactly a big talker, she was enjoying his company. And listening to him reminisce about Ray and the Bar X might possibly help her unravel the secrecy surrounding the will.

"When the ranch was going full swing, were you the only hand working for him?" she asked.

Reaching for his mug, Sam shook his head. "During the slow seasons I handled everything by myself. When calving season or roundups were going on, two other guys came in to help. See, the Bar X is small compared to some of the neighboring ranches. But acre for acre, it's a damned good one. All it needs to get going again is a herd of mama cows and a few horses."

Tessa was about to ask if he'd like to see the ranch back in production, but a woman's voice suddenly called out in the vicinity of the front yard.

The unexpected interruption quickly pushed Tessa to her feet. "Excuse me, Sam. I'll go see who that might be."

Just as Tessa started off the patio, a tall, dark-haired woman somewhere in her early sixties appeared around the corner of the house.

"Hello, there," she said cheerily. "Sorry about all the hollering. I knocked on the door but didn't get an answer. I—" Suddenly spotting Sam, she paused and then called to him. "Sam, you rusty old codger! Where have you been hiding yourself?"

Sam scraped back his chair and came to stand next to Tessa.

"Good to see you, Maureen." He greeted her with a tip of his hat.

He glanced at Tessa before gesturing to their unexpected visitor, who was dressed in a gray, double-breasted dress with a rust-red silk scarf knotted at her neck and matching red high heels on her feet.

"Tessa, this is Maureen Hollister." He introduced the two women. "She's your neighbor and owner of the Three Rivers Ranch."

Still smiling, the woman extended her hand to Tessa. "Nice to meet you, Tessa," she said while pumping her hand in a hearty shake. "And don't worry, I can only stay for a minute. I'm on my way to Prescott. My son, Joe, told me you'd arrived, so I just wanted to stop by and welcome you to the area."

"Joe? You mean Deputy Hollister?" Tessa asked.

Maureen's smile deepened. "Sorry. All his family calls him Joe," she explained, then shot a pointed look to Sam. "I hope you've been helping this young lady get settled in."

Scowling, Sam said, "Maureen, I don't need to be questioned. You know I'll see to my duties."

Maureen laughed and then said to Tessa, "He's a touchy old cuss. But he won't bite. I doubt he has enough teeth left to leave any damage, anyhow."

Sam didn't make a retort. Instead he purposely put a grin on his face to reveal he still possessed a full set of teeth.

After another laugh, Maureen went on. "If there's anything at all that you need while you're here, Tessa, just call on us. We like to help our neighbors."

So this was Deputy Hollister's mother. Tessa could only imagine what he'd told this woman about their meeting yesterday. That she'd seemed overly emotional and out of her element? He certainly wouldn't have been lying, she thought dismally.

"Thank you, Mrs. Hollister. It's very kind of you to offer. Would you like to join us in a cup of coffee?"

Maureen promptly waved away the invitation. "I'd love to sit and talk for hours. But I can't be late for my meeting."

"I understand. I hope you can come by another time," Tessa suggested.

"Oh, she'll be by." Sam spoke up in a dry voice. "She keeps the road hot. All you see when Maureen drives by is the blur of a blue truck and a cloud of dust. Roadrunners aren't even safe when she's around."

Instead of being offended, Maureen laughed heartily. "Sam, one of these mornings you're going to wake up and the gate to your goat pen is going to be standing wide open. Then we'll see how fast you go."

The man chuckled and Tessa could see he clearly enjoyed teasing Maureen. Which meant the two must have known each other many years for them to exchange this sort of banter.

"Okay, I'm off," she said, "but before I go, I'd like to ask you to join us for dinner tomorrow night, Tessa. We'll be eating around seven, but come sooner. We'll have a drink and a nice talk. And you come, too, Sam. The kids would all love to see you."

He said, "I don't—"

Before he could decline the invitation, Tessa turned and clasped his crusty hand between her two. "Oh, please, Sam. It would be extra special for me if you'd come."

Maureen must have sensed Tessa had already developed an emotional connection to the old ranch hand because she suddenly spoke up in a persuasive voice.

"You don't have to dress up, Sam. You can come just as you are. And Reeva is cooking brisket, so you don't have to worry about being fed bean sprouts."

"Well, I guess I can't fight two women at the same time," he said.

"Great!" Maureen said with a happy smile. "So I'll see you two tomorrow tonight."

As Maureen hurried away, Tessa tugged Sam back over to the table.

"Come on," she urged, "let's finish our coffee."

"I didn't plan to stay this long," he protested. "I really need to be going, too."

"A few more minutes won't hurt," Tessa argued. "Anyway, there's still lots of coffee left in the thermos. I don't want it to go to waste."

"You're hard to say no to, Tessa." Grinning, he sat back down and motioned to his cup. "Okay. Fill it up again."

Tessa returned to her seat and poured his coffee. "Thanks, Sam. I realize I'm being a nuisance. But—"

"Now that Maureen has stopped by, you want me to tell you about the Hollisters," he finished.

The sly look in his narrow eyes had Tessa smiling sheepishly. "I don't want you to gossip, Sam. But I'm a stranger around here. It would be helpful to know a little about the Hollister family before I have dinner with them."

He picked up his coffee cup. "Okay. Three Rivers is one of the biggest ranches in Arizona and the family has plenty of money. Maureen and her husband, Joel, had six kids together. Four boys and two girls. The last I heard all the kids were still living at home. Joe, the one you met yesterday, is second from the youngest."

Joe. He might be just plain Joe to everyone else, but to her he would always be Joseph, she thought. "He seemed like a very intense young man."

Sam sipped his coffee and stared off at the jagged rock cliffs in the distance. "He has reason to be that way."

The subtle insinuation had Tessa curiously eyeing the old cowboy. "Why do you say that?"

He shook his head. "You need to let Joe tell you that."

Joseph Hollister would hardly be sharing personal facts about himself with her. And that was probably a good thing, Tessa decided. The less she knew about him, the less she'd have to forget once she was back in Nevada.

But when will that be, Tessa? You're telling yourself you're going to remain here on the Bar X until you learn the reason for your inheritance. But aren't you really more interested in getting to know Joseph?

Not wanting to answer the question sounding off in her head, Tessa grabbed up her coffee cup and promised herself she wasn't going to give the sexy deputy another thought. At least, not until tomorrow night and she stepped into the Hollister home.

Chapter Three

The next day Tessa grappled with the urge to drive into Wickenburg and shop for something special to wear to Three Rivers Ranch. Yet each time she came close to grabbing her handbag and truck keys, she talked herself out of the notion. It was foolish of her to try to look extra special for Joseph Hollister, or any of his family, she'd argued with herself.

Now, as she stared at her image in the dresser mirror, she wished she'd made the trip into town. The black-and-white-patterned sheath was neat, but it was hardly glamourous, and the strappy black sandals on her feet looked like she was going to a picnic in the park instead of to dinner with a prominent family.

Sighing, she picked up the silver-backed brush and tugged it through her straight hair. Since it was almost time for Sam to pick her up, it was too late to do anything about her lackluster appearance.

Minutes later, as Sam helped her into the cab of his old truck, Tessa said, "Thank you again, Sam, for going to this dinner with me. I hope you're not dreading the evening."

As he drove the truck down the dusty dirt road, a slight grin cracked the wrinkles on his face. "It's been a long, long time since I carried a gal to dinner. I'm not dreading it."

Tessa smiled back at him then turned her gaze out the passenger window. As the pickup headed away from the Bar X and on toward Three Rivers, the land opened up into wide valleys dotted with rocks, standpipe, blooming yucca and prickly pear. The grass that covered the lower slopes was short but very green.

When the simple barbed-wire fence running next to the road suddenly changed to one of painted white pipe, Tessa asked, "Are we seeing Three Rivers land now?"

"That's right. Just a little stretch of it butts up to the Bar X. Most of Three Rivers stretches on east of here—toward the old ghost mines around Constellation and north toward Congress."

She doubted Three Rivers would come close to covering as much land as that of the Silver Horn, but it was clearly a prominent ranch. Not that the size, or the wealth of the Hollisters, mattered to her. She'd already decided that even if Joseph wasn't already attached to a woman, he was out of her league.

Minutes later they reached a fork in the road and Sam steered the truck to the left where they passed beneath a simple wooden plank burned with a 3R brand. Another two miles passed when they topped a rocky rise and the Hollister homestead spread majestically across a wide, desert valley.

As they drew closer, Tessa could see a large, three-story house with wooden-lapped siding painted white and trimmed with black. The structure was surrounded by massive cottonwoods and smaller mesquite trees. A hundred yards or more to the right of the house was an enormous work yard with several large barns, sheds and holding pens, all of which were painted white.

"Here we are," Sam said as he pulled the old truck to a stop in a driveway that curved along the front of the house. "Quite a spread, wouldn't you say?"

"It's beautiful," she agreed, then added, "but I happen to think the Bar X is beautiful, too."

Sam chuckled. "Sheriff Ray is smiling right now."

Even after they'd departed the truck and walked onto the ground-level porch running the length of the big house, Tessa was still thinking about Sam's comment. If not for Ray Maddox, Tessa would never have been in this part of Arizona, much less be meeting these people. That fact multiplied her questions about the late sheriff.

At the wide door, Sam ignored the brass knocker and rapped his knuckles against the white wood.

After a brief wait, a young woman with a dark blond ponytail and a red, bib apron tied over her shirt and jeans answered the door.

"Good evening." Pulling the door wide, she gestured for them to enter. "Please, come in. Mrs. Hollister and the others are out back having drinks. I'll show you the way."

Tessa and Sam followed her into a short entryway and through a spacious living room with high ceilings and sand-colored tongue-and-groove walls. A mix of leather and cloth furniture was the kind that invited a person to take a seat, while the cowhide rugs scattered over the oak parquet were a reminder that the ranch had been built on cattle.

At the back of the room, the maid opened a pair of

French doors and gestured for them to precede her onto a large brick patio.

"Mrs. Hollister is there by the fire pit," the maid said. "And if you two would like anything to drink that isn't out here, just let me know."

Tessa thanked the woman then focused her full attention on the group of people sitting in lawn chairs and standing around. Since the men had their backs to her, it was impossible to tell if Joseph was among the group, but the idea was revving her heart to a sickening speed.

Sam must have picked up on her nervousness. With his head bent slightly toward hers, he said in a low voice, "Don't worry. These folks won't eat you."

The two of them had hardly taken two steps before Maureen spotted their arrival and hurried over to greet them.

"Tessa, welcome. I'm so glad you could come." Instead of shaking Tessa's hand, the woman gave her a brief hug and then turned and pecked a kiss on the old cowboy's cheek. "And, Sam, if you hadn't showed up, I was going to come fetch you here myself. Come on over, you two. I want Tessa to meet everyone."

As they approached the group, Tessa saw five men rise from their chairs. Except for one, all had varying shades of dark hair and all were dressed in jeans and Western shirts. Even so, there was no mistaking Joseph. He was standing near one of the smooth cedar posts that supported the overhanging roof.

Her gaze briefly hesitated on his face before she forced it to move on to the remaining people gathered on the shaded patio.

"Sam is an old friend, so he doesn't need any introductions," Maureen said, then with a hand on Tessa's arm, drew her forward. "Tessa, this is my family."

"Wrong, Mom. Matthew isn't family." One of the dark-haired men spoke up in a joking voice. "He just thinks he is."

Laughing, Maureen pointed out a tall, blond man at the back of the group. "That's Matthew Waggoner. He's the Three River foreman. A very good one, I might add. And since he's been around here for quite a few years, we consider him a part of the family."

The man called Matthew lifted a hand in acknowledgment and Tessa smiled in return.

"Now, over here to your left—the guy with the sour look on his face—is Blake. He's my oldest son and manager of the ranch. Next to him is Holt. He's a middle kid and the opposite of Blake. He's always smiling."

"That's because he's been bucked off so many horses he doesn't know any better."

This came from a very pretty woman sitting on the edge of a redwood lounger. Her shoulder-length hair was a shiny chestnut color and her long, shapely legs were showcased in a pair of tight jeans.

Everyone laughed, including Holt.

"Thanks, sis," he told her. "I'll remember you at Christmas."

"Holt is the ranch's horse trainer," Maureen explained to Tessa. "And he has suffered a few buck-offs, but I don't think the falls have addled him yet."

Maureen gestured to the young woman on the lounger. "This is my oldest daughter, Vivian. She's works as a park ranger at Lake Pleasant."

"Hi, Tessa," Vivian replied with a warm smile.

Tessa returned her greeting before Maureen finished the last two introductions.

"That's Chandler with the yellow kerchief around his

neck. He's the doctor of the bunch. He has a veterinary clinic just outside of Wickenburg."

The stoutly built man with coal-black hair and startling blue eyes lifted a hand in greeting. Though Tessa gave him a nod of acknowledgment, every cell in her body was already buzzing as she turned her attention to Joseph. From the moment she'd walked up to the group, she'd been fighting the urge to stare at him. Now she had a reason to let her eyes rest on his familiar face.

"And the very last one standing by the post is Joseph—Joe to all of us. But, of course, from what he tells us, you two have already met."

He looked different out of uniform, Tessa decided. The sleeves of his olive-green shirt were rolled back on his forearms and instead of a gun belt and weapon, a brown leather belt edged with buck stitching was threaded through the loops of his blue jeans. This evening he didn't look like a deputy. He looked like a rancher. A very sexy one, at that.

"That's right. Joseph was kind enough to help me with all my luggage. Hello again," she said to him then wondered if her voice sounded as husky to those around her as it did to her. Oh, Lord, she had to control herself. It would be worse than embarrassing if any of them figured out she'd come down with an instant crush on him.

With a slight grin he said, "Hello, Tessa. How's the Bar X?"

"It's lovely. Especially with Sam to help me." She reached for the old cowboy's hand. "He's been showing me around the place."

"That's good." Holt spoke up. "Just don't believe any of Sam's stories. He's good at telling whoppers."

Vivian turned a pointed look on her brother. "Remember, you're addled, Holt. So Tessa shouldn't believe you, either."

Laughing now, Holt went over to his sister and gently tugged her hair in retaliation.

Shaking her head, Maureen said to Tessa, "Overlook them, please. Some of my children have chosen not to grow up. Now, what would you two like to drink? I think Sam probably wants whiskey. And you, Tessa?"

"Oh. A soft drink—anything is fine."

"You need something stronger than a soft drink to put up with us," Vivian told her. "Try the peach-flavored wine. It's good."

"And, as a doctor, I can promise, Tessa, if it makes you act like a fool, you won't care in the least," Chandler joked.

Tessa laughed softly. "I can do that without the aid of alcohol."

Maureen left her side to go fetch the drinks at a portable bar set up on the far side of the patio. Once the woman moved away, the entire group of Hollisters, plus their foreman, gathered around to shake Tessa's hand and extend their welcomes.

After Maureen had served her the wine and the group began to return to their chairs, Joseph wrapped a hand around her bare arm.

"Come with me, Tessa, and I'll show you our new family additions."

She glanced around to Sam, only to find that Holt and Chandler had already hauled the older man to the other side of the patio.

"It doesn't look as though Sam will miss me," she said.

"Sam likes to talk shop with the guys. That is, whenever we can get him here for a visit. All of us were surprised when Mom told us he'd be coming with you tonight. If you haven't yet guessed, Sam mostly keeps to himself—especially since Ray died."

He guided her off the patio and, once they rounded the corner of the house, he urged her across a small patch of ground toward a big doghouse sitting near the trunk of a cottonwood.

As they strolled along, she replied, "It's odd that you describe Sam as a bit of a loner. He's talkative with me. Except that he doesn't gossip. I think it's a rule he abides by."

Joseph smiled at her. "That's a rule we should all abide by. As for Sam being talkative, I think he's a bit smitten with you."

She laughed. "He's old enough to be my father. Maybe even my grandfather."

"That's what I mean. He sees you as the family he never had."

The sad information caused her to glance at him. "Oh. So, Sam's always been a bachelor?"

"As far as we know. Ray might've known about Sam's young years, but no one else around here does. He came to Arizona from Texas about fifty years ago. As long as I can remember, he's been Ray's right-hand man. It's no wonder Sam is lost without him."

She felt a pang of regret. Not only for Sam, but also for herself. More than anything, she wished she could've known the man who'd wanted to give her so much. "Sam is a wise man. He understands life goes on."

He let out a long breath. "Yes, life goes on."

He'd barely gotten the words out when a brown-and-white dog with long hair emerged from the doghouse. Right behind her were three little pups, the spitting image of their mother.

"Oh, how precious!" Tessa exclaimed. "Are they collies?"

Joseph squatted on his heels and gathered the mother dog in the circle of his arms. "No. Sally is an Australian shepherd. She can single-handedly bunch up a herd of cattle. But she's off work duty now."

"Maternity leave," she said, smiling at the lovely little family. "How old are the pups?"

"Four weeks. Would you like to hold one?"

"Sure! But what about Sally? She's looking at me like she's not sure whether I'm friend or foe."

Joseph chuckled. "She'll be fine as long as I'm here."

He picked up one of the pups and handed it to her.

Tessa immediately cuddled the wiggly ball of fur to her breasts and stroked a finger over its head.

"I could play with you all day, little guy," she crooned to the baby then looked at Joseph, who appeared to be watching her as closely as Sally. "Will the babies eventually be trained to herd cattle?"

"Yes. Chandler trains the dogs. He has the extra patience it takes for the job."

She gave the puppy's head a few more loving strokes before placing it back on the ground. Almost immediately, the mother nosed it into the safety of the doghouse.

"Lawmen have to deal with all types of people and situations. I'm sure that takes a load of patience, too." She straightened to her full height to see he was continuing to watch her closely. The fact made her acutely aware of the rapid beat of her heart and the strange wave of heat washing from the pit of her stomach all the way up to her throat.

He said, "I try. If I get frustrated, I do my best to hide it."

"I'd have to take acting lessons to do that. I'm not very

good at hiding my feelings," she confessed while hoping her thoughts about him weren't written on her face.

Walking over to the yard fence, she looked out at a portion of the ranch yard. At the moment it was a quiet scene with only a small herd of horses milling around in a large catch pen.

When Joseph joined her, she cast a curious glance at him. "Are none of your siblings married?" she asked.

He shook his head. "No. The only one of us who's ever been married is Vivian. But that ended a long time ago. She has a ten-year-old daughter, Hannah, from that marriage."

"Oh. Is her daughter not here tonight?"

"No. Hannah's staying overnight with a little friend in Wickenburg. Our younger sister, Camille, isn't here, either. She's gone down to live on Red Bluff. That's our other property near Dragoon."

"Is Red Bluff another ranch? Or just a summer house?" she asked then quickly apologized. "I'm sorry, Joseph. I'm being nosy."

"I don't think you're being nosy. You've just met us Hollisters. If you don't ask questions, you won't know what I'm talking about," he acknowledged. "Red Bluff is another ranch down in Cochise County. It's about half the size of Three Rivers, but very productive. In the winter we move some of our cow/calf pairs down there. The weather is warmer and the grazing is better."

"I see. So you have another crew working down there?"

"Usually about five hands stay on Red Bluff to see after things during the summer months. In winter we send extra hands."

"Your sister likes living down there? Away from all of you?"

His lips twisted to a disapproving slant. "Camille needed some time away from us and—other things. Sort of emotional healing, you'd say."

Realizing her palms were sweaty, she wiped them down the sides of her hips. "Oh. I didn't mean to pry. Sorry again, Joseph. I'll quit asking questions. It's your turn, anyway. You can ask me something personal—if you like," she added with a tentative smile.

Turning to face her, he casually leaned his shoulder against a fence post. "Okay. Why hasn't some man already put a ring on your finger?"

That was hardly the question she'd expected from him and, for a moment, she was at a loss for words. Finally she said, "I'm only twenty-four. I'm not in any hurry to be looking for a husband."

His brown gaze swept furtively over her face then all the way to her feet and back again. "I don't believe age has anything to do with it. Or that a person can go purposely looking for a spouse. It either happens—or it doesn't."

So far, it hadn't happened for Tessa. Oh, she'd had suitors and a few of them she'd dated more than once. Including Thad, who had turned out to be a jerk in the first degree. But nothing had clicked for her with any of those men. Sometimes she wondered if she was expecting too much from love. Maybe the euphoria she believed she would experience when she met the right man was all just a fairy tale.

Pushing that glum thought aside, she said, "In other words, you think you'll just run into some woman on the sidewalk and fate will do the rest. That's not very romantic."

His response to that was a husky chuckle that shivered over Tessa's skin like a caressing finger.

"No one ever accused me of being a romantic guy, Tessa."

She was trying to come up with some sort of sensible reply when Vivian suddenly appeared from the corner of the house.

"Hey, c'mon, you two. Dinner is ready."

Joseph waved an acknowledgment to his sister then turned and wrapped a hand around Tessa's upper arm. As he urged her forward, she tried not to think about the heat spreading from his fingers and into her flesh, or the closeness of his strong body as they walked across the lawn.

"I hope you're hungry," he said. "Reeva's a great cook and she goes all-out when company is coming."

"I'm looking forward to it," she told him, then suddenly found herself wondering all over again if Orin had been right about her being too young and inexperienced for this trip. Because right now Joseph was making her feel as giddy as a high-school girl on her first date. At this rate, her heart was going to take a big hit before she headed home to the Silver Horn.

The dining room in the big ranch house was furnished with a long oak table and matching chairs with seats covered in cowhides of various shades of browns, black and white. Along one wall stood a carved China hutch and matching buffet table, while the opposite wall consisted of long, paned windows that looked out at the ranch yard and a distant ridge of desert mountains.

Vases filled with a mix of fresh zinnias, marigolds and cornflowers sat at intervals in the center of the table, along with tall yellow candles that were already lit and flickering over the beautiful place settings.

The sight was reminiscent of the dinners given by the

Calhoun family on the Silver Horn. Only there, Tessa would've been helping to serve the meal rather than sitting down to enjoy it.

"Come this way, Tessa," Joseph offered by way of invitation. "You can sit by me—if you'd like."

"That would be nice," she told him.

Joseph pulled out one of the heavy chairs and helped her into it while, near the end of the table, Maureen snatched a hold on Sam's arm and directed him to the chair next to hers. "Don't try to give me the slip, Sam. You're going to be my company for dinner," she told the old cowboy.

"Don't badger Sam, Mother." Chandler spoke up. "You'll have him wanting to eat in the kitchen with Reeva."

"Reeva doesn't know how to appreciate a good man like I do," Maureen joked.

Everyone around the table laughed, except for Tessa. It was just dawning on her that she'd not met Maureen's husband and the father of this group of children.

She glanced curiously from the empty spot at the end of the table and over to Joseph. Where was Joel Hollister? she wondered. Had he and Maureen divorced? Or was he simply away somewhere on a business trip? She wanted to ask Joseph, but now wasn't the right time or place. Especially when the young woman who'd answered the door suddenly entered the room pushing a cart laden with food.

During the delicious meal, the conversation around the table never lagged. Everything from ranching to the latest world events was discussed. Eventually the subject of Ray Maddox was brought up and though Tessa learned more about the man's steadfast character through the stories that were told, no one seemed to know the connection between Tessa and the late sheriff.

The disappointment she was feeling over the matter must have been noticeably apparent on her face because once the meal was over and everyone departed the dining room, Joseph pulled her aside.

"Tessa, is something wrong? You look crestfallen. Did some of us say something that hurt you?"

Did her feelings really matter to him or was he simply being polite to a family dinner guest?

Telling herself it didn't matter, she said, "Not at all. Your whole family is so nice and likable, Joseph. And dinner was scrumptious. I guess..." She paused and tried to give him a smile. "I was thinking—hoping—that your mother or one of your siblings might be able to give me some sort of answers about Mr. Maddox. But I should've known better. If Sam can't tell me anything, then it's doubtful that anyone can."

"You've just arrived, Tessa. You've not yet had time to find the answers you're looking for." He reached for her hand. "Come on, let's take a walk. Would you care to see some of the ranch yard? We can always have after-dinner coffee when we get back."

The idea that Joseph was making an effort to lift her spirits made her feel more than special and, before she knew what she was doing, she was smiling and squeezing his hand.

"I'd love to see the ranch yard. Especially the horses."

"Great." He gestured toward a door at the end of the hallway. "No need to let the others know. Let's slip out this way."

Outside, darkness had settled in, but several yard lamps illuminated the area enough for them to walk comfortably toward the barn. With the disappearance of the sun, the temperature had cooled considerably and now the dry desert breeze ruffled her hair and slipped over the bare skin of her arms and legs.

The change in temperature must have caused her to shiver. Suddenly his arm was around her back, pulling her closer to his side.

"It's getting cooler," he said. "I should've gotten you one of Mom's wraps."

"I'll be fine." Especially when the casual brush of his hip against hers was sending all kinds of electrical heat waves through her body. "The air is refreshing, actually. And it smells like..."

She paused, trying to find the right word, and he finished for her.

"Horse manure?"

Laughing, she said, "No. Like sage and roses and evergreens. It's an odd mix, but wonderful."

"I never noticed," he admitted.

She gestured toward the barn area. "Everything looks so well-kept. You must be very proud of this place."

"I am. We all are. The history is what I'm most proud of. Three Rivers has been in existence since 1847. Generations of Hollisters have put their blood, sweat and tears into this ranch. And it's still going strong."

By now they'd reached the corral where the horses were penned. Tessa peered through the opening of the boards to gaze at the animals munching alfalfa from a hay ring.

"You have some good-looking horseflesh," she commented.

"Thanks. Do you ride?"

"Sure. I love to ride. In fact, you wouldn't consider selling me a couple of horses, would you?"

"What for?" he asked.

"I'd like to explore the rougher areas of the Bar X and I need a horse for that," she explained.

"Then why buy two?"

She turned a comical look on him. "Are you sure you're a rancher? You should know horses are a herd animal. A horse is unhappy when he's alone."

One corner of his mouth tilted into a suggestive grin. "Like people?"

"Some people." Her voice sounded oddly hoarse, like she'd just woken from a deep sleep. What was the matter with her, anyway? She'd been around plenty of hunky cowboys before. The Silver Horn was full of them.

But there's something special about this one, Tessa. Something that touched you the moment you laid eyes on him.

"I'll talk to Holt about lending you a pair of horses. No need for you to buy them if you're only going to be here for a short while."

She wasn't ready to say whether her time here in Arizona was going to be short or long. For now she was simply going to learn all about her new ranch and the man who'd so generously bequeathed it to her.

"Thank you. Please assure your brother that Sam and I will take extra good care of the horses."

He moved a step closer and the urge to slide her arms around him and tilt her lips up to his was so strong, she had to look out at the horses and draw in several deep breaths just to hold on to her composure.

He said, "Holt won't be worried about that."

She swallowed hard then forced herself to look at him. "There's something I'm curious about, Joseph. Is your father away somewhere?"

Even in the semidarkness she could see his face pale.

His reaction had her wishing she could kick herself for not keeping her curiosity in check.

"I guess you could put it that way, Tessa. Dad has been dead for five years."

The revelation touched her deeply and before she recognized what she was doing, she placed her hand on his forearm. "I'm so sorry, Joseph. Sam didn't tell me and I just assumed your father was still living. I shouldn't have asked."

"It was an innocent question. Besides, I should've told you before we went to dinner. You were probably wondering why the place at the head of the table was empty. Don't feel bad about asking."

Pained by the shadows she saw in his eyes, she said, "I'm sorry just the same. You see, I understand how it is to lose a parent. My father died before I was born. And my mother was killed in a car accident when I was only thirteen."

A frown of dismay pulled his brows together. "I never would've guessed you were an orphan."

She shrugged. "Actually, I've never thought of myself as one. You see, immediately after Mother died, the Calhouns took me in. So it wasn't like I was ever completely alone. They couldn't take Mom's place, but their love made losing her a bit more bearable."

His lips twisted to a rueful slant and then his hand was reaching for hers, enfolding it inside his strong fingers. And, like a sip of dry wine, the warmth of his touch radiated through her whole body and left her just a little too happy.

"It's good that you had the Calhouns to fill the void," he said gently.

"Yes. And that you have your family around you," she replied.

Suddenly he moved so close that the front of his body was brushing against hers. “You know, I’m getting the feeling that the two of us have more in common than just Ray Maddox.”

The husky note in his voice was so sexy it was almost like he was kissing her. The idea caused her nostrils to flare, her breathing to quicken.

“Why?”

Her murmured question put a faint smile on his face and then his head was bending downward, until his lips were hovering a scant few inches from hers.

“We’ve both lost parents. We both ride horses. And, uh, we’re both standing here beneath the desert stars—together. Like fate and the sidewalk.”

The warning bells going off in Tessa’s head were deafening, but the clanging noise was hardly enough to make her step back and away from him. Something about him was pulling at the deepest part of her, urging her to touch him in ways she’d never wanted to touch a man before.

“This isn’t fate,” she tried to reason. “It’s—crazy.”

His soft chuckle fanned her face. “It’s okay to be a little crazy once in a while.”

Her lips parted but not one word would slip past her throat. Yet losing her ability to speak was the least of her worries.

All at once, Joseph Hollister was kissing her and Tessa was certain she’d stepped directly into a dust devil. The spinning wind was quickly sweeping her off her feet and all she could do was hang on to him and wait for the whirling ride to end.

A split second. That’s all it took for desire to take over her brain and, without her even knowing it, her arms slipped around his waist, her lips opened wider. White stars were raining down on her, blinding her, consuming her with heat.

She wasn't sure if it was the shrill call of a nearby stallion or some indistinguishable sound closer to the house that caught Joseph's attention and caused him to suddenly step back from her. Either way, the abrupt separation caused her to sway on her feet.

"That was, uh, not planned, Tessa."

His voice sounded a bit gruff, as though he wasn't pleased with his impulsive behavior. But at the moment she wasn't all that concerned with what he was thinking. She was more worried about the desire roiling in the pit of her stomach and screaming at her to step back into his arms. She had to get a grip on herself before she totally lost her senses over this man.

"Um—no. I didn't think it was," she said, her voice unsteady. "Planned on your part—or mine. It was just a kiss. So let's just forget it and move on, shall we?"

Even through the dim lighting she could see he was surveying her face and she could only hope she'd managed, for once, to hide her feelings.

"Forget it. Yeah. Sure. If that's what you want."

She didn't want to forget and move on. But a girl couldn't always have what she wanted, Tessa reminded herself.

Her throat tight, she forced a faint smile on her face. "Yes. I think that's best. But just in case you're wondering—it was a very nice kiss."

He cleared his throat and reached for her arm. "We'd better get back to the house before Mom sends out a search party."

They started back to the house and as Tessa matched her strides to his, she realized the kiss he'd just given her had ruined her hopes of ever finding a special man. She'd always be measuring her dates to Joseph and somehow she knew they'd all come up lacking.

Chapter Four

The evening sun was still fiercely hot as Tessa sat on the couch, carefully studying a photo album she'd discovered in a desk in the study. Even if Sam and the Hollisters hadn't given her a brief description, she would have easily identified Ray Maddox by the sheriff's badge pinned to his chest.

The early images depicted a tall, stoutly built man with dark hair and a wide, easy smile. His wife, Dottie, had been a petite blonde with sweet, angelic features. But the accident had clearly changed things. In later photos she was always in a wheelchair and Ray was carrying a strained look on his face. Sadly, there were no images of babies or children documented during the couple's long marriage. Tessa supposed the riding tragedy had taken away all chance for them to have a family. If only the photos could talk, Tessa mused.

The mystery of her link to Ray had continued to nag

her, but not nearly as much as thoughts of Joseph Hollister. Three long days had passed since the dinner party at Three Rivers and she was still wondering why he'd kissed her and why she'd responded in such a reckless fashion. Even now she couldn't stop thinking about the way his lips had tasted, the way the scent of him had filled her head, and how the heat of his body had radiated through hers.

Darn it, she had to stop thinking about his kiss and start figuring out how she was going to ask the man for his help. If she called him, he might get the idea she wanted more of his hot kisses instead of help unraveling the mystery of her inheritance. Or would that kiss they'd shared even enter his mind? Even though the embrace had sent her senses reeling, she figured sharing passionate kisses in the moonlight with a woman was a routine thing for him. He'd probably forgotten the whole thing.

Her thoughts were suddenly interrupted by the faint sound of voices coming from somewhere near the front of the house. Lifting her head, she listened intently until she heard the voices again.

Who could that be? Sam had already come and gone for the day.

Tossing the album aside, she curiously hurried over to the window and was totally surprised to see Joseph and a young girl riding horseback up the long, dirt drive. Not only that, Joseph was leading two saddled horses behind him.

Happy excitement rushed through her as she raced out of the house and down the long row of rock steps to meet them.

"Well, hello," she called out to him, "this is a big surprise."

Grinning, Joseph lifted his hand in greeting. “That’s why I didn’t call and warn you we were coming.”

“Uncle Joe is that way.” The girl with a blond ponytail spoke up. “He likes to do surprises.”

The two visitors reined their horses to a stop beneath the flimsy shade of a mesquite tree that grew near the retaining wall. Tessa walked over to join them.

“You must be Joseph’s niece, Hannah,” Tessa said as the young girl slid from the saddle and handed the sorrel’s bridle reins over to Joseph. She was dressed all in cowboy gear, including a pair of knee-length chaps edged with long green fringe. Besides looking adorably cute, Tessa could see the girl was as comfortable around a horse as her uncle.

“That’s right,” the girl said with a wide grin. “And you’re Tessa. I can tell because everyone told me you were very pretty.”

Everyone? Did that include Joseph? Tessa wasn’t about to ask.

Smiling at the girl, Tessa said, “Thank you for the compliment. But you’re even prettier. You look like your mother.”

Hannah wrinkled her nose. “That’s what everyone says. Thank goodness. I don’t want to look like my dad. He’s a jerk.”

Joseph cut his niece a look of warning, while Tessa cleared her throat and quickly changed the subject.

“So are you two just out enjoying a ride this evening?” she asked.

“Joseph brought you a pair of horses to keep,” Hannah blurted before he had a chance to say anything. “The red roan is Rosie and the black-and-white paint is Rascal. They’re the best of friends. That’s why Uncle Joe picked them. So they’d be happy together.”

Tessa moved to a spot where she could safely view the horses without being in the way. "I see." She darted a doubtful glance at Joseph, who was busy tying the horses' reins to an old hitching rail. "But I didn't know it was safe to keep a mare with a—"

"Oh, you don't have to worry about Rosie having a baby," Hannah was quick to reassure her. "Rascal is a gelding."

Tessa could feel her face turning red. Apparently being raised around livestock had already taught Hannah plenty about the birds and bees. "Uh, I just meant that mares are sometimes ill-natured and kick at the males."

"Oh, not Rosie. She's sweet. Tell her, Uncle Joe."

"Rosie is definitely sweet." His gaze on Tessa, he walked over to where she and Hannah were standing. "Or maybe Rascal is just a lovesick pushover. Either way, you won't have any problem with them getting along."

Since Tessa hadn't seen or heard from Joseph since the dinner party at Three Rivers, she was beginning to think that he'd forgotten about her and his promise about the horses. But now as his pointed gaze met hers, she realized he hadn't forgotten anything, especially their kiss. The notion pushed her heart rate to a rapid thud.

Drawing in a deep breath, she tried to make herself relax. "It was nice of you to bring the horses. Thank you, Joseph."

"You're welcome."

A few seconds of awkward silence stretched between them before Hannah finally spoke up. "We thought you'd like to go for a ride with us, Tessa. Would you? I haven't got to see any of the Bar X in ages."

"Oh." She glanced down at her casual jeans and tank top then over to Joseph. "Do we have time for a ride?"

"Sure. The sun won't set for a couple more hours." He

glanced down at her strappy sandals. "Did you bring a pair of riding boots?"

"I did. Let me go change." She started to hurry away and then paused. "Sorry. I'm forgetting my manners. Would you two like to come in and have something to drink? Soda? Ice water?"

"Thanks, but we have cool drinks in our saddlebags. We'll wait for you out here," Joseph told her.

"Right. Okay. I'll be right back."

"I think she was happy to see you, Uncle Joe. Her eyes were all sparkly when she looked at you."

Joseph reached over and playfully tugged the brim of Hannah's straw hat farther down on her forehead. "You're silly. And before Tessa comes back, I'm warning you that you'd better not be playing cupid. If you do, it'll be the last ride you ever take with your uncle Joe."

Completely unfazed, Hannah giggled. "I'll be nice. Just don't be a stuffed shirt with Tessa. Or you'll never get her to go out on a date with you."

Joseph frowned at his niece, who, in his opinion, was growing up far too quickly. "What do you know about it, anyway, young lady? And I'm not here to ask Tessa on a date. We're here to deliver horses and be neighborly. You're only ten years old. Your mind shouldn't be on boy/girl things."

Hannah rolled her eyes and sighed. "You're so hopeless, Uncle Joe."

He was hopeless, all right, Joseph thought as he watched the horses switching and stomping at the pestering flies. For the past three days his thoughts had been consumed with Tessa and the kiss they'd shared in the moonlight. He still didn't know what the hell had come over him. It wasn't his nature to grab a woman and kiss her as though he'd known her for years instead of two short days.

Don't you mean kiss her like you wanted to carry her straight to your bed, Joe? That's the thing that's really nagging at you. The moment your lips had settled over hers it was like you'd been swept up in a fiery tornado and your feet still haven't returned to solid ground.

"Mom says Tessa is from Nevada. That's a far ways from here. Is she going to live here for very long?"

Hannah's question pulled Joseph out of his musings and he glanced down at his inquisitive niece. "I don't know how long she plans to stay. Except that she won't be here permanently."

"How come? Does she have a boyfriend up there?"

Joseph grimaced. "Hannah, one of these days when you become a grown woman, you're going to realize there are more things to life than having a boyfriend."

She pulled a face at him and started to spout some sort of retort, but was interrupted by the sight of Tessa hurrying down the steps to join them.

While she'd been gone, she'd donned a pair of red cowboy boots along with an old brown cowboy hat with a bent brim and sweat-stained band. Her long hair was fastened into a low ponytail at the back of her neck, while a pair of aviator sunglasses shaded her eyes. She looked beautiful and oh, so touchable.

Thank God, Hannah would be along as a chaperone, Joseph thought. Otherwise he'd have a hell of a fight trying to keep his hands off her.

"So which horse am I supposed to ride?" Tessa asked. "Rosie or Rascal? Or does it matter?"

"Ride Rosie!" Hannah chimed out. "She loves to long trot. Rascal is so lazy he just wants to clop along."

Tessa chuckled. "Fine with me. I'll ride Rosie." She

glanced at Joseph. "Do you want to leave Rascal in one of the corrals while we're gone?"

"Not unless you want the fence kicked down. Rascal wouldn't be too happy if we left him behind. At least, not until he gets used to his new home," Joseph told her. "Don't worry. I'll lead him behind me. It's no problem."

Seeing Hannah had already climbed into her own saddle, Joseph turned to Tessa.

"Need some help getting mounted?" he asked.

She turned a warm smile on him and Joseph's chest swelled with emotions that made absolutely no sense. A pretty girl with a sweet smile shouldn't be making him feel like he was king of the mountain.

"Thanks. I could use a little help. Rosie is rather tall."

He moved up behind her and was instantly enveloped with the scent of wildflowers and the memory of her soft lips moving against his. If Hannah wasn't looking on, he'd be sorely tempted to pull her into his arms.

"Uh, go ahead and put your foot in the stirrup and I'll give you a boost up," he instructed. Then, clamping his jaw against the taunting thoughts, he wrapped his hands around either side of her slim waist and lifted her up and into the saddle.

She was as light as a feather and graceful, too. As he handed the reins up to her, he couldn't help but notice how comfortable and right she looked in the saddle.

"Thanks." Stroking her hand along the mare's neck, she looked down at him. "Before we start, is there anything I need to know about riding Rosie?"

He forced his gaze to move away from her lips. "Her mouth is soft. And you don't have to give her much of a nudge to make her go."

Hannah suddenly reined her sorrel mount closer to

Tessa's. "Don't worry, Tessa. If you need help I'll be right beside you."

Tessa gave the girl a grateful smile and it was plain to Joseph that she'd been around children and knew how to interact with them. No doubt she'd make a great mother. One that would be loving, but also have a firm, guiding hand. But that fact had nothing to do with him, Joseph mentally chided himself. He wasn't looking for a wife or a mother for his unborn children. The only reason he was here at all was to keep two promises. One to take Hannah riding and the other to deliver the horses to Tessa.

Swinging into his saddle, he grabbed Rascal's reins and motioned for them to follow. Once they reached the ranch yard behind the house, he steered his horse onto a dim path leading off to an eastern section of the ranch.

"We'll take this trail," he said. "I've been over it with Ray before. It'll be easy riding."

"Where does it go, Uncle Joe?"

"To grazing land. Down near the river."

Hannah let out a disappointed wail. "Oh, do we have to go that way? I wanted to go to the bluffs. We might find a rattlesnake den there. I'll bet Tessa has never seen one of those."

Instead of appearing squeamish, Tessa merely laughed. "When the weather is warm, we have plenty of western rattlesnakes on the Silver Horn. But not any sidewinders like you have down here. We don't have Gila monsters, either. I'd like to see one of those—at a distance, of course."

Hannah let out a happy laugh. "Yay! Tessa's going to be fun!"

Fun? Joseph figured she was going to be downright dangerous. But he was a deputy sheriff, he reminded himself. He could handle anyone in any situation. Even a beautiful woman with a warm, sexy smile.

"We'll save the venomous reptile hunt for another time," Joseph said dryly. "Unless we're unlucky enough to accidently run into some."

Hannah let out an exaggerated sigh then winked at Tessa. "You're going to find out that Uncle Joe can be really boring. But I love him anyway."

For the past three years Tessa's time had mostly been divided between housekeeping duties on the Silver Horn and attending college classes. She'd not had many opportunities to go horseback riding. Now as she rode along with Joseph on one side of her and little Hannah on the other, she was reminded how pleasant it felt to have a horse beneath her and the warm summer wind in her face.

With its tall, stately saguaros, blooming sage and jumping cholla, the stark beauty of the Bar X was incredibly enchanting. Yet Tessa had to admit that even the majesty of the land couldn't distract her attention away from Joseph. Long-legged and tall in the saddle, he handled the gray gelding with a deftness that impressed her. Obviously he'd grown up being a cowboy and the years of experience showed in his knowledge of the land and the horses carrying them over it.

"When Ray still had cattle, I'd sometimes ride with him and Sam to check on the herd," Joseph commented as the three of them skirted around a large rock formation. "Ray loved being a rancher as much as he loved being a sheriff."

The wistful note in his voice had Tessa glancing over at him. "From the way everyone talks about Ray, I'm getting the impression he was good at both jobs."

"He didn't do anything in half measures," he replied. "I admired him for that."

So when it came to his job, Joseph liked for a man to give it his all, Tessa thought. Was that the way he'd feel about loving a woman? Would he throw all of himself into the relationship? Or maybe his job as a deputy got all of his attention?

Determined to put the questions out of her mind, she said, "Earlier this afternoon I found a photo album in the study. His uniform and her wheelchair made it obvious the pictures were mostly of Ray and Dottie. The pics had me wondering if either one of them ever had relatives living close by. They might have a clue about Ray's will."

He slanted her a thoughtful glance. "The only relative of Ray's I ever knew about was an older brother. He lived over near Apache Junction. But he died several years before Ray. And Dottie wasn't originally from Arizona. She came here from South Carolina and had a few relatives living there, but none of them ever came around. From what Ray said, her parents never approved of Dottie marrying him. And they blamed him for the accident that left her paralyzed. I doubt any of them know anything. They didn't even show up for Ray's funeral services."

"What a sad situation," she mused aloud. "Do you happen to know how Ray and Dottie met?"

"I think she'd come to Arizona to visit a college friend who'd moved out here. From what I understand, she ended up meeting Ray at the Wickenburg Rodeo."

"Wickenburg has a rodeo? I love rodeos!" Tessa exclaimed.

"I do, too!" Hannah practically shouted with glee. "And Wickenburg has a big one. We take our horses and ride in the parade, too. You'd love it, Tessa! There's a carnival, too. And all kinds of fun stuff to do on Valentine Street."

Joseph cast his niece an indulgent smile before he turned his attention to Tessa. "Hannah isn't exaggerating. For the past seventy years or so, the town has a celebration called the Gold Rush Days. The rodeo is just one of the highlights of the festival."

"It must have been a real highlight for Ray. The big, strong lawman meeting a woman, falling in love, and making her his wife." Tessa sighed and then shook her head. "Sounds like a modern-day fairy tale—until you get to the part where Dottie was paralyzed. Unfortunately life isn't always perfect."

"At least they were together."

He suddenly turned his gaze on the distant horizon and as Tessa took in his solemn profile, she wondered if his thoughts were on his parents and how their time together had been cut short.

Wanting to ease the awkward moment, she asked, "So when does this Gold Rush Days take place? Maybe I could take in part of the fun."

"The first part of February," he replied. "So this year's festival has already taken place. Maybe you can go next February. That is—if you're still around."

The month of May was just getting started. Several months would pass before February rolled around again. Was he thinking she'd still be living on the Bar X next year? Right now her future plans were little more than day-to-day.

"I have no idea where I'll be in another year," she admitted.

He leveled a pointed look at her. "No. I don't suppose you do. You have another life back in Nevada to think about."

Yes, she did have a life back there. But since she'd arrived on the Bar X, everything about her old life had faded into the background. Sure, she thought about the Calhouns and the Silver Horn and all her friends, but she wasn't exactly aching to return. In fact, she was becoming very comfortable in her new home. The feelings left her guilty and torn.

"I have quite a bit to think about here," she said.

One corner of his lips curved wryly. "Yes. For right now you do."

So he figured once she found some answers about Ray's will, she'd be skedaddling back to Nevada. His reaction stung her a bit, although she didn't know why. She wanted to tell him that she didn't take her inheritance lightly or the reason behind it. But with Hannah riding within earshot of them, she decided it best to keep her thoughts to herself.

The next few minutes passed in silence and then Joseph gestured toward a green strip of trees in the distance. "We're almost to the river," he said. "We'll take a break beneath the willows. And let the horses drink."

Riding a few feet ahead of them, Hannah twisted around in the saddle to look at her uncle. "I'm not tired, Uncle Joe. Can I ride Rooster over to the top of that ridge?" She pointed to a landmark about a quarter of a mile away, but still well within view.

"No. Sorry, Freckles. You know the rules."

The girl's lip pushed out in a disappointed pout. "Yeah. But the rules stink."

Joseph said, "I'm not your parent. So I can't be the one to let you break the rules. If your mother was here—"

"Oh, sure! She's just as bad as you are." Hannah reined her horse alongside Tessa, then said a bit sheepishly, "Sorry. I'm sounding like a spoiled brat."

"Yes. You are," Joseph bluntly agreed.

The child shrugged one little shoulder and if they'd been standing on the ground instead of riding, Tessa would've been tempted to give her a comforting hug.

After a moment Hannah said, "See, Tessa, my grandpa had an accident and died. His horse spooked and he fell from the saddle with his boot still hung in the stirrup."

Shocked by this revelation, Tessa turned a stunned look at Joseph. Why hadn't he explained this to her the night she'd visited Three Rivers? Was there something about the tragedy he didn't want her to know? A connection to Ray Maddox somehow? Judging by the grim expression on his face, it was clear he had no intention of saying more on the subject.

She turned to Hannah. "I'm very sorry you lost your grandfather, Hannah."

The girl let out a disheartened sigh. "See, that's why I can't ride alone anymore. Everybody is afraid it could happen to me or somebody else on the ranch."

The fact that Joseph hadn't wanted to share the details of his father's accident bothered her, but she did her best to ignore the feelings. After all, she'd only known Joseph a few short days.

But he'd kissed you like a lover, Tessa. Didn't that count for something? Or had he just been playing with you?

Shaking off the pestering thoughts, she studied the disappointment on Hannah's face.

"Your family made the rule because they love you and want to keep you safe," she gently explained. "Besides, it's really more fun to ride with someone. Don't you think?"

After a moment a smile slowly spread across Hannah's face. "Yeah, it is more fun with you and Uncle Joe along," she agreed.

From the corner of her eye, Tessa could see Joseph staring off to the east, where green, jagged peaks were covered with giant boulders and tall saguaro. His features matched the hard, unforgiving land and Tessa could only guess why his mood has taken such a dark turn. Was he simply annoyed with Hannah or thinking about his father?

"You know, I'd like to see that ridge, too," she said to Hannah and then cast a thoughtful glance in Joseph's direction. "After we give the horses a breather at the river, do you think the three of us could ride over to the ridge?"

Several moments ticked by before he finally acknowledged her. The blank look on his face told her he'd been so lost in thought he'd not even heard her question.

"I'm sorry, Tessa. What did you say?"

Tessa repeated her question and to her relief he responded with an easy smile. And just like that the brooding shadows on his features vanished with the warm, desert wind.

"Sure. We'll all go," he said, winking at Tessa. "Maybe we'll even see a Gila monster."

Hannah let out a happy yelp. "Tessa, you're the best!"

Joseph teased, "Hey, I thought I was the best. Aren't I the boss around here?"

Tossing her head, the girl pulled a playful face at him. "We're on the Bar X now. Tessa's the boss on this ranch."

Joseph chuckled then slanted Tessa a sly look. "I'll have to remember that. So, what do you think, boss? Think the three of us ought to kick our horses into a long trot? Or can you hang on at that speed?"

Laughing, she shot him a daring look. "A trot, huh!

I'm thinking it would be more fun to canter. That is, if you can hang on going that fast."

Overhearing the exchange between her uncle and Tessa, Hannah shouted gleefully, "Yippee! Let's go!"

The girl quickly kicked her horse into a canter and as she moved ahead of them, Joseph looked over at Tessa and grinned.

"Come on, Lady of the Bar X. Let's see who gets to the river first!"

The two of them urged their mounts into a faster gait and as they cantered side by side over the open range, Tessa felt a connection to Joseph that was unlike anything she'd ever experienced before. It was strong and warm and something she never wanted to end.

Chapter Five

By the time the threesome returned to the ranch house and dealt with the horses, the sun had already dipped behind the distant mountains, stretching long shadows across the patio where Tessa and Joseph sat sipping tall glasses of iced tea.

Moments earlier, Hannah had skipped her way to the barn to search for the cats. As quietness settled over the backyard, Tessa realized it was the first time today that she'd actually been alone with Joseph.

Since they'd taken seats in the red motel chairs, he'd removed his cowboy hat and placed it near his feet. The wind had lifted the waves of his dark hair and scattered the strands across his forehead. His strong, sexy image caused vivid memories of their kiss to parade through Tessa's mind.

"Tessa, I think I need to apologize to you."

The unexpected comment caused a wash of heat to

sting her cheeks and, before she could stop herself, she blurted, "If this is about that kiss, then don't."

"It's nothing about that," he replied. "Unless, you're thinking I ought to apologize—for the kiss, that is."

As her gaze continued to slip over his tanned features, she tried to avoid his mouth. Yet the harder she tried, the more fascinated she became with the gleam of white teeth against his lips, the faint dimple coming and going near one tempting corner.

"Um, no. I don't think that at all," she said awkwardly and then tried to give him a casual smile. "I'm just trying to figure out why you'd be feeling the need to apologize to me."

With a heavy sigh, he settled his shoulders against the back of the lawn chair.

"It's about…well, what Hannah was telling you earlier," he began. "About Dad—his death and the rule about her not riding alone. If you think I sounded too curt with her, I'm sorry."

Surprised that he'd even brought up the subject, she shook her head. "I'm not one to be judging you. The Calhoun family have babies and younger children and I often acted as their nanny. But none of those children are as old as Hannah. So I'm hardly an expert on the best way to handle a ten-year-old girl," she assured him. "And, anyway, I can understand the safety reasons behind the riding rule."

He let out another long breath then wiped a hand over his face. "That's something else I wanted to talk with you about. It's not just the fear of Hannah falling from her horse. Because—well, to be frank, I've never been convinced that Dad's death was an accident. Neither has Blake. The rest of the family doesn't say too much about it, but Mom expresses her doubts from time to time."

Stunned, she shifted around in her chair so that she was facing him and at that moment she could see dark, raw pain clouding his brown eyes.

"Are you saying you believe…someone deliberately caused him to be hurt—killed?"

His features as hard as granite, he nodded. "That's exactly what I'm saying."

Chilled by the notion that such an evil incident might have touched his family, her mind began to whirl with questions. "Ray must have been the sheriff at that time. How did he handle it?"

Grimacing, he said, "He and his staff investigated every possible angle. There just wasn't any proof that Ray could take to the DA. So, ultimately, Dad's death was ruled an accident."

Frowning thoughtfully, she said, "Legally, I can see how the lack of evidence tied Ray's hands. But what did he personally think about the case?"

"Dad could ride the rankest of broncs. And on that particular day the horse he was on was as gentle as a lamb. Major Bob and Dad were best buddies. The brown-and-white paint would follow him around like a puppy and the miles he carried Dad over the ranch would be countless. Knowing all this, Ray figured something else had taken place. An encounter with someone that turned out deadly."

Just the notion of Joseph losing his father in such a horrifying and malicious way left her heart aching for him. "Oh, Joseph. It's so horrible I…well, I don't know what to say. Except that I'm sorry. You and your family didn't deserve to have such a thing happen."

His lips twisted to a bitter slant. "An accident I could accept, Tessa. Losing your mother in a car accident was surely awful for you. But at least you know how she died and that someone didn't deliberately kill her. With Dad—we can't be certain. And the idea Dad's killer might possibly be walking among us is something that's gnawed at me for the past five years."

Tessa suddenly recalled telling Sam that Joseph seemed like an intense young man. Now she understood where some of that intensity was coming from.

"Is your dad the reason you became a deputy?" she asked curiously. "To go after the person responsible for his death?"

He shook his head. "No. I was already in training before Dad died. My uncle Gil, Dad's brother, is a law officer down in Tucson. He had a big influence on me. So did Ray. I'd always liked the idea of serving my community and making it a safer place for everyone."

"What did your father think about your job choice?"

He shrugged. "I think a part of him was disappointed that I wanted to do something outside the ranch. But he supported me. He was the type of father who encouraged his kids to follow their dreams."

She sighed. "You're lucky to have had a father like that, Joseph. Even just for a while. I often think if my father had lived, I might be a different woman now. But that's something I'll never know." She slanted him an empathetic look. "I hope someday you'll unearth the truth about your father's death. Five years is a long time. Have you found any clues as to what might have happened?"

"Unfortunately no. Blake and I still go out and search around the spot on the ranch where Dad's body was discovered. But we've never found anything helpful. The problem is compounded by the fact that we can only guess how far Major Bob had traveled with Dad hanging in the stirrup. It could've been miles. The horse was smart. He knew Dad needed help and he knew he had to get both of them home. And they weren't that far from the ranch yard when some of the hands spotted the horse with Dad dragging beneath him."

Tessa outwardly shivered at the horrific image. "I take it that your father had gone out riding alone that day."

He nodded glumly. "That was nothing unusual. Dad liked to ride alone and gather his thoughts. Especially when things were hectic. That day he'd gone out to check a water pump. Or so he told Holt. I've often wondered..." He paused then leveled a pointed look at her. "If I tell you something, Tessa, will you promise not to repeat it to anyone? Not even Sam?"

She tried not to look surprised. "Of course, I promise," she assured him. "Whatever you tell me will remain with me."

He raked fingers through his hair, then glanced out to the barn as though he needed to make sure Hannah was still out of earshot. At the moment the girl was sitting on a hay bale near the open doors with both cats vying for a position on her lap.

When his gaze swung back to Tessa, he said, "This is something I've not told anyone. Not even my family. I've kept it to myself because—I've been afraid it would do more harm than good."

The closeness she'd felt to Joseph this afternoon as they'd cantered to the river suddenly took on a far more personal meaning. He trusted her enough to share private details of his family life with her and that notion touched her deeply.

"I'm guessing this is about your father's death?"

He nodded. "It's something Ray told me not long before he died."

Confused by the mention of Ray, she said, "I thought Ray had been retired for a few years before he died."

"Even without a badge on his chest, Ray never truly quit being a lawman. All those years, he continued to work on Dad's case. Ruling it as an accident really frustrated him. He wanted closure for Dad and himself—for all of us. Not long before Ray died, he suggested to me that he was getting close to solving the mystery. Naturally, I pressed him for details, but he refused to say much. Except that he believed a woman had some sort of connection to Dad's death."

Totally shocked now, Tessa's jaw dropped. "A woman! Who? What did she have to do with your father?"

His sigh was heavy with frustration. "Ray wouldn't explain. Except to say that she was acquainted with Dad somehow and that she lived in Tucson. At least, at that time, she lived there. By now, it's anybody's guess where she might be."

Tessa looked at him and wondered how he'd lived all these years with such uncertainties. Only a few weeks had passed since she'd found out about her inheritance and the questions surrounding it continued to torment her. She couldn't imagine going for years without having answers.

"Oh, Joseph, why did Ray throw you just enough tidbits to have you wondering? He clearly recognized he was dying. Why didn't he share his whole theory on the matter with you while he was still alive?"

He shrugged. "He was waiting to gather more evidence before he laid everything out to us. See, Ray was very protective of Mom and didn't want to cause her any unnecessary grief. Not without definite proof."

"I see. So we can assume the trail he was on never developed into anything. Is that what you think?"

A grimace marred his forehead. "Hard to say. His health took a sudden turn for the worse and before I had a chance to press him on the matter, he was on a life support machine and unable to talk."

Her heart was suddenly aching for the heavy load Joseph had been carrying around. "And all this time you've not said anything to your family because you wanted to protect your mother, too," she said gently.

"Mom has already been through so much grief. If I find something concrete to go with Ray's assumption, then that's another matter. I'll have to reveal it to the family. But I'll tell you this, Tessa, Dad wasn't a womanizer. He would've never betrayed Mom."

Instinctively she reached over and rested her hand on his forearm. "After meeting your mother and most of your family I can only imagine how hard this is for you—dealing with all the doubts and questions surrounding your father. But I trust your judgment on the matter, Joseph. I also happen to believe you'll solve the mystery someday."

Smiling, he reached over and placed his hand over hers. The intimate contact was warm and comforting, yet also terribly exciting and she couldn't stop her heart from thumping with crazy pleasure.

"Thanks, Tessa," he said quietly. "And I think I ought to apologize—again. Here I am talking about finding the truth about Dad when you have all sorts of questions about Ray and his will."

She shook her head. "My mystery can hardly be compared to yours, Joseph. I was given a huge gift. You had something very precious taken away."

"Yes. But you need answers, too. Just like I do."

She said, "I admit I'm having trouble getting the whole thing off my mind. Every morning I wake up I look around at this beautiful land and nice home and it's like I'm living in a dreamworld. Without knowing Ray's reasons behind his gift, none of it seems real somehow."

His hand tightened slightly over hers and she was forced to look away before he could see just how strongly his touch was affecting her.

"Maybe you're just having a hard time accepting the idea that you're deserving of Ray's lifelong savings."

"I am having a hard time accepting the notion," she agreed. "These past few days since I saw you at Three Rivers, I've been trying to decide whether I should ask a favor of you."

She could feel his brown eyes searching the side of her face and the sensation left her with the urge to squirm upon the seat of the lawn chair.

"Why would you hesitate to ask me for a favor?" he asked.

She pulled her gaze away from Hannah and the cats to settle it back on him. "Well, um, I wouldn't want you to get the wrong idea. I mean, that I was using you—or maybe chasing after you." Her face reddened as she said the last words, but he didn't seem to notice. Or if he did, he was kind enough not to point it out.

"What is this favor?"

"Help me find the answers to Ray's will—my connection to him. You're a deputy and, I hope, my friend. You're the only person I know of who might be able to unearth the truth."

"Ah, the truth," he said softly. "Seems like we're both searching for that."

She nervously licked her lips and wondered how much longer he was going to leave his hand on top of hers. The touch was growing hotter by the minute. Pretty soon she was going to self-combust.

"Well, I don't want to put you on the spot, but I've been thinking some of the people who worked under Ray might still be working there with you. There's a chance, although I admit a slim one, that they might have heard Ray mention me or know how he might be connected to me or my family."

He finally pulled his hand away from hers and though Tessa felt a measure of relief, she also felt bereft that the warm connection was gone.

"You're not putting me on the spot," he told her. There are a few guys still on the force that worked under Ray. And also a secretary who worked with him for years. I'll ask around. See if they know anything."

Tessa gave him a grateful smile. "Thank you, Joseph. I realize it's a long shot, but I've been trying to think of every possibility. You're probably going to laugh at this suggestion, but I've even considered the idea that Ray might've somehow known my father, Asa—years ago when they were both still living."

An uncomfortable expression suddenly came over his face. "That theory crossed my mind. I've also wondered if you might have been related to Ray—closely related."

Her mouth went dry. Her heart drummed loudly in her ears. Even though that very same thought had crept through her mind, just hearing Joseph say it out loud was enough to jolt her.

"You mean—as in father and daughter?"

Suddenly he was squatting on his heels in front of her chair and his hands were curling tightly around hers, as though he already knew she desperately needed his support. "Tessa, tell me, do you think there's a chance your mother might've known Ray?"

Incredible thoughts tumbled through her mind as she lifted her gaze to his.

"The notion seems far-fetched, but I have considered it," she admitted. "Still, knowing my mother, it just couldn't be true."

"Why? It's possible there was another part of your mother's life she didn't tell you about—before she met Asa Parker?"

If his suggestion were true, then her family had never been what she'd always believed it to be. And that idea tilted her very world.

Groaning with dismay, she said, "Ray couldn't have been my father—or uncle or…well, anything. I have my birth certificate. I even have my parents' marriage license. His name was Asa Parker. And believe me, Joseph, when my mother talked about the man, you could see genuine love shining in her eyes. I have no doubts he was my father."

He studied her thoughtfully. "You told me your father died before you were born. Do you have any photos of him here with you?"

"Two. They were taken when my parents got married in Las Vegas. Unfortunately the quality is poor. But to me, Asa Parker doesn't look like a younger version of Ray Maddox."

"You've never seen either man," he noted. "I'd like to look for myself."

He helped her to her feet and Tessa instinctively glanced toward the barn.

"What about Hannah? She might come back to the patio and miss us. And it's going to be dark soon. You should probably be saddling up."

With a wry smile, he urged her toward the back entrance of the house. "Trust me, Hannah isn't shy. If she wants to, she'll come in and find us. And the horses can easily see their way home in the dark."

With that settled, they entered the house. When they reached the living room, Tessa said, "Have a seat and make yourself comfortable. Ray's album is on the coffee table if you want to take a look. I'll go fetch the photos from my bedroom."

Moments later she returned with a pair of small snapshots to find Joseph sitting on the couch, pouring through the photo album. As Tessa approached him, he smiled and, in that moment, she realized she'd come to trust this man with her family history. But that didn't mean she should trust him with her heart. No, that was a whole other matter. She desperately needed to remember that.

Easing down next to him, she handed him the photos. "I recall Mom telling me these were taken with one of those disposable cameras that were popular back in those days. Let's see, that would've been January of 1994. I was born the first of September."

Bending his head, he carefully studied the images. "They are terribly grainy," he said. "The developer must have done a crummy job."

"I'm guessing that particular wedding chapel didn't have a photographer. Or if it did, my parents couldn't afford the services. At that time she worked as a file clerk for a tire company and my father did day work."

He glanced up and Tessa was instantly overcome by the few scant inches between their faces. It was hardly enough space to allow her to breathe. But what did breathing matter when all she wanted was to lean into him and feel his lips on hers? Had she lost her mind or just now found it?

He asked, "You mean day work on ranches? He was a cowboy?"

Oh, mercy, his skin smelled like a man touched with sage and sunshine. The unique scent pulled on her senses.

Clearing her throat, she said, "That's what Mom always told me. Although she never said where. Now that I think back on it, whenever she talked about my father, it was usually about his character. Not the details of where he came from or anything about his family."

"Hmm. You didn't ever find that strange?"

Looking away from him, she nervously licked at the prickly sensation dancing across her lips.

"Not when I was small. Though, whenever I grew old enough to understand, I decided it was very strange. But my mother was so good to me and I could see that talking about Dad made her very emotional and sad. Digging at her wouldn't bring my father back to us. So I didn't see the point in badgering her with questions."

"Until now."

She glanced over to see his gaze was back on the photos.

"What do you mean?"

He continued to study the snapshots. "Just that if you had more information about your father, it might help us get to the bottom of Ray's will. Do you know how Asa died?"

"In a hospital in California, I think. But I don't know which one or where. He had some sort of acute blood disease."

"Hmm. I suppose you've searched for information about him on the internet?"

"Yes. I made a few attempts. There were several Asa Parkers obituaries, but none of them matched the information Mom had given me. I also searched for California hospital death records during the months before I was born. Oddly enough that search came up empty. But sometimes information goes unlisted or it gets erased."

He nodded. "Especially after twenty-four years."

"Anyway, I felt like Mom told me the most important things I needed to know about the man. About how responsible he was and how much he loved her and their coming baby."

Frowning, he placed the snapshots on the coffee table then looked around at her. "Sorry, Tessa, but the man's face is partially shaded in one shot and turned aside in the other. He does have a tall, burly build and the hair looks dark. I can't honestly say that it's Ray. But I can't rule out the possibility it could be, either."

Tessa didn't know whether to feel relieved or disappointed. She wanted answers, but the truth might upend her whole life. She wasn't sure she was ready for that sort of upheaval or if she'd ever be ready. "Well, it was a try."

"Would you mind if I take these to work with me?" he asked. "The crime lab has the capabilities to work on photos. I have a friend who might be able to clear them up a little."

"I'd be grateful. Thank you, Joseph."

"You're welcome, Tessa," he said softly.

She was telling herself she needed to leave the couch and put some space between them when his gaze suddenly dropped to her lips. Tense silence followed, making it easy for Tessa to hear the rapid beat of her heart pounding in her ears.

"Um, it's getting dusky outside," she said in a nervous rush. "I think I—we—should probably go check on Hannah."

Flattening her hands on the cushion of the couch, she meant to push herself to her feet, but her body seemed to be ignoring the signals from her brain. Then, before she could do something to break the paralysis, Joseph's face moved even closer to hers. So close, in fact, that she could see the amber flecks in his brown eyes and the faint stubble of dark whiskers beginning to peep through his tanned skin.

"Joseph."

His name came out more like a breathless plea than a deterrent. And instead of him pulling back, his hand wrapped gently around her upper arm, and then his lips were brushing lightly, temptingly, against hers.

A tiny moan of pleasure sounded in her throat and before she could think about resisting, she was leaning into him, inviting him to deepen the contact. He didn't disappoint. His hands settled against her back and drew her toward him while his lips opened over hers in a kiss that robbed her breath and rocked her senses.

The kiss they'd shared at the corral on Three Rivers had been hot, or so Tessa had thought. But this one was downright scorching. Heat shot from the roots of her hair all the way to the soles of her feet. Instead of backing away from the fire, she wrapped her arms around his neck and drew herself closer.

Over and over, he kissed her until the room was nothing but a foggy haze and the two of them began to topple sideways. With his hands clamped securely around her shoulders, he started to ease her downward onto the cushions of the couch. Somewhere in the foggy recesses of her brain, she knew she should pull away and give herself a moment to check the sudden rush of passion threatening to overtake her. But it was impossible to resist the taste of his lips, the warm pleasure of his hands touching her, holding her.

"Uncle Joe! Where are you?"

The sound of Hannah's voice coming from the direction of the kitchen had the same effect as an explosion going off in the middle of the room. Tessa jerked away from him and quickly jumped to her feet, while on the couch, Joseph sat straight up and raked fingers through his rumpled hair.

After a moment he called out, “In here, Hannah. In the living room.”

Tessa hastily smoothed her mussed hair and had just finished straightening the strap of her tank top when Hannah appeared in the doorway.

The girl glanced quizzically from Joseph to Tessa then around the room. “Gee. Don’t the lights work? It’s kind of dark in here.”

Still shaking from the effects of Joseph’s embrace, Tessa hurried over to a table lamp. As she clicked it on, she told Hannah, “We’ve been busy talking and didn’t notice it was getting dark.”

The expression on Hannah’s face was skeptical and Tessa figured the girl had already picked up on the tension in the room. But thankfully she didn’t start asking awkward questions. Instead she strolled over to Tessa.

She said, “I came to the house to see if you have any cat treats. I promised the cats I’d give them both a treat. Is that okay with you?”

Smiling, Tessa curled her arm around Hannah’s shoulders and urged her toward the kitchen. “Sure, it’s okay. Come on and I’ll give you a few. But not too many. Otherwise I’ll have fat cats,” Tessa teased.

They started out of the room and Joseph called after his niece. “Hannah, we have to be leaving in a few minutes. So make sure everything is in your saddlebags. I’ll catch up with you at the barn.”

“Okay, Uncle Joe.”

Moments later Tessa was placing the plastic bag of fish-shaped treats onto a shelf when the sound of Joseph’s footsteps brought her head around to see him standing in the doorway of the walk-in pantry. The sight of his long, lean body silhouetted against the kitchen light was all it took to make her heart start hammering all over again.

"Hannah's already headed back to the barn," she told him.

He took a step into the pantry and, for one wild second, she wondered if his intentions were to close the door behind them and pick up where they'd left off when Hannah had innocently interrupted them.

"I know. I heard her go out," he said. "I wanted to talk with you before I headed to the barn."

She started to move toward him then decided against it.

"I don't want us to start analyzing what just happened," she said bluntly.

"I don't, either. I only wanted to tell you—I wasn't exactly planning on things getting so out of hand."

She looked down at the floor as memories of those delicious moments flood her with heat. "I see. And now you regret it," she muttered.

"No! I just don't want you thinking I'm some sort of… wolf out to prey on you."

Looking up, she pressed fingertips to her burning cheeks. "Don't be ridiculous, Joseph. I'm not a child. And you're not a wolf."

He took another step closer and, if possible, her heart pounded even faster. He didn't have a clue about how very much she wanted him to kiss her, touch her. Which was all for the best, she thought. Otherwise she might end up falling into bed with him and that could only lead to a broken heart. Namely hers.

"No. But I can see you're emotionally vulnerable right now. I don't want to take advantage of that."

No man had ever kissed her as passionately as Joseph had a few short minutes ago. And no man had ever considered her feelings the way he was doing now. He wanted to protect her, not hurt her. The realization made her want him even more.

Her throat tight with emotions, she stepped over to him and placed her palms against his chest. "I'm stronger than you think, Joseph," she murmured. "If you seduce me, it will be because I want you to."

Suddenly his fingers were gently stroking the stray tendrils of hair away from her forehead. The tender touch made her feel like a princess being courted by a gallant knight.

"Tessa, I can't explain what's happening with us—to me. We've only known each other a short while and you don't plan on staying here for long. I shouldn't be wanting you—but I do."

A shaky breath rushed out of her. "If I told you that I didn't want you, you'd know I'd be lying. I mean, after the way I just kissed you?" Groaning, she turned her back to him then practically wilted with desire when his hands came over her shoulders and drew her close to the front of his body. "I'm not some wanton hussy, Joseph. I've not even dated that much. Now you must be thinking—"

"I'm thinking you're beautiful, and young, and that you're the first woman to come along who's made me think about things that—well, I've pretty much pushed out of my life."

Turning, she tilted her head back to look up at him. "I can't tell you what's going to happen, Joseph. I'm beginning to really like living here—like you. But my life—my friends and the people I call family—are all back in Nevada. I came down here with intentions of staying a couple of weeks at the most. Maybe I need to forget all about figuring out why Ray willed me everything he owned and simply be thankful for it."

His hands cupped the sides of her face and the tenderness she felt in his touch melted the very center of her heart. Where was she going to find the strength to walk away from this man and the feelings he evoked in her? Why would she want to?

Because there were no promises that anything lasting would ever come out of a relationship with Joseph. No guarantees that she wouldn't end up with her heart being crushed to tiny, painful pieces. That's why, she thought ruefully.

"Tessa, you can't leave here now," he said softly. "The questions about Ray and the will would always be nagging you. And maybe you'd be wondering about—us."

Her insides began to tremble. "Us? Are you insinuating we're a couple, Joseph?"

His fingertips began to caress her cheeks. "We won't know the answer to that if we don't give it a chance. You've been talking about Ray and the will and all the questions you want answered. But maybe you ought to be concentrating on me and you and what just happened in the living room. I'd like to think that's enough to keep you here in Arizona—for a while."

And it was more than enough to send her running right back to the Silver Horn where her heart would be safe from a tall, dark deputy with amber-brown eyes. But was that what she really wanted to do? Run? And then lament about what might have been?

"All right," she softly conceded. "I promise to stay—for a while longer."

A happy light danced in his eyes. "That's what I wanted to hear. So, would you like to go riding again? Just the two of us? I'll come Sunday and bring a picnic."

There was no point in trying to slow him down. Not when spending time with him made her feel happy and special and very wanted.

Laughing, she said, "I thought the woman was supposed to do the picnic part."

He grinned. "This time the man is going to supply dinner. You just be ready."

Being alone again with Joseph might prove to be her undoing, but she wasn't going to think about that now. Trying not to sound too eager, she said, "I'll be ready."

"Great." He reached for her hand and pulled her out of the pantry. "Now, come on and walk with me to the barn. I'm sure Hannah will want to tell you goodbye."

A few minutes later Tessa stood on the rock steps of the retaining wall and watched as Hannah and Joseph rode away toward Three Rivers. And as the horse and riders disappeared into the gathering darkness, she realized their visit had changed her in more ways than one.

Nothing was settled in her mind anymore. Except the powerful longing she felt to be back in Joseph's arms.

Chapter Six

"Hmm. I can't be certain. Not from these photos. But—"

Pushing aside a messy stack of papers and two coffee mugs, Louella Jamison, Ray's longtime secretary, placed the images on her desk and tapped a red fingernail to one of them.

"But what, Louella?"

The middle-aged woman with short blond hair and dark blue eyes peered intensely at the photos Tessa had given Joseph yesterday.

"I was secretary for fifteen of the twenty years Ray served as Yavapai County sheriff. When you've been around a man for that length of time, you pick up on a few of his habits."

After her boss had retired, Louella had chosen to take a lesser desk job at the substation in Mayer, a little town southeast of Prescott, where the main office for the Yavapai County sheriff was located.

Today, Joseph had just happened to be patrolling the southern command and had stopped by during his lunch break to speak with Louella.

"So," he prodded, "what have you picked up? Come on, woman, am I supposed to wait around here for the cows to come home before you tell me?"

Chuckling, she said, "Yeah, yeah, you deputies are always in a hurry. It's a wonder you don't all have bleeding ulcers from gobbling your food too fast."

Accustomed to Louella's teasing, Joseph said, "For your information, I took a whole fifteen minutes to eat. That's ages. So what about the photo? Is that Ray? Or not?"

"As I was saying before—I can't be certain. But see the way the man is standing? His right leg is slightly forward and sort of bent at the knee. That's the way Ray always stood."

Joseph leaned over Louella's shoulder to take a closer look at the snapshot. "Hey, you're right. That is the way he often stood. Now that I think about it, I remember him talking about tearing a ligament in his knee once. Some sort of accident in the cattle pen. Hmm. That's interesting."

"Might be interesting, but a lawyer would call it inconclusive evidence." She swiveled her chair around, forcing Joseph to step to one side of the cluttered desk. "Who is the woman in the picture, anyway? A relative?"

A few minutes ago when Joseph had first entered the old redbrick building and found Louella at her desk, he'd not explained anything about the photos. Except that he was trying to discern if the man's image was that of Ray. Thankfully, there was nothing in the background or about the couple's clothing that implied it was a wedding photo. And Joseph wasn't going to volunteer that much information. If any kind of infidelity had been going on with the late sheriff, he didn't want to be the one to spread such a well-guarded secret.

"I'm trying to find out what connection, if any, she might've had to Ray." He eased his hip onto the corner of Louella's desk. "I take it you haven't heard about Ray's will?"

Leaning back in her desk chair, Louella studied him with faint skepticism. "No. I assumed Sam probably wound up with everything. Ray's parents died years ago and his only sibling is gone, too. Sam was the only logical person left."

Joseph absently picked up a small can filled with pencils and rolled it between his palms. "Well, Sam got some sort of monetary gift from Ray. I have no idea what it amounted to. The rest of the estate—the house, his finances, everything—went to Tessa Parker, a young lady from Nevada."

Flabbergasted, Louella's mouth fell open. "Joseph, have you been drinking? Ray would never do something that crazy! He was a responsible, caring person. And he was sane right up until he died. If this is true, then some crooked lawyer has pulled a shenanigan of some sort. And why not? There's not a soul around to make waves about it!"

She was quickly getting heated up about the whole thing and Joseph promptly placed the cup back on the desk and rose. "Just calm down, Louella. There hasn't been anything shady going on. Tessa is just as confused as you are about this inheritance. That's why I wanted you to look at the pictures. Ray apparently had some sort of connection to the Parker family. We just don't know what it is. Think, Louella. Did he ever mention that name before?"

Louella's short laugh was full of disbelief. "Fifteen years, hundreds of cases and files, and an office that was as busy as a bus terminal. You think I can remember one name?"

"I understand it's a long shot, Louella. But I have to start somewhere and you knew Ray about as well as anyone."

Her eyes narrowed suspiciously. "Who are you doing this for? Ray? Yourself? Or the young woman from Nevada?"

He was doing this for Tessa, he realized. Because he'd promised her. And because he could see how the uncertainty and questions were nagging mercilessly at her. Just as questions about his own father continued to plague him.

"A little of all three, I suppose," he said to Louella.

"Hmm. Well, the only Parkers I recall was Wilma and Rocky, but they lived like hermits back in the canyon. Never had kids, either. Ray didn't have any sort of connection to that pair. I'm fairly certain they moved out of this area."

"No. This had to be a different Parker—from Nevada," Joseph said. "Back before I came on the force, did Ray go out of town much?"

An impatient frown twisted her lips. "Joseph, does a bee make honey? Of course, Ray went out of town from time to time! Just like our present sheriff does. As for Ray, there was always some sort of convention or meeting he needed to attend. I recall him going to Phoenix quite a bit to meet with people at the capitol. Bickering about funding, crime prevention and all that sort of thing took up a lot of his time. He didn't like it, either. Ray wanted to be out working among the citizens of the county."

Joseph realized his question sounded inane. He'd

asked it in the hope that Louella might have remembered a trip that had seemed out of character for Ray. Apparently she didn't. Still, that hardly meant that Ray hadn't had the opportunity to run into Monica Parker somewhere, Joseph thought. The chance that such a thing had happened might be slim, but a lawman didn't solve a case by following percentages. Hunches were much more productive.

"You're sure right about that. Ray's first concern was helping the folks of Yavapai County," Joseph agreed then leaned over and gathered the photos from the desk. As he pushed them into the pocket on his shirt, he said, "Thanks for your help, Louella. If you think of anything else, call me, would you?"

"Sure." She leveled a sly glance at him. "So tell me, have you met your new neighbor? The heiress from Nevada?"

Met her? Oh, Lord, he'd kissed her like there was no tomorrow. At night he went to sleep with her on his mind, only to dream about her. And when he woke in the mornings, she was still whirling around in his head. His obsessive thoughts of the woman were beginning to worry him.

"Yes, I've met her. Mom had her over to Three Rivers for dinner one evening. And before you ask, yes, she's young and beautiful and single. Oh, and smart, too."

Louella's smile suddenly turned calculating. "Hmm. Maybe she was smart enough to figure out how to con the legal system. Ever think about that?"

Tessa a con woman? The idea was laughable. She was soft and innocent and obviously very confused about her inheritance. No, if something shady had gone on with Ray's will, Tessa would be the first person to want to give everything back to his estate.

"You're barking up the wrong tree, Louella. Ray and the Parkers were connected. And I'm going to keep digging until I figure out how." He started out of the small room then, pausing at the doorway, looked back at her. "Let me know if you think of anything—no matter how trivial."

She held up an A-OK sign with her thumb and forefinger. "See you later, Joe."

Outside, on his way down the steps of the former two-story schoolhouse, a voice called to him from behind.

"Hey, Joe, going to lunch?"

Turning, he saw fellow deputy, Connor Murphy, hurrying to catch up to him.

"Done been to lunch," Joseph told his old friend. "I just stopped by to say hello to Louella."

The tall blond man slipped a pair of sunglasses over his blue eyes. "Well, darn. I thought we might grab a burger together. It's been a while since you've been over this way and I've not heard your voice on the radio. What have you been up to?"

Joseph shrugged. "Traffic violations. A few home break-ins. Poaching on the Broken Rafter and some fisticuffs at the Fandango."

Connor chuckled. "In other words, the usual."

Yes, work had basically been the norm, Joseph thought. But nothing else about his life had been the same. Not since Tessa had moved onto the Bar X.

"The past couple of weeks I've been working the northern command," Joseph told him. "The captain sent me down here today—something about Pete being off duty for a while."

Connor nodded. "Poor guy was riding his ATV on his day off and wrecked it in a ravine. Broke a couple of ribs, but managed to walk out. Nothing like being housed up with twin toddlers to recuperate," he added with a sardonic laugh. "I'd think dragging myself in to work would be easier."

Connor would think in those terms, Joseph decided. The guy's motto was to date a different woman every week and stay single the rest of his life. Being housed up with a wife and young children would be torture for a man like him.

"I'm sure Pete will be fine." Joseph pulled one of the photos from his shirt pocket and handed it to Connor. "Does that guy look like anyone you know?"

Frowning, the young deputy studied the snapshot. "Not that I can say. You need to get the lab to clean that thing up for you." He started to hand it back to Joseph then suddenly decided to take another look. "Wait a minute. You know, he sort of reminds me of Sheriff Maddox—back before his hair got so gray. Who is it, anyway? Some criminal with a long rap sheet?"

Sheriff Maddox before his hair had grayed. Yes, Connor would remember back to those days. He and Joseph had both come onto the force when Ray was still in office. Joseph's mind was suddenly spinning with all sorts of possibilities.

"No. I don't think he's a criminal," Joseph told him then decided it wouldn't hurt to give Connor a partial explanation. "Actually, I'm trying to decide if the man in that picture is Ray. And, Connor, I'd appreciate it if you wouldn't mention this to anyone right now. It's sort of a private matter."

The deputy handed the photo back to Joseph. "Sure, Joe. It's already forgotten. Hope my opinion helped in some way."

Help? What would it do to Tessa if she did learn Ray had known her mother? And if the man in the picture was actually Ray, how did that explain a wedding at a Las Vegas chapel? In 1994, Ray had already been married to Dottie for several years.

You're the only person I know of who might be able to unearth the truth. Tessa's words slipped through his thoughts like a haunting whisper. She was looking to him for help. But now he was beginning to wonder if the truth would be the best thing for her.

"It helped, Connor. Thanks." Joseph returned the photo to his shirt pocket and started down the steps. "I'd better be going. I have miles to go."

"Maybe we can get together sometime soon," Connor called after him. "Let's take some beer over to the lake and do some fishing."

"Sure. I'll call you when I get some extra time off." Joseph tossed the words over his shoulder while thinking two weeks ago the idea of an afternoon at the lake with his old buddy would sound like fun. Now the only thing he wanted was to spend every spare moment he could find with Tessa.

If that made him crazy then he'd just have to be crazy. At least until she moved back to Nevada.

"Sam, drop me off at the drugstore and I'll gather up what I need while you go to Jackson's Feed and Ranch Supply. There's a coffee shop on down the block from the drugstore. When you finish, you can pick me up there," Tessa told the old rancher as he drove the two of them down a two-lane street in Wickenburg.

"That suits me."

He slowed the truck then wheeled it into the first empty parking spot he could find near the drugstore. Tessa opened her purse and pulled out several large bills.

"Will this be enough to pay for the feed and hay?"

He took the bills and jammed them into the front pocket of his frazzled jeans. "Plenty and some left over."

"Then you might as well buy cat food, too," she told him. "And anything else you think we might need."

Sam nodded. "I'll do it. But I think you ought to know the Hollisters don't expect you to buy feed for their horses."

Frowning quizzically, she said, "Why, Sam, that's ridiculous. They've loaned me the horses. The least I can do is feed and care for them properly."

Sam tugged on the brim of his hat, a habit Tessa noticed the older man displayed whenever he was vexed about something.

"Tessa, they have bins of feed shipped in to Three Rivers. They'd never miss two hundred pounds or a half dozen bales of alfalfa."

"That's beside the point, Sam. I'm not a moocher. And, anyway, buying a little feed isn't going to break me." She unbuckled the seat belt holding her in the worn passenger seat of Sam's old truck and quickly climbed down from the cab. "I'll see you in a few minutes."

Inside the old-fashioned drug emporium, she gathered up the things she needed, plus a few toiletries that caught her eye. After paying for her purchases, she walked down the street to the coffee shop where she planned to meet Sam.

Since this was only her third visit to the quaint desert town, Tessa was still learning where certain shops and restaurants were located. For the most part, it was a cowboy town with the buildings and landscape all done in a Southwestern flavor. On her last visit, she'd discovered Conchita's coffee shop. The little pink-stucco building was located on a quiet side street and nestled beneath the branches of two large mesquite trees. A wide overhang sheltered the entrance, which was a simple wood-framed screened door. To one side of a stepping-stone sidewalk, small tables and chairs offered customers a place in the cool shade to enjoy their drinks.

Inside, Tessa walked up to a varnished wooden counter where a young auburn-haired woman by the name of Emily-Ann was sitting on a tall stool. As soon as she spotted Tessa, she placed the tablet she'd been holding in her lap on a shelf behind her and stood.

"Well, hello," she said with an easy smile. "Nice to see you again, Tessa."

Tessa laughed. "Wow, you remembered my name. I'm impressed. With all the tourists passing through here, I'd have everyone's face and name mixed up."

Still smiling, Emily-Ann shook her head. "You're giving me too much credit. Most of the tourists who come in never bother to introduce themselves. And as soon as you told me you're living on the Bar X, I knew you'd be sticking around."

Sticking around. For some reason folks around here were quick to assume she was here to stay. It was true she was beginning to love the ranch more and more and this town was quickly charming her, but that didn't mean she was destined to live the rest of her life here. Joseph didn't seem to think so. Not when he was often mentioning the fact that she'd be going back to Nevada.

Shaking away that annoying thought, she said, "Well, I will be sticking around—for a while."

"Looks like you've been doing some shopping? Have you tried the new dress shop over on Apache Street? She has some adorable retro-looking things. Like 1950's stuff. I don't have the waistline for that sort of clothing. But you'd look great."

Tessa dug into her shoulder bag and pulled out her

wallet. "Thanks, but I hardly have a pencil-thin waist, either." She handed her a small bill. "I'll take a plain coffee today with just a bit of cream and no sugar."

"Coming right up."

As Emily-Ann made the coffee in a quick, one-cup brewer, Tessa gazed longingly at the pies lined on the shelves in a glass showcase.

"Why don't you have a piece to go with the coffee?" Emily-Ann suggested. "The blueberry is to die for. Just make sure you brush the stain off your teeth whenever you get home, though. Or you'll be going around with a blue smile."

Tessa laughed. "I'd better pass this time."

The young woman was handing her the foam cup filled with coffee when the door over the shop opened and an older man and woman walked in and ordered lattes. Tessa used the interruption to make her way outside to one of the little tables beneath the mesquites.

She was sipping her coffee and enjoying the cool breeze drifting across the quiet patch of yard when the customers emerged from the shop and walked on to their car. A moment later Emily-Ann left the building and joined her at the table.

"Mind if I sit with you?"

"Please do," Tessa insisted. "I'm waiting on a friend. But it might be a few minutes before he shows up."

"Oh, boyfriend? If it's any of my business," she said slyly.

"No. Just a friend," Tessa explained.

"Actually, I wasn't thinking," Emily-Ann admitted. "For all I know, you could be married with kids."

Tessa groaned inwardly. She had Joseph. Sort of. But she had no right to even call him a boyfriend. Just because the guy had kissed her senseless didn't mean he was attached to her. "I don't even have a special guy, much less a husband or kids," Tessa told her. "What about you? Are you married?"

"Goodness, no!" She let out a short laugh. "I'm independent. I've watched too many of my friends end up with broken hearts and major cases of depression. I can depend on my dog much more than a man."

"Dogs are nice," Tessa agreed. "And some men."

Emily-Ann laughed. "I'll take your word for it." She leveled a thoughtful glance at Tessa. "The Bar X is on the way to Three Rivers. Have you met the Hollisters yet?"

Surprised, Tessa asked, "You know the Hollisters?"

With another easy laugh Emily-Ann said, "Tessa, most everyone in this area knows the Hollisters and Three Rivers Ranch. They've been a big, important family around here for many years. As for knowing them personally, I'm friends with Camille—the youngest of the kids. But she's living down by Dragoon now and I rarely hear from her. It's like she's gone into hiding."

Joseph had vaguely mentioned that his younger sister had gone to their other ranch for emotional healing. Tessa figured Emily-Ann knew exactly what had prompted Camille to leave Three Rivers, but she wasn't about to prod the other woman for information. That would be gossiping about Joseph's family and she didn't want to disrespect him in such a way.

"I have met the Hollisters," Tessa told her. "They're a very nice family. I'm lucky to have them for neighbors."

Nodding in agreement, she asked, "Is your family renting the Bar X? I guess your father must be a rancher."

Emily-Ann's assumption caught Tessa off guard. But she quickly realized it was only natural that Emily-Ann would assume she was living with her parents. Owning a ranch at her age was a bit out of the ordinary.

"Um, no. My parents both died when I was much younger. I happen to own the Bar X."

The young woman's mouth fell open and Tessa was bracing herself for more questions when she suddenly spotted Sam's truck pulling into a parking spot in front of the coffee shop.

"Oh, there's my guy." Grabbing up her bags, she rose. "Thanks for the coffee and the chat. See you next time."

"Sure. Make it soon!"

By the time Tessa reached the truck, Sam was standing by the passenger door, waiting to help her into the cab.

"Why, Sam, you didn't have to bother. I can climb up on my own," she told him.

He grinned as he took her by the elbow and helped her into the seat. "I'm practicing up on my manners. Who knows, I might get married someday."

Tessa looked at him in shocked wonder. "Are you serious? You're thinking about getting married?"

Sam chuckled as he shut the truck door. "Hell, no! But it sounded good there for a minute, didn't it?"

"Sam, you old joker!"

Tessa was still laughing as he climbed behind the wheel, but her laughter sobered somewhat as he started backing the truck out of the parking slot and she just happened to glance out the windshield. Emily-Ann was still sitting at the outdoor table and, even from a distance, the young woman's expression looked incredibly forlorn.

How odd, Tessa thought. Only moments ago Emily-Ann had seemed cheerful and happy.

Once Sam had turned onto the main street leading out of town, Tessa asked, "Do you know the young woman I was sitting with back there at the coffee shop? Her name is Emily-Ann."

A grim frown caused the wrinkles on Sam's face to

deepen. "Only in passing. I knew her parents—folks by the name of Smith. Her mother is dead. Happened a few a years ago. After that, her father left for California. Never seen him again. He was one of those big blowhards. Always talking about the things he was going to do. But that's all he was, just talk." He shook his head. "Poor little thing. She hasn't had it easy, that's for damned sure."

"Why, Sam, you're just a softie."

A sheepish look replaced his stern expression. "Sorry, Tessa. I said a lot more than I should have. And I don't mean to be judgmental, but I expect folks to live up to their responsibilities. That's all."

As they traveled back to the Bar X, Tessa thought long and hard about Sam's remark.

Did she have a responsibility to Ray Maddox and the Bar X? She'd not asked for the man's gifts, but perhaps she owed him more than just gratitude and respect. And then there was Orin Calhoun. He'd taken her in and given her a wonderful home when she'd needed it the most. He'd made her a part of the Calhoun family. And he'd also made it very clear that he wanted her back in Nevada, near him and the family. Did she have a responsibility to him? Or was she wrong in thinking she owed either man anything?

And what about Joseph? He might just be the most important man in your life right now, Tessa. Orin and Ray have kindly and generously provided for you. But they can't provide you with the things you've always wanted. A loving husband and children of your own. Maybe you need to quit worrying about showing your gratitude and start following your own dreams.

Mentally shaking away the voice going off in her head, Tessa glanced thoughtfully over at Sam.

"Sam, do you think the two of us could turn the Bar X back into a working ranch?"

She'd thought her question would elicit a look of surprise from the ranch hand. Instead his expression never wavered as he kept his gaze firmly on the highway in front of them.

"Sure do. Wouldn't take us long, either." He darted a glance in her direction. "You thinking about doing that?"

"Hmm. I've been thinking about a lot of things. If I did decide to do such a thing, could I count on your help? Or is that a silly question?"

"Damned silly."

She smiled at him and suddenly an unexpected lump of emotion filled her throat. "Thank you, Sam."

Midmorning the next day, Joseph arrived on the Bar X to find Tessa patiently sitting on the bottom step of the retaining wall. A few feet away Rosie and Rascal were already saddled and tied to the old hitching post beneath the shade of the mesquite tree. The sight of her lifted his spirits more than anything he could ever remember, making it impossible to wipe the eager smile off his face.

As soon as he stopped the truck, she walked out to greet him and, as she approached, Joseph noticed she was dressed in jeans and boots and a black long-sleeved shirt printed with tiny yellow sunflowers. Her long hair was bound in a single braid that rested on her right shoulder. She looked so fresh and sweet it was all he could do to keep from pulling her straight into his arms.

"Good morning, Tessa," he greeted.

"Good morning, Joseph," she replied with an impish grin. "I was beginning to think you were still home in bed. I've been waiting for hours."

He glanced at his watch. "It's ten. That's when I told you I'd be here."

She let out a soft laugh. "I'm teasing. You're right on time. And Rosie and Rascal are ready to go."

He glanced over at the horses. "So I see. Sam must have been here earlier and saddled them for you."

The indignant look on her face had him laughing.

"For your information, Sunday is Sam's day off," she said primly.

"I'm the one teasing this time," he said then turned back to his truck. "I have our lunch already packed in my saddlebags. All I have to do is tie them on and I'll be ready to go."

They walked over to the horses and Tessa stood to one side while he fastened the leather bags onto the back of Rascal's saddle.

"It's a beautiful morning," she said. "Not too hot and only a few fluffy clouds in the sky. Is the weather always like this down here in Arizona?"

"As summer goes on, it'll get hotter. July and August are the months we stand a chance for rain. But even then we don't get much moisture. That's why we're constantly irrigating on Three Rivers."

"Where does that water come from?" she asked curiously. "The river?"

"We're blessed to have a spring that never runs dry. We pump it from there. We also have several ponds and an endless number of water wells. It takes all of them to keep the stock watered and the fields irrigated." With the bags secure, he turned to her. "Ready to go?"

The sight of her smile affected him like nothing he could ever remember. It made everything around him seem bright and special, as though he was seeing the world through different eyes. He didn't know what that meant, except that it was going to be hell for him when, or if, she decided to leave.

"Sure. I have everything I need already on my saddle."

Her gaze met his and suddenly he couldn't stop his hands from wrapping over the tops of her shoulders or brushing his lips against her forehead. "Forgive me, Tessa, but you look so pretty this morning. And I'm very glad to see you."

The slight tilt of her face had her lips pressed against his jaw and the sweet kiss touched him somewhere deep in his chest.

"I'm very glad to see you, too, Joseph. I've been looking forward to today. To being with you."

Her admission thrilled him, making him wonder if he'd turned into a complete sap. Not wanting to dwell on that idea or give himself the chance to deepen their embrace, he stepped back. "Me, too. So we, um, better get started. Don't you think?"

She nodded and he quickly helped her onto Rosie's back. While he mounted Rascal, she asked, "Do you have a certain area picked out to ride?"

He reined the horse alongside hers. "No. You choose."

"Well, I've not had a chance to look at the southern part of the ranch. Have you ever been back there?"

"No. So we'll discover what it looks like together."

For the next hour they rode through fields covered with large patches of cacti and groves of Joshua trees, until the land began to break with deep, brush-filled arroyos. Once they'd maneuvered their horses out of the narrow gorges, they found themselves on a wide mesa covered with a carpet of green grass. In the distance, tall, rocky bluffs made a jagged line across the horizon and Tessa couldn't resist traveling onward.

"Let's ride to the bluffs. We might find a nice shade there to eat our lunch," she suggested.

He shot her an indulgent smile. "Fine with me. Let's go."

Twenty minutes later they reached the cluster of rocky hills and Tessa couldn't help but gasp with delight at the raw, rugged beauty in front of them.

"Oh, Joseph, this is spectacular! Look at the pine trees! And there's a pool of water over by that red cliff. Let's have our picnic over there. What do you say?"

"Looks like a great place to me," he agreed. "Let's go."

When they reached the natural pool, they let the horses drink their fill, then loosened the saddle girths and turned them free to graze on the patches of grass growing nearby.

"Don't worry," Joseph assured her. "The horses won't leave. They're trained to stay close."

"I hope you're right," Tessa joked. "Otherwise we'll have a long walk back. It feels like we're miles from the house, but that can't be. I only own a thousand acres. Is this land still on the Bar X?"

"Actually we're not as far from your house as it feels. We've not reached the border fence yet. I expect we'd find it behind this ridge of hills. So we're still on Bar X land."

Tessa stared in awe at the spectacular landscape. Then, realizing she must seem like a gaping child, she glanced sheepishly at him. "Just when I think I'm getting adjusted to...Ray's gift...I see something like this and... I get all choked up."

"Anyone in your place would feel overwhelmed," he said gently.

Pushing back the brim of her hat, she quickly dabbed at her misty eyes and gave him a wobbly smile. "Sorry for getting all silly on you. Come on. Let's eat. I'm starved."

"I'm starved, too. But not for food. Not just yet," he murmured.

He moved closer and the dark gleam she spotted in his eyes caused her to draw in a sharp breath. Before she had time to release it, he wrapped his arms around her shoulders and lowered his head. Tessa tilted her face toward his and that's all it took for their lips to connect.

As his mouth fused with hers, a familiar ache swept through her and with it came a jarring revelation. The aching need she was feeling wasn't just a physical urge to be close to this man; it was flowing from the very center of her heart.

Sweet. All giving. And totally euphoric. The sensations rushing through her were all those things and more. Like dangerous and reckless. Yet in spite of the risks, she was tossing her heart to him and all she could hope for now was that he caught it before it crashed to the ground.

Chapter Seven

Tessa lost count of how many times Joseph kissed her. Not that the number mattered. She could've gone on kissing him forever. But something eventually caused him to lift his head and once the contact between their lips was broken, Tessa was so dazed she could hardly focus on his face.

As he eased her out of his arms, she breathed deeply and tried to calm the desire raging inside her.

"I, uh, think we'd better get our lunch," he said, "Before..."

His awkward pause had Tessa finishing the words for him. "Before things get out of hand."

"Something like that," he muttered.

She was trying to come up with a suitable reply when he turned away and picked up the saddlebags packed with their lunch. As Tessa watched him carry the meal over to the wide pool of water, she wondered what he could possibly be thinking. That he wanted to make love to her but had decided he would later regret it?

She fought off the depressing idea and walked to where he was spreading a small square cloth on the ground.

"Is this spot okay?" he asked.

Her lips were still tingling from his kisses, her body still aching to be next to his. She didn't want to think about eating, yet she was mature enough to understand he needed space and that she needed to give it to him.

"Yes," she told him. "It's lovely. The shade from the pines is deep and cool. And I can hear water trickling. Is that coming from the mountain?"

As she eased down on her knees to take a seat at the edge of the small tablecloth, he motioned to a spot in the slabs of red rock jutting from the hillside. "Over there. Looks like you have a spring, too. I don't know if the pool stays full year round. I never heard Ray mention it, but I'm sure Sam can tell you."

"This is desert country," she stated the obvious. "The water has to be coming from somewhere deep underground."

"Look over to your right," he told her. "Deer tracks where they've been watering. I figure mountain lions show up here, too."

"Let's hope that species stays away until we eat our lunch," she said wryly.

Sitting cross-legged, he placed their meal on the space between them while Tessa made herself a comfortable seat on the thick carpet of pine needles.

He said, "Looks like Reeva packed sandwiches of pulled pork. There's also potato salad and some sort of cake for desert. And I put in canned sodas just in case you wanted more than water to drink."

"Sounds yummy. Thanks," she said as he passed half of the meal over to her.

As they began to eat, he cast a sheepish glance in her direction. "I guess you're thinking I'm crazy or something."

She lifted her gaze to his and as their eyes met she felt a soft punch to her midsection. "Why?"

He grimaced. "You're not making this easy for me, Tessa."

She said, "Look, Joseph, you ended that kissing session because you wanted to—or thought it best. I'm not going to question you about it. In fact, maybe we'd better forget it—again."

His gaze dropped to his sandwich. "Yeah. That's what we're always telling each other, isn't it? To forget it. But I don't think that's working. Not for me or for you."

He certainly had that right, Tessa thought glumly. They were long past the forgetting stage.

Tired of skirting the issue, she decided to be blunt. "Do you have this sort of problem with your other dates? You can't decide whether you want to make love to her?"

He sputtered then coughed. "Damn it, Tessa, it's been a long time since I've had *other* dates. And as for making love—there's more involved than just *wanting*—especially with you."

"Like what?"

He rolled his eyes. Then, lifting the black hat from his head, he raked a hand through his hair. "You're very young."

"Not that young," she countered.

He tugged his hat back onto his forehead. "We've not known each other that long."

"It doesn't feel that way to me."

He grimaced. "You don't intend to stay here permanently. It wouldn't be smart for us to start something that's only going to end."

Her teeth sank into her lower lip as she glanced out at the grazing horses. So he was thinking about the end rather than the beginning.

She said, "I haven't talked about leaving anytime soon."

"No. But we both know you will—eventually."

He didn't trust her to stay in Arizona and she was smart enough to know he'd never follow her to Nevada. Her throat was suddenly so thick she couldn't possibly take a bite of the sandwich, but she held on to the piece of food anyway, as though it was some sort of lifeline.

"I think we should talk about something else," she finally managed to say. "Okay?"

"Gladly."

She looked at him and felt her heart wince with longing. "So tell me what you've been doing at work."

He picked up a container of potato salad and used a plastic spoon to scoop up a bite. "Nothing out of the ordinary. I worked a quieter area yesterday. Our main office is located in Prescott and that area usually keeps the deputies hopping. Our captain keeps us rotated, though, so none of us is overworked."

"Do you like things quiet or would you rather be busy?"

He shrugged. "It's nice to have a break once in a while. But I'd rather keep busy."

She forced herself to start eating her sandwich again. After a moment she was relieved to feel some of the tension drain out of her.

"Liam, one of the Calhoun brothers, is a detective for the Carson City Sheriff's Department," she told him. "Grandfather Bart was never pleased about Liam's choice to be a lawman. And to make matters worse, a few years ago, Liam was badly wounded in a shootout and nearly died."

His amber-brown eyes were somber as they settled on her face. "That's bad. Did he recover?"

The memory of Liam's close call with death was something that would always remain with Tessa and she shuddered to think how Joseph might possibly face the same danger. That he could end up wounded and fighting for his life.

"By the grace of God, Liam recovered completely and was able to resume his job," she answered. Then, in the most casual voice she could muster, asked, "Have you ever been in a dangerous situation?"

He glanced at her. "Depends on what you call dangerous. If you mean a shoot-out, no. I've never had to draw my weapon. And I hope I never do."

His answer brought her a measure of relief. "Does your family worry about you?"

"I think Mom does, but she doesn't let on. Especially to me. And, anyway, she understands there are plenty of other hazardous jobs besides being a lawman. Like Holt's for instance. Working with young horses is far more dangerous than my job."

She picked up her potato salad and sampled a spoonful. "Hmm. That's true," she admitted. "But a badge on your chest puts a target on your back. Anyway, that's how it seems to me."

Joseph scooted backward until his back was resting against the trunk of a pinyon tree then stretched his legs out in front of him. "Yeah, it makes us a target in lots of ways."

She frowned. "What does that mean?"

His features twisted with sarcasm. "Wearing a uniform and rounding up the bad guys gives us an image that draws the ladies."

"Are you telling me that's supposed to be a problem? I thought men loved attention from the opposite sex."

He made a mocking grunt. "It's ironic, Tessa. We get the attention, but we have a hard time trying to have a long-term relationship with a woman. At least, that's the way it's been for me."

Her curiosity sparked, she studied the sardonic expression on his face. "So, being a deputy puts a strain on dating? Is that what you're trying to tell me?"

"It puts a strain on plenty of things." He picked up a tiny twig from the ground and tossed it toward the pool. "You might find this hard to believe, Tessa, but there was a time in my life when I was actually thinking about getting married and starting a family."

Now that Tessa had kissed him and held her body close to his, she couldn't imagine any other woman being in his arms. The shaft of jealously that lanced through her was unlike anything she'd felt before.

"You were engaged?"

"No. Things never reached that point. And I guess I should be thankful for that much. Neither of the women I was interested in would've made a good wife for me. The first one, Candace, turned out to be more interested in my family's wealth than me. When she learned we'd basically be living on a deputy's salary, she was outraged. And that was a damned hard pill to swallow."

"Obviously that was enough to end your relationship with her. Or did you try to work things out?"

He grimaced. "How do you work things out with a gold digger? No. I couldn't get Candace out of my life fast enough. And for months afterward, I beat myself up for having such a miserable judgment in women. In fact, for a long time I couldn't bring myself to date anyone. And then I met Willa. She was sweet and cute, and cared less about the Hollister money. She had plenty of her own and hardly needed mine. But the closer our relationship grew, the more I could see she was too emotionally weak to deal with my job. She was terrified for my safety and continually begged me to find another job. She didn't understand that being a deputy is a part of who I am."

Try as she might, Tessa couldn't feel badly about his broken relationships. Instead she was incredibly relieved that he was unattached.

"So did all of that make you put away your dream of a wife and family?"

He shrugged one broad shoulder and Tessa couldn't stop herself from imagining how he would look beneath the denim shirt. Would dark hair be sprinkled across his chest? Would the rest of his skin be as tanned as his face? Oh, lord, why was she thinking these things? Why did she want to leave her seat on the ground and move as close as she could possibly get to him?

"Let's just say after two busted relationships, I don't have much trust in women or myself," he answered.

He didn't have much trust in her either, Tessa decided. He was expecting her to pack up any day now and head back to Nevada. But how could she tell him that the longer she was near him, the more torn she felt about leaving? That would be like admitting she was falling in love with him and she was quite certain he didn't want that from her.

What does he want, Tessa? To take you to bed? Then end things whenever he decides he's tired of you?

The questions in her head put a momentary damper on her appetite, but she did her best to shake it away and force herself to eat.

After downing a few bites of potato salad, she said, "Mom always told me if I followed my heart, everything would work out right. Orin tells me the same thing. But I'm not sure if that's the safe way for a person to maneuver through the dating field. I've already made plenty of mistakes."

"You think of the Calhouns as your family, don't you?"

She glanced over to see he was regarding her with a thoughtful eye.

"They'll always be family to me. You see, other than Mom, I don't have any relatives—at least, any I know of. She was an only child and by the time she was grown, her parents divorced and left Carson City in opposite directions. Mom never got along with them, so I guess it hardly mattered that neither one could be located for their daughter's funeral. And now...well, honestly, I have no desire to look for someone who never cared about their daughter or granddaughter."

He swallowed the last of his sandwich and brushed his hands together to remove the crumbs. "What about your dad's folks? They weren't around to give you a home?"

She shook her head. "Mom explained that my paternal grandparents were up in years whenever they had my father and they'd already passed away years before she ever met him."

He looked at her with dismay. "Wow! You really were without a family when your mother died. So how did the Calhouns come about giving you a home?"

"Mom and Orin's late wife, Claudia, were close friends," she explained. "Back in the days when I was just a little girl and both women were still alive, we'd go out to the Silver Horn to visit. In my child's mind, it was like going to a palace to call on royalty. At that time I never dreamed it would become my home."

He frowned. "When both women were still alive—you mean something happened to Claudia?"

"Sadly, she fell down a long staircase and suffered a head injury. Barely a year had passed after that tragedy when Mom had the car wreck." Sighing at the memory of those black days, she shook her head. "After that, nothing was the same for me or the Calhouns."

The empathy she saw in his eyes told her he understood the upheaval she'd gone through.

"I'm sorry you lost so much, Tessa."

"It did tear a huge hole in my heart," she admitted. "But the Calhouns have given me so much. And these past few years I've tried to give back to them by working as the family housekeeper."

Surprise flickered in his brown eyes but thankfully she saw no sign of contempt.

"The housekeeper," he repeated, as though he was weighing the word on his tongue. "I understand you wanting to repay their kindness in some way, but I can't imagine the family expecting that sort of duty from you."

"The Calhouns didn't expect it or want it. In fact, Orin was dead set against the idea and I had to do some serious persuading for him to give me the job. Actually it was more than persuading—it was more like begging."

"And he gave in."

Tessa nodded. "Only because he could see how deeply I felt about contributing my share of work to the Silver Horn. Plus, he was partial to the idea of me having a job at home where the family could keep an eye on me."

Clearly intrigued, he asked, "So how long did you work as the Calhouns' housekeeper?"

"Oh, five or six years. Something like that. I was still working there when I got the news about Ray's will."

Amazed, he shook his head. "You're kidding, right?"

"Why should I joke about something like that?" she asked stiffly.

He made an openhanded gesture. "Sorry, Tessa. It's just that you're so…well, I figured with the Calhouns, you'd probably lived a privileged life."

Smiling vaguely, she said, "It was privileged in the sense that I got to live in a huge, lavish house. But the Calhouns don't exactly laze around. They all work very hard."

"And you wanted to follow their example," he said thoughtfully. "So you worked hard as the family housekeeper. Is that what you plan to keep doing whenever you go back to the Silver Horn?"

Was that a thread of disdain she heard in his voice? No. She couldn't imagine Joseph being a hurtful snob. But then she'd not expected Thad to have that sort of attitude, either. Which only proved she had a lot more to learn about men.

Unwittingly she lifted her chin to a proud angle. "Actually, Orin is in the process of looking for someone to take over my old job."

His brows lifted slightly. "Because he thinks you'll stay here in Arizona? Or because Ray's inheritance has made you wealthy enough to forget about working for a while?"

She wanted to tell him just how tacky she considered his questions. But after the very personal way they'd just kissed, Tessa decided he had a right to ask that much.

"Sorry, Joseph, both of your assumptions are wrong. A few weeks ago, I received my degree in criminal justice from the University of Reno. My plans are to find a job in that field. Perhaps as a legal secretary. I've not yet decided just which path I want to take. My degree gives me lots of options."

His jaw dropped. "Damn. I feel like a fool, Tessa. You never mentioned college and I never imagined you had those sorts of plans for your future."

She placed the small container of potato salad back on the cloth and reached for a chunk of cake heavily wrapped in clear plastic.

"Until today we've not really had an opportunity to talk about other—personal things." She shrugged. "But as far as my plans for the future? Those are currently up in the air. Right now my main focus is to resolve the questions surrounding my inheritance."

The cake was some sort of rich, apple concoction. Normally, Tessa would have relished every delicious bite, but the sexy image of Joseph and the fact that the two of them were so completely alone was making a wreck of her senses.

You little fool, Tessa. A few minutes ago Joseph pushed you out of his arms and put an end to all that torrid kissing. He doesn't want to pick up where the two of you left off. Even though you want to.

While Tessa wrangled with the chiding voice in her head, her gaze followed his over to the tiny pond.

Surrounded on three sides by flat, red rocks, a small waterfall trickled from thin slabs of rocks and made a tinkling noise as it hit the deep blue pool. Bright, colorful birds skimmed the surface, while others chirped from the branches of nearby willows. The tiny paradise surrounding them belonged to her. Even now, after all these days she'd been on the Bar X, she could hardly absorb the fact.

He suddenly spoke. "I haven't brought this up yet, but I thought you'd want to know. I've been talking with a few people who worked with Ray. Including his secretary. None of them recalled him bringing up the name Parker."

Eager for any kind of information, no matter how minute, Tessa leaned toward him. "What about the photos? Did you show them around?"

His gaze returned to her. "I left them with a guy at the lab. He thinks he can clear them up a bit, but he's limited to working on them during his own personal time. So that might take a few days. However, I did show them to a few people. Louella, Ray's secretary, thought the man's stance looked like Ray's. And another deputy thought it looked like a younger version of Ray with dark hair."

The emotions rushing through Tessa were too tangled for her to unravel. "Really? Maybe the power of suggestion had them thinking they saw something they didn't actually see."

He said, "When I showed the photos, I only asked them if they recognized the couple. I didn't offer any other information."

Tessa's mind shuttered at the possibility of Joseph's suggestion. "Oh. Well, that doesn't mean it could be Ray in the photos. You saw for yourself. They're too blurry to make an accurate ID." She swallowed hard as her voice began to wobble. "Besides, Mom wouldn't lie to me. Not about my father!

"Tessa, what I just told you—it's all supposition," he gently pointed out. "You shouldn't let it upset you."

"You don't understand how this makes me feel, Joseph. If Mom deceived me about something so important—it would make everything about my life a big lie!"

Not waiting to hear his reply, Tessa jumped to her feet and crossed the few short steps to the water's edge. She was staring into the deep pool, trying to calm herself, when Joseph's hands settled on the back of her waist.

"Tessa, I agreed to help you with this. But if finding the truth is going to cause you this much pain, then perhaps we should quit digging for answers. I'll get the pictures back and you can put all of this out of your mind."

Aghast at that thought, she twisted around to face him. "Out of my mind? How am I supposed to forget all this? The way things are now, I'm not just wondering why I was willed a small fortune, I'm having doubts about who my real father might have been!"

Ever since Joseph had arrived on the Bar X this morning, he'd been fighting the urge to make love to her. And a few minutes ago, before they'd started their lunch, he'd been well on his way to doing just that. But while he'd been losing himself in her kiss, all sorts of doubts had started wrestling with the needs of his body.

Something had kept warning him that once he surrendered his body to Tessa, his heart would soon follow. And the fear of giving that much of himself to her had ultimately caused him to end the embrace. But now, with tears swimming in her eyes, and her lips quivering with emotional overload, he forgot about what was best for him, or right for her.

"Tessa." His throat too tight to say more, he pulled her against his chest and wrapped his arms tightly around her. She pressed her cheek to the middle of his chest and he dropped a kiss on the top of her head. "Don't be sad. I want today to be special for us."

Tilting her head back, she looked up at him and he was relieved to see a shaky smile spread her lips. "Just being with you is special, Joseph."

It had been easy for Joseph to see she had mixed feelings about the circumstances of her inheritance, but she was making it pretty damn clear she wasn't confused about wanting him. And that was all the encouragement he needed to lower his head and capture her warm lips beneath his.

Soft. Giving. And oh, so delectable. Kissing Tessa was like trying to quench an unbearable thirst. No matter how much he searched her lips, it wasn't enough. When she curled her arms around his neck and arched her soft body into his, he felt sure the heat washing from his head to his feet was going to scorch him alive.

Only seconds passed before frustration had his tongue pushing against her teeth and she promptly opened her mouth to allow him inside. The intimate connection rocked his senses and instantly the kiss exploded into something much more. While their tongues clashed, his hands roamed over her back and shoulders, down her arms, then finally stopped to cradle the perky curves of her bottom.

Somewhere in the foggy haze, he recognized her hands were on an exploration of their own and, although the fabric of his denim shirt was thick, her fingers still managed to leave a trail of heat wherever she touched him. The fiery sensations made him want to tear off his shirt so he could feel her hands sliding over his bare flesh. But it was the need for oxygen that finally forced him to ease his mouth from hers.

Sucking in ragged breaths, he buried his face in the curve of her neck. "Tessa, I don't understand it. But I've wanted you from the very first moment I saw you."

"Oh, Joseph, that evening—after you left—I couldn't quit thinking about you." She lifted her face and began to plant tiny kisses along his jaw and down the side of his neck. "Now I want to show you how much I want you."

The feathery movement of her lips as she spoke against his skin sent erotic shivers down his spine. Her mere touch was seducing him and though a voice in the back of his mind was telling him to put the brakes on their embrace, he refused to listen. Making love to Tessa was the only thing he wanted. The only thing that mattered.

While common sense yielded to the heated desire of his body, Tessa's hands were at work separating the snaps on the front of his Western shirt. When the pieces of fabric parted, her hands flattened against the middle of his chest then began a slow descent until they reached his navel and the band of his jeans.

Struggling to hold himself together, Joseph wrapped his hands around hers to momentarily still the sweet torture of her caresses. "Tessa, are you sure about this?" he whispered. "We should be back on the Bar X. In your pretty white bed."

Her eyes narrowed to sexy slits as she smiled provocatively up at him. "We'll have plenty of time for the white bed—later. Besides, there's a nice thick blanket of pine needles right behind us. You're not afraid to rough it, are you?"

Groaning deep in his throat, he brought his forehead against hers. "And here I've been thinking all along that you're a soft princess."

She pulled off her cowboy hat and tossed it aside. "See, cowboy. I left my tiara home today."

Snagging an arm around her waist, he pulled her tight against him and kissed her just long enough to create a groan in her throat. Then, sweeping her up in his arms, he carried her to the shade beneath the pines. After gently placing her on the bed of brown needles, he paused a moment to look down at her.

Her eyes fluttered opened. "What's wrong, Joseph? Why are you looking at me like that?"

Something in the middle of his chest was twisting tighter and tighter, shortening his breaths to shallow gulps. "Because I'm looking at an earth angel and she's the most beautiful thing I've ever seen."

A smile tilted the corners of her kissed-pink lips and then, to his dismay, he spotted a tiny tear trickling from the corner of one blue eye. The sight pierced the softest part of him and he suddenly realized how very much he wanted to cherish and protect her, to make her world as bright and beautiful as she was making his.

He touched a forefinger to the moisture seeping into her hairline. "In case you didn't understand, that was a compliment."

"Oh, Joseph, I'm not sad. It's just being here with you like this that's making me teary."

His fingers gently stroked a few stray hairs away from her face. "I never thought this would be happening today," he said, his voice rough with desire. "And you deserve better."

"Better? It couldn't get better than making love here at this beautiful little oasis."

Reaching up, she linked her hands at the back of his neck and drew him down to her. He slanted his mouth over hers and tried to let his lips convey the rush of emotions flooding through him.

Eventually though, kissing her wasn't nearly enough, and he left her mouth to slide his lips across her cheek. Once he reached her ear, he gently sunk his teeth into the lobe and her groan of pleasure emboldened him to widen his search. Like a cat lapping sweet cream, he made a slow foray down the side of her neck until the barrier of her shirt prevented him from traveling lower.

His fingers fumbled with the top button on the garment, but Tessa brushed his hands away and quickly undid the front of her shirt.

Once the garment fell open, he pushed her flat against

the ground then eased back far enough to treat himself to a look at her. The pale blue bra cupping her breasts was made of delicate see-through lace, giving him a tempting glimpse of the brown nipples beneath. Just gazing at her was enough to send his senses tumbling end over end.

Drunk with desire, his fingers trailed along the edge of the lace then over the cups of her bra until his thumbs and forefingers were gently squeezing her nipples. The touch caused her to let out a soft mew and the needy sound had him dropping his head until his lips were touching the hollow between her breasts.

She smelled like a field of wildflowers and her skin had to be the softest thing he'd ever touched. He kissed her there then, tracing the tip of his tongue along her breastbone, he reached up and pulled both bra straps from her shoulders.

The moment they fell to her arms, she yanked the lace down from one breast then, with her hands in his hair, guided his mouth to the budded nipple.

Her boldness turned his blood to liquid fire and though he wanted to give her everything she wanted, his body was already teetering on the brink of exploding.

After a few short seconds he lifted his mouth from her breast.

"I'm…sorry, Tessa," he whispered brokenly. "I can't keep going—I have to be inside you. Now!"

Her fingers touched the side of his face. "And I need for you to be inside me. Now!"

Before he could collect his senses enough to make a move, she sat straight up and began removing her clothing. Joseph managed to follow suit and, after a few short moments, they were lying side by side on the blanket of pine needles.

"I should spread my shirt for you," he murmured as

he drew her tightly against him. "I don't want your back to get scratched."

She wrapped an arm around his neck and Joseph was instantly overwhelmed by her scent and the soft, alluring curves pressing against his bare skin.

"Don't worry about my back," she said in an urgent rush. "Just make me yours."

"Mine. Yes, all mine." He rolled until she was lying on her back and he was positioned over her.

With his hands anchored on either side of her shoulders, he paused. "You little minx. You've got me so crazy I nearly forgot to ask about protection."

"I'm on the pill. But if you're concerned…"

As her words trailed away, he groaned with disbelief. "Concerned? No, I'm relieved. Oh, babe, my only concern now is making you happy."

"Then don't make me wait."

Her raspy plea was all the urging he needed. Parting her legs with a knee, he entered her slowly, smoothly, until he was deep inside her. By then, Joseph was certain the day had turned to night and a thousand stars were raining down on him from every direction.

Nothing should feel this good or this right, he thought. But it did. Oh, it did. And just when he decided it couldn't get any better, she moaned and lifted her hips toward his, drawing him even deeper into her velvet heat.

Rocked by the hot sensuality of her body, he lowered his face until his lips enveloped hers. The connection set off a growl in her throat and then she was wrapping her arms and legs around him, anchoring her body to his.

Joseph began to move his hips against hers and she quickly followed, matching her thrust to the rhythm of his. In only a matter of moments he was transported to a hazy, distant place where there was nothing but flashes of color and waves of intense pleasure. The cool wind against his back was canceled by the raging heat inside him. The sound of the birds and the trickling water was drowned by the roaring sound of his heart drumming in his ears. All he knew was that Tessa's soft body was beneath his and he couldn't get enough.

At some point the realization that he might be hurting her pricked the back of his foggy mind. Yet when he tried to gentle his strokes, her body begged him for more. After that, he allowed her to set the pace, until it became so frenetic he could scarcely breathe and his heart felt as though it was on the verge of exploding.

Certain he was going to die from pleasure, Joseph tried to back off but she wouldn't allow it. And then, suddenly, it didn't matter. He heard her cries of relief and immediately felt himself falling over the edge of a deep gorge, spiraling ever so slowly toward a bed of white clouds.

Crying out, he clutched her tightly to him and waited for the incredible journey to come to an end.

Chapter Eight

Making love to Joseph had changed everything.

The thought kept rolling through Tessa's mind as she lay on her side next to him. His face and upper body were covered with sweat and his dark hair hung in damp, lanky curls across his forehead. He was a beautiful man with a wealth of goodness inside him and as they'd made love, she'd felt some of that goodness spill into her. Having her body connected to his had felt incredibly perfect and right, and unlike anything she'd ever felt before.

Reaching over, she touched her hand to his face and the contact caused his eyes to open and connect with hers. The tender light she saw in the brown depths made her heart ache with longing.

"Are you all right?" she murmured.

A wry smile slanted his lips. "Afraid you came close to killing me?"

With a humorous groan, she rolled close enough to

wrap her arm around his waist. "A little thing like me killing you with sex? It's not possible. But I'd like to try again—later."

A sexy chuckle rumbled deep in his chest. "Maybe I can manage to give you a second attempt. Let's finish our lunch and head back to your house. What do you say?"

Smiling, she eased out of his arms and reached for her clothes. "Better hurry," she teased over her shoulder, "or I'll eat all the leftovers."

Later, on the ride back to the ranch house, they took a different route that led them through open fields of blooming sage and an abundance of grass that somehow managed to thrive in the arid soil. Although Joseph had implied he wasn't in a hurry, several times he kicked Rascal into a long trot. Tessa had easily kept up with him, all the while wondering if he actually intended to keep his promise of making love to her again or if he was simply in a rush to end the ride.

Once they reached the ranch yard and put the horses out to pasture, Tessa didn't have long to wonder. Inside the house, he barely gave her enough time for a bathroom visit before he carried her straight to the bedroom.

In the soft, queen-size bed, Joseph made love to her at a slow, delicious pace that lasted through most of the afternoon. When it finally came to an end, Tessa relished the feeling of having her cheek pillowed on his shoulder and her body cradled in the curve of his.

Past the parted curtains, the sun was still bright, but it wouldn't be long before it turned red and slipped behind the distant hills. She had no idea how much longer Joseph planned to hang around and she wondered what he would think if she asked him to stay the night. Not that she was going to. In spite of the incredible intimacy they'd just shared, it was too early to expect any sort of commitment from him. Even a single night.

"What are you thinking?" Joseph asked "Missing the waterfall and all those pine needles?"

Drowsy and utterly satiated, she rubbed her cheek against his shoulder. "Mmm. The spot at the bluffs was so beautiful. I would love to camp there sometime. With just a bedroll and a coffeepot."

"And me?" he added teasingly.

Groaning, she turned so that her face was nestled against the side of his neck. "Naturally. It wouldn't be the same without you there."

With a thumb beneath her chin, he tilted her face up to his. "Maybe we should plan the trip soon. Before you decide to sell the place."

His comment caught her completely off guard. Obviously he was still thinking she was the here-today, gone-tomorrow type. Or, even worse, he was thinking she considered this day together as just an enjoyable round of sex and nothing more.

Frowning, she asked, "Is that what you're thinking? That I'm about to put the ranch up for sale?"

He was about to speak when his cell phone began to ring. "Sorry, Tessa, I have to get that. It's the sheriff's office."

"How do you know the call has to do with work?" she asked. "You haven't even looked at your phone yet."

"Work is a special ring," he explained as he threw back the sheet and reached to the floor to fish the cell from his jeans' pocket.

He answered the call by immediately identifying himself. Then, after a few brief words, ended the connection and swung his legs over the side of the bed.

"I have to go," he said abruptly. "There's been some

sort of disturbance over at the Fandango and the deputy handling the call needs help."

As he pulled on his clothes, Tessa hurriedly did the same.

"Fandango? Is that some sort of bar?"

"Bar, grill and dance hall all rolled into one. The place is a few miles south of Wickenburg on the highway to Phoenix."

"But this is Sunday afternoon!" she exclaimed while trying to tamp down her disappointment. "It's not even dark yet. People are already drunk and rowdy at this hour?"

"I have news for you, sweet Tessa—people get drunk and rowdy at all hours of the day. Even on Sunday."

He fastened his belt then jerked on his boots and reached for his hat on the way out of the bedroom. Tessa followed him to the front door, where he paused long enough to place a hasty kiss on her lips.

"Sorry, Tessa, I was hoping we'd have the whole evening together."

Even though she felt like she'd been doused with a bucket of cold water, his words reassured her somewhat. Doing her best to smile, she said, "Me, too. But we've had a nice day together."

"More than nice. I'll see you later." He planted another swift kiss to her lips then hurried out the door.

Tessa walked onto the porch and crossed the yard to stand in the shade of a cottonwood. By then, Joseph was already gunning his truck down the drive toward the main road. As she watched a cloud of dust swallow up the fast-moving vehicle, uncertainty crept over her. Joseph was a lawman. The fact rarely left her mind. But not until this very moment had she allowed herself to really consider everything his job entailed or how it would always affect his life.

Could she live on constant alert? Never knowing when or if he'd be called away to deal with a dangerous situation?

You need to grow up, Tessa. Just because Joseph had sex with you doesn't mean he's thinking of wedding bells. Or even love. This thing with Joseph is just temporary. Just like your life here in Arizona. The Bar X is just a place and Ray Maddox was just a man. The best thing you can do for yourself is to forget everything and go back to Nevada where you belong.

The recriminating voice made her feel even worse about Joseph's abrupt departure and, as she walked back to the house, Tessa did her best to shake away the negative thoughts. Yet as soon as she entered the living room and faced the big leather recliner with the faded headrest, the doubts and questions returned with a vengeance.

Ray was more than just a man to her, she thought. If not for the late sheriff, it was highly unlikely she would've ever met Joseph. But whether her relationship to the deputy was going to bring her great happiness, or an abundance of sorrow, she could only guess.

Nearly a week later, on Saturday evening, Joseph left his bedroom and descended the stairs to the ground floor of the ranch house. As he passed the open door of his mother's study, she called out to him.

"Joe, is that you?"

Pausing, he backed up a few steps and entered the large room furnished with a massive mahogany desk, a couch and matching armchair in cordovan leather, and bookshelves that lined two whole walls. The study had once been his father's office and Joseph could easily recall the many nights he'd spotted Joel working late, pouring over the endless paperwork that went along with running a ranch the size of Three Rivers. His father had loved the ranch and, up until the day he'd died, had dedicated his life to it and his family.

Walking over to the desk, where his mother sat beneath a small pool of lamplight, Joseph could see billing statements and receipts scattered in front of her. The sight caused a pang of regret to slash through him. His father should still be alive, managing the ranch and enjoying his wife and children. But that wasn't to be. And after five long years, Joseph was beginning to doubt the mystery of Joel's death would ever be unraveled.

Clearing his throat, he asked, "Did you need to speak with me, Mom?"

Leaning back in the desk chair, the weary smile on her face depicted the long hours she'd already put in today. "Not about anything specific. You've been away so much lately, we've only had a few minutes to talk at the breakfast table."

Joseph had always liked to think he had an especially close relationship with his mother. Not that she loved him more than his siblings. She loved all her children equally. But, rather, she seemed to understand Joseph had taken the loss of his father especially hard and she'd tried to compensate and give him as much of an anchor as possible.

Resting a hip on the corner of the desk, he said, "Sorry, Mom. We're short-handed at work, so all of us deputies have been putting in extra hours." He paused and attempted to clear the uncomfortable thickness from his throat. "And I've been seeing Tessa as much as I can."

She leveled a pointed look at him. "Yes, that's what

Blake has informed me. And if it hadn't been for him, I wouldn't have known that much."

The tone in his mother's voice had Joseph feeling like he was back in junior high school and was about to get a lecture for a miserable test grade.

He said, "Well, it's a cinch I can't talk to Holt about seeing a girl. He'd have the news spread all over Yavapai County. And Chandler is so busy, I rarely have time to say hello to him."

She let out a resigned sigh. "I guess the days when you could talk with your mother about such things are long past."

His mother was a tough cookie. She never played the sympathy card. Her uncharacteristic remark had him wondering if something else was going on that had her worried. God only knew what a heavy load she carried.

"Mom, nothing with you and me is long past," he said gently. "To be honest—I wasn't sure how you'd feel about me dating Tessa. The night of the dinner party I got the impression you liked her. But..."

Frowning, she leaned slightly toward him. "What are you saying, Joe? That you're getting serious about her and were worried about how I would react?"

Was he getting serious about Tessa? This past week he'd been desperate to spend every spare moment he could with her. Which had him wondering if he was simply suffering from a bad case of lust or something far deeper.

"I don't know how to answer that. Tessa has become very important to me. But I—"

His tangled emotions prevented him from going on. There wasn't any way he could explain the doubts that had been going through his mind. Or the fear that he was falling in love with a woman who had plans for a future that didn't include him.

"You what?" she prompted. "Aren't really sure she's someone you want to be around on a long-term basis?"

Joseph mindlessly adjusted the bolo tie positioned near the collar of his white shirt. "She's only been here for two weeks, Mom. That's not long enough to make that sort of decision."

Amused with his reasoning, she said, "Two weeks. The first time I met your father, I knew for certain he was the one."

"Yes, but you women have intuitions that tell you such things. Men have to take their time and figure them out. And I don't exactly have a good batting record with women."

Maureen shot him a droll look. "Joe, you need to be thanking God for not allowing you to end up with Candace or Willa. Both women would have been a mistake. As for Tessa, maybe you should ask yourself how you would feel if she suddenly went back to Nevada—to stay. Because that will most likely happen."

Joseph could understand his mother's concerns. She'd watched her eldest daughter suffer through a divorce. She'd seen Blake hurting over a shattered romance and little Camille was so heartsick over a man, she'd left the ranch completely. It was no wonder she might be worried that Joseph was headed down the same miserable path.

"I'm very aware of that, Mom."

"So this is just a temporary thing?" she asked. "You two are just enjoying each other's company while she's here."

It had already become far more than that, Joseph realized. But he wasn't going to heap that worrisome detail onto his mother.

"You could put it that way," he said. "She's still very much interested in finding out about Ray and his reasons for willing her the Bar X. I'm trying to help her with that."

The expression on his mother's face turned curious. "Oh. And how's that going?"

He grimaced. "I might be a decent deputy, but I'm not a detective. So far all I have is suppositions. I've been wanting to ask you what you thought of contacting Dottie's relatives back in South Carolina. Do you think they could give me any helpful information?"

Maureen's short laugh was mirthless. "You'd never hear the truth out of those people. They hated Ray and turned their back on Dottie because she wouldn't leave him."

Joseph had figured as much. But he was rapidly running out of leads. He had to try any and every angle.

He said, "Tessa gave me a couple of snapshots of her parents the day they got married. When I showed them to Louella and Connor, they both thought the man might possibly be Ray."

Maureen left her seat and walked around the desk to stand in front of him. "Joe, is this some sort of joke? Where are these photos, anyway?" she demanded. "I want to see them!"

The fact that his mother was angry and shocked over this revelation didn't surprise Joseph. Ray and Dottie had always been close friends to the Hollisters. To accuse the man of infidelity or bigamy was the same as accusing a family member.

"Sorry, Mom, I don't have the photos. They're at the crime lab. They were shot with a disposable camera about twenty-four years ago. Benjamin's trying to clear them up."

Her jaw dropped with disbelief. "Well, obviously Louella and Connor need their eyes examined. Ray was married to Dottie twenty-four years ago. Could be Tessa's father resembled Ray. That's the only reasonable explanation. And why would you even go down this path, anyway, Joe? I don't have to tell you that Ray was a good man."

Joseph stifled a groan. "Yes, Ray was a good man. But he was human and none of us is perfect, Mom. As for me going down this path, when a lawman works a case, he has to look in all directions, otherwise he might miss the truth. Think about it. Why would Ray give everything he had in the world to Tessa? A man has to have a concrete reason to do such a thing."

Maureen's head swung back and forth. "Ray adored Dottie. He would've never been unfaithful to her. There has to be another reason."

Ray might have adored Dottie in the spiritual sense, Joseph thought. But she'd been severely handicapped for the majority of their marriage. She couldn't have met Ray's sexual needs. But Joseph wasn't about to point out that possibility to his mother. She was already eyeing him like he was some sort of family traitor.

Biting back a sigh, he said, "It's just a theory, Mom. Nothing for you to get upset about. Anyway, I've got to be going or I'll be late."

Her gaze flicked over him. "You look very handsome tonight, son. Obviously you're not on your way to work."

He grinned. "I'm taking Tessa to a nice dinner in Phoenix. She's never been there and I thought she might enjoy something more than a night in Wickenburg or cooking a burger on her patio."

For a moment Joseph thought his mother was going

to give him a few more words of advice. Thankfully she must've decided against it, because she smiled and patted his arm.

"I'm sure she'll enjoy it. Go and have a good time."

"Thanks, Mom." He kissed her cheek then gestured to the desk behind them. "And if I were you, I'd put that stuff away and go relax with a glass of wine."

Chuckling softly, she looped her arm around the back of his waist. "You know, that's sounds like a good idea to me. Come on, you can walk with me to the patio on your way out."

"Joseph, you've been staring at me ever since we've sat down at our table. Is anything wrong? Do I have lipstick on my teeth or something?"

A wry expression on his face, he reached across the beautifully set table and wrapped his hand around hers. "I apologize for staring, Tessa. It's just that I've never seen you looking as gorgeous as you look tonight."

When Joseph had told her yesterday that they'd be going to Phoenix for dinner tonight, Tessa hadn't hesitated to drive into Wickenburg and shop the little boutique Emily-Ann had told her about. In the end she'd spent more than she'd planned on a lacy dress of pale pink. The circle skirt stopped just a fraction above her knees, while the fitted bodice showed off her slender waist. She'd found a pair of nude, high-heeled sandals to go with it and a rhinestone clip for her hair.

Last night she'd been wondering if her splurge on the outfit had been foolish. But now as she saw the appreciative gleam in Joseph's eye, she decided it had been worth every penny spent. Especially now that they were sitting in this elegant restaurant situated on the top floor of a four-star hotel.

When they'd arrived a few minutes ago, most of the linen-covered tables had been empty. But since they'd ordered their meal and a waiter had served them a bottle of chilled wine, several diners had filtered in and, from the looks of them, Tessa easily decided they were in the Hollisters' league, not hers.

She smiled at him. "Well, I can clean up from time to time."

Chuckling, he squeezed her hand. "That's obvious. Even though you look pretty damned sexy in ranch gear."

"Thank goodness. Since I've come to the Bar X, that's pretty much all I've worn. If the Calhouns could see me helping Sam spread feed and pitch hay to the horses, they wouldn't recognize me."

"You didn't do that sort of thing on the Silver Horn?"

She shook her head. "Too many wranglers and ranch hands around to take care of those types of jobs. And, frankly, I believe they thought I was too fragile to lift a feed bucket. Of course, no one would dare say anything like that to Sassy or Noelle. They can do anything around a ranch that a man can do. Maybe better."

"You've told me that Sassy is a sister to the Calhoun brothers, but I've not heard you mention Noelle before. Who is she?"

"She's Liam's wife. He's the detective," she added as a reminder. "Noelle owned a little ranch south of Carson City before she and Liam married. Ran it all by herself, too. She's tough, but beautiful. So is Sassy. Did I tell you that she raises horses and has a knack for starting colts?"

He looked surprised. "No. You haven't mentioned that. She must be a fierce woman. Her husband doesn't worry about her being injured?"

"Sure he does. But Jett wouldn't demand she give up something she loves. Although, I was talking with Lilly this afternoon and she told me Sassy won't be riding colts for the next few months. She's expecting again—their fourth."

Easing his hand from hers, he picked up his wineglass and took a long sip. "You miss your family, don't you?"

"A little. But I'm not homesick, if that's what you mean." She glanced to her right where a plate-glass wall gave them a panoramic view of the desert. The setting sun was dipping behind a ridge of jagged hills, spreading a magenta glow over the city. "This is so beautiful, Joseph. I wasn't expecting anything this special."

"You say that like you're not used to a man taking you to a nice restaurant."

"Not *this* nice. Housekeepers don't usually get asked out by the upper crust. At least, this one didn't. I was fed lots of fast food," she added with an impish smile. "Bad for the waistline but easy on the wallet."

A faint smile touched his face. "I'm sure you never complained."

"Why, no. I've never had any real money of my own, either. Not until Ray's will."

His expression took on a somber quality as his gaze roamed her face. "That's hard to believe. With the Calhouns being so wealthy, I figure they would've at least set aside some sort of trust fund for you."

"Believe me, Orin and Bart are always trying to give me money or make investments for me," she explained. "But I've never wanted that. After Mother was killed, they've provided me with everything I needed. Why would I want to take more? That would be taking advantage. I suppose that's why it's been hard for me to accept my inheritance from Ray. I can't see that I deserve it."

She took a sip of the fruity wine while his probing gaze continued to slide over her.

"Ray wouldn't like you thinking that way," he said. "He believed you deserved it. Otherwise he would've given everything to someone else. Sam, most likely."

She winced with a pang of remorse. "Sam," she repeated wistfully. "Everyone believes Sam should've gotten the Bar X. I even think so."

"Sam has everything he needs or wants. Especially now that you're here."

"What does that mean?"

His lips took on a wry slant. "Other than Ray and Dottie, Sam has never had anyone. Your company makes him happy."

She looked out at the rugged mountains, now shrouded in dark shadows, and tried to keep the sudden melancholy she was feeling from her voice. "Old Sam is a lot like me, I think. He's had a family take him under their wing, but he was never actually one of them. It's not the same thing as what you have, Joseph. It just can't ever be."

She turned her attention back to his handsome face while wondering what could possibly be wrong with her. She owned a beautiful stretch of land, a lovely house, and had more money in her bank account than she'd ever dreamed of having. The long, arduous task of acquiring her college degree was completed. She supposed from the outside looking in, most folks would think her life was coming up roses. Yet she'd never felt so torn or uncertain about herself or her future.

She drew in a deep breath. "After I talked to Lilly today, I got another call. From Jett—Sassy's husband. He's the Silver Horn's lawyer. The one who did all the communicating with Ray's attorney about the will."

His eyes narrowed skeptically. "Has he learned something else about the will? About Ray and you?"

"No. The call was nothing about that." Realizing she

was gripping the stem of the wineglass, she forced her fingers to relax. "He wanted to know when I might be coming home. He's offered me a job. A position, actually. As his assistant."

He remained silent for so long that Tessa felt like kicking his shin under the table…although she wasn't exactly sure what she wanted him to say. She only wished he cared enough to make some sort of reply.

She was on the verge of asking him point-blank how he felt about the news when a waiter suddenly approached with their salads.

Finally, after the young man had served them and left the table, Joseph said, "The Silver Horn must be massive if its lawyer has so much work to do he needs an assistant."

His remark reminded Tessa that she and Joseph had only known each other a short time. There was still so much he didn't know about her life back in Nevada. And so much she hadn't yet learned about his. Yet when she looked at him, the dear familiarity of his face made her feel as if she'd know him forever.

"Jett only works at the Horn a couple of days during the week. He has his own law practice in Carson City. His sister Bella used to work along with him. She's a lawyer, too. But she fell in love with Jett's ranch manager, Noah, and they married and moved to a ranch near Tombstone. Then Jett hired an assistant, Elaine, to sort of fill the void of Bella's leaving. But now he tells me Elaine is leaving in the next few days. Something to do with her husband's job being transferred out of state."

"I see. So what did you tell him?"

Actually, Tessa had been floored by Jett's proposition. She'd always admired him greatly. Not just because he was a devoted husband and father, but also a very dedicated lawyer who worked tirelessly to help people who'd found themselves in difficult situations. And although she'd often talked to Jett about finding a job, she'd never imagined having the opportunity to work directly with him. The idea was both flattering and exciting. Yet it was also very heart-wrenching. Joseph had just come into her life. She couldn't just walk away from him.

"I told him I'd have to think about it."

Without glancing her way, he shook the pepper shaker violently over the bowl of torn greens. "Why? Sounds like a dream job to me. Unless this Jett is a taskmaster or something."

"He wouldn't approve of an employee dawdling around and wasting time, that's for sure. But he'd hardly be a taskmaster." She ate a few bites of salad then said, "Let's talk about something else."

He flashed a glance at her. "All right. There's something I learned today that I've not mentioned to you yet. I was going to wait until later after we got back to the Bar X, but seeing you want something else to think about, I'll go ahead and share it with you now."

She wanted to tell him that she had more than enough to think about and that all of it revolved around him. But she kept the urge in check. Just like she'd been keeping all sorts of thoughts and feelings from him this past week. Each time they'd made love, her throat had ached with the need to tell him how much she was beginning to care about him, how very important he was becoming to her. But each time she'd held back.

Since the day they'd picnicked at the bluffs, the two of them had been together as much as his job had allowed. Not once during those long, lovemaking sessions had he come close to hinting he had serious intentions toward her. As a result she was finding it very hard to hold on to the hope that he would ever make any kind of serious commitment to her.

"Okay. I'm listening," she told him.

He dipped a fork into his salad. "I had to drive over to Camp Verde today to our eastern command center. While I was there dealing with another matter, I talked to a guy who used to work as the undersheriff to Ray. Mike was probably the closest friend Ray had on the force."

Her attention suddenly went on high alert. "Did you question him about Ray's will?"

"I brought it up. He'd not heard anything about you getting Ray's estate. And he never knew of Ray being associated with anyone by the name of Parker."

"That's the same answer everyone has given you so far," she said glumly.

"Yeah, but Mike gave me a little more. After I continued to press him, he recalled a time Ray went out of town—supposedly on a business trip—and when he returned he seemed happier than Mike had ever seen him. He said Ray even had a box of cigars and spread them around to the guys in the office. Mike thought it was odd and was thinking Ray was behaving like a man whose wife had just had a baby. Which was impossible because of Dottie's handicap."

Even though the large room was a pleasant temperature, Tessa felt a chill rush over her. "Did this Mike ask Ray what the cigars were for?"

"He did and Ray explained that he was just in a happy mood and wanted to share it with the men. At the time, Mike didn't believe it. And, frankly, I don't believe it now."

She put down her fork and stared at him. "Joseph, surely you don't believe that he—that those cigars were for *me* being born? It's a ludicrous idea."

"Why is it ludicrous? Because you don't want to believe that Ray might actually be your father?"

Her hands were suddenly trembling and she swiftly placed them in her lap just so he wouldn't see how shaken she was by this new information.

"You don't understand, Joseph. I don't have anything against Ray. Dear God, how could I? He's already given me so much. It's… I just can't bear to think of my mother—"

When she didn't go on, he finished for her.

"Being something other than what you thought?" he asked gently. "Well, I think most all children see their parents in a different light. And I figure most parents guard a few secrets of their own. Including mine. Sometimes I think my dad had some sort of secret and that's what eventually caused him to be killed."

Shivering at the thought, Tessa realized that Joseph had his own doubts and questions to deal with and, compared to hers, they were far more serious.

"What could your father have possibly been hiding? Sam tells me that Mr. Hollister was the best of the best. And since Sam doesn't talk much about other folks, that's saying a lot."

"Yeah, Dad was the kind of man every guy wants to be. As for the possibility of a secret, I've spent long hours trying to figure out what he could have been keeping to himself. I've told you how Ray believed there was a woman somehow involved. But I refuse to think Dad was doing anything wrong." He looked at her, his expression wry. "I suppose I'm like you, Tessa, I don't want to think of my father deceiving his family. No matter the reason."

Smiling gently, she reached across the table and touched her fingers to his. "It's like you said to me the night I visited Three Rivers. We have much in common."

With a faint grin, he turned his fingers over and wrapped them around hers. "Yes. Even more than sharing a kiss in the moonlight."

Chapter Nine

Tessa had been offered a job. One that she would hardly want to refuse. Like a vinyl record with a hung needle, the thought stuck in Joseph's mind throughout the remainder of the meal. And later, as they danced to a live band in the adjoining bar area, he still couldn't shake off the dismal notion.

Joe, maybe you should ask yourself how you would feel if she suddenly went back to Nevada—to stay.

His mother's words had hit home much sooner than Joseph had expected and he didn't have to ask himself how he would feel once Tessa was gone. He'd be totally and irrevocably lost. But what was he going to do about it? What could he do? She'd not said anything about loving him or making a future with him. She seemed hesitant to make any sort of concrete plans. Would that change if he told her how much she'd come to mean to him? How much he wanted her to stay in Arizona?

By the time they arrived back at the Bar X, Joseph was feeling worse than desperate and it showed in the urgent way he made love to her. When he finally rolled away from her, he was drenched in sweat, while Tessa appeared utterly drained.

"Forgive me, Tessa. I didn't mean to be so rough."

Scooting close to his side, she slid her hand slowly up and down his arm. "You weren't rough. But you did seem…far away. Is something wrong?"

He turned onto his side and immediately groaned at the sight of her flushed cheeks and swollen lips. Each time he took her into his arms, she gave him everything he asked for and more. There would never be any other woman like her in his life. Somehow he knew that.

"No. Nothing is wrong." He cupped his hand against the side of her face. "Being here with you like this… puts me in a different world. One that I don't want to leave."

She slipped an arm around his rib cage and drew herself tight against him. Joseph instinctively ran a hand down the bumpy ridges of her spine until he reached the flare of her hips.

"I don't want you to leave it," she murmured. "In fact, I've been thinking you should spend the night with me."

He'd been thinking about it, too. Over and over, he'd imagined sleeping beside her. Waking up to see her smiling face next to his. But to him, staying would be making a commitment of sorts. Was he ready to risk that?

He said, "You must have heard I cook a mean breakfast."

Chuckling, she pressed her lips to the spot where his neck curved into his shoulder. Joseph immediately felt his loins tighten with desire and the reaction made him wonder if she would always wield this much power over his body.

"Mmm. That's good to know," she murmured. "I'll take pancakes and link sausage. With plenty of syrup. Can you manage that?"

Strange how easy it was to picture himself cooking for Tessa, sitting across the breakfast table from her and sharing the last of their coffee on the patio. He could even imagine further into the future, where the Bar X corrals held a small herd of horses, cattle grazed on the flats and Tessa held a baby in her arms. His baby.

Clearing his throat, he said, "No. I can't manage that."

"Well, if that's too complicated, I can easily settle for scrambled eggs and toast."

Even though he couldn't see her face, he could hear a big smile in her voice and the sound drove a dagger of regret right through his chest.

"That's not—I'm talking about more than food now."

Her head tilted back until her blue gaze was locked on his. "What *are* you talking about, Joseph?"

The soft smile on her lips had him groaning with frustration before he rolled away from her and sat up on the side of the bed. As he pulled on his boxers, he tried to swallow away the thickness in his throat. "I'm saying I'm not ready to spend the night with you. That's all."

"Oh."

Behind him, he heard a rustle of sheets and then felt the mattress move as she rose from the bed.

While she remained stubbornly silent, he pulled on his jeans and boots, then reached for his shirt where she'd tossed it to the floor. He was jamming his arms into the sleeves when she walked in front of him.

"I'll be out on the patio," she said, her voice strained.

His hand shot out and wrapped around her upper arm. "That's all you have to say? That you're going outside?"

She glanced pointedly down to where his fingers were clamped into her flesh. "What are you expecting from me, Joseph? For me to get on my knees and beg you to stay?" Without giving him time to answer, she shook her head. "Sorry, but that's not going to happen."

His jaw clenched, he muttered, "I don't want you to beg! But I would expect you to be interested enough to wonder why!"

Pulling her arm from his grip, she backed away from him as though he was a stranger instead of the man she'd just given her body to in an oh, so generous way.

"Why?" she asked mockingly. "I don't have to ask you that question, Joseph. I already know the answer. You're afraid you might get too comfortable. And you don't want that to happen. You don't want to make the slightest commitment to me."

She'd hit the mark so closely Joseph could only wonder if he'd turned transparent or if the short time they'd been together was enough for her to learn what was inside him.

His lips flattened to a grim line as he fastened the snaps on his shirt. "That right, I don't. And why should I? You certainly don't want to make me any promises."

Her lips parted in dismay as she took a hesitant step toward him. "That's insulting! I've invited you into my arms—my bed. Maybe that doesn't count much to you, but it does to me."

Before he could react to that, she hurried out of the room. Joseph started to follow her then decided against it. Instead he made a trip to the bathroom and used a few moments to wash up and collect himself.

But as he combed damp fingers through his hair, he

stared at his image in the vanity mirror and wondered what kind of fool was staring back at him.

When Joseph finally made an appearance on the patio, Tessa was sitting in one of the lawn chairs, staring out at the starlit sky, trying to fight back angry tears. Anger at herself and at fate for bringing her to Arizona in the first place.

Easing down in the chair next to her, he said in a flat voice, "You're angry with me now."

She looked at him and the pain in the middle of her chest felt like a hand was squeezing the life right out of her heart. "No. Not at you. At myself. I should have known better than to think—I don't know what I thought—except that I believed we were growing close. Obviously it was too close for you."

He let out a heavy sigh. "What do you expect from me, Tessa? You're here on the Bar X temporarily. Am I supposed to give you my heart and then let you carry it back to Nevada with you?"

"Joseph, I—"

"Look, Tessa," he interrupted. "I made some huge mistakes in the past. First with Candace, then with Willa. I don't want to make a third with you."

Tessa wanted to leap from the chair and fling herself at him. She wanted to pound her fist against his chest until she was so spent she didn't care what he did or said.

"That's what I am to you? A mistake? Too bad you didn't realize that earlier this evening," she said bitterly. "You could have saved yourself a lot of money on dinner and wine."

"Don't be silly. This isn't about money."

Her nostrils flared as she struggled to keep her temper at bay. “Really? I’m sure you’ve not forgotten for a minute that I worked as a maid for several years.”

“Damn it, Tessa, I’m not a snob. Besides, you have money now.”

She made a mocking snort. “You can’t dress up a dandelion and call it a rose. Half of my life I’ve been an orphan. And now, thanks to you, I’m not even sure who my father might have been. It’s no wonder you don’t want to stay the night with me. I’m the kind of girl that’s only good enough for part of the night. Right?”

In a flash he was on his feet standing in front of her. “You’re the one who’s being insulting now. If you’d give me a chance to talk, I might be able to explain a few things.”

“What is there to explain?” He’d gone as far as he was willing to go in their relationship. Now she felt like a complete idiot for dreaming she could have more with this man. “You’ve pretty much stated your case already.”

“I can’t trust you, Tessa. It’s that simple.”

Incredulous, she stared at him. “Trust? You think—”

Shaking his head, he walked over to the edge of the patio and stood beneath the spiny limbs of a Joshua tree. “Hell, I’m not talking about you and other men. I’m talking about you staying here on the Bar X. So far, you’ve not made up your mind about anything.”

To him she probably did seem indecisive. But coming here to Arizona had uprooted her from the only life she’d known. He should understand she needed time to consider all the major changes she’d been dealt since her inheritance. The main one being him.

Leaving the chair, she crossed the short space between them until she was standing directly behind him. As she stared helplessly at the middle of his back, she swallowed at the emotions tightening her throat. She wanted so badly for him to understand. She desperately needed him to take her into his arms and assure her that being with her was all that mattered.

"I've not been here a month yet, Joseph." She attempted to reason. "Don't you think you're rushing me a bit? This is my life you're talking about."

He turned and pinned her with an accusing look. "It's my life you're tampering with, too! I'm not a complete fool, Tessa. I heard the wistful note in your voice this evening when you told me about the job offer. A big part of you wants to go back to Nevada. To be with your family and friends. It's home to you."

Normally, Tessa had the patience of a saint, but at the moment she could feel her cheeks burning with anger. "That's right! Just like Three Rivers is home to you. And you don't see me pressuring you to leave it, do you?"

"I think I deserve to know whether you're going to stay in Arizona or not!"

Yes, he did deserve that much, Tessa thought miserably. But she couldn't make him a promise to stay. Not when an avalanche of fear was urging her to run as hard and fast as she could from him and this place.

The amount of men Tessa had dated in her life were pitifully few and none of those short-term relationships had been even close to a full-blown affair. Now that she'd found Joseph and experienced real passion, she'd begun to ask herself just how long it could actually last. She might not be that experienced with men, but she wasn't totally ignorant, either. Taking a woman to bed didn't necessarily mean he loved her or wanted to marry her. And she was desperately afraid that if she allowed herself to believe Joseph might grow to love her, he'd decide to move on and leave her with nothing but a broken heart and memories that would haunt her for the rest of her life.

A sting of helpless tears forced her gaze to drop from his. "I'm sorry, Joseph. But I still haven't learned why Ray willed the Bar X to me! How could you expect me to know whether I'm going to stay here permanently?"

Even though the patio was partially covered with dark shadows, she didn't miss the steely look in his eyes.

"Yeah," he said with sarcasm. "I'm being stupid to expect you to give me any kind of answers. Your mind is so hung up on the past, you can't begin to think about the future! As far as I can see, Ray Maddox has nothing to do with what's going on with you and me. Maybe he's your father. Or maybe he simply picked your name out of a phone book and decided you're the lucky winner of his will. Who the hell knows? One way or the other, you need to get your head on straight!"

Her teeth snapped together. "And you ought to understand that I need time to think about this!"

"Well, I damned sure plan to give you plenty of it."

He stepped around her and stalked into the house.

Stunned, Tessa momentarily stared at his retreating back then hurried after him.

By the time she entered the house, he'd already reached the living room and was jamming his hat onto his head.

"You're leaving." She stated the obvious.

He paused long enough to glance in her direction before he headed toward the door. "I think it's best for both of us, Tessa."

Her heart hammering with heavy regret, she walked over to where he stood with his hand on the doorknob. If only he would put his arms around her, she thought dismally, and tell her he couldn't live without her. But that wasn't going to happen and she'd been stupid to think it ever could.

"I'm sorry the night ended this way, Joseph," she said hoarsely. "I'm sorry that I can't give you the answers you want."

"Yeah. Me, too." He opened the door and stepped onto the porch. "When you decide to grow up enough to make some decisions, give me a call. Otherwise, I won't be around."

Any other time, she would've suggested that he go jump in a deep gorge and take a few days to claw his way out. But surprisingly the anger that had burned so brightly in her a few minutes ago had all drained away. Now all she felt was emptiness.

"If you think on it long enough, I believe you'll decide you need to do some growing up, too, Joseph. Goodbye."

She shut the door between them, then slowly walked to the bedroom and removed her robe. The bed felt cold as she climbed between the sheets, but she could remedy that with a few extra blankets. It was the terrible ache in her heart that was going to be far more difficult to cure.

"You want to stop at Maria's for tacos? I'm too hungry to wait until we get back to Prescott to eat."

Joseph continued to stare moodily out the passenger window of the truck as Connor drove them down the main highway that ran through the tiny community of Yarnell. It was nearing eleven o'clock at night and, considering he'd not eaten since one in the afternoon, thoughts of food should have been on his mind. Instead he could think of little more than Tessa and the painful look on her face as he'd walked out the door.

"I don't care. Whatever."

"You don't care," Connor repeated in a mocking voice. "That's not a bit surprising. Maybe I'll eat the tacos and give you a piece of cardboard to chew on. You wouldn't know the difference anyway."

Frowning, Joseph glanced over at his partner. Ever since Monday, when a sniper-type shooting had wounded a deputy on the outskirts of Prescott, the captain had ordered all remaining deputies to work in pairs rather than patrol remote areas of the county alone.

Normally, Joseph would've enjoyed working shifts with his longtime buddy, but as the week had continued to pass without a word from Tessa, his frayed nerves had reached the snapping point.

Did you really expect Tessa to contact you, Joe? You more or less chopped off all ties to the woman. And you did it in a selfish, hurtful way. No. She isn't going to call you, speak to you, or even waste her time thinking of you. So forget it. Forget her.

Hating the negative voice in his head, Joseph wiped a hand over his face in an effort to clear his mind. "Put enough ketchup on it," he muttered, "and I can eat anything."

Connor wheeled the vehicle off the road and braked to a stop in front of a tiny adobe building with a flat roof and a turquoise door positioned between two dusty windows.

"Thank goodness Maria's is still open. What do you want to drink?" Connor asked as he unlatched his seat belt.

"Anything. Whatever you get for yourself will be fine with me." Joseph dug his wallet from the back pocket of his jeans and tossed several bills over to his friend. "Use that to pay for the whole thing."

"Hmm. Wonders never cease," Connor joked. "There's actually a nice guy behind that badge you're wearing."

Before Joseph could make a retort, Connor left the truck and went inside the little building to order their food.

Joseph scrunched down in the seat and rested the back of his head on the headrest, but didn't allow himself to relax to the point of closing his eyes. The radio on the dashboard continued to crackle with static and the intermittent voice of a female dispatcher. So far the night had been quiet, yet it was evident from the frequency of the radio exchanges that the department was on high alert. Every little suspicious act was being investigated and would continue to be in that manner until the sniper was identified and caught.

Tessa was living all alone on the Bar X without anyone to protect her. Not even a dog to bark out a warning. The idea had always bothered him, but since the shooting, it had become more worrisome. More than once this week he'd thought about stopping by Sam's and asking the ranch hand if he'd be willing to go up and spend the night at the Bar X. But Sam would insist on sleeping in the barn and that would be asking too much of the man. Besides, having Sam there would only be a short-term solution.

The door of the truck suddenly opened and Connor tossed a grease-spotted paper bag onto the console between the seats, then handed Joseph a large foam cup filled with ice and cola. "Here it is," he said. "Dig in."

Joseph pulled out one of the tacos wrapped in waxed paper and settled back in the seat. Connor did the same and, for several moments, the two men ate in thoughtful silence. Outside the truck, a hot night wind was kicking up dust from the dirt parking lot and swirling it around the truck. With only a few hundred people living in the area, there was hardly any activity around the buildings lining the two-lane highway, making the little town eerily quiet at this time of night.

"I hate coming here," Connor mused as he sipped his cola.

"Why? Not enough bright lights and action for you?"

He shook his head. "No. Each time I drive down 89, I think of the Yarnell Hill fire and the nineteen firefighters who lost their lives. It's sad to think about."

Four years ago, the enormous flash fire that had started from a lightning strike had not only taken many human lives, it had also destroyed more than a hundred buildings around the town. The tragedy had garnered national attention.

"Yes. But time marches on and the human spirit overcomes the loss and pain—eventually."

"Hmm. You're sounding damned philosophical tonight. At least that's better than the grumpiness I've been getting from you these past few days."

"It's been a tough week."

"Yeah. Everyone in the sheriff's department has been on edge. But the medical report on Jimmy is encouraging. At least he's going to make it." Connor glanced over at him. "Guess your mom hates seeing you head out to work."

"She's feels like the rest of the folks in Yavapai County. It's unsettling to her, but she isn't wringing her hands. She believes it was an isolated incident. Or, at least, she's telling me that just to reassure me."

Joseph forced himself to choke down another bite of taco while wondering if Tessa had been watching the local news and if she might be worrying about his safety. Or was she already forgetting him and getting ready to go back to Nevada? The questions rolling through his mind left him cold.

"It can't be easy for her," Connor said, interrupting Joseph's dismal thoughts. "Not after losing your father the way you did."

Joseph cringed. His father's death was the last thing

he needed to be dwelling on tonight. But he didn't point that out to Connor. In spite of his friend's usual happy-go-lucky demeanor, Connor's young life had been anything but a bed of roses. His mother had been an unwed teen when she'd given birth to him. Afterward she'd wound up in juvenile detentions on several occasions. Thankfully at that point, he'd had a father who was willing to step in and take over. But Brad Murphy had died suddenly when Connor was still in high school and after that he'd been shuffled back and forth between grandparents and a pair of uncles. It was a credit to Connor's own moral compass that he'd grown up to be a responsible man.

"A lot of things aren't easy for her now that Dad is gone," Joseph conceded. "But Mom is a rock."

Joseph was about to shove the last bite of taco into his mouth when he heard his phone signal that he had a personal message. For the first couple of days after he'd left the Bar X, he'd frequently checked his phone for a text from Tessa. Now, after nearly a week had passed, he didn't allow himself to hope it was her.

Dragging the phone from his pocket, he punched the screen until he reached the new message. The sender was Benjamin with the news that he'd finished work on Tessa's snapshots. Joseph could pick them up at the crime lab.

"You're scowling," Connor said. "Must be bad news."

Shaking his head, Joseph dropped the phone back into his pocket. "I'm not sure what Tessa would consider good or bad."

"Tessa? Who's she? A new girlfriend?"

Girlfriend? What he felt for Tessa couldn't begin to be described as a girlfriend. In the short time they'd been together, she'd grabbed hold of his hopes and dreams. She'd made him start wanting things that he'd long ago pushed aside. Like a home and children of his own.

"Not exactly a girlfriend. She…er, moved onto Sheriff Maddox's ranch about a month ago. Those old photos I showed you the other day—those belong to her. And Ben has been trying to clear them up for me. The message was from him. He has them finished."

Frowning with confusion, Connor dug another taco from the sack. "I don't get it. What's the deal with the photos? She doesn't know who those people are?"

Joseph gave him a quick rundown about Tessa being orphaned, the surprise inheritance and the mystery about her connection to Ray. He didn't go on to tell him that he'd ended up getting much closer to his new neighbor than he'd ever planned to.

"Tessa knows the woman is her mother," Joseph continued to explain. "The man is another matter. The photo was supposedly taken on their wedding day and the man is Tessa's father."

Connor's expression took on a shocked look as he shifted around in the seat toward Joseph.

"But, Joseph…that's—when I looked at the snapshots the other day, I told you I thought that was Ray Maddox!" He lifted the straw cowboy hat from his head and speared fingers through his blond hair as though that would clear his thinking. "Hell's bells! Reckon that could be him? But what about his wife—Dottie?"

"I don't know, Connor. None of it makes sense."

Downing the taco in three quick bites, Connor reached for the key in the ignition. "Let's head back to Prescott and take a look at those photos."

Joseph shook his head. "We've not finished our rounds. Let's drive to the county line first and then we'll head back."

Connor groaned. "You're too damned honest."

No, Connor was wrong, Joseph thought. He wasn't

an honest man. At least, not with Tessa. Otherwise he would have confessed that his feelings for her had grown into something very serious. He would've told her how thoughts of her leaving were tearing him apart. Instead he'd tried to pressure her into saying everything he'd wanted to hear. He didn't have any right to think of himself as a tough lawman. He was nothing more than a spineless sap.

If you think on it long enough, I believe you'll decide you need to do some growing up, too, Joseph.

As the two men traveled the remaining thirty-plus miles to the county line, Tessa's departing words continued to haunt Joseph. Maybe he did need to do a little growing, he thought. But he also needed a woman who knew what she wanted and, so far, Tessa didn't seem to know what she wanted most. Him or her life back in Nevada.

Chapter Ten

"For someone who was so all fired up about going on a horseback ride this morning, you've sure gone quiet on me now."

Tessa looked over at Sam as the two of them rode Rosie and Rascal across a stretch of grazing land east of the ranch house.

"Sorry, Sam. I was just doing some thinking, that's all."

"You appear to be doing a lot of that here lately. You worried about something?"

Worried? It was worse than that, Tessa thought. She'd been going around in a painful daze, asking herself how things with Joseph had abruptly turned from bliss to hell in a matter of moments. Aside from losing her mother, these past few days had been the worst in her life. What was she going to do about it?

When you decide to grow up enough to make some decisions, give me a call.

Initially his remark had infuriated her. But now that a week had passed without him, she'd thought on his words long and hard and decided he was right. Being indecisive was just as bad as making a wrong choice.

"I'm not worried," she told Sam, thinking *heartsick* was more like it. "Should I be?"

He shrugged a bony shoulder. "I thought with the shooting the other day, you might be a little worried about Joseph. But, heck, he knows what he's doing. He won't take unnecessary chances."

Her heart was suddenly hammering with fear. "The shooting? What are you talking about?"

He clamped his lips together and Tessa could see he was angry at himself for saying anything.

"A deputy was wounded. Happened somewhere west of Prescott. Some idiot shooting with a long-range rifle. Haven't caught the bastard yet, either."

"Oh." She felt like dozens of heavy rocks had just tumbled to the pit of her stomach. "I didn't know anything about it. I rarely turn on the television to hear the news."

"Well, like I said, I wouldn't concern myself about it too much. Joe usually works the southern part of the county anyway."

Like the shooter couldn't move to different areas of the county? she thought sickly.

"So they think the crime was committed by someone who was personally targeting lawmen?"

"Seems that way," Sam answered. "Still, it wouldn't hurt for you to keep your eyes peeled, Tessa. What with you living here alone."

"I'll be careful," she tried to assure him, even though

a chill was creeping down her spine. Not for her own safety, but for Joseph's.

The two of them rode on until the grassy valley ended at a ridge of jagged hills covered with blooming cholla, paloverde and tall saguaros. As they reined their horses to a stop in the shade of a juniper tree, Sam said, "That's some beautiful grass. Best I've seen in years. Thanks to the little shower we got the other night. You could graze a sizable herd on this piece of land, that's for sure."

Tessa gazed out at the wide valley blanketed with a stand of green grass and desert wildflowers. Ever since she'd arrived on the Bar X, she'd often imagined how it would look as a working ranch again. And with each passing day, the desire to restore the ranch to its former glory was growing stronger and stronger.

"That would be something, wouldn't it? To see my own cattle and horses grazing on my own land." She let out a wistful sigh then shook her head. "Don't laugh, Sam, but there's a part of me that wants to actually go for it. To purchase the cattle and horses and see if I could make the place go. With your help, of course."

A broad smile split the cowboy's wrinkled face. "Damned right, with my help," he said, then squinted an eye at her. "And why would I laugh at that idea? I've been waiting and praying to hear you say something like that. I know it'd be what Ray would want."

What Ray would want. Oh, God, if only she could know what Ray had actually wanted when he'd willed the Bar X to her. Then maybe she could understand where she truly belonged. Joseph hadn't recognized just how deeply the not knowing affected her. Maybe if he had, he wouldn't have ever turned his back on her.

"But Ray didn't know me, Sam," she returned. "He

didn't know whether I even liked the outdoors, much less if I'd be interested in owning a ranch."

"He must've figured it all out somehow. And don't ask me how or why." His gloved hand made a cross over his chest. "'Cause he never told me."

Tessa let out a weary sigh. "I believe you, Sam. And I'm beginning to believe he didn't tell anyone else, either. Not even his lawyer."

"Well, it don't matter now, Tessa. He's gone. But you and me can get this ranch going again. That is—if you plan on making it home."

Tessa's throat tightened as she recalled that very first evening she'd arrived on the Bar X. The sight of it had overwhelmed her and not just because it was beautiful. Something about the place had tugged on her heart—like she'd been coming home after a long separation. And from that moment on she'd been afraid to admit those strange feelings to anyone, even herself.

She nudged Rosie forward, but after going a few feet, reined the mare to a stop. Sam immediately rode Rascal alongside her.

"What's wrong?" he asked.

"Nothing," she said, shaking her head as she fought off the urge to drop her face in her hands and weep. "That's not true, Sam. Everything is wrong. I've been behaving like a child. I've been silly and afraid and—"

"And you and Joe have had a row. Is that it?"

Tessa wasn't aware that Sam had known about her relationship with Joseph. The older man was only at the ranch in the mornings and sometimes in the early evenings to do chores. He'd probably spotted Joseph's truck parked in front of the house and put two and two together.

"Yes. We had a big row," she said in a choked voice. Then, lifting her chin to a proud angle, she looked out at the desert land. Her land. "When I first came down here to Arizona, Sam, I expected to only stay a few days. Just long enough to look the place over and find a real-estate agent to sell the ranch for me. But from the very first day everything took me by surprise. It all felt so right to be here. And then one day led to another."

"Nothin' wrong with that, Tessa."

"No. But then I got to feeling all mixed up. I have folks up in Nevada that love me. I have a good job waiting on me—if I want it."

"You have folks that love you here, too. If you'll just give them a chance."

She looked over at Sam and the kindness she saw on his brown, leathery face caused a tear to slip from the corner of her eye. "I'm not so sure about Joseph. He doesn't trust me to stick around. And I can't blame him for that. I've been worse than wishy-washy. And now—well, even if I told him I was staying put, he wouldn't believe me."

"Are you trying to tell me you're going to stay and make this your home?"

She nodded her answer and as she did a great sense of relief washed over her. "Even if I never learn my connection to Ray, I feel certain this is where I belong."

"Men are stubborn cusses, Tessa. We have to be shown instead of told. I figure once Joe sees you're digging roots, he'll come around."

Yes, it was time she rooted down, Tessa thought. Time she showed Deputy Joseph Hollister that she was a strong woman. One who knew exactly what she wanted in life.

Smiling over at Sam, she urged Rosie forward. "Come on, Sam. Let's get back to the ranch house and I'll make us a pot of coffee. We have lots of planning to do."

* * *

Later that same evening, Joseph was sitting on the back patio, absently sipping at a glass of iced tea, when his mother walked up and sank into a chair next to him. She was wearing her jeans and boots and, from the looks of their dirty condition, he figured she'd been out with the men helping with branding and vaccinations.

Her gaze sliding over his uniform, she asked, "Night shift again?"

"Yes. It'll stay night shift until the captain decides to change the schedule."

"Well, Reeva has dinner almost ready. I hope you're hungry. She's made roast chicken and chocolate cake."

"Sounds good. But I don't have time to eat. I need to leave in ten minutes."

"I'll have her dish it up in containers and you can take it with you."

"Thanks, Mom, but I'm not hungry."

The concern on her face was the sort that could only come from a mother. "You look like you've not eaten in days. Are you still worried about Jimmy? I hear he'll be getting released from the hospital soon."

"Jimmy is going to be fine. No thanks to the bastard who took a potshot at him."

Her gaze never leaving him, she pulled a bobby pin from the knot in her hair, twisted it tighter and jabbed the pin back in place. "I've had my eye on you, Joe. Something is wrong. Spit it out."

He snorted. "You have five children. You can't keep your eyes on all of us."

With a short laugh, she left the chair and walked over to the bar. After pouring herself a small glass of wine, she came to stand in front of him.

"Mothers have eyes in the backs of their heads. And

this one can see you're miserable. What's happened? Is it Tessa?"

Staring into his tea glass, he drew in a long breath and wondered why the middle of his chest held such a constant ache. "Talking about it won't help."

"Why don't you try me?"

Smiling wanly, he looked up at her. "Okay. Your son is an idiot. I always seem to pick the wrong woman."

"Oh. So you think Tessa is wrong for you. That's funny. I had pretty much come to the conclusion that she was perfect for you."

Joseph placed his glass on a table next to his chair then used both hands to scrub his face. "She doesn't know what she wants, Mom," he said wearily. "She doesn't even know if she's going to stay on the Bar X or go back to Nevada. She says she needs time to make a decision. Well, the way I see it, if she cared enough about me, she wouldn't need time to think. She'd know right off. I told her I didn't want to see her. Not until she decided to grow up."

Maureen eased into the adjacent lawn chair. "Oh, Joe, I'm ashamed of you! Dear Lord, the poor darling has only been here for a month! Besides that, she's had all kinds of huge changes thrown at her. If you wanted to make points with the woman you should've been showing her some love and patience. Not pressuring her and making ultimatums!"

"Damn it, Mom, I know you're right. At least, I know it now. After all these days without her, I've had plenty of time to think." He looked at his mother and for one moment wished he was a small boy again. Back then she could fix any problem. Even when he'd lost his favorite horned lizard, she'd gone out and helped him find another. But he wasn't a boy anymore and Tessa was far more important than his pet horned lizard. “I don’t know what to do now. I figure she’s probably already making plans to leave.”

Maureen glared at him with disgust. “I’ll tell you what you’re going to do. You’re going to go over to the Bar X and grovel. You’re going to tell her what a jackass you’ve been and how much you still love her.”

Love her. If he’d realized just how much he loved Tessa a week ago, he wouldn’t be in this agony now.

His mother reached across the small table and placed a hand on his arm. “Joe? You look sick.”

His head swung back and forth. “I am sick, Mom. I—never told Tessa anything about loving her. How could I—when she couldn’t even tell me whether she was going back to Nevada! Besides, there’s another issue I’m dealing with now. Those photos I told you about—of Tessa’s parents. Ben did a pretty good job of clearing them up and I hate to tell you this, but the man looks like Ray to me.”

Joseph could see it was on the tip of her tongue to argue the matter, but then she eased back in the chair and took a long drink of the wine as though she needed some sort of sustenance to accept the reality.

“You’re sure about this?” she asked.

“Not a hundred percent. But Connor and I believe it’s him. Though how or why he might have been with Tessa’s mother is another matter. I promised Tessa I would help her find answers about Ray. But I’m not so sure she’s going to be happy about this news. It basically makes her mother out to be a liar. She doesn’t want to think her parents lived a lie. Or her father wasn’t the man she believed him to be.”

“You’ve told me that Tessa’s father died before she was born. So she has no perception of the man,” Maureen pointed out.

"I think Monica Parker painted Tessa's father as a very admirable man."

Maureen sighed. "Tessa seems like a strong woman to me. And she needs to know the truth about the photos. Being honest with her is the only way to start a relationship."

Start a relationship? If only he could start over with Tessa, he thought dismally. But he was deeply afraid he'd waited too long to be totally honest with her.

"Seeing her this evening is out. I barely have time to make the drive to work." Joseph's reasoning was as much for himself as his mother. "I'll show her the pictures tomorrow and try to make amends."

She reached over and patted his shoulder. "Everything will work out, Joe."

Even if the situation was hopeless, it was a mother's job to give her child words of encouragement. But this was one time Joseph desperately wanted to believe his mother was right. Because, without Tessa, his chance for any kind of happiness was over.

The next morning, while waiting for Sam to return from town with a part to repair a broken windmill, Tessa was in the kitchen making sandwiches for lunch when she heard a knock on the front door.

Frowning, she put down the tomato she'd been slicing. That couldn't be Sam, she decided as she wiped her hands on a paper towel. When he came to the house, he always knocked on the back door.

Joseph! Could it be?

Her heart hammering with hope, she hurried through the living room and into the small foyer. At the door, she hastily smoothed a hand over her ponytail, then raised up on tiptoes to peep through the small square of window. But the man standing on the porch wasn't Joseph, it was Orin.

Orin! Here on her doorstep!

Her mind too stunned to think past opening the door, she fumbled with the knob and finally managed to swing the partition wide.

"Hello, Tessa," he greeted. "Surprised to see me?"

The endearing smile on his face caused a muffled cry of joy to escape her. Then she leaped across the threshold and flung her arms around him.

"Surprised? I'm stunned!" she exclaimed. "Oh, I'm so happy to see you!"

"My, my, I was hoping I'd get a warm reception, but I wasn't expecting this!" Chuckling, he hugged her tight then stepped back and took a measured look at her. "You look great, honey. Just great."

She glanced around his shoulder. "Are you alone? Noreen didn't come with you?"

"Noreen wanted to make the trip, but she's tied up with cases and wedding plans."

"Well, it's wonderful that you're here." Suddenly aware of her appearance, she hurriedly brushed her hands down the front of her dusty jeans. "I look awful. I've been out helping Sam with the windmills and—oh, what am I thinking?—please come in, Orin." She reached for his arm and led him into the house. "So when did you leave the Horn? You haven't had time to make the drive today."

"I got to Wickenburg late last night so I stayed in a motel there," he told her.

"Oh, I wished you'd driven out here to the Bar X. I have three guest bedrooms just ready and waiting for a visitor."

As they moved into the living room, his eyes made a quick survey of his surroundings. "This is nice, Tessa.

Very nice. And the outside looks beautiful, too. I'm properly impressed."

Orin Calhoun was an extremely busy man. He'd not made the long trip down here just to look at her ranch, Tessa thought, but she didn't question why he was there. Knowing him, he'd tell her soon enough.

"Thank you. I'm very proud of the place. Just wait until you see the land." She grabbed him by the arm. "Come on and I'll show you the rest of the house."

After a quick tour of the rooms, she took him back to the kitchen, where he made himself comfortable on a stool at the breakfast bar.

At the cabinet counter, Tessa draped a sheet of clear plastic over the plate of sandwiches she'd put together. "Would you like iced tea or coffee? I have a few sodas, too. And a bottle of Irish whiskey if you need a shot of something stronger," she offered.

"Whiskey! Since when did you take up drinking? Is that what living down here has done to you?"

Normally, Orin's question would have pulled a laugh from her. But since Joseph had moved out of her life, she'd stopped laughing altogether. "No, Orin. I've not taken up drinking. I purchased the bottle for Sam. In appreciation for all he does for me around here."

"I see. Well, coffee would be nice. If it's not too much trouble."

"You've just driven seven hundred miles to see me. I don't think making a pot of coffee will be too much trouble for me," she teased. "And I was just making sandwiches for lunch when you knocked. Would you care for one?"

"No, thanks. It's too early for me. Maybe later."

As she began to gather the makings for the coffee, he

said, "So tell me again about this Sam. I'd like to meet him."

"Sam went to town to fetch a part for the windmill. But I expect he'll be back in another thirty minutes or so. He was Ray's ranch foreman for many years. And before Ray died, he made Sam promise he'd stick around and help me for as long as I wanted. He's been an angel."

She poured the water into the coffeemaker and switched on the warmer beneath.

"An angel, eh? So this Sam must be a good-looking cowboy," Orin said knowingly.

She attempted a laugh, but her battered emotions buffered the sound, turning it into more of a grunt than anything. "He's not bad for a man in his seventies. Although, he could stand to carry about twenty more pounds on his bony frame. And the wrinkles in his face are as deep as plow tracks."

"Hmm. Obviously, Sam isn't the reason you're still here."

She glanced over to see a thoughtful frown on his face. "Orin, did you make this trip to try to talk me into going back to Nevada?"

A sheepish expression came over his features. "The idea did cross my mind. I've missed you like hell. We've all missed you. But I'm not here to badger you about coming home to the Horn. I'm here because I've been worried about you."

"Worried?" She shook her head in confusion. "I don't understand. Lilly calls me nearly every day. I've been reassuring her that all is well. Hasn't she been keeping you updated?"

"Yes. Lilly gives me a rundown of the phone conversations you two have. But I can read between the lines, Tessa. You turned down Jett's offer and—"

"I didn't turn it down," she interrupted. "Not completely. I told him I'd have to think on it."

Smiling slyly, the older man shook his head. "Tessa, Tessa," he gently scolded. "If you had serious intentions about Jett's job offer, you would've already been packing and heading home."

Orin had five sons and a daughter. Tessa had never really thought the dedicated father had paid that much attention to her, a child who'd come to live in his house only because her mother had died. But apparently, over the years, Orin had taken more note of her than she'd ever guessed.

"I'm sorry, Orin. I've been meaning to call Jett and let him know I won't be taking the job. But things have been—well, I needed time to think on it."

"And now you've decided."

Sighing, she filled a mug with the fresh coffee and carried it over to him. As she placed it on the bar in front of him, she didn't have to ask if he wanted cream or sugar. She'd served him hundreds of cups of black coffee. She knew his favorite shirts and boots and how he liked his steak cooked. But more than his likes and dislikes, she understood just how much he loved his family. And that included her.

Easing onto the stool next to his, she looked at him and felt her throat thicken with emotion. "Yes. I've decided. That probably doesn't make much sense to you. Considering that I went to college four long years just to find a job like Jett's position. But you see, Orin, being here on the Bar X has changed me. And changed the direction of my life. I'm going to make this my home."

He didn't make an immediate reply. Instead he sipped his coffee and studied her shrewdly. "Lilly tells me you still haven't uncovered the facts of why Ray Maddox willed you this place. Is that right?"

She nodded glumly. "I've been hoping and praying something would turn up to explain things. But…well, so far nothing makes sense. Joseph thinks—" Her throat was suddenly so tight she had to swallow before she could continue. "He believes Ray might actually have been my dad."

To say Orin looked stunned was an understatement. "Maybe you'd better explain, Tessa," he demanded in a fatherly tone. "And you can start with telling me about this Joseph."

Drawing in a bracing breath, Tessa told him all about the Hollisters and Joseph, how she'd grown close to him and how he'd been trying to help her uncover the truth about Ray.

"Joseph took the pictures of Mom's wedding day to have someone in the crime lab try and sharpen the images. That was a few days ago. I've not heard from him since—" Unable to go on, she dropped her head and closed her eyes. "We had an argument—about whether I was going back to Nevada or staying here. I couldn't tell him what he wanted to hear."

"Why not? You didn't have any problem telling me."

Lifting her head, she looked at him through teary eyes. "That's because you understand everything, Orin. And, anyway, Joseph hadn't said a thing about being in love with me. It wasn't right that he expected me to make all sorts of promises to him."

A wan smile softened his eyes. "It's obvious to me that you're very much in love with Joseph. Maybe you need to let him know you don't plan to run away."

"Yes, I plan to tell him. I just haven't done it yet because I very much doubt he'll believe me. And I…don't think I can stand watching him walk away a second time." She left the bar stool and walked over to the sliding patio doors. As she gazed out toward the barn and corrals, she said, "I plan to buy cattle and horses, Orin. To make the Bar X a working ranch again. I realize that won't happen overnight. But I'm hoping that once Joseph sees I'm making a commitment to the place, he'll recognize that I've grown up."

Shaking his head, he left his seat to go stand next to her. "I'll be frank, Tessa. I don't like the idea that you've set your sights on a lawman, any more than I like your decision to stay here in Arizona. But more than anything, I want you to be happy. If you think the guy is worth all the effort, then you have my blessings."

Turning her head, she looked at him and the love she saw on his face reminded her that from the moment her mother had died, Orin had made sure she was never without family support. And that would never change, even if she lived many miles away. He and the rest of the Calhoun clan would always be there for her.

"You've misunderstood, Orin. My plans for the ranch aren't a ploy to get Joseph back in my life. Sure, I won't mind if it helps him learn to trust me. But that's beside the point. I want the Bar X to be productive. I want to make it a thriving ranch again—perhaps even better than before."

With his hands on her shoulders, Orin turned her so that she was facing him. "Tessa, you never showed an interest in ranching before. Yes, you always liked to ride horses and be around the animals, but you never mentioned you wanted to be…well, like Sassy or Noelle."

"I never dreamed I'd ever have the chance to do something like this. And when I was living on the Silver Horn, you never asked. You were always encouraging me to focus on my education and college. Which I'm glad of.

I'm very proud of my degree and I do plan to put it to use. Later on. After I get the ranch going."

"Cattle prices have dropped somewhat, but they're still high. And good working horses do not come cheap. It will take a chunk of money to get started. Have you thought about that?"

She nodded. "The money Ray left me is more than enough. And deep down I believe he'd be happy that I'm investing it back into the ranch."

A faint frown creased his forehead. "I can see that's important to you. Although I'm not exactly sure why it is. You're feeling beholden to a man you never met. A man you'll never know."

"That's not exactly true, Orin. The more I explore the Bar X, the more I'm beginning to see him in all the little things that make a place special. Even if I never learn who he was to me, I believe he was a good man. And that's all that really matters, isn't it?"

Smiling, he gently patted her cheek. "You've not only been thinking about things since you've come here, it's clear to me that you've also been growing. You were already a special young woman. But I can see a grit in you now, Tessa, that wasn't there before. It tells me you're a fighter and you're going to succeed at whatever you set out to do. I'm very proud of you, darlin'."

To have Orin, the only father figure she'd ever known, praise her in such a way caused tears to sting her eyes.

Giving him a wobbly smile, she said, "I realize you have all kinds of responsibilities waiting on you back on the Silver Horn, but it would make me very happy if you'd stay on a few days. Sam and I could sure use your advice."

He curled his arm around her shoulders and gave her a reassuring squeeze. "I wouldn't think about leaving now."

Through the glass doors, she spotted Sam parking his truck near the backyard fence. "Sam's home! Come on and I'll introduce you," she said, taking him by the arm and urging him out the patio door. "You two have a lot to talk about."

Chapter Eleven

Joseph was bleary-eyed as he steered his truck off the main highway and onto the dirt road that led to the Bar X and Three Rivers. The night had been extremely busy with all sorts of calls, including an outdoor basketball game that had turned into fisticuffs. He and Connor had barely had time to deal with that fracas when they'd been called to a remote area of the county to give backup to a pair of game rangers rounding up a group of illegal hunters. It wasn't until the end of their shift, when they'd returned to headquarters, that they'd learned Jimmy's shooter had been arrested without incident and was safely behind bars.

At least something was finally going right, he thought ruefully. But how was it going to go when he stopped at the Bar X and knocked on Tessa's door? Since they'd parted more than a week ago, he'd done nothing but think about her laugh and smile, the scent of her sweet skin and the touch of her soft hands roaming over his body.

There had been moments these past days that he'd questioned his own sanity. Why else would he have behaved like a pompous ass and started demanding promises from her that she wasn't ready to give?

Because you love her, you idiot! You wanted to hear her say she'd never leave Arizona. Never leave you. But instead of explaining what was really in your heart, you walked out. Now, it's going to be a miracle if she ever forgives you.

Ten minutes later, his heart beating anxiously, he turned onto the graveled drive leading up to her house. However, his nervousness was soon replaced by surprise when he pulled his truck to a stop next to a navy blue truck with Nevada license plates. Was someone from the Calhoun family here? Had someone come to help her move back to the Silver Horn?

Sick with the thought, he took the steps of the retaining wall two at a time and hurried to the front door. After punching the doorbell several times and getting no response, he went to the back of the house and gazed out at the ranch yard. Sam's old, battered truck was parked beneath the shade of a mesquite, but the only movement he saw was Rosie and Rascal milling around the hay manger.

Hastening his stride, he walked out to the barn and searched the big building, but Sam was nowhere to be found. Apparently he'd gone with Tessa and her guest, wherever that might be. Which was totally odd, given the fact that Sam wasn't a socializer. Especially with someone he'd just met. So what could possibly be going on?

Minutes later, as Joseph walked into the kitchen at Three Rivers, he was so preoccupied with thoughts of

Tessa he hardly noticed Reeva working at the cabinet counter. Nor did he see Hannah barreling straight at him until she was flinging her little arms around him and squeezing him with all her might.

Bewildered by the unexpected greeting, he glanced up to see a smiling Vivian striding toward him.

"Hannah's been worried about you," his sister explained. "We all have."

Hannah tilted her head back until she was looking up at him. "We heard on the news this morning about the man who shot the deputy. He can't shoot at you now, Uncle Joe. He can't hurt anybody else, either."

Doing his best to smile, he touched a finger to the tip of Hannah's nose. "That's right, Freckles. So you put all that worrying out of your head. And now that I think about it, why aren't you at school this morning?"

She wrinkled her nose. "I have to go to the dentist at Prescott. Yuck! Double yuck!"

Joseph patted the top of her head. "You want to be able to chew your food, don't you?"

Hannah tilted her head to one side as she contemplated his question. "Yeah, I guess so. But I mostly want to look as pretty as Mom when she smiles."

"Nobody can look as pretty as your mother when she smiles. So you'd better go to the dentist and work on it," he teased.

"Ha! You must be wanting something to hand out compliments like that," Vivian told him then pointed a finger at her daughter. "You, young lady, need to go finish getting ready. We have to leave in fifteen minutes."

With a loud groan of protest, Hannah left his side and hurried out of the kitchen. Joseph removed his hat and wearily raked a hand through his hair.

"Would you like something to eat, Joe? Lunch won't

be ready for another hour." Reeva turned away from the cabinet to look at him. "Let me fix you a late breakfast. You need to eat. You're getting downright scrawny."

"No thanks, Reeva. All I want is a few hours of sleep."

He started out of the room and Vivian followed. As the two siblings both headed toward the staircase that led upstairs to the bedrooms, Joseph glanced thoughtfully over at her.

"You haven't heard Mom say anything about Tessa having company from Nevada, have you?" he asked.

His sister's brows arched upward. "Why, no. Why do you ask?"

"Because someone is at the Bar X and I don't know who."

Vivian had climbed two stairs when she paused to look at him. "You have a phone, don't you? Why don't you call Tessa to find out what's going on over there? Wouldn't that be the easiest way?"

"It would," he said stiffly. "But since I've not communicated with Tessa in several days, I'd rather not call."

With a look of surprise on her face, she descended the steps until she was standing next to him. "Joe, I don't understand. You've been seeing Tessa quite a bit. I thought you two were probably getting close. Has something happened?"

Only everything, he thought miserably. He'd fallen in love, but rather than embrace the feelings, he'd run and hid from them like a scared pup.

"Yeah," he mumbled. "We argued."

He started to move on up the staircase, but Vivian snagged a hold on his shirtsleeve. "Joe, just a moment—"

"I can't talk about it now, Vivian." He cut her off before she could begin a long lecture. "Maybe later."

She shook her head. "I don't want to pump you for details. I only want to say that if you love Tessa, don't walk away from her. That doesn't fix anything."

The shadows of regret he saw on Vivian's face reminded Joseph how deeply his sister had been hurt by a man who'd given up on their marriage and walked away.

Suddenly ashamed of the self-pity he'd been carrying around, he said, "Thank you, sis. And, believe me, I don't intend to let Tessa get away. Not for any reason."

He gave his sister a brief hug then hurried up the stairs. It no longer mattered that he'd been up and going without sleep for nearly twenty hours. He was going to shower and head back to the Bar X. If Tessa wasn't there, he'd sit on her doorstep and wait until she showed up.

"You really should let me cook for us tonight, Orin," Tessa argued as the two of them entered the house through the back patio doors. "I have some fresh cuts of steaks. I can make salad and fries and garlic toast to go with them."

"I know that Greta taught you to be a good cook. But I'll take you up on the steaks tomorrow evening," he told her. "We've already told Sam we'll stop by his place and pick him up by seven. It's not that far of a drive to Wickenburg and the three of us will have a nice outing together. It will give Sam and me a little more time to discuss the breed of cattle we think will work best on the Bar X ranges."

For the past few hours Sam and Tessa had been driving Orin over the grazing areas of the ranch, along with checking the water supply sources.

Now as the two of them made their way to the living room, she glanced over at him. "You really do like Sam, don't you?"

"I'll tell you one thing, Tessa. I can go back home to

the Silver Horn and not have to worry about you or the Bar X being taken care of. He's a simple man with a heart of gold. And he damned well knows his way around a ranch yard. I couldn't be happier that he'll be your ranch foreman."

Yes, she could count on Sam, Tessa thought. But Joseph was another matter. He'd let her down so hard that the fall had cracked her heart. But she couldn't think about the misery of losing him now. Orin was here to help her. She couldn't waste the time whining over what could've been. She had to focus on her future. But could she ever be truly happy without Joseph in her life?

"I'm glad you approve, Orin. At least, I—"

Her words trailed away on a wistful sigh, which promptly had Orin folding his arms across his broad chest while his shrewd gaze took in her glum expression.

"You're thinking about that deputy now."

His deep voice was like that of a high school principal, stern yet at the same time empathetic. The sound helped her keep her spine straight and her chin up.

"I'm sorry, Orin. And don't worry. I'm not going to burst into tears at our dinner table tonight. I'm just—"

"Thinking it might be worth a try to reach out to him? Try and talk things over?"

Amazed that he could read her mind so well, she nodded then gave him a wry smile. "That's what I'm thinking. And that's what I'm going to do. We still have about three hours to kill before we pick up Sam. I'm going to call Joseph and see if he's willing to meet with me for a talk."

"That's my girl," he said with an approving grin. "You do that. In the meantime, I'll go fetch my bags from the truck. Which bedroom do I put them in?"

"First one on the right." As he started to the door, she

added in a teasing tone, "And, Orin, I think you've had one too many kids. You've started reading our minds."

Chuckling, he glanced over his shoulder at her and even at a distance Tessa could see a sly gleam in his eye. "And I might not be finished yet. Having kids, that is. Noreen wants a baby and I'm sure not opposed to giving her one, or two, or a dozen if she wants them. I've learned, Tessa, it's never too late to love."

He went out the door while Tessa thoughtfully stared after him. When Claudia had died so suddenly, Orin had considered his life over. He'd turned into a recluse and begun behaving as though he was an old man instead of a robust rancher, capable of keeping up with his sons. It wasn't until Rafe and Lilly had fallen in love and married that something inside Orin had woken up.

It's never too late to love. Oh, how she'd grown to realize the truth of those words.

With that thought in mind, she carried her phone to the bedroom and sat on the edge of the white bed where she and Joseph had shared a passion so deep she would carry the memories the rest of her life.

Her hands shaking, she scrolled through her contacts until she reached Joseph's number. But just as her finger was about to push the call button, Orin called out loudly.

"Tessa, come here! Quick!"

The urgency in his voice had her tossing the phone onto the bed and racing out of the room. As she hurried down the hallway, he suddenly stepped from Ray's old room, causing her to nearly barrel straight into him.

"What's wrong?" she asked. "Are you getting ill?"

"I'm okay." Without saying more, he took her by the arm and led her into the living room. "I was putting my empty bag on the top shelf in the closet and found something."

Relieved and a bit bewildered, she shook her head. "Let me guess. A dead mouse. Since the house was empty for a while I—"

Shaking his head, he said, "Nothing like that, honey. Come over here. Where we can sit."

He led her over to the couch where the open drapes shed plenty of light into the room. It wasn't until the two of them were sitting that she noticed he was holding a manila envelope in his hand.

"That's what you found? What is it? Old photos?"

A strange expression on his face, he handed it to her. "More than photos. I think this holds the answers you've been looking for."

Totally confused, she began to pull the contents from the envelope. "I don't understand, Orin. This stuff—" She stopped in stunned silence as a single sheet of thick paper fell open on her lap. It was a marriage license issued in the State of Nevada to Monica Simmons Parker and Asa Hamilton Parker. The document was an exact duplicate of her mother's marriage license! But how did it get here in Ray's house?

She stared at Orin as her mind spun for reasonable explanations. "This doesn't make sense! Why would Ray have a copy of my mother's marriage license? Unless—"

He gestured to the papers lying in her lap. "Maybe you should look everything over before you start making assumptions."

"Right—yes." Her hands shaking, she sifted through the remaining items. A photo very similar to those that she'd given Joseph to examine. A copy of Tessa's birth certificate. And a sealed white envelope with her name handwritten across the front. Like pieces of an abstract puzzle, she tried to assemble them in her jumbled thoughts.

"Why was this stuff hidden away on a shelf in the

closet?" In a dazed stupor, she continued to stare at the papers that documented her life. The fact that Ray possessed these things could only mean one thing. Yet the reality was slow to settle in her mind. "Why hadn't it been left in Ray's desk where I could easily find it?"

"I figure the man didn't want just anyone finding these things," Orin said carefully. "At least, not until you found them first."

Her hands shook as she tore into the envelope and extracted two sheets of lined notepaper. "It's a handwritten letter," she whispered numbly. "To me. From Ray."

Her voice quivered as she began to read out loud.

"'My dearest Tessa,

By the time you read this letter I will be gone from this earth and you will be on the Bar X. It grieves me deeply that I can't be there with you. I'll never feel the joy of talking with you, seeing you smile, or feeling your hand reach for mine. Still, I can die a happy man knowing I have a daughter who's grown into a lovely, responsible woman.

"'I'm sure you have many questions as to why I never made an appearance in your life and why Monica, your mother, told you I had died before you were born. First and foremost, please try not to judge her harshly. The two of us met by happenstance and I was so instantly besotted with her I couldn't reveal that I was already married to Dottie. Instead, I married Monica using the assumed name of Asa Parker. It wasn't until she was pregnant with you that I realized I had to confess.

"'Naturally, the truth angered and disappointed her, but she loved me in spite of everything. And I continued to love her, even though, I never saw her again…'"

Too choked with tears to continue reading, she handed the letter to Orin. "Please finish it for me. I can't."

Orin gruffly cleared his throat and picked up where Tessa had left off.

"'...after the night I visited her in the hospital—when she'd given birth to you. You see, my darling daughter, your mother was a wise and wonderful woman. She understood that neither of us could live with our consciences if I deserted Dottie to be with her. Therefore, over the years, she sent photos and letters of you, as a way for me to keep up with my daughter's growth. Yet, all the while, my heart yearned to be the father you needed.

"'When Monica died so suddenly, my first urge was to make myself known to you and bring you home with me. Although Dottie never learned about your existence, I'm very certain she would've welcomed you with loving arms and made you the child she could never bear. I was making plans to go to Nevada when I received the news that you'd been taken in by the Calhouns, a family that could give you so much more than I ever could. And now as I fight this disease that is taking me away, I believe I made the right choice in letting you continue to believe Asa Parker was dead. Those were your important growing years and I wanted you to have the stability the Calhouns could provide.

"'My greatest wish now is that the Bar X will give you as much pleasure as it has given me. And that someday you will come to realize how very much I loved you.

Your father,
Ray'"

As Orin slowly closed the letter, Tessa began to sob.

"Oh, Orin, all these years. I had a father—and now he's gone. I can't bring him back!" Every part of her was aching with regret and a sense of utter loss. Not just for all that she'd missed, but also for her parents, who'd made the lonely sacrifice to spend their lives apart. "Why didn't my mother tell me?"

Lying the letter aside, Orin drew her into the comforting circle of his arms and Tessa buried her face against his strong shoulder and continued to cry.

"Your mother couldn't tell you, Tessa." Orin spoke gently. "She wanted you to believe your father was a hero. And as far as I'm concerned, Ray Maddox was a hero. It takes a big man to give up the things he loves most. Why else do you think I let you come down here to Arizona without putting up a big fight?"

The gruff affection in his voice brought even more tears to her eyes. "I love you, too, Orin," she finally managed to choke out.

"Tessa! What is this?"

The unexpected sound of Joseph's voice had Tessa pulling away from Orin's embrace and jumping to her feet.

Using the back of her hand, she attempted to dash the tears from her cheeks. "Joseph! What...are you doing here?"

His skeptical gaze swung to Orin then back to Tessa's tear-stained face. "I rang the doorbell but apparently you didn't hear it. What's wrong? Who is this man?"

The shock of Joseph's arrival was enough to stem her sobs and as she wiped at the last of her tears, she walked over to him.

"This is Orin Calhoun." She gestured to Orin, who

was now rising from the couch. "He's my—Nevada father."

Joseph looked dumbfounded but managed to give Orin a polite nod. "Nice to meet you, sir."

He walked over to Joseph and extended his hand. "I'm certainly happy to see you, Deputy Hollister. You couldn't have arrived at a better time."

Looking even more confused, Joseph shook the other man's hand. "Maybe one of you should explain what's going on. Have you gotten bad news?"

Orin cast Tessa a gentle smile before he stepped over and collected Ray's letter from the coffee table. "I wouldn't call it bad," he said as he handed the folded paper to Joseph. "I found this earlier in the closet of Ray's bedroom."

"Please read it, Joseph." Tessa spoke, her voice hoarse with raw emotion. "It…explains everything."

Joseph unfolded the letter and began to read. As Tessa watched, she could see he was deeply affected by Ray's revelations. The man had been his mentor and longtime friend. The fact that Ray had hidden such a deep secret was probably even more shocking to him than to Tessa.

"This is incredible!" He shook his head in disbelief. "I had my suspicions that Ray might be Tessa's father, but when I tried to imagine my old friend holding such a secret—it seemed impossible. But now this letter makes everything clear."

Tessa collected the photo and other documents from the coffee table and handed them to Joseph. "These things were with the letter. The photo is almost like the ones I gave you."

He glanced through the items before turning his focus on her. "I brought the photos with me, but I left them in the truck," he admitted. "After my friend in the crime lab cleared them up…well, I could see the man was a young Ray Maddox. I didn't know how to tell you, Tessa, or how you would take the news."

Even though there were a few steps separating them, she couldn't mistake the warm, tender love she saw in his eyes. The sight of it propelled her closer to him.

"Is that why you're here, Joseph? To give me the photos?"

"No." He glanced uncomfortably at Orin. "I, uh, thought we needed to talk."

Orin cleared his throat. "You two don't mind me. I'll be in the bedroom."

He slipped quietly from the room and, for a moment after he disappeared from view, Tessa thought she was going to start crying again. Her nerves were on a roller coaster and she realized the highs and lows would never end until she learned what was in Joseph's heart.

Her legs too shaky to continue standing, she walked over to the couch and sank onto the middle cushion. "I had picked up the phone to call you when Orin found the letter," she admitted.

He moved over to the couch and eased gently down beside her. Tessa's first instinct was to throw herself at him, to hold him tight and never let him go. But there were so many things that needed to be said, so much to explain.

"I came by earlier this morning," he told her. "I couldn't find anyone around."

She sighed with regret. "I'm sorry we missed you. Sam and Orin and I were driving over the ranch looking over the grazing and water supply. Orin has agreed to stay on a few days to help us get the ranch restocked and going again."

The surprise on his face was almost comical. "Restocked? You mean you're going to make the Bar X a working ranch again?"

For the first time in days, a genuine smile came over her face. "I sure do mean it. Sam is going to oversee everything. And, of course, I'll be around to help, too."

His hands closed around her shoulders as his eyes delved into hers. "Tessa, only days ago you told me you didn't know what you were going to do about staying here or going back to Nevada! Am I supposed to believe—"

"This isn't some sudden decision, Joseph, although it probably looks like it to you. I think I've known from the very first moment I stepped foot on the Bar X that I would never be able to leave it. But that night—when we argued—I was afraid to admit that to myself, much less you. All that time we were together you never mentioned anything about loving me. I tried to tell myself it would be better if I went back to Nevada and forgot you. But I can't do that. I can't leave this wonderful home my father gave me. And, most of all, I can't leave you. Even if you don't love me."

With a rueful groan, he pulled her against him then wrapped his arms so tightly around her she could scarcely breathe, much less move.

"Oh, Tessa, I've been a fool. I should have told you how I really felt. But you never said anything about love and my pride kept holding me back. That and the fear that you had no real intentions of staying here permanently. Then when you told me about Jett's job offer, I sort of went into panic mode. I was sure I was going to lose you. That night we argued, I hardly knew what I was saying. But I realize now that everything I said was wrong. Can you ever forgive me? Trust me?"

Tilting her face up to his, she hoped the magnitude of love she felt for him was there in her eyes for him to see.

"We were both afraid of getting hurt," she whispered. "But that's all gone and forgotten now, Joseph. All that matters is this moment and our future. My parents didn't get to spend their lives together. But maybe I can make up for that in a little way by living the rest of mine with the man I love."

He lowered his lips to hers.

As he kissed her deeply, joy flowed through Tessa until she felt as though her whole body, including her bruised heart, was flooded with happy sunshine.

"Looks like I have a penchant for picking the wrong place and time to show you how much I love you, but I promise I'll make it up to you later." Drawing her hand to his lips, he kissed the backs of her fingers. "Will you marry me, Tessa? Will you be my wife? The mother of my children?"

More tears spilled from her eyes, only this time they were created from the sheer joy bubbling inside her.

"Yes! Yes!" She planted kisses all over his face. Then, easing back, she gave him an impish smile. "Unless you think you need more time to make sure I'm putting down my roots here on the Bar X."

Chuckling low in his throat, he nuzzled his lips against her cheek. "There isn't going to be any waiting. I'm going to put a ring on your finger as fast as I can."

Orin's earlier plans for the evening suddenly came to her mind. "Orin is taking Sam and me out to dinner tonight. I think it would be the perfect chance to celebrate our engagement. Can you join us?"

The tender smile on his lips and soft glow in his eyes said he'd pluck a star from the sky and hand it to her on a silver platter if that's what her heart desired.

Epilogue

Eight months later, on a cold, February night, the Hollisters plus a few close friends were gathered in the big living room of Three Rivers Ranch house to celebrate the beginning of the annual Gold Rush Days festival that would kick off in downtown Wickenburg tomorrow.

At least, that was the excuse Maureen was giving everyone for the dinner party. But the Hollister matriarch wasn't fooling anyone, especially Joseph and Tessa. The real reason for the get-together was to celebrate the exciting news that Tessa was pregnant. For the first time since Hannah was born eleven years ago, a new baby would soon be joining the Hollister family.

As Tessa stood next to the fireplace, soaking up the warmth from the burning mesquite logs, Joseph walked up and handed her a fluted glass of ginger ale and a small saucer holding a cluster of chocolate-covered walnuts drizzled with gold-colored icing.

"Reeva says it will be a few more minutes until dinner is ready. I thought you might like to try her gold nuggets—that's what she calls them. She makes these every year when Gold Rush Days roll around."

"Yum! Thank you, Joseph. I am famished."

"Why don't you sit down, honey?" he suggested. "There's a big, empty chair right over there by Sam and Mom. You need to rest before we have dinner."

Laughing softly, she bit into the sweet treat then washed it down with a sip of her drink. "I'm only eight weeks along, Joseph. When the baby starts growing and getting heavier, I'll probably be hunting the first chair I can find. But right now, the fire feels wonderful."

Lowering his head to hers, he murmured in a suggestive tone, "Folks around here are saying how cold this winter has been. But I haven't really noticed. Have you?"

Her muted laughter put a grin on his face. "I'd call it the warmest winter on record. We've hardly had to use the heater at our house."

His grin deepening, he slipped an arm around the back of her waist and nuzzled his nose against the top of her hair. "Happy?" he asked softly.

She tilted her face up to his. "A year ago, I was working as a housekeeper on the Silver Horn. I thought my life was about to change because I was finishing my criminal justice degree and planning to find a new job. Wow! Talk about change. Now I'm a married woman with a baby on the way. Not to mention the owner of a thriving ranch."

"Well, a year ago you were right about two things. You did get your degree and you did find a job as legal secretary for Mr. Dayton in his Wickenburg law office."

Since she'd taken the job three months ago, each day had been a learning experience about the intricate dealings of the legal system. Plus, Mr. Dayton was an elderly gentleman who was a pleasure to work with. Only yesterday she'd told him about her pregnancy and already he'd been assuring her she could take as much maternity leave as she needed. As for the Bar X, Sam was doing an admirable job seeing that every aspect of the ranch was working and producing as it should. And soon their first crop of calves would be born.

Her soft laugh conveyed just how amazed she was by the changes in her life. "Not in my wildest dreams did I imagine I'd be inheriting a ranch like the Bar X and marrying the sexiest deputy in all of Arizona."

His fingers tightened possessively on the side of her waist. "Just in Arizona? Geez, I must be slipping," he joked. "I thought I was easily the sexiest in three states."

"My mistake," she teased. "I should have said the whole southwest."

Since their simple but beautiful June wedding, which had been held on the front lawn of the Bar X with family and friends in attendance, she and Joseph had made their home in the house where Ray had lived his entire life.

Getting accustomed to Joseph's long, irregular work hours hadn't always been easy, but she was learning to make the most of the time they had together. And she could honestly say their marriage was growing stronger with every passing day.

As for her parents' affair, coming to terms with their deception hadn't been as easy. There were times Tessa deeply resented the fact that her mother had allowed all those years to pass without telling her that her father wasn't dead but alive and living in Arizona. And her resentment didn't stop there. Ray should've never deceived Monica or Dottie, or the people around him. And yet, in spite of all the mistakes they'd made, Tessa's heart would always ache for her parents' star-crossed love.

"Honey, what are you thinking about? Are you missing the Calhouns?"

She looked up at him and the tender devotion she saw in his brown eyes filled her with warm contentment. No matter the crooks and turns their lives would take in the future, she knew with all certainty that Joseph would always be at her side.

"No, we just saw all of the Calhouns when we drove up there to visit at Christmas. And Orin calls me practically every day. I was actually thinking about Ray and my mother. It wasn't meant for them to be together. Not like we are." She rested her cheek against the side of his strong arm. "Yet in spite of their deception, Joseph, I can't judge them badly."

"Of course you can't. Ray's gift to you was more than just a house, a piece of land and a bank account. It brought you here to Arizona—to me. It's given Sam a new purpose for living. And when our first child is born and, God willing, the babies that follow, Ray's gift will keep on giving to them."

She sighed. "Yes, it's given us love. And in the end I think that's all my father really wanted to do—just give me love."

Joseph was pressing a kiss against her temple when Blake and Holt walked up to them. In spite of the cocktail in Holt's hand, there was a somber expression on his face. Blake's mood didn't appear to be any better.

"Hey, guys, what's with the long faces?" Joseph asked then gave his wife a conspiring wink. "You heard Reeva was cooking chicken tonight instead of beef?"

Neither man appeared amused. Holt let out a heavy sigh while Blake's head moved negligibly from side to side.

"We have something to show you," Blake said. "Before dinner starts."

"And before we showed it to Mom," Holt added soberly.

Sensing the gravity of the moment, Joseph's grin quickly disappeared. "Okay. Where is this 'something'?" he asked.

Blake dug into the front pocket of his jeans then opened his palm to reveal a spur rowel. Larger than most, it was about two inches in diameter and rusted to a deep reddish brown color.

"I'm confused. What's the significance of this?" Tessa asked. She glanced at Joseph to see his face had taken on an unusual pallor. "What's wrong? Explain this to me, Joseph."

Joseph drew her closer to his side. "When Dad was found—that day he died, we noticed one of his spur rowels was missing. All these years we've been searching for it."

She glanced skeptically at her two brothers-in-law then back to Joseph. "How do you know this was Joel's rowel? Over the years there's surely been other ranch hands who've lost a spur or a rowel."

"Good point," Blake agreed. "But Dad's spurs were unique. No one else on Three Rivers had a set like his."

Joseph plucked the rusty rowel from Blake's palm and held it so that Tessa could have a closer look. "See, it has a lot more points than a regular rowel. And its shape resembles a sunburst. Dad's spurs were what's called Spanish Colonial. Antiques worth quite a bit of money."

"That's not the reason we were hunting the lost rowel, though," Holt quickly clarified for Tessa's sake.

"Holt is right," Joseph added. "The dollar value of the spurs is insignificant. We've always held the notion that wherever the rowel had fallen might be the spot where Dad—that some sort of altercation took place."

No wonder the brothers were looking so grim, Tessa thought. "I understand the importance now," she said. "It could be a huge clue."

"Where did you find it?" Joseph asked his brothers. "Close to where Dad was discovered?"

Blake shook his head and Holt spoke up. "Not far from the number nine well pump. Down in the arroyo. We were checking on the bulls."

"Holt needed to tighten his cinch," Blake continued to explain. "When he got down from the saddle, he spotted the rowel lying next to a boulder."

The faint frown on Joseph's face told Tessa he was thinking more like a deputy now rather than as a son. "That's close to the old road leading to the Fisher property."

"Yeah," Blake said flatly. "That's what we were thinking. Holt and I believe we should wait until everyone leaves tonight before we show it to Mom."

"I agree," Joseph said. "Seeing this thing is going to upset her. After all, she gave the spurs to Dad as an anniversary gift."

The three brothers were exchanging grim glances when Maureen suddenly stood and announced that dinner was ready to be served.

Joseph handed the rowel back to Blake. As they all began to shuffle out of the room, Tessa noticed her brother-in-law discreetly drop the rusty clue into his pocket and out of sight.

Working their way toward the dining room, Tessa caught Joseph by the arm and pulled him partially down the hallway and out of earshot.

"What's wrong?" he asked.

As she searched his handsome face, she realized the deep love she felt for her husband would always link her happiness to his. "I'm fine," she assured him. "It's you I'm concerned about. I could see your brothers' discovery of the rowel upset you. I hope you won't let it ruin our evening."

His lips slanted to a gentle smile. "I'm not going to sugarcoat it, Tessa. The sight of the rowel did bring back painful memories. But I'm much more hopeful than upset. It's an inkling to what happened to my father. One that we can build on."

"That's good. I understand how it feels to have unanswered questions gnawing at you and I keep praying that someday the truth about your father's death will come to light. Ray's secret didn't stay buried forever. Neither will Joel's."

His brown eyes glowed down at her as he cupped his hand to the side of her face. "Before I met you, my darling Tessa, I was driven to find the answers to Dad's death. I believed it would be impossible for me to be truly content until I solved the mystery and got the justice he deserved. But now, with you in my life and our baby on the way, I realize how wrong that thinking was. I am happy and contented. And I believe that's the way Dad would want me to be."

Her heart swelled with love and pride. "I'm glad. But that doesn't mean you're going to put the case to rest, does it?"

"Of course not. It just means I'm always going to put you and our children first. If the questions about Dad's death are meant to be answered, then it will happen. Just like it happened with you and Ray."

"Hmm. Sometimes I wonder if Ray carried clues about your father to his grave—more than those he shared with you. Obviously he was a man who could keep secrets."

"And his best-kept secret is now my wife," Joseph shrewdly replied.

Down the hallway, Vivian poked her head around the open doorway leading into the dining room. "Hey, you two! Get in here! Mother is ready to make a toast. And the prime rib is getting cold."

"We'll be right there," he called to his sister. Then, with a hand at Tessa's back, he nudged her forward. "Prime rib? I thought we were having chicken."

Unable to contain her laughter, Tessa looked up at him. "Oh, Joseph, you've grown into a wonderful husband, but I don't think you'd better call yourself a detective just yet."

Laughing with her, he urged her on toward the dining room. "Come on. Let's not keep the family waiting."

The family. Yes, the Hollisters were her family now, Tessa thought happily. Like Joseph had so lovingly stated, Ray's gift would keep on giving for the rest of their lives.

* * * * *

Look for Stella Bagwell's next book in the
MEN OF THE WEST *series,*
Blake Hollister's story,

HER MAN ON THREE RIVERS RANCH
coming in April 2018!

And to learn more about Tessa's friends in Nevada,
check out previous books in the series:

HER KIND OF DOCTOR
THE COWBOY'S CHRISTMAS LULLABY
HIS BADGE, HER BABY, THEIR FAMILY

Available now from Mills & Boon Cherish!

MILLS & BOON®

Coming next month

THE SPANISH MILLIONAIRE'S RUNAWAY BRIDE
Susan Meier

She laughed again. "I can't even figure out how to explain running from my wedding. It's not as if I was such a great prize myself."

"You are a great prize." The words came out soft and filled with regret that her dad had skewed the way she saw herself.

She stopped at her door, but she didn't use her key card to open it. She glanced at Riccardo, her pale pink face illuminated by the light beside her door. "I'm a twenty-five-year-old woman who doesn't know who she is."

"You have to know you're beautiful."

She caught his gaze. Her long black lashes blinked over sad blue eyes. "Physical things fade."

"You're pretty in here," he countered, touching her chest just above the soft swell of her breasts. "When you're sixty, eighty, a hundred, you'll still be compassionate."

She shook her head. "You don't know that. We just met. Aside from the fact that I ran from my wedding and my dad's a bit of a control freak, you don't know much of anything about me."

Silence hung between them as they stared into each other's eyes. The warmth in her big blue orbs touched his heart, but the lift of her lips sparked a small fire in his belly. Everything male inside him awoke. The urge to kiss her tumbled through him.

He should have turned, walked the few steps to his own room and gone inside. Gotten away from her. Instead, he stayed right where he was.